LOVE'S WONDROUS HOLD

No matter how she tried, Lorinda was helpless to free herself from Yellow Feather's hold.

"Because you have disturbed my heart," he said solemnly, "I must possess you. I cannot let you leave." Reaching a hand down to her face, he traced her features. "You are mine," he continued. "And you must learn to love me . . ."

Lorinda's heart thundered inside her. Her breath caught in her throat as his fingers touched her lips with tenderness. She was being pulled into a magnetic force of passion and need and welcomed his other hand as it lifted her chin, caressing her. She would soon be lost to him if she didn't speak to break the spell. "Are you saying that you love me?" she whispered.

Yellow Feather's lips were now near hers. "Yes," he murmured.

"If you do, then lead me back to my people," she said. But Yellow Feather did not answer her. Instead, he took her lips in a lingering kiss. Lorinda's head was swimming in wonderment. If he did return her to her people, would she be able to part with him, never to see him again?

SAVAGE OBSESSION

CASSIE EDWARDS

Zebra Books
Kensington Publishing Corp.

http://www.zebrabooks.com

ZEBRA BOOKS

are published by

Kensington Publishing Corp.
850 Third Avenue
New York, NY 10022

First Printing: October, 1983
10 9 8 7 6 5 4

Printed in the United States Of America

AUTHOR'S NOTE

The Chippewa, especially the Lake Superior bands, have been neglected by historians, perhaps because they fought no bloody wars of resistance against the westward-driving white pioneers who overwhelmed them in the nineteenth century.

Yet, historically, the Chippewa were one of the most important Indian groups north of Mexico. Their expansive north woods contained valuable resources, forcing them to play important roles in regional enterprises. They have remained on their native lands, still a proud people, and continue to develop their interests in lumbering, fishing, farming, and mining.

I found my study of the Chippewa a most rewarding and heartwarming experience. It was a pleasure to write about them!

As unto the bow the cord is,
So unto the man is woman;
Though she bends him, she obeys him,
Though she draws him, yet she follows;
Useless each without the other!

—Longfellow

One

The candle was burning low in the center of the dining table, emitting a soft glow around the one-room log cabin. Tanned and stretched animal hides were spread and nailed to hang across the two windows and one door, and the cracks between the logs showed the mixed mud and straw that had been used as clay to keep out the rain and cold.

The floor was of tramped earth and was always the cause of Lorinda Odell's feet being damp and cold, even through the protective covering of proper shoes. Hurrying around the cabin, she straightened patchwork quilts on the beds. She had yet to sleep comfortably on her own bed, which had pieces of rope instead of springs, strung on pegs between the side rail and the walls. But nothing about the pioneer way of life was easy. Lorinda's life in New York State had been much more pleasant. At seventeen, she was wondering if she would even reach her next birthday. Her Aunt Rettie Odell's tales of savage Indians who still roamed this land always turned Lorinda's heart to ice.

Mavis Odell spoke softly from behind Lorinda. "Lorinda, honey, would you please pour the tallow for the candles for a while?" she said. "My back, it aches from standing so long."

Lorinda swung around and felt a sadness course

9

through her veins, seeing her mother standing there so tiny and frail. The pioneer way of life had begun to take its toll on this woman in her mid-forties. Her skin was deeply tanned and tightly drawn from working outside in the sun all day, side by side with her husband Derrick, as they readied the land for plowing and seeding. She had even helped driving the oxen to pull out the stumps and boulders from the land when they had first arrived in the Minnesota Territory three years before.

During Mavis and Derrick's marriage of twenty-seven years, seven babies had been conceived and five had been lost. The first to be born in Minnesota was Amanda Marie, who was now five months of age and very much a picture of health. But Mavis continued to be weakened by it all and could hardly join her husband behind the horse and plow any longer.

Lorinda rushed to her mother and helped to ease her onto a chair. "Mother, I so worry about you," she said. "Since Amanda's birth, you seem so drained of energy. You work too hard. If only I could do more to help you."

Mavis's pale green eyes assessed her daughter. Lorinda had become a young lady the past year. Her body had ripened, with silky-soft swells of breasts, a tiny waist, and gently rounded hips. Mavis lifted her callused fingers to Lorinda's hair and combed through it, feeling its lustrous satiny texture. Ah, at one time, Mavis herself could boast of having such brilliant auburn hair hanging to her waist. But she was now gray-haired and aging much too quickly.

"Darling, I've tried so hard to protect you," she said wistfully. "Life has to have more in store for you than working day and night in the house and the fields. Look at you. You're so pretty. You must agree to return with your Aunt Rettie to St. Paul for more schooling. Only by doing so can you have a chance to lead a better life than I have led. You may, by chance, even meet a gentleman of means."

Lorinda fell to her knees and placed her head on her mother's lap. She wrapped her arms around her. "But, Mother, if I leave, you won't have anyone to help you with the chores and with Amanda," she said. Her gaze traveled to the wooden cradle that sat in the darkness of the far wall. Amanda was a good baby. When she wasn't suckling from her mother's breast she was either napping or lying peacefully in her cradle, looking around with her sky-blue eyes, absorbing life.

Lorinda had often worried about the future for her sister. Would Amanda be strong enough to live through the hardships ahead? Would she even reach Lorinda's own age of seventeen? Minnesota was *not* New York.

"I musn't go with Aunt Rettie," Lorinda quickly added, feeling suddenly protective of her innocent baby sister. "It seems I've only just returned home."

Caressing Lorinda's thick mane of red hair, Mavis felt tears creeping from her eyes. She had missed her daughter this past school term. She would miss her again. But she had to encourage Lorinda to go. "Lorinda, listen to me. You must. When Aunt Rettie arrives with her buggy, you *must* return with her," she said. She lifted Lorinda's chin with a forefinger so they both could gaze into one another's eyes. Mavis was proud of this daughter whose brilliant green eyes danced beneath a veil of thick lashes and whose tiny nose had a cute way of wrinkling when she laughed.

But Lorinda's smile, usually so charming, would sometimes reveal another, daring quality about her, as her serene expression changed suddenly to a strange blaze of fury when she was given cause to grow impatient or angry. It was this quality about Lorinda that urged Mavis to do everything possible so that Lorinda had the opportunity of meeting a proper gentleman. The Norse blood in Lorinda's veins made her much too adventurous, daring, and imaginative. Lorinda's restlessness could surely be quelled by the proper man!

"But will you truly be all right, Mother?" Lorinda murmured. She couldn't help but think of the cold winter months ahead and the hardships that accompanied them. Lorinda had escaped such hardships by living with her Aunt Rettie in her aunt's two-story frame boardinghouse in St. Paul during the school term. Fireplaces in each room had been a luxury Lorinda hadn't even had in New York State. But now, her main concern was for her father, mother, and baby sister, who had only one fireplace, which served for both cooking and heating in their one-room, drafty log cabin. Pneumonia had snuffed out many lives, and, also, there was always the fear of Indians.

"Your father will provide," Mavis said. "Your father has always provided."

The sound of buggy wheels and a horse approaching outside the cabin drew Lorinda to her feet. She quickly checked her appearance, wanting to look neat when her Aunt Rettie came through the door. She ran her fingers over her dress. It was of a green-flowered printed calico material with a tight-fitted bodice and high neck and was buttoned down the front. The waist was cut like a separate jacket and came to a sharp point in the front and back. The skirt was long and full, but lacked the many petticoats that were worn by more well-to-do women in the villages and cities. Lorinda had discovered long ago that petticoats were not practical in a log cabin where space was limited.

With an anxious heart, Lorinda went to the door and pushed the animal hide covering aside, watching her Aunt Rettie being assisted from her fancy black buggy by her brother Derrick, Lorinda's father. Lorinda had to smile inwardly, seeing once again the difference between brother and sister. Attired in his faded coveralls, Derrick towered over Rettie. He was stoutly built and though in his late forties had a thick head of rust-colored hair and sported quite a handsome, full auburn beard.

Rettie, on the other hand, was quite short, pleasantly plump and spunky, with gray hair circled in a bun pulled away from the lines of wrinkles on her very round face. When she had become widowed, she had chosen to reclaim her maiden name and had loved her independent status ever since. Her raspy voice resounded through the air as she greeted Derrick with a hug around the neck, roughly pulling him down to meet her shorter height.

Lorinda couldn't help but silently admire the magnificence of her aunt's attire of a navy blue satin material. The bodice was trimmed with braid and had bell-shaped oversleeves with full undersleeves of finely tucked muslin. The high neck was finished with a white collar and was fastened with her aunt's favorite cameo brooch. The full skirt was held out by stiff petticoats, and, as she now moved hand in hand with her brother toward the cabin, the skirt rustled voluptuously.

"There's my girl," Rettie said in her grating voice. She released her hand from Derrick's and went to Lorinda, pulling her roughly from the doorway to draw her into her arms. "How's my precious?" she said, as one would speak to a small child.

"I'm just fine," Lorinda murmured, hugging her back. Lorinda had always liked the special attention from her one and only aunt, but she had only recently begun to think herself too old for such fussing over. She inhaled the sweet fragrance of her aunt before working herself free. She knew this fragrance by heart. Lily of the valley. She could remember the many times she had seen her aunt dab this sweetness behind each of her ears and at the hollow of her throat.

The aroma now clung to Lorinda's dress as she stepped back away from her aunt smiling, yet not as cheerfully as she knew her aunt would expect. Oh, Lorinda did *so* want

13

to go to St. Paul, but she felt such a strong commitment to her family. Surely she was needed! Could she refuse them the extra pair of hands?

Lorinda leaned a bit against her father as he slid his arm about her waist. Oh, she already missed him!

"Ain't she just too beautiful, Rettie?" Derrick boasted, squeezing Lorinda closer to his side. "Ain't she grown up over the summer?"

Rettie reached up and gently touched Lorinda's face. "She sure has, Derrick," she said. A frown caused her wrinkles to deepen. "Maybe even a mite too beautiful for her own good."

"Eh?" Derrick said, scratching his head briskly.

"The men in St. Paul. Derrick, so many are huntin' wives. Some are a mite too anxious for their own good. I'll have to keep a closer eye on Lorinda. We don't want no riffraff touchin' or soilin' her."

"You mean she might'n be safe there with you, Rettie?" Derrick said, eyeing Lorinda and then Rettie.

"She'd be safer if you'd move into town yourself to watch after her," Rettie grumbled.

Derrick's face reddened. He moved away from Lorinda and with an angry jerk lifted the animal hide covering at the door. "Don' start again, Rettie," he stormed. "I should've known what you were gettin' at. Now just don' start on me again." He went on into the house and slouched onto a chair at the dining table. Mavis sat down opposite him with Amanda at an exposed breast.

"Keep your anger down, Derrick," Mavis said quietly. " Rettie means no harm. She's just concerned about our welfare."

"Hell," Derrick grumbled, lighting a pipe.

"You just won't listen," Rettie said, moving on into the cabin, puffing from the exertion of carrying her weight and her cumbersome attire around. She stopped to admire baby Amanda affectionately, then settled onto a

14

chair, eyeing the hollowed-out beets spread across the tabletop that were being used for molds to make candles. She set her jaws firmly. She would never understand her brother and why he had chosen the harder way of life. In New York State he had had a good spread of land and a comfortable house to match.

Yet Rettie couldn't help but feel a mite responsible for his move to Minnesota. If she hadn't written to him about her loneliness after her husband's death, Derrick and his family probably never would have ventured out here to this new way of life. After that, it had seemed that their life-styles had reversed. Rettie had succeeded in starting a thriving business in the house left her by her husband, and Derrick had started from scratch.

No, Rettie didn't understand it. Derrick could have purchased a tract of land in St. Paul and could have become a prosperous businessman in his own right. Instead, he had chosen a different course in life, one he might one day baost about, when he transformed the barren land he had claimed into the finest homestead in Minnesota Territory.

Lorinda could feel the tension in the air as she stepped into the cabin. She glanced quickly from her father to her Aunt Rettie, knowing to expect to hear the same arguments. Deep down inside her she wished victory for her aunt. If this one-room drafty log cabin could be left behind, wouldn't it be the answer to many things? Yet Lorinda couldn't help but remember the pride in her father's eyes at each day's end after he had transformed another small piece of wilderness into his dream. Each fresh callus on his hands meant a day closer to succeeding. Could Lorinda truly wish to deprive him of his own victories? Oh, she was so confused. Life could be so hard at times.

"Coffee anyone?" she said, reaching with the protective shield of a pot holder for the coffee pot that was warming in the coals of the fire of the fireplace. Tincups were always on the table ready for coffee. Lorinda poured coffee into three, not wanting any for herself. She eased onto a chair also at the table, watching her baby sister peacefully suckling and making soft, pleasurable mewing sounds of contentment. Lorinda would miss her sister. It had taken many years for a sister to arrive on the scene. It was hard to have to think of being away from her. It gave Lorinda a strange emptiness to think of having to say goodbye.

Lorinda tensed when she heard the battle of words heat up between brother and sister.

"You are a stubborn man, Derrick Odell," Rettie accused. "You should've at least built your house in the shadows of Fort Snelling if you refused to move into St. Paul. You are the same as askin' for Indians to come knockin' at your door by livin' way out here with no neighbors in yellin' range."

Derrick took a swallow of coffee then slammed his cup down onto the table. "There ain't no Indians within miles of this place, Rettie," he scoffed. "Neither Sioux nor the Chippewa have caused the white man problems lately. Don't you know they've been plumb scared off? They know the land has been handed us by the government. The papers have been signed and legal by them big shots in Washington."

"You don't seem to understand, Derrick," Rettie argued further. "A signed paper means nothin' to Indians who've never had schoolin'. I'm tellin you. You're on land that's been an Indian's land for way too long. You've chosen a piece of land too far from Fort Snelling. I wish you'd listen to reason. The Sioux especially cannot be trusted. In the past, they've left a trail of blood."

"I'm on land that's now part of a state, the great state of Minnesota, as of May Twelfth of this year," Derrick said, puffing angrily on his pipe. "President Buchanan signed the admission bill on May eleventh. We've

16

nothin' to fear from the Indians now. They've agreed to move north. The government has paid 'em well for their land. I feel safe here on my own patch of land.''

"You still ain't safe," Rettie persisted.

With his pipe hanging loosely from one corner of his mouth, Derrick shoved his chair back and rose from it angrily. He clasped his hands behind his back and began pacing the floor. "You let me be the one decidin' what is and what ain't safe for my family," he grumbled. He flashed Rettie a raised-eyebrow look. "And how is it you feel safe to travel the miles alone by buggy from St. Paul to here? Ain't you afraid of an Indian jumpin' out on you? Eh? Don't you think they'd want a gray scalp to show off? Eh?"

"I can take care of myself," Rettie said, rising. "I have me a shotgun at my side at all times. And, anyway, I haven't brought sadness to the Indians' hearts. I haven't taken their land. I'm on government land in town. There's no reason for me to fear Indians."

Derrick doubled over with laughter. "You think the land you're on is less to the Indians because it's close to Fort Snelling and that fancy capital building they've built in that St. Paul town? Rettie, your ignorance surprises me.''

"You're known as a squatter, Derrick," Rettie said firmly . "There's a difference in how you've come by your land. Though the treaties have been signed with the Indians, you, personally, have never properly paid for your piece of land.''

Derrick went to stand before the fire on the hearth with his back to his family. "You know it took all my savings to get here from New York," he said. "And I'm not the only one to claim squattin' rights.''

Rettie went to stand beside him, wringing her hands. "Yes. I know," she said. "But it don't make it any safer for you. And, Derrick, I feel responsible.''

17

Derrick swung around. He glowered at his sister. "Rettie, I'm my own man and only I am responsible for what I do."

"But I *did* urge you. . . ."

"You may think so but I had decided long before your husband's death that I had to have more in life than what I had found in New York State."

Rettie drew in a deep breath. "And this life you've found is better?" she gasped. "In a log cabin that don't even have fit'n doors and windows to keep the cold out?"

Derrick took his pipe from between his lips and spat into the flames causing a low sizzling sound to surface. "No. Not yet, it ain't," he said in a near whisper. "But I'm gettin' there. One day you'll see."

Rettie placed a hand on Derrick's arm. "Until then, can I still take Lorinda home with me to see to her proper schoolin'?" she asked quietly. "I want to at least do that."

"You owe me nothin'," Derrick growled. "I don't want *no* handouts from my kin. I'm my own man."

"For Lorinda then?" Rettie said, pleading with the dark of her eyes.

" 'Cause of Indians or 'cause you really want to see to her education?"

" 'Cause of both, I reckon," Rettie said, dropping her hand to her side. "So? Can she return to St. Paul with me again? She can do as in the past. She can work for her keep. This is what she's always wanted, to earn her keep. And Lord knows I can use all the help I can get."

Derrick swung around. His gaze met Lorinda's and held. He would miss her. Mavis would miss her. But how did Lorinda feel? It was hard for him ever to know her true feelings. Her complex personality and changeable nature made it hard for anyone to penetrate her thoughts. She was like a damn Indian, that one, so hard to understand. "Lorinda?" he said, walking toward her. He placed his pipe on the dining table then took both of Lorinda's hands in his. "Honey, what do you want to do? Tell your Pa your true feelin's for once. Eh?"

Lowering her thick veil of lashes, Lorinda felt a blush rising. How could she tell her father she was torn between wants? Would he feel that she was betraying him? If he had had a son to work by his side, things would have been different. She had been all they had . . . until Amanda.

Remembering Amanda gave her a small sense of security. They *did* have Amanda now to love and fill their long, dull evenings with. Her heart pounded as she began to speak. "Father, I do enjoy schooling," she said. "I *do* enjoy learning."

"Eh? You do?"

"Do you understand, Father?"

He squeezed her hands more tightly, feeling how callus-free her fingers were. Yes, this was what he wanted for his beautiful daughter. Yes. She *had* to go with Rettie. It was Lorinda's rightful place in the world, *not* a one-room log cabin where life had proved to be hard. It was too late for him and Mavis, but not for Lorinda.

"Yep. You're right to choose schoolin'," he blurted. He drew her into his arms and held her tightly, strangely feeling it might be their last time to enjoy such an intimate embrace. He burrowed his nose into the depths of her red hair and smelled the freshness of creek water in it, then let her free to pass her hugs around to her mother and baby sister.

"And you'd best get on your way 'fore the sun gets lower in the sky. Mornin' has a way of turnin' to night quite fast this month of September," Derrick said, eyeing the already filled carpetbag waiting beside the door. He had known all along that Lorinda was prepared to leave, but they always seemed to have to go through the same rituals of outwardly showing doubts and guilts. He under-

19

stood this. It was the way of families . . . families who had tight bonds among themselves.

Mavis rose from the chair, securing Amanda in the crook of her left arm and tucking her breast inside her dress with her free hand. She was choked with emotion, already envisioning the long days and nights of winter without Lorinda. But it was necessary. It was necessary. She stifled a sob when Lorinda reached her arms out for Amanda and when Mavis eased Amanda into Lorinda's arms, she held her tears intact and relished this moment of her daughters together. She trembled inside, wanting to hug them both to her, to never let them go. . . .

"Sweet baby sister," Lorinda cooed as she pulled the thin yellow-striped blanket away from Amanda's face. She let her gaze move slowly over the tiny features, oh, so delicate, oh, so pink. Amanda's blue eyes squinted as she studied Lorinda back. For a moment, time seemed to stand still as sister studied sister, as though memorizing one another for some future use. Then Lorinda leaned her lips against Amanda's brow and kissed it gently, tasting and smelling the sweetness of the delicate baby's flesh. "When I return, you will even be walking, baby sister," Lorinda said. "Maybe even talking. Won't you be such a big girl then ?"

"Come, precious," Rettie encouraged. "The sun does have a way of creepin' toward the horizon much too quickly this time of year."

Lorinda handed Amanda back to her mother, feeling an ache circling her heart. She swung around to face her father with wide eyes. "Father, maybe the winter won't be so harsh," she said eagerly. "Maybe you could travel in to St. Paul so I can see Amanda occasionally. Maybe I can even come home. . . ."

Derrick clasped her shoulders roughly. "You don't *ever* consider travelin' back here unless you're escorted by your Aunt Rettie," he said firmly. "Do you hear?"

Lorinda gulped hard. "Yes, sir. It was just an idea."

"You must never travel alone," Derrick warned further. "*Never.* Too much can happen."

"Then you *are* afraid of Indians?" Lorinda said quietly.

"Indians?" he said darkly. "Who said anythin' 'bout Indians? Did I say anythin' bout Indians? It's the white man with lust in his heart for a beauty like you that I'm a-worryin' 'bout ."

"Then you might come into town, since I can't come home?"

"We'll see," he said. "We'll see."

"Lorinda . . ." Rettie fussed.

"Yes, ma'am," Lorinda said. "I'm coming." She made her rounds with hugs and kisses, then grabbed her carpetbag and followed her aunt and climbed aboard the stately, fringe-topped black buggy that was to be led by a lone black stallion.

With a rapid heartbeat and tears surfacing, Lorinda looked toward her mother and father standing arm in arm. She said a final goodbye as Rettie encouraged the horse to move away from the house with a loud shout of "Hahh," and with the jerk and slap of the reins.

Lorinda continued to wave until Rettie commanded the horse around a bend, leaving only a railed fence at both sides of the clearing as proof of the energy with which her father daily labored. Stubs of trees poked through the ground as far as the eye could see, where her father was preparing the land for future crops of corn and beans. A spring, rippling clear and fresh along the inside of the fence railing reminded Lorinda of the times she had carried butter and milk to place in the coolness of the water for safekeeping. She had even been instructed how to dig holes near the spring so that food could be stored in a cool place without getting it wet. These were the primitive ways of life that she was leaving behind. In St. Paul, merchants had learned to cut ice from the river in winter to keep food cold, and to sell it in different-sized "cakes" to village residents. And not only did Aunt Rettie have occasional cakes of ice on hand, she also had a cast iron, woodburning cooking stove in a separate room where the cooking was done, and separate, private rooms for everyone, with iron beds and soft feather mattresses. It was a different world for Lorinda at her aunt Rettie's and she couldn't help but feel bubbles of excitement growing inside her the closer the horse drew to the village.

"You're a bit flushed, Lorinda," Rettie said, glancing sideways toward her. "You're not gettin' ill on me, are you? Might you need to wrap a shawl around your shoulders or place a bonnet on your head? You're not used to this bumpy ride by buggy."

"Aunt Rettie, don't you realize that my flush is from excitement?"

"Then you are glad to come home with me again?"

"Oh, so much," Lorinda sighed, lifting her face, inhaling the heady fragrance of the afternoon. The crisp, cooler evenings had already caused the maple trees' leaves to turn to blazing red, and floating webs sparkled from tree to tree limb, catching in their stickiness small unsuspecting insects and loosened, fading fluff from the cottonwood trees.

A shrill shriek from a bluejay overhead caused Lorinda to jump with a start. She had never heard such a loud call from a bluejay before. It had seemed to silence all the other birds' nervous chatter in the treetops. Lorinda shuddered a bit, feeling suddenly strangely alone. Something compelled her to glance quickly back towards where her parents' log cabin stood, now hidden from her sight by a protrusion of trees.

Lorinda shuddered again, not knowing why. Then she realized that the birds' chatter above her head in the shadows of the trees had resumed as a bluejay swooped suddenly down to rest on a limb next to where Rettie and Lorinda were passing. Its beady black eyes shone sparks of danger in them, and again Lorinda did not know why.

"We'd best enjoy the music of the crickets while we can," Rettie said as she snapped the horse's reins harshly. "Won't be long now and their voices will be stilled by the heavy cover of autumn's first frost."

Ignoring her aunt's idle talk, Lorinda hugged herself as she glanced on all sides of her. She hadn't thought much about it before, but she was now realizing that the forest could hide many things . . . maybe even . . . Indians. Her heart raced, wishing to see houses in the distance instead of more trees. She suddenly felt very vulnerable and too alone in this vast wilderness. Her excitement was changing to fear. She then looked toward the shotgun loaded and ready on her aunt's lap, but felt no safer. Indians were swift. One gun would *not* be enough.

"Lorinda, did you hear what I said?" Rettie said impatiently. "Precious, where *is* your mind wanderin' to?"

Lorinda forced a laugh. "You said the crickets' songs would soon be stilled," she said.

"Yes. Somethin' to that effect," Rettie laughed.

"This is the one thing I don't like about the autumn of the year," Lorinda murmured.

"And what is that, precious?"

"Death," Lorinda said, trembling a bit. "Death comes to so many things. . . ."

"My, oh, my, but you sound morbid," Rettie said. "Precious, you're much too young to be thinkin' on such things as death."

"I guess it's just because we're so alone," Lorinda replied softly, glancing around her again.

Rettie cackled throatily. "It's the Indians," she said. "I've done and got you afraid of Indians. Land sakes, precious, it's just like your pa says. They've been peace-

23

ful enough lately. You don't have no true reason to fret. I just use those tales to encourage your pa to move into town where he can make a decent livin'. That's all.''

"If you believe that, why the loaded gun?"

Rettie's brow furrowed. She glanced at the gun, then at Lorinda. ''Don't hurt a soul to be prepared for anythin' that might jump out at you while you're on the trail,'' she said. ''Since becomin' widowed, I've had to learn to protect myself.''

"Then you truly don't worry about Indians?"

''Harumph,'' Rettie said, then clucked to the horse and sat in silence until the edge of town was reached. Only then could Lorinda relax and let excitement begin to build inside her again.

As Rettie maneuvered the horse and buggy down one rut-filled dirt street after another, Lorinda became all eyes, seeing once again the bustling city whose population totaled more than ten thousand. With only gossip of a railroad coming through, the main mode of travel remained the steamboat. There were at the present time sixty-two steamboats that could make more than a thousand landings in a year's time, bringing new settlers, mail, and supplies.

Most of the houses were small squares of planed lumber, but many were the kind of log cabin that Lorinda was leaving behind. Above all the houses that were scattered unevenly about, Lorinda could see the dome of the first capitol building of this new state, and she knew that her Aunt Rettie's house stood nearby.

Aunt Rettie's two-story frame house was becoming well known. Congressmen and senators slept over there when they were unable to return to their own private housing because of pressing issues that required them to remain close to the Capitol, where laws of the land were being laid out. But there were still undesirables, as well, who sometimes managed to get a room at Lorinda's

24

aunt's house, and as Rettie guided the horse and buggy to a halt, Lorinda saw just such a man standing on her aunt's front porch. Lorinda knew him, and she had hoped he had moved onward.

She tensed and gripped the edge of the seat, remembering this Scandanavian lumberjack, Lamont Quinby, with his wild, sandy-colored hair, gray eyes, and thick blonde mustache. When he arrived to St. Paul the past early summer, before Lorinda had gone back to her parents' homestead for the nonschooling months, Lorinda had thought he was just passing through. He *had* originally been traveling toward the new settlement which had been named Duluth, where trees were nearby in abundance for felling. But after having seen Lorinda, Lamont Quinby had delayed his plans of moving on northward, and had begun, instead, a pursuit of her, though quietly, behind Aunt Rettie's back. Lamont's rough hands and roving eyes disgusted Lorinda, yet she hadn't revealed any of her worries about this man to her aunt. Lorinda had felt capable of fending for herself. But now, she was filled with dread, realizing that Lamont Quinby just hadn't given up all that easily.

"Precious, we made it safe and sound, just as I knew we would," Rettie said as she lifted the shotgun from her lap and climbed from the buggy. Puffing, she lifted the skirt of her dress and moved up the steps to her porch. She eyed Lamont Quinby questioningly. She had yet to figure him out. He had no true business in St. Paul, yet he continued to hang around. "See you're still here, Mr. Quinby," she said, lifting an eyebrow as she peered upward, intensely, into his face.

"Didn't say I wuz leavin'," he said, flicking ashes from a thick cigar. His eyes hadn't left Lorinda. He had waited a full summer for her and by damn he would soon make her his. He'd wasted enough time. No courtin' ritual would be used. He'd seduce her then worry her into

25

marryin' up with him. He already felt the heat rising in his loins just thinking on it. By damn, he would have her, and soon, aunt or no. No aunt would cause his planning to go awry. If'n Lorinda hadn't been with her ma and pa all summer, Lamont just knew he'd already be in Duluth with his beautiful, red-haired wife at his side, the envy of all the lumber camp.

"No. You didn't say you were leavin'," Rettie said, resting the barrel of her shotgun in the crook of her left arm. " But sure don' know what's holdin' you here. You don't have business at that fancy capitol buildin' nor have I heard you makin' plans to start a business of your own in town. What *is* your attraction to my boardin' house, Mr. Quinby?" She felt a sudden chill ride her spine when she became aware of his steady gazing at Lorinda. Was he attracted . . . to Lorinda. . . ? She set her jaws firmly. She should've known! Why hadn't she suspected?

"I pay my way, don' I?" Lamont growled, snapping his bright red suspenders that held up loose-fitted, gray, coarse-materialed breeches. His red plaid cotton shirt reflected reds onto his face, making his complexion appear blotchy. But Rettie recognized the flush of heated desire in a man when she saw it, and she now knew to be on guard for Lorinda at all times.

"Yep. Guess you do at that," she said quietly. "Yep. Guess you do pay your way. But don't 'spect to receive anything but board and keep for that pay."

"Eh?" Lamont asked, this having drawn his attention from Lorinda. "What's that you say, ol' woman?"

Rettie slipped the shotgun from its resting place on her arm and let the barrel point toward Lamont. In her raspy voice, she said, "Mister, I think you know exactly what's on my mind." She turned her gaze to Lorinda who had sat, as though hypnotized, through the battle of words. Rettie nodded her head toward her. "Come on, precious," she said. "Let's get you settled in your room.

Just ignore this vermin standin' so smugly on my porch.''

"Yes, ma'am," Lorinda said. She lifted her carpetbag and climbed from the buggy and hurried up the steps. As she passed by Lamont Quinby, she could feel his eyes undressing her and she dreaded him even more. When Rettie moved on into the house ahead of Lorinda, Lorinda took the opportunity to turn to Lamont.

"You leave me be," she hissed. "You leave me be. Do you hear?"

He chuckled and walked away from her, leaving her to stand alone with hate in her heart.

Two

The soft fluff of the featherbed and the smell of the clean patchwork quilt thrown luxuriously across Lorinda gave her just cause to not want to rise from her bed. But the splash of morning sunrise through the one window in her room spoke to her of her first day back in St. Paul. She not only had household chores to do for her aunt, but she was also anxious to go to the schoolhouse to take a quick peek through the paned glass window to see if preparations were being made to open its doors for another autumn term.

As far as Lorinda could gather, this could be the last of her schooling. It was hard to tell, with all ages of children studying together in one room, and only one teacher over them all. But Lorinda did feel prepared for life from the teachings she had managed to procure in bits and pieces, from town to town, and schoolhouse to schoolhouse.

A shuffling of feet outside Lorinda's closed bedroom door made her rise slowly on one elbow. Her hair cascaded in its auburn reds across the shoulder of her cream-colored, high-necked cotton night sack, competition now for the brilliant colors of the morning sunrise rippling on the door in pinkish reds.

Lorinda pulled the patchwork quilt up to her chin when she saw a slow movement of the doorknob. It turned one way and then the other, reminding Lorinda of her brief escape of the previous evening. When she had decided to turn in for the night, Lamont Quinby had been waiting for her, lurking in the dark shadows of the hallway. The

29

heavy footsteps of her aunt's approach had been Lorinda's reprieve for that moment. But now? Was it Lamont Quinby again?

"Surely not in broad daylight," Lorinda whispered. But she knew the early hour of the day. Since this was a city and there were no farm chores to pull one from bed at the crack of dawn, most slept until a more convenient time for rising, which would give Lamont complete freedom to move about without being detected.

"And Aunt Rettie sleeps even later, Lorinda worried aloud. "The cook is the first to rise. . . ."

Lorinda then sighed, remembering more about the previous evening. She knew that she should feel safe enough, having bolt-locked the door, but the continuing turns of the knob were slowly unnerving her. She crept from the bed and across the room . "Who's there?" she said quietly, leaning her ear to the door.

A raspy voice spoke softly back to her, making Lorinda smile and flip the bolt lock aside. When the door flew widely open before she even had the chance to open it herself, she jumped back, startled. She then felt a weakness in both heart and knees when she discovered that the voice she had heard had *not* been that of her aunt. Lamont Quinby had managed to fool Lorinda by the clever disguise of his voice. In one quick flash of movement, he was inside Lorinda's room.

"You!" she gasped. "Mr. Quinby, what *do* you think you are doing by first pretending to be my aunt and then bursting into the privacy of my room?" She tried to stop the shakiness in her voice by clearing her throat. She squared her shoulders and thrust her chin haughtily into the air. "*And*, Mr. Quinby," she continued as he stood with a half-smile of mockery lifting his blonde mustache from his lips, " if you do not turn and leave this room at once, I shall scream."

With the toe of this boot, Lamont inched the door shut.

"An' be fuel for scandalous gossip in this capital city called St. Paul?" he laughed. "No, you wouldn't be foolish enough to do that." The wildness of his sandy-colored hair matched that in his gray pools of eyes as he now towered over Lorinda, even larger in size than her father. He reached for her and drew her roughly into his arms and crushed his lips against hers.

Lorinda's heart pounded with outrage and hate. She struggled to free her arms that were pinned against this steel brute force of a man and she worked even harder at freeing her lips. She couldn't stand the smell of him. He reeked of cigar smoke and whiskey. The wetness of his open mouth and the way his tongue was exploring inside her mouth made Lorinda feel as though she might retch.

Without giving up his tight hold on her arms and lips, Lamont began to inch Lorinda back toward the bed. Soon he would have her. After he took her sexually, even her aunt would welcome a wedding band from him on her niece's finger.

Ah, yes. He would see to it that Lorinda would be his. Wives were hard to find in these parts . . . especially a wife that would be as pleasing to the eye as Lorinda.

Lorinda struggled and squirmed some more, finally able to catch her breath when Lamont eased his lips from hers. "You filthy man," she hissed. "Let me go or you'll be sorry." She flinched as one of his hands lowered and began stroking a breast through the coarse material of her night sack. His other hand guided her downward, onto the bed.

"Sweetheart, nothin' will stop me now," he said in a passion-filled voice. "I've waited roun' for you all summer. I ain't waitin' no longer. Come on. Relax. Let me show you the enjoys you can get from my body next to yours." He lowered himself over her, holding her immobile against the soft feathers of the mattress.

"Why me?" Lorinda argued, becoming breathless

31

from her continued struggles. "Why not a woman who is willing? Mr. Lamont, I've never been with a man before. Please leave me be."

His mouth left wet trails of kisses all over her face as his left hand lowered to lift her night sack to her waist. "Why you?" he laughed. "Damn it, sweetheart, ain't you ever looked in a mirror? You're beautiful and *so* damn desirable. And knowin' I'm the first man to take you don' matter to me. You're ripe for showin' *how*. It's bes' to marry up with a woman you've showed how to love."

Lorinda's breath caught in her throat. "Marry. . . ?" she gasped. She was mortified, not only by his words, but by what his hand had managed to do with her night sack, now realizing how exposed she was to this man of no morals. No man had ever seen her *ankles,* let alone other completely private parts of her anatomy.

"You're goin' to be my wife," he said, panting with heated desire. He lowered his mouth to the peak of a breast and nipped at a nipple through her night sack. "Nobody else's. Ever," he added, in a threatening tone of voice. "I can't let *any* man have you. You're mine. . . ."

The bedroom door burst open with a loud crash as it banged back against the wall. The quick rush of feet and rustle of skirt alerted Lorinda to the fact that she was soon to be rescued by her Aunt Rettie. Her eyes widened when she saw the stiff bristles of a broom lift into the air and crash down on top of Lamont's head with a loud whack.

"You low-down ugly brute, I knew you had no good on your mind when I first seen you," Rettie growled. "I seen it in the shiftiness of your eyes." As she talked, she continued to raise and lower the broom atop his head. When he swung suddenly around, the broom's bristles caught him in the face with such a fierce blow, blood was drawn in tiny, round spurts, causing Lamont to let out a loud wail. He jumped from the bed, holding his face between his hands, growling.

"You damn ol' woman," he said darkly. "You bitch. What have you done to me?" He began to stumble towards the door, still groaning, but before he left the room, he turned and stared toward Lorinda, now revealing the full extent of his injuries to her as he dropped his hands to his side. His face looked as though a dozen snakes had pierced his flesh with their forked tongues, as blood continued to trickle from the wounds in tiny rivers of red.

"Don' forget what I said, sweetheart," he said icily. He doubled a fist into the air and held it out before him. "Nobody but me. Ever. . . ."

Lorinda felt a chill encompass her, seeing the cool glint of evil in the depths of his steel-gray eyes. It was quite apparent that his pursuit of her had not been brought to a halt by the blows of the broom. She moved to cover herself with the quilt as she saw his gaze settle on the lower extremities of her that he had so wickedly uncovered with the coarse, rough touch of his fingers. She winced as her aunt raced across the room, swinging her broom anew.

"You scalawag," Rettie raved, landing a blow on his shoulder. "You get your things and get out of my place. Now! Do you hear?"

Lamont cowered, covering his face with his arms. "Yeah. I hear," he grumbled. "You fat ol' woman, I hear. I'm gettin'. I'm gettin'. Just lower that damn broom. I don' want to have to hurt you none. Do *you* hear?"

"Just you try," Rettie laughed hoarsely. "I'm stronger than most men. Just try me. It'd be fun showin' you."

Lamont scurried from the room, leaving Lorinda a bit trembly, yet amused by how her aunt had handled the situation. She only wished now that it had been *she* showing such spunk. But she had been at a disadvantage, having

33

been held by force beneath the wide expanse of a man who would always cause her insides to turn to stone.

She rose from the bed as Rettie closed the bedroom door. But when her aunt turned and gazed intently toward Lorinda, Lorinda was suddenly afraid that possibly her aunt might think that Lamont had been teased into the room purposely. Wasn't that what was in the depths of her aunt's dark eyes? An accusing? The bolt lock on the door *had* been slipped aside. . . .

Lorinda lowered her lashes, turning her eyes from her aunt. She could even feel the heat in her cheeks, realizing that she was blushing. She felt as though she was in a trap, though not one of her own making, and wondered if her aunt would really believe her if she denied having any part in what had just happened.

"Lorinda, how . . . ?" Rettie spoke softly, still standing stiffly by the door in a lilac velveteen night robe. Her hair was set free from its bun and hung in wiry gray masses across her shoulders and down her back. The aroma of her cologne overpowered all other smells in the room as though a garden of lilies of the valley was spread at Lorinda's feet.

"He forced his way in here," Lorinda replied, now quite determinedly meeting her aunt's steady gaze.

"The lock. He couldn't have. . . ."

"I can't believe you are actually doubting me," Lorinda said. She hated it that her lower lip was trembling, but she felt deceived by her aunt and her show of lack of trust and faith in her.

"I don't want to doubt you," Rettie said. She went to Lorinda and lifted her hair from her shoulders, openly admiring it. "Precious, all I know is that I found this man in your room, on your bed, with an unlatched door provin' how he had made his entrance. You're a beautiful thing now, all filled out and ready for love, and how am I to know that mebbe you wanted to see what it was like to

34

be with a man? It'd be only healthy, you know."

"Aunt Rettie," Lorinda gasped. She slapped her aunt's hands away from her hair. "I never . . . would *never* . . . ." she quickly added. She turned abruptly on a heel and hurried toward her wardrobe to choose her day's apparel. She *had* to get away. *Now.* She was suddenly seeing a different aunt.

"Lorinda, precious, I'm sorry," Rettie said. She rushed to Lorinda's side, watching almost frantically as Lorinda jerked clothes angrily from inside the wardrobe. She further watched as Lorinda slipped into a riding skirt and blouse and pulled boots onto her feet.

"What are you doin', Lorinda?" Rettie said thickly. She tensed as Lorinda briskly pulled a brush through her long streamers of red hair, then moved toward the door after throwing the brush on top of the bed.

"I need some fresh air," Lorinda said. "I feel as though I've been cruelly attacked by two people this morning instead of just one." She ran from the room, leaving her aunt standing alone, gasping with horror. Lorinda covered her mouth with her hand, feeling suddenly ashamed of her outburst of words. It *was* disrespectful of her, yet she would never forget the look of distrust in her aunt's eyes. Oh, it wasn't fair! Lorinda had never teased a man. *Never!* It was not in her nature to do such a thing. Why hadn't her aunt known this?

Rushing on down the staircase, Lorinda didn't stop to take in the convenient luxury and pleasantness of her surroundings. The previous evening, as soon as she had arrived, she had openly admired the neatly papered walls with their leaf design; the gleam of the hardwood floors; the paned-glass windows with the lacy white curtains draped luxuriously across each one, and the gracefulness of the upholstered sofa and rosewood tables and chairs. In her heart she hoped that one day her parents would have such possessions as these. Only her father's stubbornness could stand in the way. He had his *own* dreams.

The aroma of sausage and eggs frying almost side-tracked Lorinda into the kitchen, but her need to get away, to think, was even greater than the hungry ache at the pit of her stomach. She ran from the house and around to the back where her aunt's beautiful black stallion was housed in an outbuilding all its own. The fresh smell of damp straw greeted Lorinda as she reached for a blanket and saddle, and when she had the horse ready for this early morning romp, Lorinda mounted him and urged him quickly away before her aunt could give chase with the raspiness of her voice.

Lorinda knew the streets of the city quite well, and this early in the day she had them mostly to herself. She rode past the Chapel of St. Paul. It had been erected by members of Father Lucien Galtier's small congregation in 1841. The settlement that had become the state's capital city had taken its name from this chapel. It was small, one story, with few windows, and a gold cross above its double doors, but it was still one of the main centers of social life among St. Paul's proud settlers. The church was a meeting place, where the pioneer families saw their neighbors socially. At other times they worked together on different projects, for instance, when the women gathered in one of their homes for a quilting bee.

Lorinda rode on past the capital building, noticing that some fancy carriages were already drawn up to the steep steps of the front entrance, discharging men in formal attire—black waistcoats, black pants, and top hats. Lorinda had been told by her aunt that those who arrived earlier were the ones who were the most dedicated to improving the laws of the land, among them possibly one who might one day become president of the United States. At this moment, this was the least of Lorinda's concerns. She had almost been successfully seduced by a man this morning, and she had lost a bit of admiration for

36

the aunt whom, only the day previous, she had held in such high esteem.

She clucked to her horse and thrust her knees into his side, not caring when the wind lifted her skirt to an almost daring height just below her knees. No one was looking her way. After having left the capitol building behind her, she felt almost alone in the world.

She kept the horse at a steady gallop until she reached an embankment that overlooked the muddy waters of the Mississippi River. Dismounting, she secured the horse's reins to a lower branch of a stately elm and moved through the dew-dampened grass until she stood at the edge of the embankment, looking downward at the quiet, steadily flowing water. A steamboat became visible around a bend in the river, emitting black coughs of smoke upward into the sky. Lorinda sighed, smiling. She was remembering the past spring. The winter had been long and tedious, frosty and intense with cold temperatures. The snow had set in on the first of November, and, from that time until April, all the hills, valleys, and lakes had been shrouded with the white mantle of winter, and the river had been bound in icy fetters. Communications had been cut off and all had awaited the arrival of spring, which, when it finally happened, was in the form of one of the fiercest storms in St. Paul's history.

Towards evening on that ninth day of April the clouds had gathered, and, just at dark, a violent storm of wind, rain, and loud peals of thunder had begun. The darkness had been shot through with vivid flashes of lightning. Then, in a sudden, momentary lull of the wind, the silence had been broken by the never-to-be-mistaken groan of a steam engine. In another moment, the shrill whistle of a steamboat had thrilled through the air, cutting through the heavy booming of heaven's artillery. Another moment had passed, and then a bright flash of lightning had revealed the welcome shape of a steamboat just

37

rounding the bluff. Regardless of the pelting rain, the raging wind and pealing thunder, the population of St. Paul had rushed to the landing as the fine steamboat, the *Dr. Franklin No. 2,* dashed gallantly up to the landing.

"And that's the first time I saw that terrible Lamont Quinby," Lorinda hissed, doubling her fists to her side. She had been one of the throng, watching the boat unload its passengers, and, even then, when Lamont had stepped out onto the snow next to where she stood, his gaze had met and held hers.

"Oh, how I hate . . ." she began, but was stopped by the rough feel of a callused hand suddenly covering her mouth. Her heart leaped inside her, as she felt even more than the hand on her mouth. She could feel the barrel of a gun causing quite a discomfort in the small of her back. Lorinda cringed and felt her knees grow weak when she recognized the voice of her assailant.

"Now, just you do as you're tol' and things'll be all right," Lamont Quinby said darkly.

Lorinda worked with her mouth, uttering soft mumblings of protest against the still tight clasp of his fingers. Again she recognized the smell of him by the scent of cigars on his yellow-stained fingers. She strained her body away from him as he began forcing her to turn around. Again she was reminded of the gun when he thrust it even harder into her stomach as she found herself with a freed mouth, and now facing him.

"You have to be crazy to do what you're doing," she said, licking her lips, clearing them of the foul taste of his hands. Her gaze moved to the pearl-handled pistol resting against her body. "And a gun? Sir, you *must* be daft."

Her gaze moved back to his face. She could see dried droplets of blood where he had been attacked with the broom. His eyes appeared to be hazed over with a strange mixture of anger and passionate desire. Lorinda had bravely spoken her mind, but, inside, she was a mass of ripples. The gun . . . his determination . . . were just cause for alarm. Still she knew that she *had* to defend herself. She had chosen an isolated place to do her thinking. She hadn't thought to watch, to see if she had been followed. With a quick jerk of the head, she looked in another direction and saw a black carriage and brown mare standing behind a cluster of ground cedar, and she wondered what Lamont Quinby *did* have planned for her if she didn't escape.

"Daft?" he chuckled. "Sweetheart, smart's the word to use. You're comin' with me now. Your aunt ain't here to stop me. An' when you stop puttin' up such a fuss and take to lovin' me, you'll be glad I made you my wife."

Lorinda laughed amusedly, glancing once more at the gun then back into his face. "Wife? *Sir,* I would *never* exchange vows with the likes of you," she said. She spat at his feet and lifted her chin haughtily.

"When we get to Duluth, you'll have no choice in the matter," he said. He poked her with the gun and urged her to move toward where the carriage waited. "You'll be in a camp of love-hungry gents, and if'n you've not spoken vows with me, all the men'll be clamoring to get their hands in yore breeches."

Lorinda's face reddened. She now knew for sure what his plans were. He was kidnapping her. *Kidnapping her!* The thought of traveling with him . . . sharing a bed roll with him . . . and even more . . . set her heart to thumping wildly from angry disgust.

Out of the corner of her eye, she watched him. He moved with her, occasionally poking her with the gun to urge her on even faster. She lifted her skirt to step over a large rock, then took in a deep breath as she purposely tripped and landed awkwardly onto the ground. She eyed him speculatively as he abruptly stopped above her, waiting. She feigned hurt. She groaned and reached for her ankle, still watching him.

"Damn it, girl, get up," he grumbled, shifting his feet nervously.

"I can't," she said, forcing a whine to her voice. "My ankle. It hurts so." She rubbed her ankle, moaning.

Lamont looked on all sides of him, grumbling to himself. Then he leaned down on one knee next to her, and, just as he did, Lorinda kicked the gun from his hand, kicked him in the face with the heel of her boot, then scooted up away from him and began to run in a stumbling fashion until she reached her horse.

Panting for breath, she untied the horse's reins, but just as she was about to mount him, she was jerked away and sent tumbling onto the ground with Lamont standing over her. She was afraid but smiled inwardly, seeing his bleeding nose and lip.

"I'm beginnin' to wonder if you're worth all the trouble I've been through this mornin'," he said with his hands on his hips and his legs widespread. "First I let the ol' woman get me with 'er broom and now *you* bloody my nose and lip. Two wildcats if'n I ever did see any." He wiped the blood away with the back of his hand, then leaned down and pulled her up next to him. "But I likes 'em full of fire," he chuckled.

Lorinda cringed and struggled against him when his lips crushed down upon hers. She tasted his blood and felt his roaming hands on her body. Again she kicked with her boots but this time only succeeded in angering him more. He pulled his lips free and bent and reached beneath her skirt and ripped some petticoat away and quickly had her hands tied behind her back with it.

"Now. If'n you even get away, you can't get far with tied hands," he laughed. "You can't mount yore horse, and as soon as I get you in the carriage, I'll even tie yore ankles."

"Then what?" Lorinda hissed.

"As I said. You're goin' with me," he said, jerking

her roughly along until his carriage was reached. "You're goin' to be Mrs. Lamont Quinby sometime real soon. Tha's what I've planned all summer whilst waitin' on you and nothin' is goin' to stand in my way. Not even yore cantankerous aunt, *nor* yore temper."

"You cannot force me to wed."

"By the time we reach Duluth, you'll want my name. It'd be the only proper thing to do once I take your virginity from you. You'd not have anythin' to save and flaunt to a 'proper fellow'—or whatever you'd call a man *you* might take a fancy to in the future."

"What . . . ?" she gasped.

Lamont placed his hands around Lorinda's waist and lifted her up into the carriage and onto the padded seat. "I bought this fine carriage especially for yore trip with me, sweetheart, " he said, ripping more material from her petticoat. He held her ankles still as he tied them securely together. "I know the fact that I have to tie you ain't so nice, but in such a fine carriage, at least you won't have to bounce around so."

Looking desperately around her, Lorinda was realizing the reality of what *was* happening to her. Her pulse raced, as she struggled with her secured ankles and wrists, only succeeding at causing them to become raw and sore. She thought of her aunt. What *would* her aunt do when the day passed without Lorinda's arrival back home? Surely she would go immediately to the sheriff! Lamont Quinby would be searched out and possibly even hung for this evil deed!

Ceasing to struggle, Lorinda eased her back against the plump softness of the carriage's interior. She had to think that she would soon be rescued. She couldn't lose hope. She sat in silence as Lamont slammed the carriage door behind him. Tensing, Lorinda watched his movements through the small space of the door's window. He was now guiding her aunt's black stallion toward the carriage

41

and when Lamont walked from view with it, Lorinda realized that he wasn't only kidnapping her, but also abducting the horse. But that made Lorinda smile smugly. With a horse trailing along behind, their escape would be slower, and also, it would make it easier for the sheriff to distinguish this traveling carriage from any others. This black stallion of her aunt's was one of only a few of its stately breed in St. Paul.

The too sudden jerk of the carriage as it began moving over clumps of weeds jolted Lorinda from the seat, causing her to bump her head against the flooring as she crashed downward onto it. Stunned, she lay there for a moment, then, with a slow, progressive achiness, she managed to get herself back on the seat. She inched her way to the window, hoping someone would ride close by. She wanted to yell for help. But Lamont was clever. He never once drew his carriage within yelling distance of a house *nor* a horse and buggy, and he was already directing the horse to the outskirts of town.

Tears sprang to Lorinda's eyes. She had never felt so utterly helpless. But she had to keep reassuring herself that she had tried as best she could to defend herself, and had to continue believing that this inconvenience was only momentary. The sheriff would soon be on the trail. She *would* be rescued! She *would!* NO evil man could get away with this. It just wasn't right! It just wasn't fair!

Lorinda took a fast glance from the window, then another. She swallowed back her tears and felt an inner ray of hope rippling in warm flashes throughout her. Lamont was now traveling on a country road quite familiar to her. She knew it from the many trips to and from her parents' homestead. She had been on this very road only the day before and was now seeing the same scarlet-reds of the maple trees' leaves and the golden-browns of the towering oaks.

She was so happy to see it, the sparkle of a stream at

the side of the road could have been diamonds. She knew that the chances were great that her father would be working the ground outside his homestead close to this very same creek this time of day and would recognize her screams for help. *Then* she would show this terrible Lamont Quinby. Lorinda knew her father well enough to know that he would give Lamont the beating of his life before handing him over to the sheriff.

Sighing heavily, Lorinda could relax a bit. She knew that they did have a distance to go before rescue would become imminent. She eased her back against the cushion but never took her eyes off the side of the road, watching for the familiar railed fence that her father had built, and when she caught sight of that very first rail, she scooted back to the edge of the seat and anxiously waited.

Wide-eyed, she felt the slick nervous perspiration of the palms of her hands and felt such a racing of her heartbeat she wasn't sure if she could stand it. She was only moments away from seeing her father . . . and from being rescued from this vile creature. She only hoped that he would hang from a rope for all to see, to scare off any other men who might have such evil lurking in their hearts.

Now counting the rails and seeing the tree stumps in the fields on both sides of her, Lorinda knew that at any moment she could see her father with his horse and plow. The morning sun was quite high now and she could envision him tall and stout, attired in faded overalls, with sweat beads glistening on his brow beneath his thick head of auburn hair. His full auburn beard would even have sparkles of sweat on its ends as he would be urging his horse to help pull the plow through the root-infested land he had become so proud of. He hadn't let a fear of *any*thing stand in the way of his dream. . . .

An aroma of burning wood captured Lorinda's keen attention as it floated leisurely through the open windows of the carriage. But then she smiled. She knew that she wouldn't find her father plowing this day, but instead, using the horse to pull stumps from the earth, having already set fire to those he had pulled free.

As the smell grew progressively stronger and was even causing a foggy haze on all sides of the carriage, Lorinda's heart raced wildly. At any moment now, her father would be in full view. How dumb this Lamont Quinby was to keep urging his horse onward into this smoke-infested area. Surely he *had* to know that where there was smoke there was fire and where there was fire there was man.

Lorinda laughed confidently. "Oh, what a surprise you have in store for *you,* Mr. Lamont Quinby," she whispered.

Her heart skipped a beat when she felt the slowing of the carriage. Had Lamont seen her father at the side of the road before even she could see him . . . to yell . . . at him . . . ? Was this Lamont Quinby not so . . . dumb . . . after . . . all . . . ?

Almost toppling from the seat in her haste to see further from the window, Lorinda struggled, succeeding at balancing herself again, then managed to lean her head through the window, only to wish now that she hadn't. With shock registering inside her brain like a million stabs from a knife, she saw the reason for Lamont's having drawn the carriage to a complete stop. The aroma of wood burning hadn't been from tree stumps, but . . . but . . . from her parents' one-room log cabin and one outbuilding.

As Lorinda sat, stunned into continued silence, she looked anguishedly around her. All that remained of the log cabin was charred ruins and a lone chimney reaching ghostlike into the sky . Then her wits returned and her thoughts were of her family. "Mother, father, Amanda. . . ." she whispered, then began screaming their names over and over again while struggling to free herself of her bonds to go in search of them. When Lamont hurriedly opened the carriage door and looked at her questioningly, she screamed out the truth of whose house they had just discovered.

"God," Lamont said. "Jesus . . . God . . ." he said again, standing immobile, glancing at the charred ruins, then back again toward Lorinda.

"Set me free," Lorinda cried. "You must set me free. I must find my family. Surely they are all right. They have to be nearby unharmed. They have to be. . . ."

Lamont's eyes darkened. He felt a queasiness at his stomach. From his higher perch on the carriage seat he had seen farther onto the land surrounding the log cabin. And what he had seen hadn't been pleasant. Damn it. How could he have known that this road would lead him straight to Lorinda's kin? How could he have known that this kin would be found scalped and with arrows piercing their flesh? How could he allow Lorinda to see the . . . bodies . . . ? But how could he not?

"Sweetheart, let's just move on," he encouraged. "Yore kin are prob'ly back in St. Paul now, safe and sound. Just you settle down and let us be on our way."

"No. Let me free," Lorinda yelled. "I've got to be allowed to see to my family. I've got to. Mr. Quinby, surely your heart isn't so cold that you can't understand. . . ."

Lamont glanced in the direction of the bodies then into Lorinda's green pools of eyes, seeing the pleading. "Oh, all right," he grumbled. "But only briefly. I don' intend to stay 'round these parts for long. I don' hanker for an Injun's arrow to be *my* way of dyin'. . . ."

Anxiously, Lorinda watched Lamont untying her bonds. "Indians?" she said. "Why on earth would you . . . mention Indians? " Something grabbed at her heart. The log cabin . . . ? Had the fire been purposely set?

45

Had it . . . not . . . been an accident? Her guts twisted, remembering her aunt's warnings.

"There. You're free. But I don' think you're gonna—" Lamont grumbled as he watched Lorinda scurry from inside the carriage. He stood back away and watched her fast approach to where he had seen the bodies. His body stiffened and he closed his eyes when he heard her mind-boggling screams.

Lorinda stooped over her mother, still screaming. It was as though it wasn't real, that she was experiencing some sort of nightmare. Her mother *couldn't* be lying there in a pool of blood with many arrows piercing her tiny, frail body. It couldn't be her mother whose facial expression was so twisted, so grotesque, so frozen in appearance, with her soft green eyes open, staring wildly, showing the horrors of her last moments of life on earth when an Indian had rid her of her long tresses of gray hair. . . .

"Oh, God," Lorinda said, lowering her face into her hands as her screams changed to body-wracking sobs. "Oh, God, Mother. Why? Oh, why . . . ?" Through the cracks between her fingers she caught sight of another body, close to the burned outbuilding, where all her father's farm implements had always been stored.

Crawling on her hands and knees, Lorinda went to her father. She swallowed back a bitterness rising in her throat when she saw him in the same condition as her mother, except that he was lying on his stomach with the arrows sticking straight up from his back.

"He didn't even have the chance to defend himself," she cried further into her hands. "The cowardly Indians had to sneak up on him from the rear." Again she felt as though she might retch when she couldn't help but stare at his scalped head. She gulped and gulped, so aching now from grief, remembering her father's pride in his thick head of rusty hair at his age of forty-nine. The hair

46

was now in the possession of some savage, murderous renegade Indian!

"Lorinda," Lamont said from close behind her. "We've gotta get out of here and fast. Those Injuns could return."

Lorinda cast him a look upward. "I've got to bury my parents," she said stiffly.

"No. You can't. . . ."

"I must," she said. "I cannot leave them. . . ." Her eyes grew wild and her heart jumped with alarm. She rushed to her feet, stumbling, looking frantically around her. "Amanda . . ." she whispered. "My God, how could I . . . have . . . forgotten my baby sister. . . ?" She began running around the yard, kicking at the charred remains of the house, sobbing wildly.

"Amanda . . . ?" she now screamed. "Oh, Amanda. Sweet little Amanda. Where are you . . . ?" Her insides felt empty. She had lost so much so quickly. And now? Had she also lost her sister?

"What is it, Lorinda?" Lamont said, going to her, breathless. He kept watching around him, truly fearing the Indians' return.

"My sister," Lorinda cried. "I can't find her. . . ."

Lamont lowered his eyes. "Maybe she died in the fire."

Lorinda's breathing ceased momentarily. She swung around and looked intently toward the smoking remains of the house. " Please, no," she prayed. Not worrying about the heat penetrating the soles of her boots, she made her way through the smoking debris to where her sister's cradle had always sat. With a pounding heart, she looked down onto the charred skeleton of the cradle and breathed more easily when no bones or skeletal remains of her sister could be found. But then she still had no answer. With weakened knees she went back to her mother's lifeless body and this time noticed Amanda's

47

yellow-striped blanket peeking partially out from beneath Mavis, miraculously free of bloodstains.

Dropping to her knees, Lorinda began to weep openly again. She pulled the blanket free and cradled it against her chest. She rocked back and forth on her knees, mourning all her losses, now realizing the fate of her baby sister. The Indians . . . had . . . taken her. . . .

Three

The campfire flickered in many shades of orange and the aroma of coffee made the dew-damp air of night seem warmer and cozier. But Lorinda wasn't warm or cozy. She tried to snuggle more deeply into her bedroll by the fire, wishing to stop trembling, but her thoughts continued to haunt and chill her, through and through. Would she ever be able to place the horrors of her parents' death behind her? The two days of travel since hadn't helped. It was as though she was living a nightmare that had no end. Even now as she closed her eyes, she could see the lifeless bodies . . . the pierced arrows . . . the scalped heads. And Amanda? Oh, how it tore at Lorinda's heart thinking about her baby sister Amanda. Had the Indians killed her ? Or were they even possibly . . . abusing . . . her . . . ? She reached for Amanda's blanket and hugged it to her.

"Still awake?" Lamont asked as he stooped next to her, rubbing his hands over the fire.

Lorinda didn't answer. She instead flipped over and placed her back to him. Not only had he kidnapped her, he had refused to let her bury her parents. He had even refused to take her back to St. Paul to let her report the massacre to the sheriff. Her hate for Lamont Quinby matched her hate for the Indians. But one day, she would get her revenge . . . on . . . *both* of them.

"Come on, sweetheart," Lamont said thickly. "It'd be cozier if we'd share one bedroll. I've let you alone these past two nights because of your grievin', but it's time to put that behind you and live for the livin'." He reached over and touched her hair. In the dancing shadows of the campfire, it was many shades of red. He licked his lips hungrily.

Lorinda slapped his hand away. "Leave me be, Lamont Quinby," she hissed. "You're no better than a renegade Indian. Only a heathen would leave bodies unburied. My parents deserved the peacefulness of graves with the proper Christian words spoken over them. I tremble to think that a wolf might. . . ."

"Don't think on it so much," Lamont grumbled. "Someone'll come along, Your kin'll have what's proper done to 'em."

Lorinda flipped over and eyed him angrily. "And you should have gone back into town and reported the massacre," she said scornfully. "You are less than human. You truly are. There's hardly ever anyone on that cleared road where my father chose to homestead. No one will find their bodies . . . if . . . there's any bodies left after the animals—"

"Hush, woman," Lamont said, reaching and grabbing one of her wrists. He jerked her to a sitting position, then closer to him. "I did what I had to do. I explained that to you. If'n I had gone back to St. Paul to tell of our findings, I would've walked right into a noose around my neck. Kidnappin' is *not* a minor offense and you know that. No. I had to think of the livin', namely *me*."

"I'm sure you're the only one you ever think about," Lorinda hissed, flinching when he squeezed her wrist even tighter.

"Tha's not quite true," he growled. "My mind is also full of you." He pushed her down and leaned down over her, letting his free hand begin unbuttoning her blouse. "And since I *am* thinkin' on my wants and needs, I refuse to let another night get past me 'fore havin' you."

Lorinda's breathing became erratic, hating the feel of

him pressing against her and the coarseness of his fingers as they were now touching the flesh of her breast. The smell of him, the mixture of perspiration and tobacco, caused her to cough and roll her head from side to side as his lips sought hers out. "I hate you," she screamed. "I hate you . . . hate you. . . ."

She was unable to say any more. She now not only smelled him but tasted his spittle as the wetness of his lips and tongue attacked her own. She gagged and began fighting. She was able to jerk her wrist free and with both hands began to shove and jerk at him. When that didn't work she chose to use her nails against the flesh of his face and at the same time raised a knee quickly into his groin.

"Yeow," Lamont yelled, rising. He rubbed at the raw wounds of his face and stood glowering down at her. "I guess I'll have to teach you who's boss," he growled. He began removing his belt but a sudden movement in the brush behind him caused him to swing around just as an Indian raised the butt of a rifle and came down with it across Lamont's right temple. Lamont stood as though in a daze for a brief moment, seeing a flash of yellow from a feather hanging from a coil of the Indian's hair before staring into the dark, expressionless eyes of the Indian. He then gave way to unconsciousness as he tumbled to the ground.

Lorinda watched in terror. She covered her mouth with her hands. She had the need to scream, but found that no sounds would surface. Her pulse raced both from fear and hate when she watched the Indian move stealthily toward her. She had never been close to an Indian before and couldn't help but let her gaze move slowly over him. He was tall, lean, and copper-skinned, with handsomely squared shoulders. His facial features were stern and his smoldering brown eyes flat and expressionless. His blue-black, coarse hair was cut in a fringe across the forehead with the remainder in two severely long braids that hung down his back, to his waist. A fillet of beads was stretched across his forehead and around his head to keep his hair in place, and a beautiful yellow feather hung distinctly from a coil of his hair.

When he moved to stand over her with legs widespread and with his rifle barrel resting in the crook of his left arm, she was quite aware of his attire—a breechcloth worn over tight, fringed leggings that extended from the ankles almost to the hip, where they were held in place by a thong tied to a belt. The bands for the leggings were made of beautiful woven beadwork, with a long fringe of yarn for tying them around the knees. His beaded doeskin moccasins were wrought intricately in patterns of porcupine quills dyed rose, green, and blue, and he wore no shirt, only narrow bands of fur around his wrists, the ends hanging and decorated with beads.

Lorinda's hate for him ran deep, yet she couldn't help but feel a strange stirring beginning inside her as he continued to stand over her in silence, now so obviously studying her back. He was handsome, so handsome his dark, fathomless eyes caused her heart to race. But then she forced herself to remember . . . remember her parents . . . her sister Amanda. This savage was probably the one responsible. He was the first Indian to make his presence known to them on this dreadful trip to Duluth.

Feeling the need to show courage and strength, Lorinda pushed herself up from the ground and placed her hands on her hips. She could feel the wobbling of her knees but knew that he couldn't see them beneath the protective coverings of her skirt, so she grew bolder and spat at his feet, then tilted her chin haughtily into the air. She cringed when he spat at her feet and stood his ground, still expressionless, unnerving her so much that she stepped back away from him. She dropped her hands to her side. "What do you want of me now that you've already done

52

harm to Lamont Quinby?'' she asked weakly.

She looked toward Lamont, not truly caring that he lay lifeless in the grass. The Indian had at least done her *that* favor.

Yellow Feather felt threatened in a way new to him. He had yet to see such a beautiful *ee-quay*. With her dancing green eyes beneath a veil of thick lashes, *she* was the cause of his feeling threatened. He didn't understand the thumping of his heart nor the weakness in his knees. No Indian maiden had ever affected him in this way . . . not even his two wives that he so proudly possessed.

His gaze moved back to Lorinda's hair and how it hung, unbound, like lustrous satin in its brilliant auburn colors. There was no denying it . . . the flame of her hair matched that of his heart, and he knew that he had to possess her, to call her only his. He would call her *Mis-kwah-wa-bee-go-neece*. Yes , *ay-uh,* Red Blossom was a perfect name for her. It was only right because of the color of her hair.

He took a step forward, towering over her. He motioned with his left hand toward the brush from whence he had come. ''*Mah-szhon,*'' he ordered stiffly. He preferred to speak in his Indian dialect, wanting to appear superior to her, never having felt that an Indian looked intelligent while stumbling over the *chee-mo-ko-man's* way of speaking.

Lorinda swallowed hard as she inched away from him. ''What?'' she said in a near whisper.

''*Gee-mah-gi-ung-ah-shig-wah,*'' he said forcefully, still motioning toward the darkness of the brush.

''You . . . want me . . . to go with you? Is that what you're saying . . . ?'' Lorinda said. ''Where are you planning to . . . take . . . me . . . ?'' She glanced quickly around her, wondering about the opportunity of escaping. But the darkness of the forest and the baying of the wolves in the far distance caused her to think better of

53

it.

She looked back at the Indian, wondering now why he hadn't used a bow and arrow when attacking Lamont and why he hadn't scalped him? And why hadn't he attacked her? Hadn't she seen the way he had looked at her hair and how it had caused goose pimples to ripple along her flesh? She had thought she would be scalped at any moment. If he was the Indian responsible for her parents' death why was he being different now? Then her thoughts went to Amanda. Could he lead her to her sister?

Yellow Feather went to Lorinda and began shoving her away from the campfire. "Okay, okay," she murmured, stumbling. She looked at what lay on the ground next to her bedroll. She leaned down and grabbed Amanda's baby blanket and tucked it in the crook of her right arm as Yellow Feather succeeded in pushing her into the density of brush beneath the soft flutter of the maple tree's leaves.

When Lorinda saw her aunt's black stallion and Lamont's horse already loosened, standing next to the Indian's own sleek brown mare, she realized that his hunt had at first been only for horses. She had to wonder when he had changed his mind. Had he seen Lamont attacking her? In his savage way, had the Indian decided to rescue her?

But no. If he had meant just to save her from Lamont's assaults, the Indian wouldn't be forcing her to go with him. He would have stopped her assailant and either would have attacked her himself or let her be. But he was doing neither. *He* was *also* kidnapping her.

"As he did Amanda?" she worried to herself. She eyed the Indian with hate. If not for the possibility of being led to Amanda, she would fight him until her death, if need be. She could claw at those dark, expressionless eyes. She could yank at his pigtails, which looked to have been braided with such care and skill, or she could attempt grabbing his gun. . . .

Her thoughts were interrupted by the Indian's forceful words as he motioned toward the black stallion with the barrel of his gun.

"*Bay-bay-shee-go-gah-shee,*" Yellow Feather said. "*We-weeb.*" He looked back toward the dancing orange shadows of the campfire, eager to leave the *chee-mo-ko-man* behind. Yellow Feather had seen this man's attack on Red Blossom and had felt a hate so deep that it would have been a pleasure for him to have separated this man's sandy-colored scalp from the rest of him. But Yellow Feather's first interest lay with the beautiful white woman in distress. At his first sight of her, he had been compelled to move closer, to study her satiny-white skin and the flame of her hair. When he had seen her struggles with the evil white man, he had quickly put his hunt for horses behind him.

Lorinda knew what he wanted. He wanted her to get on the horse. Her heart raced, wondering how far she would have to travel side by side with this Indian. What *did* he have in store for her? Would he take her away from this campfire to have the privacy to attack her himself? Or was he planning to take her to his people, to put her on display, maybe even to torture her? She had seen his eyes assessing her over and over again.

Swallowing hard, Lorinda was thinking once more about escaping. Maybe it was best to take her chances in the dark of the forest and try and find her way back to St. Paul alone, to seek help in finding her sister, instead of foolishly thinking she could go with the Indian to find her. What if she *did* find Amanda in the Indian village? What would she even be able to do? She would be one white woman against *many* Indians. . . .

As Yellow Feather's eyes were momentarily turned from her, Lorinda threw her baby sister's blanket onto the black stallion and quickly mounted the horse. She clung

55

to its thick mane since there were no reins and thrust her knees deeply into the horse's side, relieved that no words were necessary to get it to begin moving farther into the darkness of night. She leaned low over the horse, breathing heavily, yet trembling, feeling the cold rush of the air against her face and the thin cotton fabric of her long-sleeved blouse.

The horse moved around the fragrant pines and beneath the darker shadows of oak and maple trees. The horse's hooves were muffled by the soft bed of pine needles and the fallen leaves of autumn. Even the horse now carrying Yellow Feather made no sound as it moved next to Lorinda's. . . .

Lorinda's breath left her momentarily as she felt his arm of steel around her waist. For a moment, her heart even ceased to beat as she felt as though she was flying from one horse to the next. Then, as she blinked her eyes nervously, she found herself on the Indian's horse, being held next to the Indian's bare, heaving chest. Though the night was black, she could feel his dark eyes upon her as he continued to hold her there so close to him. She could feel the thundering of his heartbeat against her own chest and she could feel his breath hot upon her face. He smelled of the outdoors, all fresh and clean, and when his lips suddenly came down upon hers, Lorinda felt a strange stirring of warmth inside her, a sort of painful, yet sweet ache, where no feelings had ever existed before. Closing her eyes dreamily, her head swam with delight, having never known such a tender kiss before. She would never forget the wet, horrible, brutal kisses of Lamont Quinby. . . .

Lorinda's eyes grew wildly open, suddenly remembering just *who* it *was* kissing her. It was a savage, renegade Indian! An Indian she hated . . . one who may even have murdered her . . . her . . . parents. . . .

With all the strength that she could muster, she jerked

her mouth free from his and began swinging her arms and legs, yelling wildly at him. "Let me go," she yelled. "You're nothing but a savage Indian. I can't stand to have you touch me. Let me go!"

Surprisingly Yellow Feather *did* let her go. Quite abruptly. He loosened his grip from around her waist and let her drop clumsily to the ground where she landed in a heap. She pushed herself to a sitting position and sat there for a moment, stunned. She rubbed an aching arm, eyeing him questioningly. First he was gentle with her, then he was rough. She was slowly discovering the complexities of this Indian's personality.

"You heathen," she hissed. "I hate you. If you could understand English, you could hear me tell you how much I hate you."

Yellow Feather smiled smugly to himself. He had felt her response to his kiss and knew that she could never truly hate him, as he also could not hate her, though he did feel such intense hatred and bitterness toward most *chee-mo-ko-man*. The white man had wronged his people. Many times. He had never thought to have feelings other than revulsion for *any* paleface liars, until moments ago . . . until Red Blossom.

Reaching a hand to Lorinda, Yellow Feather said, "*Mah-bee-szhon.*"

Lorinda's eyes blazed. She inched away from him, scooting on the dew-laden leaves beneath her. "I don't know what you're saying," she said stubbornly. "But you won't get me to do anything without a fight first."

Again Yellow Feather smiled to himself. He liked her spunk. He liked the fire in her words. He wouldn't have expected a white woman to be brave enough to fight back. He would have expected her to be weak and weeping from fear. He had heard that most white women feared the Indians, though it was common knowledge that his tribe of Indians, the Chippewa, also known as the

57

Ojibway, were nonwarring and had always made peace with the white man.

But she may think I am Sioux, he thought to himself. He had heard of the recent bloody Sioux raids and the scalps being taken and laughed about. Yellow Feather had silently envied the Sioux this show of strength, having been taught differently by his peaceful father, Nodin-gah-skah-nah-soon, Chief Wind Whisper. But if I had been on a raid other than that of stealing horses, I would not have thought before killing Red Blossom and then I would not have experienced such pleasure as I did while kissing her, he thought further.

He smiled. At this moment, he was thankful that his father had taught him the more peaceful way of life. He once more motioned with his outstretched hand toward Lorinda. *"Mah-bee-szhon,"* he said more forcefully. In time he would show her his way of speaking the English language. But now it was more important to appear as all Indian to her, to get her used to *his* way of life—since he would never allow her to return to the *chee-mo-ko-man.*

Lorinda rose slowly to her feet then swirled around and began to run blindly through low hanging branches and thick ground cover, fussing loudly when her skirt would catch momentarily on a twig or scratchy briars. Her heart beat thunderously inside her and her chest ached as she began panting for breath. She wiped at her brow, feeling the cold perspiration lacing it. Chills coursed through her the deeper she went into the damp, cold forest.

"I've *got* to get my breath," she whispered. She stopped and leaned her back against a tree, looking around her, wondering why the Indian hadn't followed her. Had he given up? Had he felt her not worth the chase? A disappointment caused an emptiness at the pit of her stomach. She had felt something in the way he had held her and kissed her. There had been no resemblance to how she had thought a savage would treat her. He had been gentle . . . even . . . sweet . . . ?

Turning her eyes to the black forest ceiling, she whispered, "What am I doing thinking good things about this Indian?" she whispered. "He is my enemy. He may have killed . . ." she screamed in terror when Yellow Feather was suddenly there beside her. His moccasined feet had cushioned his approach and he was now taking her hand and guiding her back from whence she had come. She struggled and kicked at him but he moved steadily onward with his shoulders squared handsomely and his jaw set strongly.

"Whatever your name is, I want to go to my aunt," Lorinda said, now growing weak in voice as well as limb. She strained, trying to pull her wrist free. "Don't take me to your Indian village. Your people. They will hate me. They will despise me." She then felt shame. If she didn't go to the village, then maybe she would never get the chance to rescue Amanda. Oh, she was so confused. She felt tears surfacing for the first time since the day she had found her parents' bodies. She was now feeling their loss all over again. She so wanted to have her father to run to . . . to be able to fall into his arms . . . to protect her from all harm. Instead, she had an Indian by her side who probably hated her as much as she hated him.

She sniffled a bit and tried to see his full features once more, but with the dark shroud of night all about them, only his outline and the determination in his walk could be seen. She stumbled once more as the fullness of her skirt enfolded her legs, binding them, but Yellow Feather continued to move onward, pulling her along with him, until they reached the horses.

Without hesitation, Yellow Feather placed his hands on Lorinda's waist and lifted her onto the black stallion. He looked unwaveringly into her eyes for a moment as though silently ordering her to stay on the horse. Lorinda swallowed hard as she scooted to be more comfortable, then let her gaze move to the crumpled baby blanket at Yellow Feather's feet. She didn't speak, just pointed, and in the blink of an eye he handed it to her and then walked away from her, toward the two other horses.

As Lorinda folded the blanket and placed it beneath her, she watched Yellow Feather secure a rope about Lamont Quinby's horse's neck, then guide it next to his own. His rifle was inside a leather pouch, secured to the horse's side with leather strappings, and beautiful red-designed blankets were thrown across it instead of a saddle. He tied Lamont's horse to his own horse's reins, then went to Lorinda's horse and made her some reins from some leather rope that he had pulled from somewhere inside his leggings. Lorinda breathed more easily when he handed her the attached reins. She had dreaded having to make the journey with only her horse's mane to cling to. At least, having reins, she might possibly be able to encourage her horse to a faster escape if the opportunity presented itself to her again. She couldn't give up. She just couldn't!

"Geen-mah-szhon," Yellow Feather said firmly as he mounted his own horse.

When Lorinda eyed him quizzically, wishing he could speak English, Yellow Feather spoke more sharply as he pointed toward a small clearing ahead of them. *"Mah-szhon,"* he said, kneeing his horse, watching her to see that she was ready to obediently obey him. His heart warmed and he smiled inwardly as she clucked to her horse and snapped the reins, to move alongside him with head held high.

With a straight face and expressionless eyes he watched her outline as the moon's rays broke free from the dark cover of clouds, filtering now through some leafless branches overhead. He admired the way she sat straight-backed on the horse, as though proud and sure of herself, even though she had just become his captive. He

60

watched the long, thick tresses of her hair rise and fall with each of the horse's movements, wishing it was the sun instead of the moon casting dancing shadows all around them. He was anxious to see Red Blossom's hair in the full blazing reds that only the daylight hours would afford him. He was anxious to touch it . . . to smell it . . . .

His gaze traveled lower, watching how the wind lifted her skirt above her knees revealing the smooth, clean shape of her legs. He was surprised that she wore no leggings to cover herself as most Indian maidens did, but the rapid beat of his heart was proof to him of how glad he was that Red Blossom was different. It was this difference that made him know that she would never belong to another. . . .

Four

Red sandstone cliffs loomed boldly above the gentle blue water of the St. Croix River, while pleasant hills and stately elms, cedars, and pines also cast their reflections along the shores, suggesting a quiet peacefulness. Goldenrod and asters and cardinal flowers of purple, gold, and crimson colored the landscape cheerfully as Lorinda continued to travel side by side with the Indian. Though the air was fresh and sweet, smelling of lake water and the Norway pines that lined the bluffs, she was in no position to enjoy it.

"I am so tired," she sighed, slumping a bit over her horse. She and the Indian had traveled for two days and nights, stopping only long enough to receive nourishment from wild berries that Yellow Feather had so skillfully found. Wearily, Lorinda cast him a watchful glance. He had yet to reveal his name to her, and what few times he had spoken to her, it had only been by way of his usual Indian jargon. She licked her parched lips, knowing that her complaints were settling on deaf ears, and continued to move next to him, no longer fearing the end of the journey. Her sore achiness made her anxious to arrive anywhere, just so long as she was allowed to climb from the horse and stretch out, to get some badly needed sleep.

She looked toward Yellow Feather once more, seeing how straight he still sat. He seemed as though in a trance, as though he was willing himself to move onward, to not require any rest. Forcing herself, Lorinda straightened her own back. "I'll show him that I have strength to match his," she whispered. "I shall not complain again.

63

I will show him that I am also a person of strong will. I shall beat this Indian. I *shall.* . . .''

Yellow Feather could feel Red Blossom's eyes on him and understood her thoughts. She was tired, as he also was. But he had to guide her in a different direction from his village, and this special journey had required more days of travel. He had decided against revealing his captive to his father Chief Wind Whisper. His father would not approve of Yellow Feather's decision to take a third wife, *nor* of the fact that this future wife was a white woman. Chief Wind Whisper was ill, and Yellow Feather did not want to upset him unduly.

So he would take her to his secret sacred cave, he had decided. She would be safe there, and she would be his alone.

Frowning, he thought of his father's weakening condition and knew that one day soon it would be himself who would be chief and who would be making the decisions for his people. At that time, he would proudly present his new wife to his people, and, since he would be chief, no one would dare challenge his decision to bring a white woman into the St. Croix band of Indians.

Seeing the familiar winding blues of the St. Croix River and the jutting cliffs, Yellow Feather knew that their destination was near, where the sunshine of the meadow met the shadow of the forest, and where his guardian spirit had guided him that very first time, oh, so many years ago. If he thought about it hard enough, it was as though he was being transported back in time, a small boy again, when he had been called Ah-gah-sah-dee-bee-gee-zis, Little Moon. . . .

Minnesota Territory: Spring, 1846

The fire had grown cold through the night. Outlined by

logs, it now lay in black ashes in the fire space in the center of the wigwam. Little Moon leaned up on one elbow, glancing quickly around him. The smoke hole at the top of the wigwam was emitting soft splashes of early morning light downward, enough for Little Moon to see that the rest of his family were still asleep, covered by tanned bear hides on their cedar bough beds.

Each slept with feet toward the fire space, wearing moccasins and fully clothed, in order to stay warm as possible through the night after the fire died down.

Little Moon smiled, seeing the exact arrangement of his family in the wigwam, having been taught that each member of the family had a possessive right to certain parts of the dwelling. The space where sisters and brothers would have lain had always been vacant, and Little Moon's grandmother's space had been vacated many moons ago.

On opposite sides of the closed entrance flap, Little Moon's father and stepmother lay. Mee-chah-bah-pin-ah-nung, Big Laughing Star, had played the role of mother to him since he was a papoose, so his heart was warm for her. She was the merriest of all the Indian maidens and shook all over when she laughed. She was toothless, short and fat, and waddled when she walked. Little Moon would always hold a special place for her in his heart.

When Little Moon looked toward his father, Chief Wind Whisper, he thrust his chest out proudly. He felt honored to be the son born to this man who was the chief of the St. Croix band of Chippewa Indians, a chief with only one son, though he had had two healthy wives during his reign. His first wife had borne him his one son late in life, then had died shortly afterwards. Big Laughing Star, his second wife, had been unable to bear him anymore children, but she had made his life happy in many other ways with her sparkling and merry personality.

Ay-uh, yes, Little Moon was proud to be the next chief-in-line, and now that age thirteen was only days away, he had to prove his worth to his Great Father by participating in the required prepuberty fast. It was time for Little Moon to establish good relations with the spirit world, in hopes that he would acquire a guardian spirit that would henceforth provide sound advice, knowledge, and even power to influence the course of Little Moon's future life.

Little Moon needed a dream to appear. If he wasn't afforded a sacred dream, his power would not be strong. He knew that all great things came from dreams. He knew that if the guardian spirit promised him help, he would be a great hunter! He would be a great warrior! He would be . . . a . . . great . . . chief . . . !

As Little Moon began to creep from his cedar bough bed, he was wondering in which form his guardian spirit would appear to him. Would it be by way of a person? A bird? Or an animal? He had to wonder how many days of fasting would be required. He shuddered a bit in the cool of the morning, not so much from the cold, as from the fear of possibly being one who wouldn't be blessed by a sacred dream. He had heard about young men such as himself going deep into the forest and remaining for many days and nights, only to emerge pale of color and drained of energy and emotion, having been deprived of the honor of such a dream.

"It would disgrace me before all Chippewa brothers and sisters," he whispered, now crawling stealthily toward the fire space. "I cannot let that happen. It is *zee-gwun*. Spring. The perfect time for my fasting. I will succeed. *Boo-chee-goo-nee-gah-ee-shee-chee-gay*. I will."

Knowing the required ritual of blackening the face for the fasting rites, Little Moon reached his fingers into the warm ashes in the fire space and began spreading the black charcoal from the coals onto his face, soon changing his copper color to black with only his brown eyes showing through. Though still young, Little Moon was already quite tall, very lean, but with handsomely squared shoulders. His facial features had already become stern and unchanging, with a visible self-restraint. He had learned early how to throw an impenetratable veil over his emotions with an iron self-control, having been taught such self-restraint from infancy. His smoldering brown eyes remained flat and untouched at all times. He already had the hatred for the white man growing inside him, though his father Chief Wind Whisper was a gentle, nonwarring Indian who had always boasted of being friends with the white man.

Little Moon rubbed the charcoaled ash more angrily around his mouth and nose. He could not understand his father. He could not understand how his father could have continued to let the *chee-mo-ko-man* push his people farther and farther into the forest. The cold winters had already lain the icy hand of death on many of the St. Croix band of Indians. Even Little Moon's grandmother and grandfather were lying cold in an Indian burial ground that had been left behind when the village had been forced to move farther north once more.

"If I were chief, no white man could come near my people," Little Moon whispered. "Oh, it makes me so *nee-shkah-dee-zin*. How can I *not* be angry?"

With his face fully blackened now and his blue-black hair smooth from bear's grease and pulled back into two waist-length braids, and attired in breechcloth, leggings, and moccasins, he felt ready to move on outside the wigwam and into the depths of the forest.

Moving on hands and knees, he glanced once more toward his father with a racing heart. The next time his father would see him, Little Moon would be boasting of his successful fast. He would reveal to his father his newly acquired spiritual name that would then be his for the rest

67

of his life. His guardian spirit would instruct him of this new name and the power that would go along with it, which would make Little Moon courageous and strong.

Ay-uh, one day *he* would stand firm against the white man. *He* would see to it that his village of Indians would be close to the wild rice for easy harvesting and the St. Croix River for catching fish. These had, at one time, been the main resources with which his band of Indians had thrived so well. Since their move farther and farther north, the hunt for food had become harder and harder.

Lifting the entrance flap, Little Moon crept on out into the misty haze of morning. Rising from his knees and hands he stretched his arms above his head and yawned deeply, shivering when a cool breeze caressed the bare flesh of his chest. The air smelled fresh and clear, with only a slight aroma of smoke rising from the larger outside fire that had dimmed to glowing orange embers.

A hazy mist sparkled like a million jewels as the sun rose in shadowy oranges from behind the distant bluffs and towering tall pine forest, and at Little Moon's feet, dewdrops appeared to be tears dripping from small dog-tooth violets and, his favorite, the bloodroot with its red root and sap, its solitary leaf and its beautiful white flower.

Ay-uh, all seemed to be all right with the world this morning. It was a perfect day to begin his fast. He headed for the forest, not looking back, knowing that it was still dark enough this early morning for the giant owl to swoop down with its large claws to carry him away.

He laughed a bit nervously. He knew that the tales of the size of the *koo-koo-ko* had been highly exaggerated. No one had truly seen an owl of such size. Little Moon had figured out long ago that it was a tale of Indian mothers to their children to discourage the little ones from wandering off into the darkness of the forest. The sound that had been called the swooshing of large wings in the night had in truth been the angry wind spirits lashing the tree's limbs about. *Ay-uh,* Little Moon already knew so much of life. He was anxious to see how much wiser and stronger he would be after having spent time with his own private guardian spirit.

His heart began to pump more vigorously and his footsteps hastened, yet he couldn't admit to not being a bit afraid. He had left his weapons behind him, feeling that to enter his days of fasting unarmed could be even more impressive to the spirit world. Wouldn't it show his bravery? His seriousness at what he was doing?

The forest seemed to grow blacker the farther Little Moon traveled. His footsteps were cushioned by damp beds of leaves and deeply piled pine needles, and his nostrils flared with the pure sweet smell of cedar and pinewood. The forest trail that led him beneath maple, oak, and hickory trees was narrow. Spring buds appeared on some branches, and gray beards of moss, dripping from early morning dew, trailed down from others.

An occasional gold dusting of the sun flickering through the overhead branches marked the morning's true awakening, along with the stirrings of wild life on all sides of Little Moon. Chipmunks scampered noiselessly over fallen trunks of trees, bluejays resounded shrilly, echoing their warning to all corners of the forest, and spider's webs sparkled like diamonds in the still clinging damp mist.

Little Moon began to run slowly, pushing low branches aside, jumping over others, greeting the damp rush of the wind upon his face. His feet tried to slow him by tangling in the brush, but nothing would stop him now. He was deep into the forest. Forests were sacred places, full of shadows and unseen spirits. Little Moon would pull strength from this forest where spirits were free to move about, away from men and all the interferences of life.

"Great spirit Wenebojo, spirit who made the world, I have come alone," Little Moon said aloud, glancing all around him, relieved to see more sun splashes on trees and shrubs. "I have come to be blessed. I have come for my vision. Please bless me, Wenebojo. I do not mean to anger you by moving so far into your forest. I come alone. Me. Just one little boy."

Little Moon paused, breathing hard. He wiped his brow with the back of his arm, now wishing he had thought to bring some tobacco to offer the spirits. That would have assured him a peaceful journey. But in his haste, he had only thought to deliver himself.

A deer suddenly bounded through the thicket, startling Little Moon. His heart thundered, as like a drum, then he smiled as chickadees settled down in front of him onto wintergreen berries that showed red against their glossy leaves of green.

"I think I've gone far enough," Little Moon said. He began studying the trees, wondering which would be the appropriate one in which to build his 'nest' for the duration of his fast, for whatever length of time it might take. A tree meant purity, manhood, and strength. He would find one that had already blossomed with leaves. It would prove to be the hardiest of them all, one that he could depend on to house him until his dream had come and gone.

His search came to a sudden halt when he saw a giant maple tree towering above him. It was mighty in build, with its arms reaching up into the heavens, and its leaves were freshly green and swaying gently in the awakening morning breeze.

"Its limbs are like stepping stones," he murmured. "I can climb from one to the other with such ease. *Ay-uh*, this is to be my fasting tree."

With eagerness, Little Moon began to gather sticks beneath the tree, carried them by the armload to the upper branches and began building himself a platform on which

70

to lie on while waiting for his dream to come to him. He tied the sticks into place with strips of basswood, then made himself a bed on this platform with layers of ferns and boughs of cedar trees.

"Now to test it," he whispered. "It must be strong."

He held onto the trunk of the tree and cautiously stepped onto the platform, glancing quickly to the ground below. Though a bed of damp leaves lay beneath the tree, they would not be enough to cushion a fall.

"I must be brave," he said aloud, squaring his shoulders. "The spirits of the forest must see my bravery. The spirits must *feel* my bravery."

With jaws set, he began stomping around on the platform, testing. Then his lips curled into a smile, proud. *Ay-uh,* the fasting platform was strong. It was solid. It was firm. He swallowed back a rush of emotion in his throat as he gazed upward through the leaves of the tree, toward the blue ocean of sky above him. He stilled his feet and crossed his arms over his chest as he began a soft prayer, speaking to the spirits of the world. He prayed to this cloudless sky of blue, then turned and faced all four directions, speaking to the wind, the sun, and the unseen moon and stars. He spoke to the birds and animals of the forest, the trees, the flowering plants and the streams that flowed serenely from the red sandstone cliffs in the far distance. All these things he spoke to, knowing that spirits abided in them all.

He prayed, saying, "Oh, spirits, hear my prayers, know that I am ready to be shown the trail of my life. I do not only pray for better skills in hunting but for courage and strength to lead my people to a better life. I wish to be wiser and stronger, to be prepared when my time comes to become chief of the St. Croix. I need your advice, spirits. I need your knowledge. I pray that you will be kind enough to grant me much power to guide my people back to the days of the great wild rice harvest and to where the fish are plentiful. Oh, great spirits, hear what I say. Come to me. Bless me. I am alone. Bless me for the future of my people.''

With a wild, thumping heart, Little Moon kneeled on his platform, glancing quickly around him for any signs of his prayers having been heard, but when everything was as usual, he stretched out, straight-legged, on his back and watched the weaving of the tree's limbs drawing patterns against the sky.

The bird chatter in the trees was all around him and an occasional rustling of the brush below him was evidence of some animal moving on past. He saw a squirrel scampering across a tree's limb, stopping to eye him quizzically, then move on to the next tree, leaving Little Moon to lie alone again with only the thumping of his heart as his companion.

The blue sky began fading into a dull gray and suddenly night was upon Little Moon. He looked around him, now seeing just how black a forest could be in the night. It was the blackest black he had ever seen and it was the quietest quiet. He leaned up on an elbow, looking around him, shivering. The air was heavy with a cold dampness. He lifted some cedar boughs from beneath him and placed them over his bare chest and arms and stretched out once again to stare upward at a few stars that could be seen through the branches.

Hunger was upon Little Moon and his lips were dry from need of water. He closed his eyes thinking of gooseberries and grapes, hating it when his stomach growled hungrily. His eyes flew open widely, hoping the spirits hadn't heard. He knew that at night spirits were abroad. It was common knowledge that ghosts of the dead wandered through the forests, sometimes even with whistling cries. Little Moon shuddered. Surely this night, he would know his guardian spirit.

He closed his eyes and didn't awaken until the next

72

morning when a bluejay squawked suddenly above his head. He rubbed his eyes and pushed himself up on one elbow, disappointed that a full night had passed and he was no different than before.

"*Ay-uh*, I am to still be called Little Moon," he argued to himself. "It is *not* a proper name for a chief. But, oh, *nee-bah-kah-day*. I am *so* hungry. Is this truly only my first day of fasting? Can I last?"

He stretched back out on the platform, shivering. He wasn't only hungry but *cold*. But he couldn't let the spirits know this. He had to appear strong . . . willing to make *any* sacrifices.

The day faded away into another black velvet night, and the night then lightened into another lacy day of spring, where nature was quickly transforming the lifeless branches of the trees to rebirth and the air was heavy with the sweetness of maple sap.

Little Moon was almost lifeless now from hunger and thirst. He now spent both his days and nights in a half-sleep. It was on the third day, along with a dizziness in his head, that he heard the loud swooshing of wings above him. He worked at opening his eyes, with, oh, such an effort, with such a weakness throughout his body, but when he did manage to look upward, the blue of the sky was being hidden from his eyes by a magnificent outspreading of gray wings.

Little Moon blinked his eyes nervously, steadily gazing at this monstrous, hovering, gray bird. And what was he seeing? A lone bright yellow feather among the gray plumage? It was so bright, it momentarily blinded Little Moon. When he reopened his eyes, he found himself being lifted from his fasting platform and cradled into the curved talons of the powerful bird .

Little Moon was then alert enough to realize what bird it was who now held him! The *koo-koo-ko! Ay-uh*, he was captive of the giant owl he had always scoffed about. His pulse raced and he tried to be set free but found that the bird's hold on him was way too powerful.

Little Moon felt terror in his heart but he wouldn't let it be revealed to the spirits who were seeing this mighty bird now soaring above the treetops with Little Moon as its captive. The talons had enwrapped Little Moon very carefully, cradling him like a baby, and had done him no harm. It was as though the owl with the yellow feather was trying to say something to Little Moon as its head turned and its eyes blinked with slow, yet heavy movements.

Something grabbed at Little Moon's heart. Was this his guardian spirit? Was this truly his dream? Was he not in this giant owl's talons, but still asleep on his fasting platform? Was he finally being blessed with his special dream?

"*Ay-uh*, it has to be so," he whispered. Though this bird with the large eyes was said to be active only at night, it had chosen to make an exception this time for Little Moon. He gazed strongly back into the owl's penetrating eyes, proud that he hadn't been forgotten by the spiritual world. The owl was forever to be his guardian. And the yellow feather? What did *it* mean?

As his heartbeat raced, Little Moon said, "Oh, mighty spirit, giant owl of the forest, show me the way. Show me the trail of my life. Thank you for blessing me with your presence. Now, please show me how to lead my people."

The owl's gaze moved from Little Moon to look straight ahead as it began gradually to climb higher into the sky. When the treetops were left behind and Little Moon was able to see for many miles in all four directions, the owl leveled off and began to soar with wide, lazy strokes of his wings away from the forest and away from Little Moon's village. The sun was bright and warm in the sky and the wind was a challenge as it whipped harshly against Little Moon's face. But he continued to gaze rapturously around and below him in a trance of wonderment, that his fasting could bring him such a magnificent dream. It was a vision of all visions. It was a proud thing to tell his grandchildren, even his great-grandchildren.

With widened eyes, Little Moon watched as the owl began to lower itself from the sky, to begin circling around a body of water. Little Moon stretched his neck and studied the sparkling, rippling blue line beneath him. On both sides, bluffs of reddish brown dipped into the water, and pine trees were in abundance where some of the land dropped off into bluffs and some sloped gently into the water.

"What are you trying to tell me, Great Owl?" Little Moon said. *"Weh-go-nen-dush-wi-szhis-chee-gay-yen?"*

The owl moved onward, following the line of water. Little Moon's past began to flash before his eyes . . . a past lived by the flowing waters of the St. Croix River until the white man had given strange papers to Chief Wind Whisper to place his mark on. After that, the St. Croix band of Chippewas were instructed to move farther into the forest, leaving the river more accessible to the white man and his steel axes that felled the beautiful trees.

"But where is the white man now? I recognize the St. Croix River," Little Moon said. He grew tense and silent as the owl carried him farther and farther, where the land lay peacefully undisturbed by man, where the deer seemed to be in abundance and where the fish splashed freely in the river. Then Little Moon leaned a bit forward when he saw the long, green plants of wild rice in the shallow inlets of the river, swaying to the lapping of the water.

"It is *manomin*," he said. "It is the good berry. Wild rice. And see how much there is? It is a *jungle* of wild rice. It could feed my people for years."

The owl swooped lower and began circling over the greenish-yellow swaying stalks, and then over the clear water of the river, as though trying to relay a message to Little Moon, but Little Moon could not understand. *Ay-uh*, he had seen the plentifulness of the wild rice and the fish, but he knew that the papers signed by his father would keep his father from taking advantage of this abundance of resources even though it hadn't yet been found by the white man.

The owl continued to circle. His large, lazy eyes were now turned to Little Moon.

"Great magnificent owl, my guardian spirit, if only you could talk," Little Moon said, sighing. "*Gah-ween-nee-nee-sis-eh-tos-say-non.* How can I know how to lead my people if I don't understand you?"

The owl's eyes held Little Moon in a trance and suddenly Little Moon could feel what the owl was feeling and could understand why the owl had brought him to this particular place. It was meant for Little Moon to guide his people to this place when he became chief. The spirits would keep the white people from interfering. It would be reserved for Little Moon, the next chief-in-line of the St. Croix band of the Chippewa.

"But why not now, giant owl?" Little Moon asked. He felt the answer being transmitted to him. It was not for Little Moon to return to his father to reveal that Little Moon knew more about life than the great Chief Wind Whisper. *Gah-ween.* Chief Wind Whisper had had his own dream and vision in his youth and he had led his people wisely in *his* way. It would be in a different way that Little Moon would lead *his* people. Little Moon would not let the white man intimidate him. He would stand firm. He would be strong, wise, and courageous in his *own* way. The wild rice and fish would be Little Moon's people's blessings.

"*Ay-uh*, I understand, my very generous guardian

spirit,'' Little Moon said, and knew the giant owl heard him because it began to fly away from that river and began to hover over an opening at the side of a hill. It circled and circled, causing Little Moon a bit of fright. Was the giant owl going to drop him and possibly leave him there? But no. That could not be part of his dream. He would awaken in his fasting ''nest,'' not in, or on, a cave. But why was the owl continuing to circle? What did the cave have to do with his future? Then when the owl began to climb into the sky once more, leaving the river and the wild rice behind, Little Moon took one last look at the cave and felt a skipping of his heartbeat when he saw the evening's sunset framing the cave's opening in brilliant reds. In only an instant, Little Moon saw the face of a beautiful woman, with long, flaming red hair blowing gently in the wind. . . .

Little Moon closed his eyes and shook his head then looked toward the cave entrance once again, this time seeing only a dim gray. He smiled, knowing that this face he had only briefly seen *had* to be a part of his spiritual dream, and he had to wonder if there truly was such a woman, with such a beautiful, breathtaking color of hair.

He settled himself as comfortably as possible in the cradle of the owl's talons, feeling grateful and pleased about his spiritual blessings. He now had faith in himself as a leader. He would never doubt any instructions given him by his guardian spirit. He was now eager to return to his village and declare to his father that he had indeed been blessed. When Little Moon emerged from the forest, he would be a *man*.

The forest was now below Little Moon and he could feel the force in which the giant owl's wings worked against the wind as it glided downward, until Little Moon felt the owl's talons loosen and Little Moon found himself falling . . . swirling . . . breathless . . . until he awakened with a start and found himself lying peacefully

77

on his bed of ferns and boughs of cedar trees.

"Where am I?" he whispered, glancing quickly around him, feeling strangely full in the stomach and no longer thirsty, though it had been three days since he had eaten. He looked upward through the tree's limbs and saw an orange-reddish cast to the sky and knew that another night was fast approaching and dreaded it. Then something yellow and flashing at his side caught his eye. He gasped as his fingers crept slowly toward the yellow, almost glowing object.

"A *mee-gwun?*" he murmured. "It is truly . . . a . . . feather . . . ?"

His heartbeat raced when his fingers touched the softness of the feather. "It is. A beautiful, yellow feather! But . . . how . . . ?"

His eyes grew wide and he began to tremble, suddenly remembering his spiritual dream and the one lone yellow feather in the giant owl's plumage. "I *did* experience it," he said. "I *did. Ay-uh,* there *was* such a great bird. It is an omen. It left me the feather to remind me of what the future holds for me and my people."

A cool splash of air rushing across his face caused Little Moon to tremble. He looked frightfully about him and saw nothing, but now suddenly understood a further purpose of the yellow feather. It was as though the great owl was with him now, saying, "From this day forth, you will be called Yellow Feather. . . ."

Tears misted in Little Moon's eyes as he placed the feather to his chest and held it there against him. "Thank you, Wenebojo, great spirit who made the world," he said quietly. He turned his head slowly. "Thank you, all spirits of the forest. Thank you, oh, mighty guardian spirit, giant owl of the forest. Little Moon is grateful."

Seeing the shadows lengthening all around him, Little Moon began to move downward from the tree, all the while holding the yellow feather tightly to his chest. He began to run, jumping over fallen logs and twisted brush, and shouted to the wind: " It is I, Yellow Feather, who thanks you now, friendly spirits," he called. "Little Moon is no more. He was left behind on the fasting platform. It is I, Yellow Feather, who will be speaking to you from now on!"

He laughed gaily, already envisioning the feast that would be held in his honor for having become a man.

Yellow Feather shook his head, delivering himself from his semitrance. He glanced quickly toward Lorinda and saw her almost glowing beneath the steady warm rays of the sun. Then, suddenly the cave's entrance was outlining her as they approached it! Yellow Feather felt a quiver of warmth inside himself, realizing that all along *she* had been a part of his childhood dream. It had been *her* face that had been revealed to him on that magical night. It had been *her* long, flaming red hair blowing gently in the breeze. . . .

His heart thundered wildly, knowing that his mighty guardian spirit, the giant owl of the forest, had led her to him. He felt humble as he lifted his face to the sky.

Five

A deer bounded into the thickets as Yellow Feather led Lorinda down a steep slope and up another, until a cave greeted them, its open mouth emerging from pine and junipers. The huge virgin pines along the horizon on all sides of them were catching the last rays of the sun in their tops, which made them appear to be aflame, while the dew of evening was already appearing as crystal droplets on the tips of the grass.

Lorinda shivered, having learned to dread the evenings away from a fireplace's warmth. Blankets loaned to her by the Indian had been only a weak substitute and she longed for the time that she could once again feel the deep contentment that came from being close to a fire.

Yellow Feather drew his horse to a halt and stretched his neck a bit, looking eagerly about him. Since he had not arrived back at the village at the designated time, he would now expect to find his best and faithful friend, Shah-kah-skayn-dah-way, Flying Squirrel, to greet his approach at their private meeting place, Yellow Feather's sacred cave. Three days ago, they had gone their separate ways, with only a hunt for horses on their minds this particular time. But now that Yellow Feather had taken a much longer time to return from his hunt, he knew that Flying Squirrel would know to expect him at the cave. Flying Squirrel would also expect Yellow Feather to be triumphant, possibly proudly showing off some beautiful jewels or blankets taken from the white man's stagecoaches or carriages that were now making frequent trips toward the newest settlement in Minnesota, called Duluth.

But Yellow Feather had something of more value than any of the white man's household goods. He had *Red Blossom*. He now knew that it was right that he had brought her here to his sacred meeting place. She had been sent to him in his dream. She was a *part* of his sacred dream. But he would only share his delight at having found her with Flying Squirrel. Flying Squirrel could be trusted. Flying Squirrel knew that his allegiance lay with Yellow Feather, the next chief-in-line.

"Why have we stopped here?" Lorinda said, shivering even more. The wind was whipping in cold splashes against her face and on the exposed flesh of her legs. She glanced toward the cave. It looked even colder. It was desolate and gray and surely only housed families of bats. She looked slowly around her, wondering how much farther they would have to travel before reaching his village. Would this forced journey ever end? Oh, she was so bone weary! All that was within eye's reach besides this cave were more forests on one side of her and meadows on the other, with only the steady flowing water of the river disrupting this land of tranquility.

Yellow Feather glanced quickly toward Lorinda, seeing her trembling. He climbed from his horse, pulling a blanket from it, and went to her and helped her down from her own horse. With extreme gentleness, he wrapped the blanket around her shoulders and led her to the cave's entrance.

Lorinda hesitated, smelling a damp pungency from inside the cave. But then she smelled something else. She sniffed and recognized the aroma of smoke filtering outward through the tangle of brush that only partially blocked the entrance into the cave. Her eyebrows arched as Yellow Feather guided her on inside, where she stumbled a bit over loose rock and gravel. She sniffed again, smelling the stronger aroma of smoke. So far, all that she could see were the damp dark walls and ceiling of the cave as Yellow Feather urged her onward, deeper and deeper into darkness. Then as they rounded a turn, the flickering of a fire from somewhere farther ahead was reflected in gay oranges on all sides of Lorinda, and when she was directed around another turn, she yanked herself free from Yellow Feather. She stood, stunned. She first gazed intensely into the eyes of another Indian warrior, then quickly on around her and at what the fire's glow was revealing to her.

Her hands covering her mouth in amazement, she saw that this back end of the cave was filled with many conveniences of the white man. There were stacks upon stacks of beautifully designed blankets and patchwork quilts, kitchen utensils such as coffee grinders, pleating irons, wooden bowls and spoons, candle molds and fancy glazed pottery kettles with covers.

There were stacks of books, both large and small candles, and sparkling jewelry of all sizes and shapes spread across a wooden, three-legged table. Then she saw the flash of steel and recognized the glare from many rifle barrels as they stood, threateningly, against another wall. Her insides grew cold with fear. She didn't know what to think or do. But when the Indian who had obviously built this large campfire took one step toward her, she turned to run, falling instead against the steel wall of Yellow Feather.

Trembling even more vigorously, she gazed upward into his eyes, seeing that they remained the same as the very first time she had seen him. They held no expression. Was he as unfeeling as his eyes represented? Until now, she had begun to feel that he would let no harm come to her. Now he was with another Indian. Two Indians together could mean her possible demise. Surely they had killed many white people to have gathered together

83

such a collection of white man's belongings. She struggled as Yellow Feather grabbed her by the shoulders to hold her still.

"*Geen-ee-shqueen,*" he said firmly.

"I don't know what you're saying," she screamed. "But I know that I don't want to stay in this cave with two Indians. *You* were enough to have to get used to. I had begun to not fear you. But two? No. I must escape. Let me go, you animal." She kicked and reached for him with flailing arms and hands but softened her struggles when she heard Yellow Feather direct some words toward the other Indian.

"*Shah-kah-skayn-dah-way, mah-szhon,*" he ordered, nodding his head toward the cave entrance.

Flying Squirrel stepped to Yellow Feather's side. The two represented extremes in size. Flying Squirrel was short and small-boned, with a blemished face and no headdress, but dressed the same as Yellow Feather in other respects. His dark eyes showed confusion. "*Ah-neen-dush?*" he said softly. "*Ah-way-nish-ah-ow?*"

"*Bay-kah ah-gwah-ching,*" Yellow Feather stated flatly.

Flying Squirrel turned and studied Lorinda momentarily, then lifted a rifle into the crook of his left arm and obediently walked from the cave, leaving Yellow Feather and Lorinda alone.

Lorinda was relieved when Yellow Feather released his hold on her. She pulled the blanket more snugly around her and rubbed her sore arms where he had held her so tightly, watching in silence as Yellow Feather began arranging a layer of blankets beside the fire. When he came back to her and took one of her hands in his, his gentleness caused her to follow along with him as he led her to the blankets.

"*Nee-ban,*" he said, releasing her hand. "*Mis-kwah-wa-bee-go-neece, nee-ban.*"

84

Now doubting his intentions, remembering how he had kissed her earlier, Lorinda inched back away for the blankets. She began shaking her head back and forth, trembling inside from the fear of what the next moments might hold in store for her. Would he force himself upon her, then hand her over to the other Indian? She gathered her skirt about her as he took a step toward her.

"*Nee-ban,*" he repeated, pointing to the blanket. His jaw was set firmly and his eyes were two dark pools of determination.

When she again cowered away from him, Yellow Feather moved swiftly and lifted her into his arms and carried her back to the blankets. Once there, he held her a moment longer and gazed intensely into her eyes. Lorinda's heart began to thump wildly, feeling again the strange sweetness that his closeness could create inside her. She felt as though hypnotized, and when he placed her gently on the softness of the blankets, something compelled her to reach and touch his face. The touch was electric. She could feel the sensation of excitement pass from his skin to hers and pulled quickly away, again afraid. She seemed to have no control over these strange feelings that had suddenly become a part of her life. She tensed even more when Yellow Feather reached to touch her face. She held her breath, wondering what would happen next, then sighed with relief when his hand dropped, then lifted a patchwork quilt over her, to her chin.

"*Nee-ban,*" he said. His hands went to her eyes and urged the lids shut. "*Nee-ban,*" he repeated softly. His lips brushed against hers and then he rose and moved swiftly from the cave, leaving Lorinda in a dazed wonderment. She couldn't understand how this Indian, this savage, could cause her body to react so shamefully. Every time he had touched her in his gentle way, it had seemed to ignite small fires along her spine. *No* man had

85

ever made her feel such things, and this wasn't even a *man* she was responding to. This was an Indian . . . a savage Indian . . . a murderer. . . .

The sweet sensations aroused inside her that still lingered, the warmth of the fire, and the softness of the blankets were having a sudden euphoric effect on Lorinda. The days and nights of travel had caused such a tiredness in her limbs. She stretched out and sighed as sleep peacefully overcame her, causing all worries and confusions to slip from her mind, not even wondering where the Indian had slipped off to.

Yellow Feather found Flying Squirrel pacing nervously at the cave's entrance. He understood his friends disquiet. Bringing the white woman to the cave was indeed out of character for Yellow Feather. He usually had more power over his emotions and actions. But he *was* the son of Chief Wind Whisper. He *did* have the right to do as he wished. If another wife was part of his plan, then Flying Squirrel would have no right to question this. Yellow Feather was allowed more than one wife because he was the next in line to be chief and could support several families. He *must* have Red Blossom. His love for her was growing into a burning passion. He could not control such a feeling. He *would* not.

"Flying Squirrel, did you have a good hunt?" Yellow Feather said, stopping his friend's nervous pacing by clasping his shoulders affectionately. He could read the confusion in his friend's eyes. He frowned at this. Flying Squirrel hadn't learned early in life how to mask his emotions with a forced veil drawn across the eyes. Instead, his friend not only laughed, but talked and worried with his eyes. It was a weakness in his friend that Yellow Feather had hesitatingly learned to accept long ago.

"And can I ask you the same?" Flying Squirrel grumbled.

Yellow Feather dropped his hands to his side and

stared upward onto the gray dusky clouds of evening. "*Ay-uh,* I had a rewarding hunt," he said, sighing heavily.

Flying Squirrel went to the horses and stroked the mane of one, then the other. "You speak of the horses, Yellow Feather?" he said flatly. He turned and glowered at Yellow Feather. "Or do you speak of that . . . of that . . . white woman . . . ?"

"Both," Yellow Feather laughed. He then grew somber. "You do not approve. I can read it in your eyes."

"And should I?"

"She is more than a captive, Flying Squirrel," Yellow Feather said quietly. He went to the horse she had traveled on and lifted the small blanket from it, wondering why she seemed to treasure it so. It was bland in color and so tiny it could give no warmth. Yet he could remember her cradling it in her arms as though it was a baby. He placed it over his shoulder and began caressing the sleek black mane of the stallion. This beautiful, stately horse was his *next*-best catch on this particular hunt.

"What do you mean more than a captive?" Flying Squirrel said, moving to Yellow Feather's side. "What plans do you have? Her red hair? You haven't taken a scalp for many moons now."

"Scalp?" Yellow Feather said, turning abruptly to look down upon the face of his friend who hadn't yet even taken one wife. Were Flying Squirrel's thoughts of women so far from his mind that he couldn't notice how beautiful in flesh, not only in hair, Red Blossom was? Did Flying Squirrel only have dreams of successful hunts? He said, "Flying Squirrel, no one will ever scalp Red Blossom!"

"Red Blossom?" Flying Squirrel gasped. "You have already given her an Indian name . . . ?"

"Why should I not?" Yellow Feather stated flatly, squaring his shoulders more. "I plan to make her my

87

wife."

Flying Squirrel stumbled back a bit. The shock of Yellow Feather's words showed in the wideness of his dark eyes. "You will make a white woman your wife?" he stammered.

"*Ay-uh*. My wife," Yellow Feather boasted, lifting his chin haughtily.

"It has never been done before in our St. Croix band of Chippewa," Flying Squirrel said, a strain evident in his voice.

"*Ay-uh*. I know. Red Blossom will be the first."

"Chief Wind Whisper? What will *he* say? What will he *do*?"

"I will worry about that later."

"Later?"

"For now, Red Blossom will stay here. At the cave. I do worry about my father's reaction. I know he is not strong."

"Winter is fast approaching, Yellow Feather."

"Red Blossom will be at my side before the snows begin to fall," Yellow Feather said stubbornly.

Flying Squirrel went to the cave's entrance and peered inward. "And why fool her with speaking in Indian tongue?" he said. "Why not speak in English to her? Wouldn't it be simpler? Our people learned English long ago from the fur traders. Aren't you proud of this?"

"*Ay-uh*. I am proud," Yellow Feather grumbled. "And I will choose the correct time to reveal this to her."

"And what am I to do now?" Flying Squirrel said, going to Yellow Feather, standing with spread legs and crossed arms.

"You are to take the two horses I have brought here on to the village. But be sure to keep them far enough away so that my father does not see them. He would be unhappy about the adventures you and I have been having."

Flying Squirrel's eyes wavered a bit. "If Chief Wind

Whisper ever found out about this cave . . . ."

Yellow Feather clasped his hands onto Flying Squirrel's shoulders, gripping firmly. "He will never know," he said. "My mighty guardian spirit instructed me long ago that it isn't meant for Chief Wind Whisper to know of this place. Only myself. I took it upon myself to share this with only you, Flying Squirrel. You know, as I do, that these things we've taken from the white people will be used soon to better our people."

"After Chief Wind Whisper's death?"

"*Ay-uh*. If it takes many more moons, so be it ."

Flying Squirrel lowered his eyes. "It will not be long now," he said. "He has weakened more even since our departure of only three days ago."

"You met with my father?"

"No. It is in everyone's soft whispers how your father is weakening."

"I will return home. Soon," Yellow Feather said. He glanced toward the cave. He first had to see to Red Blossom's comforts and make sure that she was taught to be obedient to his commands. He did not wish to return from his village to find her gone. Teaching her this valuable lesson would take more time than he desired, since he had the need to return to his father, but it was necessary. His guardian spirit would understand and would see to it that Chief Wind Whisper's life would still be his a while longer. Red Blossom was now a part of the St. Croix band of Indians' future as surely as Chief Wind Whisper had been a part of their past.

"Should I tell your father that you will meet with him soon?" Flying Squirrel asked, mounting his brown mare.

Yellow Feather guided the two captive horses toward Flying Squirrel and handed him the reins for both. "No. Do not tell him anything," he said. "What I have in my plans could take too long. No need to worry my father if I don't arrive in the village as he might be expecting me to.''

"I will do as you ask," Flying Squirrel grumbled. He glanced toward the cave, frowning. "I do not like what you do, but I will do what you ask."

Yellow Feather slapped each horse and watched, crossed-armed, as Flying Squirrel disappeared into the dark of the forest. He looked toward the rippling waters of the St. Croix River and felt a deep gnawing hunger at the pit of stomach. He took the small blanket from his shoulders and placed it on the ground at the cave's entrance. Then with a skilled speed, he made a spear from a tree twig and went and fished beneath the soft rays of the rising moon, which was now being called the "Turning of Leaves Moon" by all Chippewa. It was at this time, in September, that most Indian villages broke up into smaller groups to venture to the wild rice fields to prepare for work.

Yellow Feather grumbled to himself. It had been some time now since his St. Croix Indians had traveled to any such rice fields. The white man had seen to that. But soon. Soon. He would guide his people to the richest wild rice field—that *no* man had found yet, except himself. Yellow Feather hadn't even shared this secret with Flying Squirrel.

Looking on past the cave to where the river curved to run behind it, Yellow Feather knew that the wild rice waited in the shallow inlets, with their heavy tops, bending low, waiting for a time when the *Manomin* ritual could be held by his band of Indians, when the *Manomin-gisiss*, the wild rice moon, would just begin to rise. . . .

This had been a dream of Yellow Feather's since the night his guardian spirit had revealed this place to him. It had been hard not to tell his father Chief Wind Whisper about the abundance of fish and rice that waited untouched here, but Yellow Feather had to believe that all guardian spirits knew what was best and had since carried this secret close to his heart.

He now watched a ripple in the water and a shadow of quick speed that he knew was a fish welcoming the satin glow of the moon that was enticing it closer to the surface.

With a quicker speed than that of the fish, Yellow Feather lunged his spear into the fish's belly and pulled it splashing from the water. Over and over again he performed his skills at fishing, and, when enough were caught, hurried to the cave's entrance while some fish still jerked and splashed on the spear's end.

"There's enough flesh on these to feed both Red Blossom and myself," Yellow Feather boasted to himself as he rushed on inside to where the fire still cast off a warm glow.

Tiptoeing, Yellow Feather looked toward Lorinda, seeing that she was still fast asleep. Even asleep she was hauntingly beautiful, causing his body to yearn for her in such strange ways, he was almost forgetting what had been taught him from childhood. Self-restraint. He had always been proud of his disciplined self-control. Could one woman cause his longtime iron self-control to shatter? She wasn't even of his people, yet watching her now caused a wondrous hungry desire to shoot through him. He looked at her hair. It was spread out about her head as though a part of the fire itself. *Ay-uh*, the flame of her hair continued to match that of his heart and he could hardly wait to wholly possess her.

"But I *must* practice self-discipline," he whispered. "I have to gain her trust, for to not do so would be only to half-possess her."

He chose a *chee-mo-ko-man's* frying pan from his collection and squatted down before the fire, balancing himself on his heels, Indian fashion, and began cooking the fish, all the while watching Lorinda. When she stirred, his heart jumped and his stomach quivered strangely.

Lorinda was drawn awake by the smell of food. She opened her eyes slowly and suddenly remembered where she was when she found the dark eyes of the Indian upon her. Memory of the days previous haunted her in a quick flash and she felt her hate for the Indian renewed inside her. She put her back to him, trying to ignore the tantalizing aroma floating around her. Oh, had she ever been so hungry? Could she stand it much longer with true food so nearby, smelling so heavenly? Berries! She hoped to *never* see berries again. They were not fit to be anyone's steady diet, as they had been hers the past two days and nights.

She closed her eyes and licked her lips, trying to not think about the fish sizzling over the fire. She would not let this Indian use any of his ways to draw her closer to him again. Though it appeared that he had ordered the other Indian away because of her fear of him, she couldn't let her defenses down again to let him believe that she trusted or depended on him. She would die first!

"And maybe I shall," she whispered sullenly to herself, feeling the complete emptiness of her stomach.

"Wee-si-nin." Yellow Feather spoke suddenly from beside Lorinda.

With a wild beating of her heart, she slowly opened her eyes and found him squatting close to her, offering her a wooden bowl of fried fish.

"Wee-si-nin," he encouraged, motioning with the bowl next to her face.

Forcing her eyes closed again, Lorinda shook her head back and forth stubbornly. She would *not* obey his commands, even if they were for her own good. She had to show him that she was strong. She would eat only when *she* was ready. . . .

Her eyes flew wide open when she felt something at her mouth, forcing her lips apart. She watched in total shock as the fingers of Yellow Feather's one hand held her mouth agape while the other hand busied at poking fish between her teeth. She choked and spat as he continued his forced feeding. She managed to sit upright and began beating a fist against his bare chest, then attempted to push his hands away from her face, only succeeding at causing herself to become even more choked from the fish that she had managed to swallow.

"Geen gah-wah-nan-dum," Yellow Feather said angrily, rising. He stood with crossed arms, glowering. *"Gah-ween-nee-nee-sis-eh-tos-say-non."*

Lorinda wiped the excess grease and fish away from her mouth with the back of her hand. "Just leave me alone," she shouted. "First you confuse me by treating me so gently, like a man who is in love with a woman, then you treat me so mean, even like a baby, by force feeding me. Just leave me alone." She stretched out beneath the patchwork quilt, shivering again. "I hate you, you savage," she murmured. "I wish I was home with my parents or my aunt." Tears rushed to the corners of her eyes. She turned her face from him, refusing to let him see this true show of weakness. She felt like a small child, lost.

Yellow Feather had understood her words and wondered about her mention of love. He felt a soaring within, wanting to fall to his knees and draw her into his arms. If she had not felt something for him when they had exchanged tender touches, then her mind would not be thinking of love between man and woman. Now he knew that the chances of her eventually accepting him as her husband were better than before. She *would* accept him in the blankets with her. She *would* openly invite his touches and caresses. His heart raced with excitement. He would win her over. He would.

His eyes misted a bit, seeing how she missed her white family so. Wouldn't he miss his as much, if he had been taken captive by the white man?

"The blanket. The *wah-boo-wah-yon*," he whispered, remembering Red Blossom's strange attachment to the small blanket that he had left outside at the cave's entrance. He knew that this blanket had somehow to represent "family." Turning, he went and got the blanket and returned to Lorinda's side with it. Almost reverantly, he dropped to his knees and offered the blanket to her. *"Wah-boo-wah-yon,"* he said softly, holding it toward her. His heart warmed when her eyes slowly opened and saw what he offered.

Lorinda leaned up on an elbow, confused. He seemed to understand so much about her. How did he know that this blanket could comfort her? How had he known that she was missing her parents? He was making it almost impossible for her to continue hating him. Surely he wasn't the Indian who had . . . killed . . . her parents. He was too gentle. He was too kind.

She let her gaze move to the blanket, again remembering Amanda. If not this Indian, most surely one of his tribe . . . ?

"Wah-boo-wah-yon?" Yellow Feather said once more, offering the blanket again.

"Thank you," she whispered, accepting his gesture of friendship. When their hands touched, Lorinda's skin tingled, causing an involuntary shiver to race through her. She was keenly aware of his closeness and she could see fire burning in his eyes. Her heart was beating with a nervous pounding as he reached upward and stroked her cheek with his fingertips. The sweet pain was beginning inside her again and it was then that she realized that she wanted his lips upon hers. Dropping the blanket, Lorinda reached for him and guided his face downward. When their lips met, she felt as though she was melting inside. Desire shot through her as he drew her into his arms of steel and pressed her against him. But when he began lowering her to the blankets, panic took precedence over

94

hungry desire and she began fighting him anew.

Yellow Feather imprisoned her against him as his hands gently traced her face, then went lower to touch the outline of her breasts through the thin cotton material of her blouse. He ached with want for her and knew he could have her fully, but he would not, not while she was fighting him. He could not understand her. First she would not give in to her hunger for food, and now she would not give in to her hungry desire of the heart, though her eyes were pits of dark passion. He had felt her response and knew that she had been near to surrendering herself to him. But now? She was fighting like a tigress. No. He did not understand this Red Blossom who seemed to have a temper to match the flame of her hair.

With abruptness, Yellow Feather rose from Lorinda and went to spread his own bed of blankets by the fire. It would be hard sleeping so close to her without occasionally touching her, but he knew that, in time, they would share everything.

"Tomorrow I will teach her how to be obedient to my commands," he whispered, stretching out, placing his feet to the fire. His thoughts went to Chief Wind Whisper, hoping that if his father lived for many more moons, he would understand this new Yellow Feather. "But how can he?" Yellow Feather wondered. "I no longer know myself. . . ."

Lorinda snuggled into Amanda's blanket, trying to forget Yellow Feather's effect on her. She turned slowly, seeing him looking so smug with his eyes closed, already peacefully asleep. She was surprised that he trusted her enough to leave her there untied while he slept.

"Again he knows me so well," she sighed. "He knows the dark of night would stop my escape." She looked toward the cave's entrance. "But there is morning, you dumb Indian," she laughed to herself. "I'll escape then. . . ."

Six

The damp, clinging coldness awakened Lorinda with a start. She bolted upright, seeing nothing but total blackness on all sides of her. Growing frantic inside, her pulse raced. "Where am I?" she whispered, glancing anxiously around her. Then a sudden sparkle of orange in the smoldering ashes of the fire next to her was a cruel reminder of where she had spent the night.

"The cave," she whispered. "How could I have for one moment forgotten that I was in this cold, drafty cave?"

Her face and arms were clammy to the touch and she trembled uncontrollably as she also remembered the Indian. She looked in the direction of where he had fallen asleep. The total blackness made it impossible for her to see him. Throwing the patchwork quilt from on top of her, Lorinda crept on all fours around the fire's ashes. She slowly reached a hand to the layer of blankets that had served as the Indian's bed, but when she found them empty she gasped and quickly drew her hand away.

"Where is he?" she whispered. She reached again and grew bolder this time as she let her hand travel over the entirety of the top blanket, sure now that he was gone. She frowned darkly. She had hoped to escape while he still slept. *Now* where could she expect to run into him? Hopefully, he had left for his village. Maybe his interest in her had faded and he no longer cared what happened to her. A strange disappointment coursed through her veins, puzzling her. Did she want him to care? Had she even hoped to see him again?

"But no," she said aloud, rising. "This is my chance to return to civilization as *I* know it. I'll be able to guide the sheriff and his men to this land of the Indian. *They* will be able to find the village where Amanda may be."

Lorinda went back to her own makeshift bed of blankets and felt around until she found Amanda's baby blanket. It was her only link to sanity, it seemed. She draped it across her arm. Then, remembering the cold of night in the forest, she secured a much heavier blanket about her shoulders.

The aroma of fried fish had lingered on her clothes causing her stomach suddenly to begin to ache from renewed hunger. How could she have been so foolish as to have refused to eat when the Indian had offered the fish to her? And how humiliating it had been to have him force feed her! But then she remembered how he had not forced him*self* on her when she had become almost completely defenseless to his lips and caresses. She tingled now, remembering.

"Oh!" she said, stomping a foot. "How I hate him for confusing me so!"

She began inching her way to where she could now make out a bit of light drifting lazily along the dampened side walls of the cave. Her feet were unsteady and kicked a spray of rocks aside. The noise that she stirred up echoed shallowly on all sides and behind her, causing her to tense even more inside. Fearing the Indian might have heard, she hurried her pace until the cave's entrance was finally upon her. Panting, she almost fell through the large space of light, so glad to feel a touch of freedom within her grasp.

Steadying herself against the outside wall, Lorinda squinted from the extreme change from the dark of the cave to the brilliant light of morning. She shielded her eyes with a hand, looking cautiously around her. She expected the Indian to pounce on her at any moment now. Surely he wouldn't have gone to so much trouble to capture her, to let her then go free so soon afterward. It didn't make any sense to her.

"But what *does* make sense about *any*thing an Indian chooses to do?" she said aloud.

Her eyes still searched about her and she saw that even the horses were gone.

"*He* is gone if the horses are gone," she said, feeling free to move on out into the open. "It was only the horses he was after in the first place. Now I know that."

She stepped out of the cave, still glancing cautiously about her.

"But why didn't he leave me with Lamont Quinby if his only attraction was to the horses?" she argued to herself. "Surely I only slowed him down. . . ."

She shrugged and made her way to the river's edge. She dropped her blankets to the ground and fell to her knees, leaning her face over the clear blue of the water. When she saw her reflection peering back at her, she flinched as though she had been shot. She couldn't believe her disarray. Her hair was in bad need of a brushing, and her blouse was crumpled so, even the wrinkles had wrinkles.

"How horrible," she whispered. She looked farther down and saw the dust stains and rips on her dark travel skirt. "I shall never be the same. Never."

She eyed the water again. It looked crisp and cold, yet inviting. She bent her head farther over it and lifted water into her cupped hands and splashed it onto her cheeks. A chill trembled through her, yet it was invigorating.

She felt an inner strength building inside herself, knowing that this was what she needed to get her through the coming days alone in the dangers of the forest. She not only had the cold to dread, but there was the constant threat of wild beasts as well.

"And whatever shall I eat?" she murmured aloud, combing her fingers through her long auburn tresses. She lifted her face to the sky and shook her hair free from her shoulders to settle in lustrous waves down her back. She closed her eyes as she whispered, "Berries, oh, how I dread more meals of berries." But she knew that when her stomach ached badly enough, she would welcome anything to quell her hunger.

A splash in the water close to Lorinda drew her quick attention. She watched a fish flipping around in the warm rays of the sun trickling in golden rivulets along the water's surface. She was once more reminded of the fish offered her by the Indian. She was reminded of his gentleness. When she let herself remember their shared kisses and embraces, she determinedly pushed herself abruptly from the water's edge and forced her thoughts elsewhere. The next time she would see the Indian, it would most surely be in the company of St. Paul's sheriff, when she and the sheriff would arrive in the Indian's village.

"*Then* try to capture me again," she said, laughing.

Her laughter faded to a strange awkward smile. She wanted to feel a steaming hatred for the Indian with the cold, unwavering eyes. But there was always something there, standing partially in the way of such feelings. Instead, she longed deeply to have the same delicious feelings inside her that his touch had aroused . . . .

I am so unbelievable, she thought angrily to herself. First I hate, then I . . . I . . . think I may . . . love him even. . . .

Reaching for her two blankets, Lorinda studied the directions from which to choose for her dreaded journey. One would take her back from whence she had come and one would possibly take her to the Indian's village.

With determination, she straightened her back and lifted her skirt and began retracing her journey of only the day before. If she studied the ground cover closely

100

enough, she could surely see where the horses had trampled the grass and weeds. She thought of her aunt's sleek black stallion and missed its comforting presence. If she had the horse with her now, her travels would be completed in half the time, and she could relish the warmth of its body against her legs.

But now? She had only herself to depend on. It was a first for her. She had never, no never, been totally alone in life before. Tears sparkled at the corners of her eyes, and she felt the emptiness her loneliness made at the pit of her stomach.

She wiped her eyes. She had to be brave. She had to be strong. Focusing her thoughts on other things could possibly be the answer. She glanced first at the sky. Only a few puffy white clouds were disturbing the satiny blue backdrop. It was almost as if she could reach upward and run her fingers over the smoothness of it, to find that it was in reality a canvas, the artist's brush having created the delicate blue color. If the wind blew against the small dots of clouds, surely the whites would smear in large, damp streaks!

Lorinda moved farther and farther away from the river, leaving its fresh, clear scent behind to be replaced by the overpowering aroma of pine and cedar trees thickening around her. She silently admired the deep reds of the oaks and the gold of the birch trees. The artist's strokes had moved from his canvas in the sky to the many trees in the forest. As Lorinda moved deeper and deeper into the forest, she looked upward and saw that the sun was trailing along above her, its welcome strips of yellow glowing downward through the tops of the trees, while nuthatches and sparrows flew into the sunshine with shimmerings of excited wings and song.

Tangled barberry bushes with tufts of crimson berries slowed Lorinda's approach as her skirt persisted in getting snagged and caught. She shuddered when forest spiders' webs with their glistening spokes clung to her hair and skin. But the darkening shadows of the forest encouraged her to fight off her aggressors, to move on and on. She now even ignored the forest floor's occasional garden of delicate, exquisite flowers, partially hidden in the shade under the damp thickets of young balsams.

No. She could no longer force herself to enjoy any of this adventure of which she was an unwilling victim. There were more important things on her mind. There was the lack of food . . . the lack of water! The farther she traveled, the hungrier she became. She searched for eatable berries and found only few. Her knees and ankles were weakening from the constant demand she was putting on them and she was fast becoming disoriented.

"Where am I?" she murmured, watching the sun creeping lower and lower behind the trees. She fell to her knees, looking anxiously for signs of crushed brush, but knowing she would not find any. She had lost her way on the trail long ago. She was lost.

The bed of leaves and pine needles beneath her was damp and cold and sent chills deep inside her. She spread her skirt beneath her and settled down onto it, then wrapped her two blankets around her shoulders, trembling so hard her teeth began to chatter.

Listening to the sounds around her, she was glad that most were emerging from birds nestling in for the night. A squirrel raced up a tree beside her and a chipmunk called to another somewhere in the distance. But these animals did not pose a threat to Lorinda. It was the bears, coyotes, and wolverines that were known to wander these northern woods that frightened her the most. Without a fire, she was in mortal danger. But not having had to fend for herself before, Lorinda didn't know the skill of firemaking without the aid of matches. Her night would have to be spent in total darkness.

Exhaused from worry and her travels, Lorinda chose a

fat trunk of an oak tree to rest her back against. She would make herself stay awake. She would *not* lie down. She would keep watch all around her and if anything tried to sneak upon her she would surely hear the crush of the leaves . . . or . . . the snarls of . . . the . . . beasts. . . .

But the black of the night and her sluggishness from intense hunger sent her into a fitful sleep that was visited by nightmares about her parents and her sister. She fought the battle of anguished loss over and over again in her dreams through the night, and then at the crack of dawn she was awakened quite abruptly by a shower of acorns falling on her head. Rubbing the sleep from her eyes, she gazed upward at a family of squirrels nibbling away at acorns, enjoying their first meal of the day.

Lorinda's stomach ached agonizingly. She groaned as she managed to push herself up from the soggy ground. Having been caressed by the night's lacy dew, her clothes clung to her and her hair hung in dampened ringlets across her shoulders.

"I must move onward," she murmured, swinging the blankets around her shoulders more snugly. She pushed herself upward and began to inch her way along the forest bed. Each footstep seemed to be heavier than the last. Her shoulders sagged from weakness and her lips were parched from need of water. She remembered the fish . . . she remembered the water . . . then felt a spinning of the head as she gave way to a confused dizziness and crumpled into a heap onto the ground.

"I can't," she said, beginning to cry softly. She pounded her doubled fists against the leaf-covered earth. "I can't . . . I can't. . . ."

A stirring in the brush behind her drew Lorinda's head around, yet she saw nothing. She swallowed hard, afraid. She tried to push herself upward, but her knees would no longer hold her. She now realized that the two days on the

103

trail with the Indian with only occasional berries for nourishment, her refusal of food when she had had the opportunity to eat her fill, and the past whole day and night without food had finally taken their toll. She could no longer fight the weakness engulfing her.

"Red Blossom. . . ."

Lorinda tensed, having heard the words, but not knowing from where . . . or from whom. She began frantically scooting along the slick surface of the leaves then stopped abruptly when Yellow Feather appeared in her way. So swiftly had he moved, it had been quicker than even the wind.

"You . . ." Lorinda whispered, more glad than afraid. He had saved her once. Was he going to do so again? Her heart thumped wildly as he stood there with crossed arms looking down at her with the dark of his eyes. She no longer cared that her destination would no longer be St. Paul. At least she would arrive alive . . . wherever he chose to take her. She was once more his captive . . . an alive captive.

Her gaze moved quickly over him and saw that he carried no rifle with him this time. Instead, a bow was positioned across a shoulder and a quiver of arrows was at his back. Then she suddenly remembered the words he had just spoken. Red Blossom? He had spoken . . . in . . . English. . . .

Yellow Feather's heart had become a drum, pounding . . . pounding. . . . His eyes assessed Lorinda and knew that he had won.

She was now ready to be obedient to his commands. His lesson had been slow, but sure. She would know never to wander from the cave again. She would know that to do so could be the cause of her death. This would be the *only* time that he would be there to follow her, to look after her. He only took time to teach a loved one a lesson once . . . only once.

104

Moving even more quickly, he scooped Lorinda and her blankets up into his arms. "You are weak, Red Blossom," he said huskily. "Yellow Feather will carry you back to the safety of the cave."

No matter how happy Lorinda was to see him, she just couldn't give in to him so easily. She had to try to fight him. Show him that she would not be pushed around so easily. "Let me go, you savage," she said weakly, swinging her legs and hitting at his chest with doubled-up fists.

"Red Blossom will grow weaker if you kick and hit at Yellow Feather," Yellow Feather grumbled, holding her more tightly.

Lorinda became breathless and let her legs and arms relax. She could no longer fight him. She didn't even want to. Instead, she snuggled into her blankets and wrapped her arm about his neck. Then her eyes widened as she leaned away from him a bit and looked quizzically into his dark pools of eyes. She was once more realizing that he had spoken in English!

"You . . . you speak English?" she murmured. "Did you . . . ?"

"Ay-uh," he said. "As well as you do most of the time." He began to run in a trot, bending beneath low branches and jumping over thorny brush.

"Why . . . ?"

"I have my own reasons why I did not reveal this to you sooner."

"How did you . . . you just happen along this morning?" she asked guardedly.

"I've been with you. All along. Since you left the cave," Yellow Feather said, looking straight ahead as he kept his steady pace.

"You . . . what . . . ?" Lorinda gasped.

"Ay-uh," he said. "I had to teach you that to escape from the cave to go into the forest is a thing you should

105

not do."

Lorinda once more began struggling in his arms. "A test? You were testing me?" she screamed.

"No. No test. It was a lesson."

"Lesson . . . ?"

"To be obedient to my commands from here on out," Yellow Feather stated flatly. "When I tell you to stay in the cave, you stay. . . ."

"Why, you savage . . ." Lorinda shouted, regaining her strength because of her anger. "You planned this all along. I could have been eaten by a bear for all you cared."

Yellow Feather stopped abruptly. He held Lorinda's hands as though in a vise as he spoke back in anger. "I told you. I was there. All the time," he said. "I watched you all night. No animal or man could have drawn near to you. I was there. You would not have been harmed."

Lorinda ceased with her struggles. "You didn't sleep all night? Because . . . of . . . me . . . ?"

"Red Blossom, I would never let harm come to you."

"Red Blossom?" Lorinda murmured, feeling the strange sweetness stirring again inside her, realizing how important she had become to him, someone she should hate, but was oh, so afraid someone she loved. "Why do you call me Red Blossom? My name is Lorinda."

Yellow Feather set her hands free then lifted one of his to her hair. "Because of your hair. It is like that blossom of the rare red August poppy that I've always admired for its delicate beauty and gracefulness," he said. "In Indian you will be called *Mis-kwah-wa-bee-go-neece,* which means Red Blossom."

"That is beautiful," she whispered. "But my name is Lorinda, not Red Blossom. It is Lorinda."

Yellow Feather drew her closer to him and began trotting through the forest once more with his head held proudly high. "Red Blossom. I no care for the American name Lorinda. Red Blossom has special meaning.''

"In American, Lorinda *also* has special meaning,''
Lorinda argued stubbornly. "It stands for 'the laurel,' the
symbol of victory.''

"Red Blossom,'' Yellow Feather stated flatly. "I will
call you Red Blossom. Nothing else.'' He did not wish
her to feel victorious. Not while in *his* presence.

Weary and oh, still so hungry, Lorinda rested her
cheek against Yellow Feather's shoulder. "I don't know
what to call *you*,'' she said. "Surely you will tell me your
name.'' She could vaguely remember his calling himself
by a given name but she just couldn't remember. There
was so much getting in the way of her being as rational as
she wished to be . . . most of which was oh, the closeness of him . . . .

"O-zah-wah-mee-gwun," he answered quickly.

"What . . . ?'' Lorinda gasped.

"I spoke my name, Yellow Feather, to you in Indian,''
he said, glancing down at her, seeing her brilliant green
eyes studying him. His stomach rippled strangely and for
a brief moment he thought he might be guilty of letting
her read something in the depths of his eyes. He forced
his eyes straight ahead. He could not let her know of his
deepest feelings about her. He was the man . . . she the
woman. He had to remain the strongest in her eyes.

"Yellow Feather?'' Lorinda murmured. She raised her
head and glanced upward at the yellow feather in the band
at his head. "Is that why you wear a yellow feather?''

"Ay-uh. . . ."

"Did you say yes or no in Indian?'' she asked softly.

"Ay-uh. I said yes.''

Lorinda's weariness kept attacking her in small doses.
She languidly placed her cheek back against his shoulder,
marveling at the tightness of his muscles. She was no longer afraid. She even felt as though she *should* be in his
arms, talking as though they were friends . . . instead of

107

enemies.

The picture of her dead parents and Amanda's burned cradle flashed before her eyes, reminding her of her place in this world of Indian and white man. She trembled a bit and clamped her eyes tightly closed. In his arms, she didn't want to think about the tragedy of her family. She didn't want to think about her Aunt Rettie, who must be frantic with worry. She just wanted to feel the Indian's warm breath upon her cheek and the tender way in which he held her to him. She didn't want to think that he could kill anyone. He had proven that he cared too much for life. Hadn't he saved her? Even . . . twice . . . ?

She dozed peacefully as he continued trotting at his steady pace, and, to her complete surprise when she awakened, Yellow Feather had left the forest behind and was running along the St. Croix River's edge. Lorinda was amazed at his agility and speed. It had taken her a full day to cover the same amount of ground. She had even slept a full night. And now? Was he even drawing close to the cave? She lifted her head from his chest and gazed around her. Beneath the brilliance of the sunlight, the trees in the distance were dotted in different bold colors, resembling a patchwork quilt all fresh and newly sewn to perfection. She looked downward. In the more shallow waters of this great winding river, she could see translucent, silvery-gray moss agate rolling up and down with the water, showing quite clearly how the moss clung inside, at the heart of the stone.

The neighing of a horse drew Lorinda's head in another direction. She stiffened a bit when she saw a lone horse pawing at the ground at the cave's entrance. Why hadn't she seen it before? But then she remembered Yellow Feather's words . . . how he had planned all of this ahead of time. He had most surely hidden the horse from sight before her escape from the cave. When she had begun her blind adventure into the depths of the forest, he had felt quite free to tie his horse back at the cave's entrance. He had known her return would be with him.

She looked quickly around for a second horse, seeing none. Yellow Feather *was* intending to keep her in the cave. She was *still* not going to be taken to his village.

But she should have known this. Hadn't he told her that the lesson that had been taught her was that of knowing to stay at the cave? He hadn't said "village." She felt her inner strength crumbling. Was it meant for her to be forever only a part of a cave? Had Yellow Feather rescued her only to imprison her in such a cold, drafty place? Why wouldn't he take her to his people? Was he forbidden to?

Lorinda shivered as Yellow Feather trotted on inside the cave, to where embers were glowing orange in the firespace.

"Only Flying Squirrel knows of this cave. He must have returned," Yellow Feather said as he eased Lorinda from his arms and onto the softness of spread blankets. "His fire is still warm. I will make it burn again, then go and get you food."

Lorinda hugged her blankets to her. "Flying Squirrel?" she murmured.

Yellow Feather busied himself at placing more sticks and larger logs across the fire in the center of the firespace that was circled by round gray rocks. "Flying Squirrel is my faithful friend," he said. He dropped to his hands and knees and blew onto the glowing orange coals. When a crackling and popping proved that the smaller twigs were catching fire, Yellow Feather raised to a squatting position, intensely watching the flickering of flames.

"Flying Squirrel is my most trusted friend. You saw him yesterday," Yellow Feather said. "When I saw that his presence upset you I sent him to our village. He has probably returned to the cave again so soon with news of my ailing father."

Lorinda's shivering smoothed out to a nothingness as

109

the fire grew more brightly upon her face. The warmth gave her a soft glow inside, as Yellow Feather's presence also did, who now looked at her with his smoldering, dark eyes. "Your father?" she said, hating it when her voice trembled a bit. But he *did* unnerve her so.

"Chief Wind Whisper. My father," Yellow Feather said quietly. "He has been ailing. It is his age. His heart has grown tired of beating."

Lorinda's own heart skipped a few beats. "Your father is the chief of your band of Indians?" she gasped. She gazed at him with more respect. She understood the greatness of an Indian chief and what he meant to his people. "And . . . you say he is ill? Is he possibly . . . dying . . . ?"

"He is chief, and, *ay-uh,* he is dying," Yellow Feather said sullenly. He rose abruptly to his feet. "But no more talk of my father. I must see that you eat before I return to my village of saddened people."

Lorinda looked around her. "Where is this Flying Squirrel now?" she asked softly. She still couldn't let herself trust *two* Indians alone with her.

"He's of an impatient heart," Yellow Feather growled. "He probably grew tired of waiting for my return."

Lorinda's thoughts were full as Yellow Feather lifted his bow from his shoulder and turned and left. She scooted closer to the fire, enjoying its steady warmth. She rubbed her hands over the flames, thinking further about what Yellow Feather had revealed to her about himself. If his father died, then *he* would . . . be . . . chief. . . ?

"Chief Yellow Feather," she whispered, liking the sound of it.

She smiled and began tugging and pulling at her boots. When she had them removed and her toes curled next to the fire and the blankets dropped from her shoulders, she watched as Yellow Feather returned with a skinned rabbit, ready for the frying. With open admiration, she watched further as he showed his skills at preparing food for her, the woman. Was this usual? Or was she . . . truly . . . special to him . . . ?

"Please tell me more about your band of Indians," she encouraged, tossing her hair back from her shoulders. If not for her hunger, she could even have felt peaceful inside. Somehow, Yellow Feather caused her trust in him to magnify with each added moment she spent in his presence.

Yellow Feather rose from his haunches and went to the back of the cave. He got a small drawstring leather pouch and went back to the fire to settle down next to Lorinda. "Here's something to give you strength until the rabbit is cooked," he said, offering the bag to Lorinda.

"What is it?" she murmured.

"Small cakes of maple sugar. My people make these each spring."

Lorinda accepted the bag and shook one of the cakes out onto her hand then thrust it inside her mouth. She closed her eyes and ate several more, already feeling the strength returning to her limbs. "Hmm. It's so good," she whispered. "So sweet and good. Thank you, Yellow Feather. Thank you."

Smiling, Yellow Feather once more began tending the spattering rabbit in the white man's frying pan. "You asked about my people," he said. "I am of the Chippewa." Pride was thick in his voice. "We are the St. Croix band of the Ojibway."

Lorinda felt a strong ray of hope. She remembered her aunt's talk about the Minnesota territory Indians. Aunt Rettie had said that the Chippewa were nonwarring and that it was the Sioux who left a trail of blood wherever they traveled. She felt lucky indeed to be in the presence of a Chippewa Indian rather than a Sioux. Didn't it even confirm her belief that Yellow Feather couldn't have

111

done her parents harm? But yet, she could never be sure. She had always thought that an Indian was an Indian no matter what tribe. . . .

"And where is your village?" Lorinda asked cautiously. She watched his expression darken a bit. She placed the last maple sugar cake inside her mouth and chewed anxiously.

"A day's ride away," Yellow Feather murmured. "My people have been pushed farther and farther north by the white man's signed papers," Yellow Feather murmured. "This has not been good for my people. My people have suffered."

Lorinda's face flushed a bit. She lowered her eyes. "I'm sorry," she said. Then her eyes raised quickly, revealing a flashing anger. "But you are *not* the only one who has suffered," she stormed. "The white man has also suffered by the hand of the Indian."

"Your suffering could never match ours," Yellow Feather argued.

Lorinda felt tears surfacing. She dropped the empty bag to the floor as she rose quickly. She rushed away from the fire, sobbing. "My suffering is almost unbearable at times," she said, wringing her hands, feeling a desolate sweep of loneliness overtake her. At this moment, she was being transported back in time, standing over bodies, seeing the arrows . . . .

Seeing her sudden showing of grief, Yellow Feather was confused. What had she meant by saying the white man had suffered because of the Indians? The white man had only profited! Didn't they now own most of the streams? The richest of the rice fields? The animals? The trees? The land? Even . . . the mountains . . . ?

Yet Lorinda looked as though she had suffered. His insides ached for her in another new way. He felt a keen stirring of sympathy for her, something he had *never* felt for a white man or woman. He pulled the skillet free from

112

the fire and hurried to her. Hesitatingly, he placed his hands on her shoulders and turned her slowly around to face him. "You are sad?" he whispered. "Why are you?" His heartbeat raced as she lifted her eyes to him, revealing sparkling teardrops at the tips of her long, thick lashes. Her lips were quivering and her cheeks were rosy. Oh, how he wanted her at this moment. His need caused such a painful ache in his loins.

"Why?" she murmured, swallowing hard. "Do you really want to know?"

"*Ay-uh.* . . ."

"My parents. They are dead because of Indians," she said weakly. "I found them . . . with . . . arrows piercing their flesh and their . . . their heads scalped. . . ." She lowered her eyes, not able to say anymore. It was too painful.

"When did this happen?" Yellow Feather asked firmly. He was remembering the talk of Sioux raids. He no longer envied their boastings. He now saw the results.

"Four . . . five . . . days ago," Lorinda said. She shook her head slowly. "I'm not sure. It seems I've lost count of the days and nights since my abduction from St. Paul."

"Abduction . . . ?"

"Yes," she said. "The man you found me with on the trail?"

"*Ay-uh.* . . ."

"He had kidnapped me."

"And then I . . . ?"

"Yes. . . ."

"And your parents . . . dead. . . ." Yellow Feather murmured. "Life has been cruel to you, little one." His fingers dug into her flesh. "You must know that it was *not* the Chippewa who murdered your parents," he said with force. "We are nonwarring. We made peace with the white man long ago. We could *not* harm your people."

113

Lorinda's gaze traveled quickly to the back of the cave. Doubts assailed her, seeing once again all the possessions of the white man. "How could you gather together such a collection, if not by harming the white man?" she said flatly. "How can I truly believe what you say? How?"

"I move mostly by night," he said quietly. "While the white man slept I took most of what you see here. Then there were other times when I found things discarded at the side of the trail. I do not harm the white man."

Lorinda shot him a questioning glance. "The man I was with. You . . . harmed . . . him. . . ." she said guardedly.

"That white man was causing you discomfort. I saw. I heard. Yellow Feather rescued you from the evil white man."

"But now I am *your* captive. . . ."

"Because I have never found my heart so disturbed before by any woman," he said thickly. "I couldn't leave you behind. I had to possess you. *Ay-uh,* I had to. I meant you no harm. I haven't harmed you."

"You are as evil as that white man if you continue forcing me to stay with you," Lorinda said, even more guardedly, testing his reaction. "It is not right to abduct a woman just because you find her attractive. No, you have *not* harmed me physically, but mentally, I am shattered."

"No matter what you say, I cannot let you go," Yellow Feather said, reaching a hand to her face. He traced her features. "You are mine. You must learn to love me. . . ."

Lorinda's heart thundered inside her. Her breath caught in her throat as his fingers touched her lips with tenderness. She was being pulled into a magnetic force of passion and need and welcomed his other hand as it lifted her hair, to caress it with his eyes. She would soon be lost to him if she didn't break the spell. "Are you saying that you love me?" she whispered, closing her eyes as his lips were suddenly there, warm on her forehead.

"*Ay-uh*. . . ." he murmured.

"If you do, then lead me back to my people," she said, now wondering if she would ever be able to walk away from him, to never see him again.

"You must understand that is impossible," he said, now kissing the hollow of her throat. "My death would be swift and sure. The white man would never understand my reasons for bringing you here with me. Though I am Chippewa, the peaceful Indian, the white man would forget that and also accuse me of your parents' death."

"Not only are my parents . . ." Lorinda said, but didn't complete her sentence, thinking better of speaking of her sister. If by chance Yellow Feather did not know all the Indians of his St. Croix band as well as he thought, with one having possibly been responsible for her parents' death, then Lorinda thought better of revealing her sister's plight to Yellow Feather. It would be of no use to tell the sad story to him. Only time could reveal all truths to Lorinda . . . to Yellow Feather about his people.

But at least Lorinda believed that Yellow Feather was innocent of the massacre. She could tell that he spoke from the heart. He was sincere. And, oh, he was so handsome and knew just where to place his lips to make Lorinda forget her sorrows . . . her hunger . . . her weariness. She threw her head back in ecstasy as he succeeded at unbuttoning her blouse. She didn't struggle as she had done with Lamont Quinby. Instead, she let his lips devour the flesh of her breasts that had been so deftly removed as her blouse, skirt, and undergarments fell to the floor of the cave.

"What are you doing to me?" she sighed, brushing all thoughts of guilt aside. She had known from first contact with his copper flesh that he would be the one to take her virginity and she did not dread it. She was all aglow and warm inside as his fingers moved silkily over her. She became a mass of rapturous trembles as his lips moved from one breast to the other, then lower, as he stooped on one knee before her, to plant a kiss on the soft flesh of her abdomen. All those tumultuous feelings for him that had so often left her so confused had finally merged into one . . . that only of love.

This first true awakening of love caused Lorinda to bend and reach her outstretched arms to him. In one liquid movement he lifted her into his arms and lowered his lips to hers with a wild desperation.

The tormented feelings he had held intact were now being set free, with his self-control fast placed behind him. His hand molded her breast and his lips were on fire, hot and demanding. When he heard a low moan surface from deep inside her, he carried Lorinda to the bed of blankets and spread her there to feast his eyes upon her.

With a rapid pounding in his temple, he removed his breechcloth and leggings and stood proudly above her, letting her eyes take in the strong, powerful part of him that would soon give her pleasure. When he saw her blush, he knew that he was the first. He slowly moved over her, then bore down upon her in a fiery, lengthy kiss. . . .

Lorinda's heart was pounding so, she thought she might suffocate. But when his lips possessed her again, her mind drifted to a different world that was only inhabited by Yellow Feather and herself. The whirlwind of passion that she was caught up in was causing her to be filled with a beautiful, wondrous desire that his lips and hands had created by their skillful manipulations. She no longer cared that she was his captive. If she had her way, she would stay imprisoned against his responsive body forever and ever.

"Red Blossom, I do not want to force you," Yellow Feather suddenly whispered into Lorinda's ear, while his hands continued to caress her, lifting her up, as though on

116

a cloud, drifting, floating, melting. . . .

"You are not forcing me," she whispered back, tracing his back, loving the ripple of muscles. "I do this willingly with you."

Yellow Feather forced her gaze to meet his and she could see the intensity of passion etched in his, yet there was still a veil of sorts, separating passion from cool restraint.

"You are not like the Indian woman," he said softly. "The Indian woman does not share so openly my caresses. You moan with feelings. You give me back my kiss. You enjoy. . . ."

"Never before have I done this with a man, Yellow Feather," Lorinda said, blushing. She reached to touch his lips, oh, so full, so inviting. "Only you. Only you, my sweet savage love. I surrender my all, only to you."

"I'll be gentle," he said, slowly lowering himself into her. He found the entrance difficult but kissed her worry and pain away as he finally succeeded at making complete entry.

Lorinda gasped from the short instant of pain, then sighed as the pain merged into a sweet ecstasy. She lifted her hips to him and eased her arms about his neck and clung to him as his body moved slowly inside her. With reckless desire, he pressed his lips to her throat and circled his fingers into her hair. Lorinda was drifting once more, as her needs were fulfilled. He was no longer an Indian, she was no longer white woman. They were one. Their climaxes were reached together. And only when their bodies were sated did Lorinda's face blaze with shame, causing her to turn her head from him.

Yellow Feather saw this and forced her face around to look at him. "Do not let shame ruin what we have found together," he said. "It was *mee-kah-wah-diz-ee*."

Lorinda blinked her eyes nervously, still feeling a tingling of desire between her thighs. *"Mee-kah-wah-*

diz-ee?'' she whispered. "What does that mean?"

"Beautiful. In Indian it means beautiful."

Lorinda's cheek quivered with a nervous smile. "Yes. It was," she murmured. "But I shouldn't have. I feel I have done such a wrong."

"You love Yellow Feather?"

"Yes. . . ."

"I love Red Blossom. We've done no wrong," he reassured her. He drew her into his arms and held her there with their heartbeats rapid against each other's chest.

"I want to stay in your arms forever," she sighed, caressing his neck with her fingertips. "I do love you. I do."

Yellow Feather was reminded of time . . . and his father. "I want you also in my arms forever," he said. "But I must leave you for a while."

Lorinda leaned back, eyeing him closely. "You will still leave me here in this awful cave?" she said, shivering now from her nudity.

Yellow Feather lifted a blanket around her then rose and pulled on his leggings and breechcloth. "I must go see to my father," he said, straightening his yellow feather in his headband.

Lorinda rose, clinging to the blanket. "Please take me with you," she begged.

"I cannot. . . ."

"And why not?"

"My father. He would not understand."

"Why not?"

"He doesn't even know about this cave and what is in it. He would *not* understand about how I have captured me a white woman."

"But, Yellow Feather . . ."

Yellow Feather squared his shoulders and glowered at her. "No more words," he said flatly. "What Yellow Feather says to you, you listen. You obey."

118

Anger flashed in Lorinda's eyes. She stomped a foot angrily. "All I am to you *is* a captive," she shouted. "I was a fool to think you loved me for *me*. You only want my body."

Yellow Feather grabbed her to him, causing the blanket to fall to the ground. "If a body is all I want, I have two wives to offer that to me," he grumbled.

"Two . . . wives . . . ?" Lorinda gasped. Her face flushed crimson. "You . . . are . . . married . . . ? Twice?"

"*Ay-uh.* I am next chief-in-line. I *must* have wives."

"Oh, you . . ." Lorinda cried, struggling. But her defenses melted away when Yellow Feather's lips proved his feelings for her. He trailed kisses from her forehead to her breasts, then shoved her gently away.

"I will leave now," he said. "You have rabbit to eat."

He walked to the back of the cave, then brought another leather drawstring pouch back to Lorinda. "Inside you will find several smoked fish rolled in birch bark. Eat this also," he said. "I will return before you are hungry again."

Lorinda's eyes traveled quickly around her. "But what if a bear . . . ?" she said.

Yellow Feather went to the guns and pulled a rifle free from the many. He held it toward her. "Here. Use this," he said. "I keep this one loaded at all times."

Lorinda felt a weakness in the knees. "This gun is loaded?" she said, accepting it.

"*Ay-uh.*"

Slowly, she pointed the barrel toward him, feeling strangely odd standing before him in the nude, aiming a rifle at him. "You were wrong to trust me," she said, consumed suddenly with heartbeats. Her finger went to the trigger.

"I think not," Yellow Feather said confidently. He placed his back to her as he began walking toward the cave entrance.

Lorinda dropped the gun to the floor of the cave. She lifted the blanket around her and ran after Yellow Feather. "Please take me with you," she begged.

He swung around and faced her. "You are not going to shoot Yellow Feather in the back?" he teased.

She lowered her lashes. "You knew I could not," she whispered.

"As I cannot take you with me," Yellow Feather said flatly. He left Lorinda standing, staring blankly after him.

"I will never truly know or understand him," she said aloud.

Slowly, she went back to the fire. She eyed the cooked rabbit, suddenly ravenous again. As she consumed the meat, her mind wandered back to what she and Yellow Feather had shared. It had been beautiful, yet mysterious. She couldn't believe that she had given herself so willingly . . . and . . . to an Indian.

"But I will again," she murmured. "I know I will. My hunger for him will never be quelled. . . ."

She then remembered something else. "Two wives?" she whispered. "He has . . . two . . . wives . . . ?"

Her heart ached . . . so very, very jealous. . . .

Seven

The wheels of the stagecoach fell in and out of bumps on the scarcely traveled road that had been carved through the thickness of the forest. Rettie moved with the swaying of the stagecoach, quite aware of eyes on her. The only other passenger was a man . . . a man who Rettie found handsome, thinking him to have quite an intelligent look about him. Though she had housed many men in her boardinghouse, this man was the first to create anything akin to romantic stirrings inside her since she had become widowed.

"My name's Matthew Toliver," the man said suddenly, breaking their strained silence. He leaned forward, resting his full weight on a gold-tipped cane. His fingers clasped and unclasped on the cane's handle. "What's your attraction to Duluth?" he added. "Business?"

Feeling the outline of the pearl-handled pistol inside her purse, Rettie tilted her chin and smiled smugly. "Yes," she replied. "Business."

"What sort . . . ?" Matthew asked.

Rettie flashed him a nervous glance, seeing the whole of him in one rake of the eye. His thick crop of gray hair matched the gray of his waistcoat and breeches and the cravat neatly tied at his neck. His blue eyes spoke of a warm friendliness and his added weight and the grooves on his face, revealing his age as probably early sixties, didn't make him any less attractive to her. Rettie knew the extent of her own wrinkles and how she had bloomed out in her later years, so she could most surely accept a

121

man who had aged in the same manner.

"What sort of business is drawing you to the town of Duluth?" Matthew persisted.

Rettie let her fingers travel over the shape of her pistol again, having thrust it inside her purse before leaving her boardinghouse in St. Paul. "Personal business," she said in her raspy tone of voice.

"Thinking of starting a boardinghouse there like the one you own in St. Paul?" Matthew said, smiling. He relaxed his back against the seat, watching her intently.

Rettie's brows tilted. "How did you know about my boardinghouse?" she asked, shifting in the seat as the stagecoach made a turn in the road.

Matthew laughed amusedly. He lifted his cane and rested it across his lap. "Everyone knows about Rettie Odell's boardinghouse," he said. "I've heard tell that it's the best in St. Paul."

"And, sir, were you in St. Paul long?"

"A week. . ."

"If you had heard so much about my boardinghouse, why didn't you make your presence known there?" Rettie said stiffly.

"If my plans had been to stay in your fair city longer, I would have."

"And what do you do for a livin', sir?"

"I'm a newspaperman. From Boston," he bragged.

"How nice," Rettie said quietly. She felt a heightening of uneasiness as his blue eyes continued to bore down upon her. She had left her skills at flirting back in the years of her youth. She wasn't about to make a fool of herself by trying to charm this man when she knew what little charm was left to pass around.

She glanced quickly down at her attire, seeing how her knitted shawl hid most of her filled-out blue velvet dress from his wandering eyes. Her fingers self-consciously went to her cameo brooch at the white collar of her dress and absently toyed with it.

"Delightful cologne you're wearing, ma'am," Matthew commented warmly. "Lily of the valley. Am I right?"

Rettie felt like a schoolgirl when she couldn't control a blush from rising on her cheeks. Her fingers went to the tight bun that circled her head and worked with a loose strand of gray hair that had escaped from it. "Why, yes," she said softly. "It is lily of the valley. It's all I ever wear."

Matthew closed his eyes and inhaled deeply. "I can imagine myself in a garden," he said. "Lovely, ah, lovely."

Feeling the need to change the subject, to talk of less personal matters, Rettie circled the purse on her lap with her hands and held it tightly. "You say you're a newspaperman, sir," she said, tilting her chin. "Why are you travelin' these parts instead of a more excitin' territory?"

Matthew placed his cane before him and leaned onto it. "Shall we dispense with the formalities of addressing one another as ma'am and sir?" he said. "Why don't you call me Matthew and I'll call you Rettie? We'll be in each other's company for some time before reaching Duluth. I'd much prefer being on a first-name basis. What do you say?"

Feeling a bit flustered by this man's attention, Rettie shifted her weight around on the stagecoach seat. One of her hands went to the shape of the gun in her purse, reminding her that she needed to keep her wits about her. She could let nothing stand in the way of her shooting that evil man Lamont Quinby. He most surely was responsible for Lorinda's disappearance. Hadn't he disappeared from her boardinghouse the very day Lorinda had?

Her thoughts traveled back to St. Paul . . . to the day Lorinda had run from her house in anger. Rettie's day of waiting had been long, and when she had driven out to

Derrick's house to tell her brother of Lorinda's disappearance . . . he . . . would she ever be able to put the gruesome, bloody sight from her mind . . . ? What if Lorinda had returned home that day? What if the Indians. . . ?

No. She couldn't let herself believe the Indians had abducted Lorinda as they had seemed to have done with tiny Amanda. No. It was Lamont Quinby! He had tried to have his way with Lorinda. When he hadn't succeeded, wouldn't his next move be to force himself upon her in other ways?

Duluth, Rettie thought angrily to herself. Lamont Quinby had said that his true destination was Duluth. It had also become hers.

"Well? What do you say?" Matthew persisted. "First names okay?"

"Yes. That'd be fine," Rettie finally answered. "Please do call me Rettie."

"I believe you asked why I've traveled to these parts," Matthew said, leaning against the back of the seat, relaxing.

"Yes, I did. . . ."

"I needed a change. Some new excitement."

"And you thought you'd find it here?" Rettie scoffed. "Most the winter, St. Paul and Duluth's froze in. Not much excitement to write about, I'd say."

"There are the Indians," Matthew said, frowning. "Only five days ago I wrote about the misfortune of a family being massacred by renegade Indians. Now wouldn't you say that was newsworthy enough?"

Rettie paled and her insides began a slow twisting. "A horrible thing," she murmured, lowering her eyes. "A tragic, horrible thing." Pulling a handkerchief from the sleeve of her dress, she sniffed into it.

Matthew leaned forward. "Did I say something wrong?" he said quietly. "You seem suddenly . . . so

. . . so distraught.''

Rettie swallowed hard. She was not about to discuss her woes with a complete stranger. Especially not a newspaperman. When Lamont Quinby's slain body was found, most surely this newspaperman's thoughts would wander back to her and cause him to point an accusing finger her way.

"I'm fine," she murmured. "Just this drafty stagecoach. That's all."

"I could come and sit by you and help keep the draft from you," Matthew said.

Rettie's eyes widened. "No. That's not necessary," she murmured. She could feel the color rising back into her cheeks and was glad. She then tensed as Matthew pushed his weight from his seat and settled next to her.

"No bother," he said. "No bother at all."

Rettie glanced a bit sideways at him, catching him staring at her. Together they laughed amusedly, then relaxed against the back of the seat and continued with becoming more acquainted.

"Usually the stagecoach is so packed, one hardly has space to move," Matthew said, thumping his cane against the floor of the stagecoach. "I guess the Indians have scared people away from this mode of travel."

"Reckon so," Rettie said flatly.

"But not you," Matthew said. "Why is that? Aren't you afraid of Indians?"

"There are two sorts of savages in this world," Rettie grumbled. "There's the red one and then there's the white."

"Oh?" Matthew said, tilting a brow. "And you're not afraid of either, I take it."

"Correct," Rettie spat, straightening her back. She heard Matthew clear his throat nervously. She viewed him curiously with a sideways glance. His shoulder was on a straight line with hers and if he leaned just the least

125

bit . . .

"Why isn't your husband accompanying you to Duluth?" Matthew asked, glancing her way again.

"I'm on my own. That's why," Rettie grumbled.

"Oh?"

"I'm a widow."

"Oh."

Rettie glanced toward him. "And you? Where's your wife? Did you leave her behind, in Boston?"

"Yes. I left her in Boston. . . ."

Rettie's pulse faltered a bit. She looked quickly away from him. "Oh," she mumbled. "I see."

"I'm a widower," Matthew quickly added. "I've left my wife buried in Boston."

Rettie's face brightened. "That's too bad," she said. "Sorry for your misfortune."

Matthew sighed heavily. "I'm over it," he said. "It's been two full years now."

"You're lookin' to settle in Duluth?" Rettie asked, touching the outline of the gun again. "I hear land's going for $2.50 an acre."

"Thought I'd check it out."

"You didn't like St. Paul?"

Matthew chuckled good-naturedly. "Now I didn't say that."

They talked and talked for what seemed hours until bright splashes of orange from the evening's sunset came in like streamers of satin through the windows of the stagecoach. The stagecoach shimmied a bit as its wheels slowed.

"Seems we're stoppin' for the night," Rettie said, straightening her shawl around her shoulders.

"Ever been asleep on the trail before?" Matthew asked, peering through the window.

"Not without some kin at my side," Rettie grumbled.

"Where is your kin? In St. Paul?"

Rettie's chin showed a sudden quivering as her heart began a slow ache. She turned her face from Matthew and forced her jaw to set firmly. "The stagecoach has come to a full halt," she murmured, avoiding his question, knowing that to answer would mean to relive that day in her heart all over again. "Let's get out and see what our surroundings are to be for the night."

Matthew leaned in front of her and opened the door. "Be careful stepping down," he said.

"I'm used to takin' care of myself," Rettie said flatly, wheezing a bit as she took the long step to the ground. She lifted the skirt of her dress in one hand and held her purse tightly with the other. She turned to see Matthew now standing next to her, admiring him anew and the way in which he held himself . . . so straight . . . so proud. Her gaze moved to the cane, wondering. . . .

"Shall we?" Matthew said, offering her an arm. "Let's just see how hard this ground is that we're to sleep on tonight."

Their feet made scarcely a sound as they walked on the deeply piled pine needles that had fallen from the stately Norway pines. Carrying with it a promise of a snappy night, the air was fresh and cool. The shadow of the forest lay all about them and tangled barberry bushes slowed their approach.

Rettie shivered a bit, hearing the whistling wind among the branches and seeing the ebbing red flames of the sun's rays among the maple and ash trees. When footsteps approached from behind, she turned with a start, then smiled an eager welcome as the bearded stagecoach driver came toward her, carrying a rifle.

"We'll have a fire goin' in no time flat," he said. He lifted a hat to her. "Frank's my name. If'n you needs anythin', don' be too bashful to ask."

"Thank you," she said, then watched his spirited walk as he began making a small clearing beneath the thick cover of trees.

Matthew leaned his weight against his cane as they stopped to gaze about them. "Once we get us a campfire built, things'll look a bit brighter," he said.

"That's what I'm afraid of," Rettie said, glancing quickly around her.

"What do you mean?"

"Indians. A campfire could attract Indians."

Matthew chuckled. "Thought you weren't afraid of Indians, Rettie," he said.

Rettie tilted her chin haughtily.

"I ain't," she murmured. "But I don't hanker to share my bedroll with them, neither." She marched away from Matthew, feeling his eyes watching her. She liked him. Yes, she liked him. But how did he see her? Was he thinking she was just a stubborn ol' woman who no longer had carin' in her heart for a man? She glanced over her shoulder at him and smiled, then felt her heart begin to pound as he began following her.

She focused her attention elsewhere, once more watching the stagecoach driver, suddenly feeling guilty for letting pleasure enter this journey of hate and revenge. Here she was with her brother and his wife dead . . . her two nieces missing . . . and she was thinking about feelings for a man!

When Matthew stepped next to her and reached for one of her hands, Rettie irritably jerked it away from him and went and helped to ready the campsite for the night ahead of them. She would stay away from Matthew. She had gotten by without a man since her husband's death . . . she would continue to do so. She had grown to like her independence. A man would only get in the way. She chose to not let herself think about the lonely side of her life. . . .

Feeling a sudden chill, as though the breath of death

128

had passed across her cheek, Rettie stirred from her bedroll. With a pounding heart, she inched her way to the campfire and held her hands over it, warming them. She glanced around on all sides of her, seeing Matthew soundly asleep in his bedroll snuggled as closely to hers as she had allowed, and Frank lay on the far side of the fire with his rifle positioned close by.

The fire caused weaving shadows on all sides of her and the branches of the trees tossed, creaked, and groaned. Rettie had thought the recurring dream of her family had awakened her, yet she felt there was something else. It was the restlessness of the two horses tied away from the campfire.

"Must be my 'magination," she whispered. "I'm lettin' myself get spooked for no good reason."

A crushing of leaves in the forest drew Rettie quickly around. She squinted her eyes and peered into the darkness, seeing nothing. She sighed with relief and inched her way toward the horses to see if they were securely tied. The thought of being left without a horse in this wilderness made added shivers ride her spine. Just as she was ready to reach a hand to touch one of the horses, another noise behind her caused her to stop, and suddenly she found herself the captive of a hand sealing her mouth and another twisting her arm painfully behind her.

Struggling, kicking and mumbling against the steel force of the hand, Rettie was dragged a bit farther into the forest. Her pulse raced but her anger and humiliation were greater than her fear. When she felt the hand leave her mouth she started to scream at her attacker, but then something else's being secured around her mouth kept all her sounds from surfacing. She worked her teeth and lips on the gag that now circled her face and she swung her arms and kicked her feet at the person she had yet to see.

Stumbling now, she was pushed toward a tree. Though she struggled still, she was soon tied to the tree and was finally able to look upon her abductor as he stepped into full view with legs widespread and hands resting on hips.

An intense hatred surged through Rettie's veins when her gaze met that of an Indian. The firelight gleamed on his copper-colored skin and in the dark flash of his eyes. She wanted to scream out at him. She wanted to claw at his dark, unwavering eyes. He was short and small-boned. How had she let him capture her? She usually had the strength of a man! Her gaze traveled to her bedroll, remembering her pistol. Why hadn't she thought to carry it with her for safety?

The Indian took a step forward, causing Rettie to look his way again. She froze inside, seeing his steady stare at her throat. The only weapon she had seen on him was a knife at his waist. Was he planning to cut her throat . . . then . . . scalp her . . . ?

When he reached his fingers toward her, Rettie groaned and struggled anew, then rested against the tree, motionless, as the Indian took her cameo brooch from her dress and walked away with it. Eyes wide, and barely breathing, Rettie watched the Indian move stealthily around the campsite, stealing first Frank's rifle then Rettie's shawl and purse.

Seeing her personal belongings—especially her pistol—taken away caused Rettie to begin a fresh battle with her ropes until her wrists throbbed from pain. Then suddenly the Indian was gone as fast as he had appeared.

The whinnying of a horse drew Rettie's quick attention. The Indian hadn't taken both horses! He had been thoughtful enough to leave one behind. Rettie's brow lifted in puzzlement. What kind of Indian would be so generous? And why hadn't this Indian slain them all? Why had *they* been spared when, only five days ago, others had been massacred . . . ?

Weary now from her struggles, Rettie closed her eyes. It wasn't something for her to figure out. No one understood Indians or why they did anything. She had always known this. That was why she always warned Derrick about the Indians. Though treaties had been signed, what did a piece of paper mean to a savage? What did anything mean to a savage? If they wanted it . . . they *took* it! This Indian tonight had taken her pistol. Now how could she confront Lamont Quinby . . . ?

Her eyes slowly opened, seeing how peacefully the two men still slept by the fire. It was apparent that neither Frank nor Matthew would awaken to rescue her from her discomforts until morning. She was left too alone with her thoughts. Tears rose to her eyes, once more remembering her family, feeling a bit guilty that she was the one to have been spared. If only she hadn't talked Derrick into leaving New York State. Oh, how old she suddenly felt. Oh, how beaten. . . .

"Rettie . . . what the . . . ?"

Rettie's eyes flew open, seeing Matthew's shadow against the backdrop of the fire. She began struggling with her ropes and grumbling beneath her gag, so thankful that Matthew had not slept the full night while she suffered alone, bound against the hard, rough bark of a tree.

"My God," Matthew grumbled as he worked with the ropes. "I reached over to check you and by damn when I found you gone, I . . ."

Rettie began coughing when the gag was quickly removed from her mouth. "An Indian . . ." she gasped, pointing toward the dark recesses of the forest. "He did this to me. . . ."

"An Indian . . . ?" Matthew said throatily.

Rettie began rubbing her sore wrists and moving her feet, relieved to feel the blood circulating in the right directions again. "Yes, an Indian," she raged.

Frank hurried to her, wiping sleep from his eyes. "What the hell's goin' on here?" he shouted. He ran his fingers across his shaggy red beard.

"Seems we had a visitor," Matthew growled, leaning against his cane.

"An Indian," Rettie fumed. "And while you two stand there, half asleep, the savage is gettin' away."

Frank swirled around. "The horses . . . ?" he blurted.

"He only took one," Rettie said, shaking the skirt of her dress. "He also took your rifle . . . and . . . uh . . . some of my belongings." She couldn't reveal that the loss of her pistol meant more to her than any other loss she had sustained, even that of the cameo brooch she had always treasured.

"Get everything together," Frank said, hurrying away.

"What . . . ?" Rettie gasped.

"We're leavin' this place and fast," Frank shouted from across his shoulder. "Get your gear together."

Rettie's eyes widened. "But . . ."

"You heard the man," Matthew said, taking Rettie by the elbow. "Let's get to it."

"But the Indian . . . ?" Rettie murmured, stumbling as Matthew directed her toward the stagecoach.

"He's long gone," Matthew grumbled. He opened the stagecoach door. "Now you get in there. I'll get your bedroll for you."

"I can take care of myself," Rettie said stubbornly.

Matthew chuckled amusedly. "Now, Rettie, whether or not you want to admit it, a man *can* do a few things for you, and I'm here to do the honors."

Rettie's face reddened. "Well, all right," she said. "But when I get to Duluth I have matters of my own to take care of by myself."

"We ain't goin' to no Duluth," Frank interrupted, hurrying the lone horse to attach to the stagecoach.

"What do you mean we're not travelin' on to Duluth?" Rettie fumed. "My way's paid. You *must* take me

132

to Duluth.''

Frank swung around, glaring. "Lady, this here's my stagecoach and what I says goes," he said darkly. "And I'll be damn if I take another of my stagecoach runs until these Indians are found and dealt with."

"Why I never . . ." Rettie hissed, stiffening her back.

"Rettie, get on inside," Matthew encouraged. "The sooner we get out of here the better off we'll *all* be."

"It's probably the damn Sioux. Sure as hell ain't takin' no chances with them warrin' Sioux," Frank argued aloud.

"There was only one Indian and he was a puny sort," Rettie grumbled. She took a step upward and settled herself on the seat.

"But where there's one Indian there are usually more," Matthew said. He patted her hand affectionately. "Now, Rettie, just settle down and I'll be right back."

Rettie sat waiting, feeling beat. When Matthew finally moved in next to her and eased his arm about her shoulder to comfort her, she accepted his gesture of friendship.

"I couldn't find your shawl," he said softly.

"I know," she said. "The Indian took it."

"I hope you understand about me agreeing to return to St. Paul," he further stated. "Without a gun, we have no way of defending ourselves."

"I understand," she grumbled. "But that don't make me like it any better."

The swaying of the stagecoach as it began moving along the road was welcome to Rettie. If she couldn't go to Duluth she was eager to return to St. Paul . . . to be alone with her grief.

"I have to ask you why the determination to reach Duluth," Matthew said. He swung his cane up and placed it across his lap.

133

"It's a private matter," Rettie snapped.

"Is it something that can wait?" Matthew said. "That is, since there won't be a stagecoach traveling that way for a while."

Rettie pulled her handkerchief from the sleeve of her dress. She dabbed at her nose with it, sniffling. She had always thought crying was for weak folk, but somehow it didn't matter much to her anymore, because she had the desperate need to cry. "It's really so terrible," she began, wiping tears.

"Rettie, what's so terrible?"

Rettie began by telling him about Lorinda's angry flight from her house and continued until the whole miserable story was told.

"So you think this Lamont Quinby abducted Lorinda?" Matthew said.

"I'm not sure what I believe anymore," Rettie sobbed. "There is also the problem with the Indians. Maybe Lorinda went back to Derrick's house that day and the Indians took her and Amanda away together?"

"But you were on your way to Duluth?"

"I had to find Lamont Quinby and see if Lorinda was with him."

"Did the sheriff . . . ?"

"He and his men searched for two full days and nights. They said it was all they could do."

"Did they go to Duluth?"

"No. I didn't think about Duluth until later," she said softly. "Then when I did, I thought it was something I could take care of myself."

"And now that you can't?"

"I guess I'll just have to go home and wait," she said sullenly. "Snows are due anytime now. Even the sheriff wouldn't want to head out again."

"Waiting is hard if you have to do it alone."

"I'm used to being alone," Rettie said flatly.

134

Matthew twirled his cane on his lap. "If it wasn't for my game leg, I'd head out for Duluth by horseback myself," Matthew said, smacking the thigh of his right leg. "I'd find this Lamont Quinby for you."

Rettie's gaze went to his leg. "Been wantin' to ask why your need of the cane," she said. "You walk straight with no limp. Don't see no visible sign of a bad leg."

"Got thrown by a horse," he growled. "Just tore the hell out of some muscles. That's all. But I haven't been on a horse since."

"I'm sorry to hear it," Rettie said.

"I've made my mind up about something," Matthew said quietly, glancing a bit sideways at her.

Rettie returned the glance. "And what might that be?" she said.

"I'm choosing St. Paul for my newspaper business," he said thickly.

A slow flush rose on Rettie's face. "You . . . are?" she said in a near whisper.

"Yes," he said. He eyed her back. "And, Rettie, I'd like to spend some time with you. That is, if you'd let me."

Rettie's voice weakened a bit. "Why, Matthew . . ." she whispered.

"That's a yes, I presume," he chuckled.

Rettie lowered her eyes. "I think maybe I *have* grown tired of bein' alone," she murmured. "I feel so responsible for what's happened, especially to Lorinda. If I'd have made more effort to stop her that day she ran from my house in anger, then she'd be with me now. Safe and sound." She swallowed hard. "Yes, this waitin' ahead could get mighty hard, alone."

"You won't be alone," Matthew said, squeezing her shoulder affectionately. "I'll wait right along with you."

Rettie sniffed a bit. "Do you know what's the hardest

135

thing to wonder 'bout?'' she murmured.

"What's that, Rettie?"

"Who holds Lorinda captive?" she whispered harshly. "The white savage . . . or the red . . . ?"

Eight

The birch-bark dome-shaped wigwams of Yellow Feather's village sat nestled in a dense growth of pines and hemlocks. These trees served as a perfect shelter from the north and west winds of winter, while the south and east sides had been left open to the warm splashes of the sun.

Yellow Feather held his head high and shoulders squared as he entered the village on horseback. He was proud of his band of Indians. They were dependable and hard working. He could see that everything was being readied for winter. The circular base of each wigwam had been completely banked with moss and cornstalks weighted down with large stones, a generous wood supply had been piled high against the great pines, and golden corn lay heaped in sunny spots in front of the wigwams. Before the snows began, the corn would be ground in a long hollowed log with a grinding stone, and it would be eaten sparingly until spring.

Yellow Feather proudly looked into the distance, seeing pumpkins dotting the land in their merry oranges. Some had already been harvested and had been cut into strips for drying. Closer to where Yellow Feather's horse moved steadily onward, little girls were spreading pumpkin seeds out on logs to also dry in the sun. These would be dainty nutty-flavored special treats around the winter fires.

Yellow Feather glanced further around him. Small boys were gathering acorns, hazelnuts and beechnuts,

137

while older boys were still in the process of husking and storing away more corn. Even the old women were busy. They were gathering medicinal herbs, which if not hurriedly picked and stored, would soon be withered and black and covered by snow. Meat, as well, should now be ready for each household's long winter. The meat would have been hung either in the sunshine or over the fires to be dried, so that it could keep without spoiling. For Yellow Feather's Chippewa, it was an unending struggle to satisfy the basic needs, particularly the need for food, which constantly drove them to the hunting grounds, berry patch, and forest for wild plants.

Yellow Feather now looked straight ahead, focusing on Chief Wind Whisper's wigwam. He didn't want to feel guilty about the cave and all that was hidden there. He would not let guilt bother him, he thought angrily. Chief Wind Whisper gave in to the white man too easily. It was wise that he had kept the land of his sacred dream a secret. If his father had known about it, he surely would have given *it* too, to the white people by signing a paper.

Yellow Feather had watched in silence as his father had placed a bold 'X' on the white man's papers those many years ago. Yellow Feather had seen the pride in his father's eyes, knowing that his father had felt as though he was doing a great thing, by showing the white man that he, too, could "read" and "write," having pretended to know what the white man's words had said.

"I will *never* be as yain," Yellow Feather whispered. "Never."

Snarling, wolfish dogs came suddenly nipping at Yellow Feather's ankles. If not for the snows of winter, requiring one to have to travel by sledge, Yellow Feather would have seen to it that these wolflike creatures had no place in his village. They weren't to be treated as pets. They were even sometimes vicious. But they were hardy and could pull a sledge and a heavy pack for many miles over the snow fields without giving in to weariness. *Ay-uh,* they were necessary.

He swung a foot at one of the dogs and they all turned and slinked away to hide in the brush. "To think that those dogs are Chippewa," he scoffed. "Where is their pride . . . ?"

"Yellow Feather, you have returned. . . ."

Yellow Feather's head swung around, seeing one of his wives, Happy Flower, standing at a wigwam's opening. Normally, as she was so tiny, Yellow Feather feared that a strong wind might lift her from the ground and carry her away from him. But this day he saw something else about her. Her deerskin dress was not confined at the waist by a belt or sash and its highly decorated front flap no longer hung straight from the weight of colored beads. Instead, she was proudly displaying the rise in her abdomen, which would be the first child born to Yellow Feather.

"*Ay-uh,* Happy Flower," Yellow Feather said, drawing his horse to a halt. "And how are you? Are you still ill in the mornings?" His gaze assessed her anew, as though seeing her for the first time. Her blue-black hair was pulled back to hang in two long, neatly pleated braids, and the bones of her cheeks were prominent. Her skin was of a soft copper color. Her dark eyes showed a passiveness, reflecting her eagerness to always please Yellow Feather.

A necklace ornamenting the front of the dress with graduated rows of different-colored beads hung around her neck, and the leggings that extended above her knees were decorated with beads in line patterns and edged with more beads, as were the moccasins on her feet.

She was tiny, innocent and beautiful, but she had never stirred Yellow Feather's heart to such a burning intense passion as Red Blossom had done. Each time Happy Flower had shared his bed of blankets, he had taken her swiftly and unemotionally, only for the release this awarded him. He had only this day discovered that there was more to making love than a few brief thrusts inside a woman. With Red Blossom . . . so *much* more had been shared.

"Gah-ween," Happy Flower murmured, smiling brightly as she reached for his hand after he had dismounted and was standing next to her. "No. I am no longer strangely ill," she laughed. She glanced down at her stomach then slowly placed his hand on the swell of it. She then gazed upward into his eyes, again smiling brightly.

"It is our baby," Yellow Feather said thickly, proud. He had oh, so wanted to have a son before his father left this world, but now he doubted this could happen. Six more months was much too long a time for waiting.

"Ay-uh. Ah-bee-no-gee," Happy Flower sighed. "I will give birth to a son. You'll see. Our son will be next chief-in-line after you."

Yellow Feather's hand wandered over and around the small ball, marveling at it, trying to envision a baby snuggled inside. Then his heart skipped a beat. What would Red Blossom think of one of his wives being with child? He remembered her reaction when he had revealed that he was married. Was the white man's way different? Didn't they have more than one wife to take pleasure from. . . ?

Remembering Lorinda made him also realize that he couldn't take too long in the village. He did not want her to become afraid. He did not want her to become lonesome.

"My father? How is he?" he asked quickly.

"He is no better," Happy Flower said, sighing sadly, when Yellow Feather's hand left hers. She had hoped that a child would draw them closer together, but he was a man of many moods and one who was hard to please. Her body hadn't been enough to keep him from taking a second wife. A child. Maybe when the child was born, the child could fill her lonely moments.

"I must go to him," Yellow Feather said. A stirring behind him drew him abruptly around, causing him to come face to face with his second wife, Foolish Heart. He saw the familiar set to her jaw and fire in her eyes and once more wished that this one wife would go from his wigwam and never return. Having been the second chosen of the two wives her jealousy of the first kept trouble brewing between them all, at all times.

"You have finally returned," she stormed. She crossed her arms and lifted her chin. She was taller and fleshier than Happy Flower, but could never be as beautiful. Her personality was like that of a demon, always ready to explode. "I see no animals. What kind of hunt were you a part of, Yellow Feather?"

"It is of no concern of yours," Yellow Feather stated flatly. He pushed the horse's reins toward her. "*Mahszhon.* Go. See that my horse is watered and fed."

Foolish Heart took a step backward. *"Gah-ween,"* she hissed. "Let Happy Flower do it. Or is she too delicate?"

"Happy Flower is with child. Do you not see?" Yellow Feather stormed. "I will not have her doing work you can do."

Foolish Heart glared toward the swell of Happy Flower's stomach. *"Ay-uh,* I see," she said sourly. "She will give you the first baby. I don't. That makes her more special in your eyes."

Yellow Feather leaned down into her face. "Foolish Heart, I've been away. Now I am home. See to my horse. *Ah-Szee-gwah.* Now."

Foolish Heart grumbled beneath her breath as she yanked the horse's reins from Yellow Feather's hand. She sauntered off with the horse trailing behind her.

Framing Happy Flower's face between his hands, Yel-

141

low Feather spoke gently to her. "Has Foolish Heart treated you badly while I was gone?" he asked.

"Gah-ween."

"If she ever does, Happy Flower should tell me," Yellow Feather said thickly.

"I think she's angry with the world," Happy Flower laughed. "Rarely does she smile."

"She was not like this when I took her as my wife."

"She is jealous. I *am* with child. If it be a boy, he will be chief-in-line after you, not Foolish Heart's child when she has one."

Yellow Feather did not wish to think of wives and jealousies. He was now full of worry about Red Blossom and whether *she* could accept the rivalry of two other wives besides herself. But he knew that he had to place a different worry first. He must first get her to *be* his wife.

He glanced toward his father's wigwam. He also had *that* worry that was great in his mind. . . .

"I must go to my father," he said sullenly.

"Go. I understand," Happy Flower said, touching his cheek.

"You'll be all right?"

"I know how to take care of myself, Yellow Feather. Go. See to Chief Wind Whisper."

Yellow Feather brushed the tip of Happy Flower's nose with his lips then gazed intently toward his father's wigwam. With wide strides he moved toward it but was stopped again, this time by Flying Squirrel's approach.

"What is it, Flying Squirrel?" he asked, seeing the worry in his friend's talking eyes. "I come home to trouble with my wives. Do you also have trouble for me?"

Flying Squirrel sidled up next to Yellow Feather, glancing cautiously all around him. "It is the American trader. Silas Konrad," he whispered. "Word has spread that he was in the village yesterday snooping about."

"What does it mean, Flying Squirrel?" Yellow

Feather said, suddenly angry. "Since my father's ailment, Silas Konrad has been told to meet us only where we keep the horses." Yellow Feather had never trusted Silas Konrad. Chief Wind Whisper had mistakenly smoked the big pipe with this white man, and ever since, the shifty-eyed man had continuously caused Yellow Feather problems. If he wasn't complaining, he was snooping.

"I think he has guessed that we take more than horses on our raids," Flying Squirrel added. "He is snooping to see where we keep our white man's treasures."

Hatred caused Yellow Feathers' eyes to narrow. "Where is he now?" he said flatly. He knew that if Silas by chance found the cave, he could not be allowed to leave alive. No white man could know of the riches of the land, the water, and in the cave that waited for the small band of the St. Croix Indians. No papers would ever be signed to give the white man what was meant to be the Indians'. If it meant having battle with the white man, so be it.

A tremor of strange excitement fluttered inside Yellow Feather. It was instinctive, the ancestral thirst for vengeance, a hereditary hatred that was setting his blood to warming to such thoughts as wanting victory over the white man. Then he thought of Lorinda . . . his Red Blossom. Wasn't . . . she . . . white . . . ?

"He is gone," Flying Squirrel said. "First he is here, causing the squaws to scamper to safety inside the wigwams, then he is quickly *gee-mah-gah.*"

"*O-nee-shee-shin,*" Yellow Feather sighed heavily. "Good. Maybe he will stay away for a while since he found no things of the white man here."

"You have been wise, Yellow Feather, to encourage me to not bring white man's things to the village as gifts to my family," Flying Squirrel said. "You will be a wise leader, one the St. Croix will be proud to call chief."

Yellow Feather raised a hand and placed it heavily on Flying Squirrel's shoulder. "*Mee-eewh*. Enough," he murmured. "We must no longer speak of my being chief while Chief Wind Whisper's heart is still beating."

"I am sorry," Flying Squirrel said, lowering his eyes. "I do not think at times."

Yellow Feather's eyes narrowed. "You were at the cave. You left warm coals in the firespace. Why were you there, Flying Squirrel?"

"Flying Squirrel better not say," Flying Squirrel mumbled, again lowering his eyes.

"Flying Squirrel better say," Yellow Feather said sternly.

"A campfire drew me away from my journey back to our people," he said quietly.

"Campfire? What do you mean . . . campfire. . . ?"

"I was angry at Yellow Feather for bringing a white woman to our sacred cave," Flying Squirrel grumbled. "I didn't travel straight back to our village. I rode hard and long in another direction and . . ."

"Min-eh-wah . . . ?" Yellow Feather persisted.

"I carried out a midnight raid without you," Flying Squirrel said, slowly lifting his eyes to see Yellow Feather's reaction. He quickly added: "It was successful. I got one horse, many guns, a woman's wrap and some jewelry. This is why I returned to the cave . . . to add to our collection. . . ."

"You are a fool, Flying Squirrel," Yellow Feather said angrily. "You should never work alone. One Indian is not enough against white man's guns."

"I waited until they were asleep. . . ."

"So no one saw you . . . ?"

Flying Squirrel once more lowered his eyes. "One woman . . . only. . . ." he stammered.

Yellow Feather dug his fingers deeply into Flying

Squirrel's shoulder. "A woman?" he spat. "I thought you said they were asleep.

"I thought they were. . . ."

"What did you do with this white woman?"

"Flying Squirrel didn't harm her. . . ."

"What did you do?" Yellow Feather insisted.

"Gagged her and tied her to a tree. . . ."

"She knew you were Chippewa . . . ?"

"It was dark. . . ."

Yellow Feather dropped his hand from Flying Squirrel, grumbling. "You are never to go on raids again without me," he said. "Yellow Feather commands you. You listen."

"*Ay-uh*, Yellow Feather. . . ."

"*Gee mah-gi-on-ah-shig-wah*," Yellow Feather said sullenly. "My father. I must see him then return to the cave."

Flying Squirrel's gaze met with Yellow Feather's. "The cave?" he said quietly. "I did not ask. Is she. . . ?"

"*Ay-uh*. She is still there," Yellow Feather said flatly. "I followed her into the forest and brought her back with me." He turned and moved on away from Flying Squirrel, feeling Flying Squirrel's eyes on his back, like hot coals burning him.

Ay-uh, he understood his friend, but he still could not understand himself, this new person, this self who hungered so after the pale-skinned, flaming-haired white woman. He shook his head to clear his thoughts then stooped and lifted the entrance flap to his father's wigwam and peered inward. He squinted his eyes, hardly able to see Chief Wind Whisper through a foggy mist that hung heavily in the air. Stepping on inside, Yellow Feather felt the perspiration break out on his brow and upper lip. He glanced toward a pile of hot stones in the center of the firespace where a fire usually burned and

145

watched the steam rising from each. It seemed that Chief Wind Whisper's wigwam had temporarily been changed into his own private sweat lodge, where most men went to take a cure for whatever ailed them. Yellow Feather knew that his father only used the miraculous mists to relieve the physical and mental fatigue that approaching death had handed him.

Yellow Feather's nostrils flared, smelling the familiar aroma of the liquid concoction that had been made from boiled bark and evergreen boughs and sprinkled on the hot coals. Then a hacking cough drew his attention to the squatting, cross-armed, naked figure at the far side of the lodge. As the swirling mist opened to Yellow Feather's steady stare, his heart ached for what he saw old age had done to his father.

Chief Wind Whisper's coppery face wasn't round any longer, but thin, with the skin stretched tightly over his hawklike nose and large cheekbones. What had at one time been jet-black hair was now hanging down his back in wiry grays, and his stooped figure was dried up, like a leaf of autumn.

Another round of coughs from Chief Wind Whisper tore through Yellow Feather like many arrows piercing his flesh. "Father?" he said, inching his way toward him. "It is I. Yellow Feather. I have returned."

"My son, hand your father a blanket," Chief Wind Whisper said in his mixed scratchy and coarse chatter of Chippewa and English.

Peering around him, relieved that the mist was lifting, Yellow Feather could now see the deerskins and blankets rolled up neatly at the side of the ledge, the hand drum hanging on the wall, and the strips of meat and little bundles of aromatic herbs and roots dangling from a pole over the firespace.

He could also see that the rush mats on the floor had been recently swept and that Chief Wind Whisper's bed of balsam boughs and cattail mats had been readied for his return after his relaxing steam bath.

Yellow Feather smiled to himself, knowing that Big Laughing Star still loved and cared for her husband. Though toothless, short and fat, she had made Chief Wind Whisper a good wife. She had learned to be obedient to his commands since even before they had shared the marriage feast.

With care, Yellow Feather chose a blanket and took it to Chief Wind Whisper and placed it gently around his shoulders. Then, with affection, he helped Chief Wind Whisper up and over to his bed, where the chief groaned weakly as he eased down to stretch out upon it.

"And the traps? Did you check them to see if we will have many furs to trade, my son?" Chief Wind Whisper asked, breathing shallowly.

Yellow Feather squatted beside the bed, hoping to not reveal the guilt he felt inside. He had not checked any traps. He hadn't even placed any in the forest for some time now. There had been too many trappers. The animals had become scarce, like everything else since the coming of the white man. *"Ay-uh,"* he said, with steady eyes, but a pounding heart. "I have enough to trade. Maybe for some white man's tobacco. Maybe some blankets for winter."

Chief Wind Whisper lifted a bony hand to Yellow Feather and patted his shoulder. "You are a good son," he said. *"Ay-uh,* you will make a great chief." His body began to jerk in spasmic coughs until tears became rivers on his cheeks.

Yellow Feather felt a desperation rising inside him. "Father, where is your medicine bag of herbs and roots?" he asked anxiously.

"It is here. Beneath the cattail mat."

"Shouldn't you wear it around your neck?"

"No," Chief Wind Whisper stated flatly.

147

"Do I call a shaman? Do you want a medicine man?"

"No. There is no remedy for dying of old age, my son," Chief Wind Whisper said quietly, crossing his arms proudly over his chest as the blanket fell away from him. "I do not want any chanting or words of sorcery spoken over me. I want to be left here, to die in peace."

"But, father. . . ."

"Hear my words, my son," Chief Wind Whisper ordered. "No human enemy has directed this illness of old age my way. There is no one the shaman could redirect this sort of illness back to. I am dying of old age. It is a natural thing. You one day will understand."

"What *will* you have me do, Father?" Yellow Feather said, bending, speaking more into his father's face.

Chief Wind Whisper's eyes were dark and unflinching as he captured Yellow Feather's full attention. "You must keep peace when I am gone, my son," he said sternly. "The white man has come to be a part of this northwoods country. We must be their friends. Always. Do not forget this."

"I do not understand how you can speak so kindly of the white man," Yellow Feather argued. "Where are our rice fields now? Where are the animals? What I see and hear makes my heart turn to stone."

"What do you see and hear, my son?" Chief Wind Whisper said, turning his head as he began another fit of coughs.

Yellow Feather waited, then spoke. "I hear white men in the trees with their axes. They are ridding the forests of their beautiful trees. They are scaring the deer away," he said. "The white man's wagons make what they call roads and get closer and closer to where we now make our village. What will be left for the Indian, father?"

"Wenebojo, the spirit who made the world, has always looked after the St. Croix. You must have faith," Chief Wind Whisper grumbled. He trembled a bit, then reached for his blanket and wrapped it snugly around his shoulders once more. He closed his eyes. "I must sleep, my son. I must sleep. . . ."

Yellow Feather rose from beside the bed, feeling remorse both for his father and for his father's words. Yellow Feather could never promise his father that the St. Croix Chippewa would remain passive. They had a future to be lived . . . to be enjoyed. He rushed from the wigwam to where Flying Squirrel and Big Laughing Star stood waiting.

Yellow Feather embraced them one at a time then squared his shoulders as he spoke first to Big Laughing Star. "He will die soon," he said thickly. "Make him comfortable."

Big Laughing Star's face was somber. "I will boil some cedar bough water. It will keep evil spirits away."

"And, Flying Squirrel, it is your duty to see that no medicine man be allowed in Father's wigwam," Yellow Feather stated flatly.

"No medicine man." Flying Squirrel gasped. "I don't understand you."

"It is not me you are to understand," Yellow Feather said. "It is Chief Wind Whisper's command. It is for you to obey."

"And you? Where are you going, Yellow Feather? You have only just returned," Flying Squirrel said, showing renewed anger in the flashing of his eyes.

"I have a mission," Yellow Feather said flatly. His gaze went to Big Laughing Star. "Big Laughing Star," he said. "I will return. Soon."

Yellow Feather rushed away from them at a soft trot, watching all the St. Croix Chippewa around him. He could see the trust . . . the faith . . . in their eyes as they watched him back. They all realized that soon *he* would be the one making the decision for them all. He would be their leader. Doubt crept through him, but he knew that

149

was a natural thing to feel. To succeed, one had to have at first felt doubt. . . .

A shrill shrieking drew his thoughts from himself. He stopped and looked quickly around him. When he saw Happy Flower run screaming from their wigwam with her hands covering her head, Yellow Feather rushed to her and then stopped abruptly as he saw Foolish Heart step boldly from the wigwam displaying a clipped blue-black braid in each hand.

Happy Flower swung around and tore beads from Foolish Heart's dress. "My beautiful hair," she wailed. "You ruined my hair!"

Feeling a keen revulsion for what Foolish Heart had done to Happy Flower, Yellow Feather stepped between his two wives facing the one he no longer wanted. He crossed his arms and stared in cold silence first at the limp braids in Foolish Heart's outstretched hands, then into the cruel depth of her eyes. "You do this thing to Happy Flower out of jealousy?" he said darkly. "You take knife to her braids?"

"Ay-uh," Foolish Heart bragged. "She is first in your heart, I am last in your bed. I have shown her who is the bravest."

Yellow Feather knew that these things did happen among jealous women of the St. Croix, but he would not let either of *his* women behave in such a way. He did not want his wives to be gossiped about over late-hour campfires. *"Mah-szhon,"* he ordered, pointing toward the forest. "Go into the darkness of the forest."

"What are you going to do?" she whispered. She put the braids behind her and her face was etched with a sudden fear.

"What am I going to do? I am going to take you into the forest with me where I will leave you to find your way home alone," Yellow Feather said icily. "It will be your punishment for cutting Happy Flower's beautiful hair."

"Happy Flower, I'm sorry," Foolish Heart said anxiously. She tried to force the braids into Happy Flower's hands. "Here. Take them. I'm sorry."

Happy Flower shook her head back and forth, still sobbing. *"Gah-ween,"* she sobbed. "No. I don't want them. You keep them. My braids look like you now. They are ugly."

"Come," Yellow Feather ordered. He grabbed Foolish Heart by the arm and shoved her ahead of him. "You now walk until I tell you to stop. Your name fits you right. You are a foolish, hateful woman."

Yellow Feather glanced back at Happy Flower. "Stay. I will soon return to comfort you," he said. His worries were for his unborn child. He had seen the lifeless babies delivered by Big Laughing Star. Birthing for the Indians was hard and he didn't want anything to happen to his own firstborn.

He looked straight ahead now, as though putting a wall between him and the audience on all sides of him that the shouts and cries from his two wives had created. This made his anger toward Foolish Heart swell to even larger proportions. He would take her far. He would lose her where the spirits of the dead would fly and whistle around her. When she stumbled and fell to the earth he stood crossed-armed like stone above her until she scooted to her feet and moved on into the damp undergrowth that led her farther and farther away from the familiar sounds of the village, into the strange, muted sounds of the forest.

"Yellow Feather," she pleaded, glancing back at him. "Foolish Heart is tired."

"Go," he said, shoving her. They traveled beneath the gnarled limbs of giant oaks, beside sprouts of young maples whose leaves were golden-brown, and toward the cool, dripping vines that curled from branch to branch overhead.

"My feet will not carry me farther," Foolish Heart

151

wailed as she dropped to the ground in a heap at Yellow Feather's feet. She held the two braids up, offering them to him. "Take them. I don't really want them," she whined.

Yellow Feather took them glowering. He then looked slowly around him, checking the brush for any signs of dangerous animals. He didn't want harm to come to Foolish Heart. He just wanted to frighten her into obedience. He looked back toward the village and could see traces of smoke spiraling upward from the wigwams. He hadn't brought her as far as he had planned, yet far enough for her to fear the wrath of the spirits.

"I am going now," he stated flatly. He turned and began a fast trot away from her, leaving her wailing and pleading behind him. He knew that if she rose quickly to her feet, she could soon follow after him. He put more speed into his steps until he reentered the village, where he then walked with head held high to his wigwam where Happy Flower waited. He lifted the entrance flap and went inside, finding Happy Flower sitting before the fire. The swell of her stomach cast shadows at her side. Yellow Feather went to her and touched the swell, then Happy Flower's hair that hung disgracefully short.

He sat down next to her and drew her into his arms, to let her rest her cheek against his chest. "I share your sorrow," he said softly. He placed her braids in her hand. "Your hair. You must keep it. It is too beautiful to throw away."

"Will Yellow Feather stay with Happy Flower tonight?" Happy Flower asked, wiping tears from her eyes with her free hand.

Yellow Feather stiffened, remembering Lorinda. He would make an offering of venison to her when he reached her again the next morning. If she accepted, their future . . . ah . . . how great it would be!

Happy Flower touched his hand gently. "You'll stay?

You'll share your bed with Happy Flower tonight? You proved your deeper love for me by taking Foolish Heart away."

Her words stung his insides. His love for her was not what she thought. He only truly loved Lorinda . . . his Red Blossom. He had to think of a way to make Happy Flower understand why he would not be sharing a bed with her again. Red Blossom knew ways of making love so that no other wife was needed.

Yet Happy Flower *is* my wife, he thought carefully to himself.

His gaze settled on her swollen abdomen. He remembered many wives who sent their husbands from their beds because of the fear of causing harm to the unborn child. It *was* a valid worry . . . especially for a next chief-in-line . . . who felt the importance of having a healthy son born to him.

"I cannot," he said quietly. He saw the hurt flecks in her dark eyes. He framed her face with his hands. "The baby. I no longer feel it's safe to share man-and-woman bonds of the flesh. You should sleep without me. At least until the baby is safely born."

"You want the baby so much?"

"*Ay-uh.* A son. I want a son."

She lowered her eyes. "I understand," she said. Then her gaze met his again. "Does this mean that you will take Foolish Heart to your bed when she returns?"

"No. I will send Foolish Heart from our wigwam," he said flatly. "She will not be my wife." He set his jaw firmly. "I should have told her this, but I only now made this decision."

"She will hate you, Yellow Feather," Happy Flower said softly. "Her hate for you *and* me will be strong."

"This does not matter," he said stiffly. "She is now only another Chippewa woman to me."

Loud shouts and laughs drew Yellow Feather and

Happy Flower to their feet. Together, they went outside and stood in silent disbelief at what they saw.

"Foolish Heart?" Yellow Feather whispered. He watched as Foolish Heart attempted to make her way through a crowd of Chippewa women but fell suddenly to the ground when several began pulling and ripping her dress.

"Yellow Feather, we must stop . . ." Happy Flower said, taking a step forward.

"No. We will let Foolish Heart receive her full punishment," he said icily. "It is the way of the Chippewa women when they see wrong done to one of them. They fight for your honor, Happy Flower. Be proud."

Foolish Heart flailed her hands and arms, but made no sounds as the attackers laughingly pulled and tugged at her dress, until she lay alone, unclean and half-dressed, with her face hidden behind her hands.

"We must help her," Happy Flower said, pleading with her eyes as Yellow Feather looked down upon her.

"No. She has been taught her lesson. We must not make it less, by helping her now," Yellow Feather said. He watched as Foolish Heart pushed her way up from the ground. She watched him with cold, set features as she moved past him and into the wigwam.

"Stay," Yellow Feather encouraged Happy Flower as she started to follow. "Give Foolish Heart time to make up her mind what she should do next."

He crossed his arms and watched the entrance flap intently, then took a step backward when Foolish Heart finally emerged with a small bundle in the crook of her left arm. He smiled to himself. Foolish Heart did not realize how easy she was making life for him. If she had known, Yellow Feather knew her well enough to know that she would not do this thing.

He watched her as she left the village and until she became only a dot on the horizon as she made her way

154

across the straight stretch of meadow, away from the St. Croix village of the Chippewa.

"It is done," he said. "She has chosen her own way. She chose to no longer be my wife *OR* of the St. Croix."

"Where will she go?"

"Where the four winds will carry her. . . ."

"I didn't hate her, Yellow Feather," Happy Flower said, wringing her hands nervously. "I didn't hate her."

"She hated herself," Yellow Feather said. "She hated herself." He guided Happy Flower by an elbow. "Come. You must get warm by the fire and then I must go."

"For long?"

"For as long as it takes, I will be gone. . . ."

His heart was already with Lorinda, his Red Blossom, beating out the moments until they would partake of the venison feast . . . which meant so much more than just food to be shared. . . .

Nine

After placing more logs on the fire for both warmth and light, Lorinda crept to the back of the cave and stood before the Indian's stolen goods. Anger rose inside her for what Yellow Feather had done to her people. Not suspecting they were being watched, the travelers had fallen into an Indian's trap. Upon rising from a peaceful night of sleep on the trail, they had found their personal possessions gone. Had they suspected an Indian to be the thief, or did most believe that if an Indian was near, more than possessions would have been taken? Did the Sioux share these raids with the Chippewa . . . ?

Lorinda shuddered a bit, thinking of her parents. The Indians had been greedier *that* day. . . .

Shaking her head to clear her thoughts, Lorinda began to sort through a heap of discarded carpetbags. One, with a beautifully embroidered design on its canvas backing, drew her attention away from the others. Flowers in bold reds and yellows had been sewn onto the carpetbag with silken floss and felt smooth and cool to the touch as Lorinda's forefinger traced a pansy and then a daisy with a dark brown center.

"It's so lovely," she whispered. She settled down onto the floor of the cave and placed this one carpetbag on her lap. "I wonder who the owner was. Only someone delicate and pretty could have owned such a travel bag as this."

Guilt plagued her as she slowly opened it, knowing that she was invading someone's privacy. One could carry the most precious and private of one's belongings on a journey. Should Lorinda dare to see what this particular woman had chosen? It was lost to the owner, forever, and Lorinda had not been the cause of *that* misfortune. It was not Lorinda's fault that such a beautiful carbetbag lay on her lap, enticing her.

With trembling fingers, she reached inside and felt around, touching many things that made her heart leap with joy. She could feel the familiar satiny texture of a sheer undergarment. She could even feel the delicacy of lace that was stitched onto it! Her fingers moved on around inside the carpetbag, discovering a hairbrush when its stiff bristles prickled her fingers, then she felt the smooth coldness that had to be a mirror.

Growing too excited to wait any longer, Lorinda began pulling these prized possessions from the bag, thrilling at each newest discovery. She placed the hairbrush and mirror on the floor next to her then slowly rose as she pulled a silken dress upward and held it to her, overjoyed that it was not only terribly pretty, with its lowswept neckline, tucked waist, and tiny rosebud design, but that it also was of her size. She just knew that it was, without ever having tried it on. As she continued to hold it to her, she lifted the fully gathered skirt away from her and twirled around, feeling suddenly carefree and gay. Wouldn't Yellow Feather be surprised when he returned and found her transposed into a different lady? Oh, wouldn't the silk feel so good to her flesh that had had only the coarseness of her travel fabrics against it for way too long now?

No longer feeling guilty, Lorinda placed the dress carefully on her bed of blankets then fell to her knees and continued to explore further inside the bag. Her fingers again discovered the lacy undergarment. She pulled it free and held it to her face, running the satiny texture against a cheek, but cringing a bit when she sniffed an aroma of cologne, reminding her, once more, that it was not her undergarment, but someone else's.

"But I cannot let myself think about it," she whispered, placing the undergarment next to the dress. She was far from home, from civilization even. She had to make do for herself. She couldn't continue wearing one outfit day in and out, especially now, since she had found a way to make herself feel human again.

"I will change into this," she argued to herself. "I will!"

She eyed the other carpetbags, especially one that was made of what appeared to be expensive tan leather. She chose to open it also and found it full of man's clothing. She pulled a pair of dark breeches and matching jacket from inside it then dropped them to the floor, shrugging. She didn't care about men's clothing or what else might be in the bag. Her thoughts were now on the beautiful dress . . . the hairbrush . . . and the mirror. Her eyes widened, remembering the river so close to the cave's entrance. "A bath," she murmured. "I shall take a bath in the river before I place these delicate clothes next to my body."

Seeing a pile of various household items, Lorinda ran to them and began sorting through them until her search ended with a round bar of soap. She placed it to her nose and sniffed it, relieved to find that it had not a lye scent, but a slightly sweet aroma, possibly having been dropped from a "lady of the night's" travel bag.

"Jasmine. I shall smell of jasmine instead of the trail," she said, scurrying around, grabbing a blanket to use as a towel, then following splashes of daylight until the cave's entrance was upon her. Creeping slowly with the blanket and bar of soap held next to her, she looked cautiously around the outside of the cave. She inhaled the heady fragrance of the outdoors, having been forced to grow accustomed to the damp mustiness of the cave. The sun beat down upon her in welcoming warmth. She had just stepped back out into one of those September days when it seemed nature was struggling one last time to retain its summer glow. Before long, the warm, delicious days would be replaced by a cold, gray dreariness.

She spied the gentle ripples of the lake then glanced quickly around her for any signs of movement in the tangled undergrowth. Not seeing anything that could indicate a human presence, she sighed and rushed on down the steep slope until she reached the sandy water's edge. She dropped the blanket and soap to the ground and quickly removed her boots, but, feeling as though she was being watched, hesitated before unbuttoning her blouse.

Her eyes scanned the upper embankment. She couldn't see anybody but she *felt* a presence. With a wild beat of her heart she moved stealthily behind a bush and huddled there, trembling, still watching. The sounds of the forest beyond filled her silence with the chatter of birds on the wing, and the rattling of dried leaves that hung from dead oak trees reverberated around her, as though a million feet were skipping in tune with the music the wind continuously played in this north country. From somewhere behind her, a loon's laughter, sounding human, bounced across the river, echoing over and over again until the sound was only a soft quiver, growing softer and softer, until it was gone.

Suddenly above her there arose from the ground a covey of partridges with a great whirring of wings, disappearing then just as quickly into the stately maple trees where the sun's lengthening rays shimmered like tongues of flame against the backdrop of blue sky.

"I'm being so foolish," Lorinda scoffed, straightening her back. "There is nothing here but me and nature. Yellow Feather will surely not return so soon."

Her face flushed, wondering why she would feel the need to be modest *now* in Yellow Feather's presence even

160

if he did arrive before her bath was completed. He had seen her nude. He had even caressed her complete nudity with his skilled eyes, hands and . . . lips.

"Oh, I must not let myself think about it," she sighed, letting her clothes fall, article by article, in a flutter to the ground. Feeling lighthearted and oh, so free in spirit, she grabbed the soap and stepped quickly into the water, anticipating the sudden shock of cold against her flesh. The river had already been touched by the icy fingers of old man winter farther north where the mountains set free from their icy gorges the streams and waterfalls that fed the rivers and lakes of Minnesota.

"Oh, it is so cold!" she said aloud. She had yet to let the water level cover her breasts. She shivered as the water lapped at her lustrous white mounds whose dark nipples had swollen to stiff erectness from the occasional kisses of the flirting icy liquid. "But I must wash my hair, cold or no cold," she added.

Tightening her lips and closing her eyes, she slowly tilted her head backwards and let the water capture her hair until it spread in brilliant reds all around her head. The sun felt caressingly warm on her upturned face, causing her tremors to subside a bit. She lathered the soap into her hair, rinsed it, then ran the bar of soap over and around each breast. She continued soaping the rest of her body until she felt completely refreshed and eager to return to the cave and to the dress she had found.

She drew in a quick breath when she heard an unfamiliar sound from somewhere near. It was a different sort of rustling, as though made by someone falling. Feeling her heartbeat quickening, her teeth began to chatter from both the cold and fear. But when she saw a deer come into full view, she laughed nervously and hurriedly moved, splashing, from the water. She stood straight-backed, absorbing the rays of the sun into her flesh as she patted herself dry with the blanket. Then in one sweep she had her clothes and boots and was headed back inside the cave, welcoming the intense warmth from the fire as she began to dress in the beautiful clothes that she had found. After she was dressed, her hair dried and brushed to gleaming, she felt as though one thing was missing. She had no appropriate lady's shoes to wear with this silken dress, which meant that she had to slip her feet back into her riding boots or take the chance of getting down sick from exposure.

Once the boots were on, Lorinda lifted the mirror she had found before her and saw dancing green eyes and lustrous flaming hair that hung sensuously across her shoulders. She pinched her cheeks for color then turned with a start when she felt a sudden presence behind her.

Her face felt hot when she found Yellow Feather standing there studying her intensely with the dark pools of his eyes. Lorinda's hands went to her throat, then lower when she saw Yellow Feather's gaze stop at her heaving chest, where her breasts rose and fell almost ceremoniously.

"Yellow Feather," she murmured. "You have returned."

"Ay-uh," he replied, standing with his legs widespread and his arms crossed.

Under his steady gaze, Lorinda's own eyes wavered a bit. It was as though he was assessing her anew, as though she was a different person dressed in this skimpier attire that showed the full shape of her breasts and the smallness of her waist. Hadn't he seen such a dress before? Didn't the Indian squaw dress so . . . so . . . daringly . . . ?

Swallowing hard and clasping her hands before her, Lorinda said, "And your father, Yellow Feather? How did you find him?"

"He is weaker," he said, finally uncrossing his arms. He reached to remove a bow from his shoulders and also

162

his quiver of arrows and placed them on the cave floor at his feet. "Come," he said in an ordering fashion, yet offering her a hand.

Lorinda took a step backward, eyeing the loaded gun that she had leaned against the outside wall of the cave. She wanted to trust him. Oh, she so badly wanted to trust him, but he seemed different now, and Lorinda did not know why. Had Yellow Feather's father ordered him to bring this captive to the Indian village? Would the chief's disapproval of her be the cause of her death?

"Come," Yellow Feather said more firmly, pointing toward the cave's entrance. *"Wee-wee-be-tahn."*

Though his words were forceful, his facial features seemed less stern, and did Lorinda even see a slight lifting of the corner of his lips? Was he actually finding this humorous? She had yet to see him smile, even after making love. She *had* to believe that his slight show of humor meant that he wasn't going to be delivering her to her death.

She quickly forgot the need of a gun and inched her way toward him. "You want me to leave the cave with you?" she asked quietly, blushing anew when his gaze swept over her again, causing his brown eyes to smolder even more.

"Ay-uh," he said.

He walked determinedly away from her. Lorinda was compelled to follow him, wondering just what he did have on his mind. Maybe it even meant that she was no longer to be a prisoner in this dreaded cave. Then when he broke into a trot and left her behind, a renewed fear crept through her in icy shreds. He seemed to be playing some sort of game with her . . . one she did not understand.

She lifted the skirt of her dress and hastened her pace, relieved when the light of day met her at the cave's entrance. She stopped suddenly when she saw that Yellow

163

Feather was already outside, facing the cave, in his usual Indian-style pose. Then she almost went tumbling into the brush when she moved on a bit and ran into something lying in a heap at her feet.

"My word," she gasped, framing her face with her hands. She had been too absorbed in Yellow Feather and where he now stood to notice the slain deer curled with eyes peacefully closed on the cave's rock floor. Her glance shot quickly toward Yellow Feather again, seeing how nervous he appeared as he shifted his weight from one foot to the other.

"A deer?" she said, lifting an eyebrow curiously. "Is it for me to prepare for supper? Is that why you've brought me to the cave entrance? Is that why the deer is here?"

"No. It is my gift to you. I will prepare it for our feast if you will accept it. Do you, Red Blossom?"

"A gift . . . ?" she stammered, looking once again at the deer and at the small punctured hole in its side where blood oozed in bright reds from it.

"*Ay-uh,*" Yellow Feather said. "Will you share a feast of venison with me this night?"

Lorinda laughed awkwardly, knowing she would never understand him or his customs. "*Ay-uh,*" she said, proud of her knowledge of at least one Indian word. "I will be glad to share this gift with you, Yellow Feather."

She paused, then stepped over the deer and went to Yellow Feather to look up into his eyes. "But I do wish you would call me Lorinda," she sighed. "Lorinda is my name. Lorinda."

He shook his head angrily. "*Gah-ween,*" he grumbled. "While at my side, you will be called Red Blossom." He let his shoulders and facial muscles relax a bit. "Red Blossom is beautiful." His hands moved slowly upward and began tracing her facial features, causing her to become breathless. When his fingers worked lower and touched the exposed flesh of her breasts, Lorinda's breath caught in her throat, reminding her once more just how this Indian could control her without even speaking a word.

"*Neen-gee-wee-oo,*" he said hoarsely. "*Wi-yee-bah.*"

"Please speak in English," Lorinda whispered, hating it when he stepped away from her. She hungered for his touch . . . his embrace. Now to be without it would mean to be only half alive. She knew this was wrong. Soon she would most surely never see him again. It was not meant for a white woman and an Indian warrior to become lovers. It was not normal in any sense of the word. *Ay-uh,* it would be sad . . . saying goodbye. . . .

Yellow Feather drew a knife from a leather sheath at his waist. He bent to his knees and thrust the knife beneath the deer's hide and skillfully began sliding it around, ignoring Lorinda's question. He could *not* translate into English what he had just spoken to her. To tell her that she would soon be his wife could cause her possibly to attempt fleeing again. Yellow Feather did not want to have to force her again, with anything. They would partake in the feast of venison, *then* he would tell her. It would be too late for her to flee then. She would already be *his.* . . .

Lorinda's knees grew weak and her face paled as Yellow Feather continued his art of removing the deer's beautiful fawn-colored coat. She turned her eyes from him and covered her mouth, then ran back inside the cave, panting for breath where she found the fire such a welcoming presence. It splashed color back into her face.

"A feast," she whispered. "How can I stand to eat the meat after seeing. . . ."

She swallowed hard and forced the picture of the bloody deer from her mind. Instead, she placed more logs on the fire and prepared the dishes and frying pan for Yellow Feather's return. She *was* hungry. She could not say no to such a treat as venison. She turned as he carried some cut-up meat toward her. And after this small portion of venison was fried and served, Lorinda felt a keen sense of wonder as Yellow Feather continued to watch her with a burning passion in his eyes. Not once did he take his eyes from her as they shared the meat in silence beside the dancing flames of the fire. Lorinda's insides were a mass of quivers of sensuous desire for him, yet they both continued to eat until only a few bones lay scattered about.

"The rest of the deer. There's so much yet to be cooked," Lorinda said, breaking the silence.

"You can prepare it to dry over the fire as all Indian women know to do," he said flatly.

Lorinda's eyes flashed angrily. "You seem to forget. I am *not* an Indian woman," she said sharply.

Yellow Feather rose and drew her up next to him. "No. You are not an Indian woman," he said. "But you are now an Indian warrior's *gee-wee-oo*."

"I am . . . what . . . ?" she said, furrowing her brow, studying the intensity with which he looked at her. "Why must you confuse me with your Indian words?"

"You are now my woman . . . my wife," he said, taking her by the wrists, urging her into his arms. "This is what I say to you."

"Your . . . what . . . ?" she gasped, growing weak inside. Yes, she loved him. But . . . to be called . . . his wife . . . ? How . . . ? Why would he think he could do this thing to her? Did Indians have no marriage ceremony? Or could a chief's son just order a woman to be his wife?

She then remembered his other two wives. Oh, how could she *ever* let herself forget? "You already have two wives," she stormed, struggling. "Let me go. I am *not* to be a third wife. I am *not!*"

He held her wrists tightly, holding her against her

166

struggles. "You *are* my wife," he said thickly "You accepted my gift of a deer and then you partook in the feast of venison, which both were ways of agreeing to be my wife. Since you are white, there will be no wedding celebration in the village. The celebration is here, between Yellow Feather and Red Blossom. My spiritual guardian blessed this union many years ago. All that's been required to make you my wife has been done. You *are* Yellow Feather's wife."

"A gift? The deer . . . ?"

"*Ay-uh.* You accepted my gift. You accepted my proposal in marriage when you accepted my gift. The feast was our wedding feast. You are now mine."

Lorinda's voice trailed off to a whisper. She glared at him and circled her fingers into two fists. "Why, you tricked me" she then screamed. Her face grew red with anger. "You savage beast, you tricked me again."

Yellow Feather's heart ached with frustrated hurt. He hadn't expected such anger. *Ay-uh,* he had worried about her reaction, but never had he thought to cause her to hate him. "Red Blossom, I . . ." he began, but she continued assaulting him verbally.

"And don't think for one minute that we are truly man and wife," she stormed. "A preacher's words were not spoken. Only then do a man and woman become man and wife."

"I will show you what *truly* makes man and wife," Yellow Feather said thickly, reaching to curl his fingers through her hair. He yanked her head forward in a quick jerk and crushed his mouth to hers, silencing her furious words.

Lorinda's struggles grew fainter as she felt his body of steel pressed against her and his lips demanding an obedience from her that he knew would be forthcoming. A lightheadedness swept over her as his free hand moved between them and cupped a breast, molding it in his

167

hand. As though in a hypnotic trance, she laced her arms about his neck and clung to him, letting his hand work at freeing her of the dress she had only recently been eager to wear.

She shivered as the last of her clothes fell to the floor, and, when his lips moved lower to kiss the hollow of her throat, she was lost to everything but him. She was enraptured by this man of the copper skin and strange customs. She twined her arms about his neck as he lifted her into his arms. He carried her to the bed of blankets and gently placed her there where he knelt and let his gaze sweep over her as his fingers slowly followed, causing flames to erupt and simmer on her with his each added touch.

A slow smile lifted his lips as his fingers found her boots still on. "A woman with men's boots?" he said softly. "My next gift to you will be moccasins."

Lorinda's insides felt aglow, seeing his smile. He could actually smile! She leaned down and traced his lips with a forefinger. "You are even more beautiful when you smile," she said silkily.

A frown erased the smile from his face. He squared his shoulders proudly. "A man is not beautiful," he grumbled. "Only a woman is beautiful."

Lorinda laughed softly. "I don't care what your stubborn Indian pride forces you to say," she said. "But *I* can say *I* think you're beautiful, because you are."

She reached her arms to him, begging with her eyes. His response was to stand and fully undress before her, then lean slowly down over her and gather her gently into his arms.

"Neen-nee-dah-ee-een," he said huskily. "You are all mine. No other man ever dare touch my Red Blossom."

His fingers worked through her hair while his eyes worshipped her, causing Lorinda to feel feverish with desire. She moaned throatily when he lowered his lips to a

168

breast and flicked his tongue over the erectness of the nipple. His hands lowered from her hair. One found the other breast and the other found the soft cushion between her legs. In unison he began caressing both, causing a wild excitement to grow to immeasurable heights inside Lorinda. Her body yearned for him in a sudden tormented way. She melted when his lips moved over hers in a hot, demanding fiery kiss. And when she felt the hardness of his manhood seeking entrance where his one hand had just been, Lorinda sighed with ecstasy and welcomed him there.

"I know I shouldn't," she whispered as his lips parted from hers. "But I cannot help myself. I love you, Yellow Feather. *Ay-uh,* I . . . love . . . you. . . ."

Yellow Feather felt suddenly victorious! Her wildness had been tamed! He smiled down at her, realizing that she had just proven that she was ready to accept him as her mate. Hadn't she once more professed her love for him? Hadn't she spoken a word in Indian? One day she would be able to speak all words in Indian. One day she would bear him many sons.

He felt her rapid heartbeat echoing his own against his chest and he smelled the wildflower scent of her skin. He nibbled the silken flesh of her shoulder, ah, tasting the sweetness. The warmth of her breath upon his cheek caused a singing in his heart and a quivering of aliveness in his loins. He began to move himself inside her, now consumed with an aching need. He could feel her response with the lifting of her hips, meeting him, enjoying him. She was once more surrendering herself as no Indian woman had ever done, and he knew that no other woman could be so alive, so passionate . . . so exciting. . . .

"Mis-Kwah wa-bee-go-neece . . ." Yellow feather said thickly as he felt release so near, and when she shuddered wildly and cried out his name, he joined her with a violent passion that exploded as never before, leaving

169

him breathless, with the sweetest joy in his arms . . .
Red Blossom . . . his . . . woman . . . forever. . . .

Lorinda clung to him, still feeling the sweet pain of
him inside her. When his quivering lips found hers, she
felt as though she was still soaring above herself. She
hated it when he broke the magic spell by rolling away
from her to only be at her side. She glanced toward him
and blushed when she felt a continuous gaze from the intense dark of his eyes. She laughed nervously as she
traced the muscles of his shoulders. "Why do you stare
so?" she murmured softly.

"You. Your hair," he said. "I am lucky I was hunting
for horses that night when I found you. But if I hadn't
found you that night, I would have another."

"Why do you say that?"

"I told you. You were led to me by my spiritual guardian. We were meant to meet."

"I don't understand, Yellow Feather."

"One day I will explain many of my customs to you,
then you will know, as one day I want you to tell me of
your customs."

Lorinda lowered her lashes, remembering just how
their lives differed. She wondered about his family. She
wondered about his . . . two . . . wives. . . .

He lifted her chin with a forefinger. "Why do you look
so suddenly sad?" he asked softly. "Did I not make you
happy moments ago?"

Casting him a look through her lashes, she once more
marveled at his handsomeness and how gentle he could
be, though he *was* an Indian with savage ways. She
couldn't help but envision a beautiful copper-skinned
squaw anxiously waiting at his village to share the same
sort of gentleness and caresses. Jealousy tore pieces of
her heart away, yet she knew this was wrong. She had to
keep believing that she would one day find her way back
to her aunt's house. She had to believe that she would

have Amanda safely with her on that joyous return.

Yellow Feather's eyes studied her even more intently. "I ask you. Did I not make you happy?" he repeated, lifting an eyebrow quizzically.

"Oh, yes," she finally answered. "*Ay-uh,* you did. But there are too many things to spoil such a happiness we have found."

"What do you speak of? Tell me."

"Not now," she whispered, lifting a forefinger to his lips to seal them. "Not now," she repeated. "Just hold me, Yellow Feather. Please let me spend this entire night in the peacefulness of your arms." She lowered her finger and worked into his embrace.

"*Ay-uh,* Red Blossom. *Ay-uh.* . . ."

Ten

Sparks stirred from the coals in the firespace, awakening Lorinda from her deep sleep in Yellow Feather's arms. Yawning, she glanced around her, then she rose quickly to her feet, screaming, when she saw a set of eyes studying her nudity from above the orange shadows of dying embers.

"Ah-neen-ay-szhee-way-bee-zee-en?" Yellow Feather shouted, rising, grasping Lorinda by the shoulders. He saw the wildness in her eyes and turned and saw why. "Flying Squirrel, you come like a ghostly spirit in the night to frighten my Red Blossom? Why!?!"

Flying Squirrel squatted and again stirred the coals with a stick, adding some twigs to the small tongues of flames lapping back at him. He wouldn't look Yellow Feather directly in the eyes. He kept his head bowed as he spoke almost reverently. "It is no longer night," he said. "It is morning. . . ."

Yellow Feather lifted a blanket around Lorinda's shoulders and guided her back down, to sit beside the fire. He squatted next to her, now studying Flying Squirrel. "I did not ask you to come to this cave this morning, Flying Squirrel," he said. "Did my father send you for me?"

A look of pain registered in Flying Squirrel's eyes. When he lifted them to gaze in sorrow toward Yellow Feather, no words were needed. Flying Squirrel's talking eyes had already spoken of the sad news he carried to Yellow Feather.

173

Yellow Feather's heart hammered against his chest. He rose and gathered his clothes and hurried into them. "We must go. Now," he directed toward Flying Squirrel. "I am needed. I must help to . . . prepare . . . my father. . . ."

Lorinda secured the blanket around her and rose to her feet, glancing quickly at Flying Squirrel, knowing that she would never forget how he had been watching her. She shivered and rushed to Yellow Feather. She clung to his arm as he stopped to lift his bow over his shoulder. She hadn't seen him with a gun since the night of her abduction. Somehow he had looked less warriorlike without his bow and arrows. "Your father. He is worse?" she asked. .

"My father . . . Chief Wind Whisper . . . awaits to be readied to join the Dance of the Ghosts. Then he can take the long journey across the sky to get to his happy hunting grounds," Yellow Feather said solemnly.

"What you are saying is that Chief Wind Whisper is dead?"

"Ay-uh," Yellow Feather said, lowering his eyes.

Lorinda's heart ached for him. She understood his grief. She still had the same sort of grief locked within herself. She had not only lost a father . . . but also a mother. Her thoughts switched to Amanda. Hadn't she also lost her?

With tears sparkling in the corner of her eyes, she held the blanket together with one hand and with the other reached and touched his lips. "I am sorry," she whispered.

"I must go," he said, gently grasping her shoulders. "I have the duties of son *and* chief awaiting me."

"Can I go with you?"

"No. It is not the right time."

"I hate this cave."

"I will soon return. Understand. I must return to my

174

village only in the company of Flying Squirrel.''

"You will return soon?"

"Ay-uh. . . . ." Yellow Feather said, kissing her briefly on the cheek. He nodded toward Flying Squirrel who followed quickly and obediently after Yellow Feather as he began to move toward the cave's entrance.

Not worrying about the rocks stabbing the bottom of her feet, Lorinda followed after them and watched them as they rode in the direction of the swaying, goldenrod-spread meadow. She watched until they were only dots on the horizon, then paused a bit longer to gather some fresh air around her, though this day was one of gray and low-hanging, swirling clouds that made her welcome the cave and the shelter it could give her. She went back to the fire and sat down next to it. She leaned over and placed more logs into the flames, wondering what life had in store for her next. She had to wonder if her aunt was frantic. Were there many men now on her trail? Oh, how could she leave . . . Yellow Feather . . . ?

She spied the silk dress and undergarments that Yellow Feather had so skillfully removed from her the previous night. She dropped the blanket from around her and reached for the undergarment but footsteps approaching over the gravel cave floor made her eyes light up and her heart race with glee. Yellow Feather had changed his mind. He wasn't going to leave her alone in the cave any longer. He was going to take her to his village.

Jumping to her feet, Lorinda spoke his name with a thrill. "Yellow Feather . . ." But her further words caught in her throat when she saw a stranger step out of the dark shadows. She realized her nudity when she saw his dark, shifty eyes moving over her.

"Well, well . . ." he chuckled. "What have we here?"

Lorinda bent to reach for her blanket but was stopped by the barrel of the rifle that this short, very round man

175

was carrying. In the fire's glow, the man's bald head shone like orange glass. "If'n you can parade around nude for an Injun, so's can you for me, pretty lady," he said, narrowing his eyes to two slits. "Or are you just an Injun lover? Eh? I don't see no ropes holdin' you here in this cave."

Showing spirit, Lorinda shoved the gun aside and grabbed the blanket. Tipping her chin haughtily, she snuggled back into it. She managed to hide her tremors of fear, knowing that this stranger had her at a disadvantage. He had a gun.

Her eyes suddenly widened and her pulse raced. She glanced toward the gun Yellow Feather had left loaded for her. She *also* had a gun. . . . She had placed it beside her bed of blankets earlier. If she could just get to it. She was glad that it was partially hidden from view by the dress that had so hurriedly been discarded. Only she knew where it was.

Focusing her gaze back on this man whose eyes showed that he was someone never to be trusted, she knew that he was not anyone she could ask to lead her back to St. Paul. Though he was white, he reminded her too much of Lamont Quinby.

"Who are you? What are you doing here?" she hissed.

"Silas Konrad. One of Yellow Feather's oldest friends," Silas said, laughing mockingly. His gaze moved on around her and he licked his lips as he walked toward the back of the cave. "Well, I'll be damn," he said hoarsely. "Just as I expected. That damn Injun and his raiding partner has done and got themselves quite a collection of goodies here."

Lorinda inched her way toward her gun, watching his greed show as he began sorting through the household items. She tensed when he swung around, pointing the barrel of his rifle at her. "Now don't you go and get feisty on me," he said darkly. "Me and you? We have some

176

gettin' acquainted to do."

His eyes raked over her anew. "How *do* you happen to be here in this dungeon, pretty lady? You ain't no prisoner. I can tell that. Why are you here? Who are you?"

Lorinda trembled more beneath the blanket. Her eyes wavered, ignoring his questions. She would not confide anything in him. She knew that this man was not Yellow Feather's friend as he professed. If he had been a friend, he would not have waited for Yellow Feather to depart. He would have come in and they would have met peacefully around the fire. He would have known what this cave was being used for. No. She preferred to keep her lips tightly sealed to this man. But she had to watch out for his next move. She didn't care to have his hands against her body. Only Yellow Feather would be allowed such privileges. She let her gaze settle on his gun. He would . . . try . . . to force . . . her . . . ! Did all white men do this to women. She would never forget Lamont Quinby's wet kisses and coarse hands. . . .

"Cat got your tongue, eh?" Silas said boisterously. He motioned with the barrel of his gun. "Come here. Let me take a closer look at you."

Once more Lorinda tilted her chin haughtily. She stood her ground, watching his every move. He glanced toward the household possessions and the arsenal of guns, then back toward Lorinda, appearing to like what he saw in her the best of all else scattered about.

"Well, if'n you won't come to me, guess I have to come to you," he said, laughing. His eyes showed a hungering that Lorinda had become familiar with. She knew that he did have lust on his mind. She was soon to become a victim of his sick passions of the flesh.

Her glance moved to her gun, seeing the shine of its barrel reflecting back at her. She smiled almost wickedly as she looked toward Silas but felt a sick quivering at the pit of her stomach when she noticed that he had seen the smile and had taken it as an open invitation to come ahead and take advantage of the situation at hand.

"That's it, girlie," Silas said thickly. "Let papa show you that an Injun's way of love is filth. Let papa show you how it can be all roses and music."

He dropped his gun to the floor and reached for Lorinda only to find that she was much quicker than he as she stepped back away from him. "So's you don't want it gentle? You're used to the Injun's ways, huh?" he snarled. He took a quick step forward and grabbed Lorinda and yanked the protective covering of the blanket from around her.

"Now ain't you a sight to see?" he said, stepping back, admiring her soft curves and crevices.

"Yellow Feather will seek you out and kill you for doing this," Lorinda hissed. She tried covering herself with her arms and hands but to no avail, and when Silas reached for her this time, she had not been fast enough. He yanked her next to him and squeezed a breast with one hand while holding her immobile with the other.

"Ah, you are quite a beautiful woman," he said hoarsely. "The Injun wenches I've caught and played around with ain't nothin' to compare with the likes of you."

"Let me go," Lorinda squealed, kicking, struggling. "You are evil. How did you even know about this place?"

"I'm one of Yellow Feather's faithful traders," he laughed. "I *thought* he was holdin' out on me. I knew that he had stolen more than horses from the white man. So's I followed Yellow Feather yesterday. When I saw this here cave, I ventured on ahead of him and saw you takin' a bath in the river. I held back and watched, knowin' Yellow Feather would be soon arrivin'. But I knew then that I had some explorin' to do in this here cave when I saw you run into it."

Lorinda remembered the noises she had heard before and during her bath. It had been this man . . . *watching!* She felt a renewed sick feeling circling inside the pit of her stomach. "Then you were here all night? You were just watching for Yellow Feather to leave?" she said sullenly. "All along, you knew I was here."

"I never did see you leave, so's I had to bet you were still here," he chuckled. His eyes narrowed as his free hand traveled over her. "Was worth the waitin'," he said thickly. "First I'll have my pleasures with you, then I'll carry off some of these goods and get some greenbacks for them in town."

"You'll never get away with *any* of this," Lorinda said stiffly. "Yellow Feather will return soon. His father is dead. That is the only reason he left here this morning. But he will return soon and I'll tell him what you have done to me and his things."

"Don't think you'll be a-doin' that," Silas said darkly. "You see, I'm gonna take you with me. Who knows. Maybe I can even sell you to some woman-hungry gent. Women are quite scarce in these parts. Ain't fair that the Injun has one of our white women. He has his pick of squaws back at his village. Think he even has two wives he can call his own."

He lifted a brow. "An' you say the old fella Chief Wind Whisper died? Tsk tsk. Too bad. Now, *there* was a dumb Injun. He did more for the white man than even some white men will be willin' to do. Just have to wonder what kind of chief Yellow Feather'll make."

"You won't be alive to find out," Lorinda hissed, spitting at his feet.

"Want to get nasty?" Silas fumed. "Well, girlie, I can show you nasty." He slapped her face and threw her on the bed of blankets. She watched in cold silence as he began unbuttoning his breeches. She knew what was next if she didn't act. She inched her hand toward her gun, and,

179

just as he let his breeches drop to his ankles, she lifted the rifle into the air and pulled the trigger.

Lorinda would never forget the sound of the bullet striking . . . nor the look in Silas's eyes as he lurched and grabbed at his chest. She watched in horror as he tumbled to the ground where he then crumpled up in total silence onto his stomach. . . .

"Oh, what have I done?" she wailed, dropping the gun beside her. She lay on her back, stunned, watching him for any signs of life, too afraid to move herself. She had shot a man . . . actually . . . shot a man. . . .

"I have . . . to . . . get out of here," she sobbed frantically, inching her way up from the blankets. "I can't stay here . . . with this . . . person . . . I've shot. . . ."

With eyes wild, she hurried to scoop her clothes up into her arms, then stopped, knowing that a silken dress would not be appropriate attire to wear for the journey ahead. "I won't be able to make it alive," she said aloud. "I tried it once. I will die. I just know I will die."

But determination made her move onward. She eyed the men's clothing that she had removed from the leather bag the previous day. Yes! That was the answer. At least she would be warmer clothed in this manner. And if anyone came upon her on the trail, she would no longer look the defenseless woman. She would find a man's hat also, and, dressed in this fashion, she would just be another man, someone to tip a hat to, not try to wrestle to the ground, to take sexually.

With a fierce trembling, she dressed, feeling quite awkward in the loose-fitted breeches and matching dark jacket. She searched through a pile of carpetbags and sighed with relief when she found a man's hat, crushed, yet wearable, and placed it on her head. Hurrying further, she worked her hair beneath the hat and tied a rope around her waist to help hold her breeches up, then knew that she had best leave before she wretched all over the place from the torment eating away at her insides for having killed a man.

She refused to look his way again. She, instead, lifted the rifle's barrel to the crook of her left arm, searched for and found Amanda's blanket, and hurried away from the gruesome scene that Yellow Feather would soon find and not understand. She felt an emptiness engulf her, knowing that she would not be there waiting for his return. Would he seek her out? He did care that much. She knew it.

Panting from having run from the cave, Lorinda rushed on outside to where the gray clouds had lifted to reveal a sky of blue and the sun to warm her cold feelings of dread. Would she even be alive by evening? If so, would she be the next evening? Her fate was questionable. She knew this.

A low whinnying drew her attention to the side of her. With an eager heartbeat, she knew that her chances for survival had just increased. She had forgotten that this evil man Silas Konrad had surely arrived on horseback. And there was the proof, standing pawing at the ground and eyeing her back with the soft brown of its eyes.

"I may have a chance after all," she said, feeling the ache lightening around her heart. She went to the horse and unfastened its reins from a free limb. She patted its soft gray mane and whispered into its ear as she threw Amanda's blanket across the saddle and thrust the rifle into a leather pouch at the side of the horse. She pulled herself up onto the saddle and held her back straight, trying to conjure up courage to move onward. She was bone weary from the adventure that had so cruelly been thrust upon her. Yellow Feather had been the only pleasant part of these days of mounting confusion in her life.

"Now which way do I go?" she whispered, leaning forward, glancing toward the forest, then across the meadow where she had last seen Yellow Feather. "If I choose to go back to St. Paul, I will be back home, to the way of life I am accustomed to, where Aunt Rettie surely frets and stews over me."

Then shreds of doubt tore through her. "But if I do return, I will be doing so with a white man's death heavy on my conscience. How can I do this? How can I tell anyone that I took a white man's life, and not an Indian's?" she whispered aloud. Hadn't this white man Silas Konrad been after the same thing as the Indian? Hadn't she shot the white man over the same thing that she had given so willingly . . . eagerly . . . to an Indian?

She hung her head sadly. No. No one would ever understand. Though she knew that she wouldn't have to tell the whole truth about herself and the Indian, she knew that the truth would be there, in her eyes, whenever she spoke his name.

She gazed intently across the meadow to where the goldenrod swayed gently in the breeze. She knew where her heart must carry her. She would go to Yellow Feather. She would tell him of this white man who had found his cave and what his intentions had been.

Out of the corner of her eye, she caught sight of Amanda's blanket as a corner lifted into the breeze. "I have not forgotten you, baby sister," she whispered. "Maybe by going to the Indian village, I will also be somehow led to you."

Not looking back toward the cave where she had found a new birth through love . . . but also where she had dealt out death—hate . . . she moved onward.

"Hahh," she yelled to the horse and let it carry her to the meadow where bees buzzed madly from flower to flower and the pungency of the flowers' fragrance hung heavily in the air.

"I will follow you, Yellow Feather, my love," she whispered to the wind. "Maybe your spiritual guardian is now looking over me.''

She lifted her eyes to the sky. "Hear me, spirits of this north country. Carry me to your mourning son Yellow Feather. Let me help to lift the burden of death from his shoulders.''

She bowed her head, with tears heavy on her lashes. "And forgive me for what I have done, my own Lord and Savior,'' she prayed to God. "I have sinned. I have killed. Oh, please forgive me. . . .''

Eleven

While Yellow Feather bent over Chief Wind Whisper, washing his father's face, he could smell the sage and cedar boughs as they burned in the firespace, purifying the air. Behind him, Big Laughing Star wailed noisily as she swept the floor clean, readying the wigwam for the last dinner for the dead chief of the St. Croix band of the Chippewa.

Yellow Feather continued his duties to his deceased father by meticulously braiding his father's hair that was shining with bear grease. A round spot of brown fungus was then placed on each of Chief Wind Whisper's cheeks and over this was painted a horizontal line of vermillion. His moccasins had been painted brown and Yellow Feather had also already painted brown streaks on his father's blanket.

Yellow Feather could remember the first time his father had explained how this custom had originated. As Yellow Feather's grandfather had been in the process of being readied for burial, Chief Wind Whisper had explained to Yellow Feather that a Chippewa squaw of importance had long ago gone into a self-imposed trance for half a day, and, upon recovering, had said that she had been to the ghost land where the northern light ghosts had been rising and falling in the steps of a dance, and that the ghosts had held this fungus in their hands and had painted their faces in stripes with it. Thus, since then, the Chippewa had been prepared in the same manner as the squaw witnessed in her trance, to join the dance of the ghosts, where the northern lights were shining. . . .

Chief Wind Whisper's most official costume was now chosen by Yellow Feather and carefully placed on him. His white doeskin tunic and leggings were beautifully embroidered with beads and porcupine quills, and his five-foot-long Chippewa tribal headdress lay about his head, its brightly colored feathers stitched onto the leather.

Chief Wind Whisper lay with arms folded across his chest. Where his hands met, Yellow Feather chose to place his father's spirit bundle for the dead chief to take with him on his long journey west to his camping ground of eternal bliss.

With trembling fingers, Yellow Feather lifted his knife to Chief Wind Whisper's hair and removed a lock of it to place in his own spirit bundle. This bundle would always represent father. It would be the same as having his father at his side, seeing the good that Chief Yellow Feather was going to do for his people. In life, Yellow Feather had been forbidden by his spiritual guardian to share secrets with his father. In death, he and his father would walk . . . as . . . though they were one.

Big Laughing Star ceased her mournful wails and came to stand beside Yellow Feather, peering down at her husband of many years. The outward signs of her mourning were the ragged clothes she had chosen to wear and the short length of her hair, which she had clipped only moments before Yellow Feather's arrival back in the village.

Yellow Feather had painted his face completely black. He rose to his feet and straightened his back. "It is time for the last dinner for Chief Wind Whisper," he said flatly, trying to show courage and strength and no visible emotions in his eyes or on his face. "The wigwam is now full of spirits. I can feel their presence. They will look after my father and protect him on his journey."

"He looks asleep," Big Laughing Star murmured.

"My husband looks just peacefully asleep."

"He is anticipating his one last adventure," Yellow Feather said. "Somehow he knows that this will be greater than all his travels on earth."

Big Laughing Star began to wail again and waddled away to where she had heaped bark dishes with a feast of berries, pumpkin seeds, venison and wild greens. Yellow Feather went and lifted the flap of his father's wigwam and looked outside, seeing the mournful faces of his band of Indians. He swallowed hard, realizing the responsibility that now lay before him. But he had his spiritual guardian, and now his father's spirit, as well, to ease the heavy burdens of life.

Raising a hand, he spoke to the heads of each household. "Enter," he said. "Chief Wind Whisper awaits."

He stepped aside as they filed in one at a time and settled in silence around the fire. Some glanced toward Chief Wind Whisper who was stretched out on a plank at the back of the lodge, and others stared blankly into the fire, almost hypnotized by mournful grief.

Still wailing, Big Laughing Star passed horn spoons and birch-bark bowls of heaping food around the circle. Refusing food, one Indian turned a water drum upside down to moisten the skin covering, splashing the water about inside. Another picked up a buckshot rattle and soon they were all chanting along with the hush-ah-hush of the rattle shaking to the thump-thumping of the drum.

Yellow Feather's eyes followed a medicine man as he entered and went to Chief Wind Whisper to begin speaking in low chants over his body. This continued for a while, then Yellow Feather rose and coughed and spat into the fire, causing a sudden awed silence weighted with sorrow as all eyes turned back to their new chief.

"We are having our last meal with you, my Father," Yellow Feather said solemnly, facing Chief Wind Whisper's body. "Your trail will be long. We will place food

187

on your grave to help you along your way. We will also place some tobacco on your grave for you to give to my grandfather and your grandfather before him.''

Yellow Feather looked toward the medicine man and shook his head, okaying the medicine man's continuation of his low murmurings while the other Indians rose from their feet and joined in dancing when the drum and rattle began again. Their heads bobbed up and down to the rhythm of the drum, and they chanted *"Hai! Ay! Ay!"* while Yellow Feather stood over the fire with arms crossed and his head raised in prayer.

"Spirits of the world, aid and protect my father on his long journey," he cried. "Give him the gift of eternal life when he arrives in his happy hunting grounds."

One by one the Indians stopped their dancing and mournful songs to go and take turns sitting beside their deceased chief, each whispering advice to him: to be careful to avoid certain turns in the road to the spirit land, or to trust certain spirits who would meet and assist him. They spoke with extreme rapidity, punctuating the words with occasional sharp beats from the drum. One said, "Your feet are now on the road of souls, my Chief. . . .''

With a heavy heart, Yellow Feather lifted a hand to stop the ceremony then went to the flap and raised it, where the rest of his people watched and waited. *"Mah-bee-szhon,"* he said. "It is time to say your final goodbyes to my father, your chief."

He stepped aside as one by one they moved silently into the wigwam and on past Chief Wind Whisper. When this was finished and only Yellow Feather and Big Laughing Star remained in the wigwam, Yellow Feather ignored Big Laughing Star's further mourning rituals of self-mutilation as she tore at her flesh with her fingernails. This was the Chippewa wife's way of showing her deep loss and sorrow. Yellow Feather had his own sorrow, and he had further duties to his father. He had to wrap his father's body in a fetal position with thick birch bark and tie it securely with basswood cord before he could be carried to his grave. Yellow Feather had wanted to place his father on a high scaffold for a few days, not wanting to lose sight of him so soon. But Yellow Feather knew that was not good, for even tomorrow, his St. Croix band of Indians would be gone from this place, never to be a part of it again. . . .

After his father was securely wrapped, Yellow Feather got the assistance of Flying Squirrel, and soon they were carrying Chief Wind Whisper to the burial grounds while the medicine man danced around them, singing, and while all the other Indians followed along behind. When they reached the shallow grave, Yellow Feather and Flying Squirrel placed Chief Wind Whisper into it facing west, the direction for Chief Wind Whisper's spiritual travels.

Big Laughing Star stepped up to the grave and fell to her knees. Wailing still, she placed Chief Wind Whisper's beautifully decorated bark quiver filled with arrows into the grave, followed by his hunting spear and knife and one of his traps and showshoes. Each head of household then filed by the grave and placed their own gifts inside it for Chief Wind Whisper's long journey across the sky, then stood back to make room for Big Laughing Star to begin dancing around the open grave, dancing until she fell beside the grave exhausted and breathless. She lay there in forced silence, showing that she was now "of a strong mind," and watched as the shallow grave was filled, then covered with weighted bark sheets and rush mats, upon which food and an offering of tobacco were placed.

A pile of wood had been readied beside the grave site earlier in the day. Yellow Feather faced west as he set the wood to flame. "Go now, my father. It is now time for

189

you to begin your long journey. I have kindled this fire to light your way," he said. "All our ancestors will come across the bridge of light to meet you and will be with you on your long journey to the happy hunting grounds. Go in peace, my father."

Mournful cries met Yellow Feather's ears. He understood, but it was now time for his people to put sadness behind them and place hope in their minds and hearts. He turned and faced them, determination strong in his voice. "We will now move to the council house," he flatly stated. "Everyone come. I, Chief Yellow Feather, have much to share with you."

He watched as everyone obediently moved toward the council house that stood at the edge of the forest on a large cleared space of ground where his band of Indians had always held their tribal dances and powwows.

Yellow Feather and Flying Squirrel followed side by side behind the silent throng of Indians. Yellow Feather looked toward the council house where only his father had presided as chief over the affairs of the St. Croix. It was the most attractive lodge in the village, a long narrow structure of handsomely fashioned bark. The ends were beautifully rounded and the roof gracefully arched. The snow-white birchbark sides were decorated with striking totemic designs in brilliant but harmonious colors. Chief Wind Whisper had held court there many times, calling together his council to settle disputes among the tribesman and to impose penalties when wrongs had been proved.

"You think our people will understand what you say, Chief Yellow Feather?" Flying Squirrel asked softly, sidling next to Yellow Feather. "Will they wonder why they haven't been directed to this place of food and wealth earlier?"

"They may wonder but they won't question it," Yellow Feather replied flatly. "I am now their chief. No.

190

They will not question it."

"And the white woman with the hair of flame?" Flying Squirrel persisted. "What will you . . . ?"

Yellow Feather shot Flying Squirrel a look of anger. "She will sit at my right side as I lead my people," he said. "My people will also not question that."

He glanced back at his father's grave momentarily. "Even *he* may not have questioned it if he had known the love I felt for this woman."

"What if she refuses . . . ?"

"She will not. . . ."

Yellow Feather stepped up to the council house door and lifted the flap and entered. He moved determinedly toward a raised platform spread with bearskins, strewn balsam boughs and cushions that ran entirely around the wigwam next to the outer wall. Once settled upon it with legs crossed, he bowed graciously, bending from the waist, and raised his hand in greeting to all who now sat on the floor, waiting.

Focusing his eyes straight ahead now, Yellow Feather said, "My people, I know of a place. . . ."

Twelve

The procession of the St. Croix band of Indians was led by Yellow Feather on his just recently acquired black stallion. Flying Squirrel was on his right and Happy Flower, sitting side saddle on her smaller Indian pony, was on his left. The forest trail was narrow, but Yellow Feather knew that the wide expanse of meadow that waved with yellow blossoms was not so far away. A full night's journey longer and his people would fulfill the spiritual dream of his youth.

Yellow Feather raised his head to the forest ceiling, seeing the dwindling light of day casting ghostlike shadows on the gold tips of the maple trees. "Spirits of the forest, hear my cry," he whispered beneath his breath. "Make my people brave. Make my people strong. The day has been long. The day has been sad."

A rush of sudden wind, like breath upon his face, made Yellow Feather shiver, yet smile, understanding this way of the spirits. They had heard. They were with him and his people. All would be well. Soon . . . all would be well. His people would no longer suffer. The word *famine* would be a stranger to his people's lips.

Turning his head to glance behind him, Yellow Feather felt a deep sense of pride, seeing how faithfully his people followed after him. After he had met with them in council and told them of this place of his youthful vision, they had shown hope in the quiet dark of their eyes and had obediently obeyed when he had told them to prepare their belongings for a journey of life and happiness. Each wigwam had been quickly dismantled. The bark covering had been removed and rolled up to take to the new campsite. The ironwood frames had been left behind in the ground, like so many skeletons to haunt this land that had at one time seen so many births and deaths of this band of Chippewa . . . the Obijway . . . the peaceful Indian.

"Chief Yellow Feather, how far will we go tonight?" Flying Squirrel asked, moving his horse closer to Yellow Feather's.

"All the way," Yellow Feather said flatly, thrusting his knees into his horse's sides, causing it to gallop away.

Flying Squirrel drew to his side again. "Our people. They are tired," he said, glancing back, seeing how some shoulders hunched heavily forward on their horses. Some older Chippewa were on drags, sleeping. The youngest trotted along, heads still held high.

Yellow Feather once more turned his head and let his gaze travel from one family to the next, seeing a determination etched onto each of their faces as they moved along with their own family's possessions. Some traveled by horseback and some by foot. A drag, a travois, had been made by some of two long, strong branches, with which to carry and drag their household belongings. Even all the food they had gathered and had stored for winter, to the last sunflower seed, had been packed upon the drags.

Remembering the river and how he would have easy access to it now, Yellow Feather had seen to it that the old canoes, which had during these past years housed only creeping wild vines, were being carried along too, soon to feel again the caress of water against their birch-bark sides. Though old, he knew they could be relied upon. They had been constructed to be tough, their frames sewn with the roots of a species of spruce that would not rot and the seams sealed with spruce gum, and flexible pieces of white cedar thinned and shaped into the ribs and floorboards.

Yellow Feather closed his eyes, already feeling the flexing of his muscles as he would man the oars to pull the low-riding canoe away from the shore. Ah, the canoe would move so gracefully across countless watersheds and open waters. . . .

Ay-uh, his people would soon know all the riches of the earth and river. The thundering hooves of horses drew Yellow Feather's eyes quickly open. How could he forget the horses following behind? Didn't they already prove riches that most of the St. Croix Indians hadn't known they had possession of? Only Yellow Feather, Flying Squirrel . . .

"And Silas Konrad," Yellow Feather thought angrily to himself. He wondered if Silas Konrad would come snooping further when he found the village deserted. . . .

"Yellow Feather . . ." Flying Squirrel said loudly. "We must stop. Our people must rest."

Yellow Feather thrust his knees into his horse and urged it onward. "My people must continue with their journey of the heart," he grumbled. "We must not stop."

"It soon will be dark," Flying Squirrel said quietly, once more moving next to Yellow Feather.

"I know my way in the dark. My people will follow me full of trust . . . full of hope," Yellow Feather said proudly.

"It has been a long, tiring day, Yellow Feather," Flying Squirrel grumbled. "The women. They need rest. Happy Flower clutches her stomach so. Maybe the child will be born too early."

Yellow Feather drew his horse to a halt and reached for Flying Squirrel's reins and yanked them angrily from him. "Do you forget who is now chief?" he spat, eyes flashing.

Flying Squirrel hung his head. *"Gah-ween,"* he murmured. "No. I do not forget."

"Do you forget the strength of our Indian women?"

"Gah-ween," Flying Squirrel replied. "But I feel it is not because of our people you travel so hard."

"What . . . ?" Yellow Feather said in dismay.

"You are anxious to be with the white woman again. This is why you push our people so hard."

Yellow Feather's heartbeat hastened. He *was* anxious to be with Lorinda . . . his Red Blossom. *Was* she the reason for his haste? No. It was for his people.

He argued silently with himself. No, it *was* because of Red Blossom. He ached to hold her in his arms, to smell the sweetness of her breath upon his cheek.

He set his jaws firmly and squared his shoulders. "Flying Squirrel, you speak out of line to your chief," he said flatly, yet not looking Flying Squirrel's way. He was afraid that it would be his own eyes that would speak truth to Flying Squirrel this time.

"I am sorry, Yellow Feather. Sometimes I speak too hastily. Sometimes I even say foolish things."

"Ay-uh, you do, Flying Squirrel. But you must remember. Our people have waited for too long for this land I am guiding them to," Yellow Feather said more softly. He handed the horse's reins back to Flying Squirrel. "I will not stop now until I have presented this gift of love to them. By morning our village by the St. Croix will already be established."

"You will have the wigwams erected in the night?" Flying Squirrel gasped.

"Ay-uh. We will build large fires to work by," Yellow Feather said. "You see, Flying Squirrel, snows will soon be upon us. We have the wild rice to harvest and fish to catch and smoke. . . ."

"Wild rice?" Flying Squirrel said quickly. "What

196

wild . . . rice . . . ?''

"It is a true secret I've kept locked within my heart," Yellow Feather said, once again moving onward as Happy Flower guided her pony to his side.

The air hung heavy with the smell of pine and damp underbrush. The night had fallen quickly, leaving the trail black, yet Yellow Feather continued to guide the way, having become familiar with every tree and ground slope in this land that had been shown him those many years ago. He had even become familiar with the delicate exquisite flowers that marked the seasons and especially with the springtime in this country so rich with promise. This coming spring he would be sharing it with his people . . . the way the green shoots would reach sunward through the melting snows . . . and the way the infant animals would totter from their winter nests to bear the future of their species. Chippewa children would likewise be born . . . even *his* child would be a part of this next new spring . . . the new birth. . . .

A shimmering of orange from a campfire's blaze in the distance caused Yellow Feather to draw his horse quickly to a halt. He reached for Happy Flower's pony's reins with one hand and turned and raised his hand to his people with the other. As he faced his people, his heart pounded against his ribs, having never before seen man on this sacred trail to his cave.

"No-gee-shkan," he ordered stiffly. "Stop. There is danger ahead. I will go and see who it is blocking our way."

He handed the reins back to Happy Flower. *"Ee-shqueen,"* he said quietly. "Stay and do not be afraid. I am sure it is only a hunter who has lost his way."

"I *am* afraid, Yellow Feather," Happy Flower whispered, tremoring. "Our child. If there is trouble. . . ."

Yellow Feather reached a hand to the swell of her stomach and touched it softly. "Nothing will happen to our child," he said. "The spirits are with you, protecting both you and our child from harm. I shall return. Soon. Then we will travel onward. You will be resting in a wigwam in our new village this time tomorrow evening. I promise you that."

"I'm still sad for Chief Wind Whisper," she said, lowering her eyes.

"Do not be sad. He is already on his journey. He has his journey . . . we have ours. . . ."

"You are a wise chief," Happy Flower whispered.

"I must go," he said, nodding toward Flying Squirrel, motioning for him to travel along beside him as they moved their horses noiselessly over the deeply piled leaves of autumn. They didn't speak as they pulled their rifles from their side leather pouches, letting the campfire's glow guide them onward through brush and beneath low-hanging branches of trees that were dripping dew from them. An occasional firefly's flash resembled eyes glowing momentarily then disappeared just as quickly as it had emerged from the thicket.

Yellow Feather drew his horse suddenly next to Flying Squirrel's. "We must go the rest of the way by foot," he whispered.

"What if there are many?"

"Then I will stay while you return to our people and instruct the best of our warriors."

"And if there is only one?" Flying Squirrel asked, dismounting along with Yellow Feather.

"I can think of only one white man in these parts who would be traveling alone."

Flying Squirrel's eyes suddenly lit up. *"Ay-uh,"* he mumbled. "Silas Konrad. He has found our trail."

"Possibly our cave," Yellow Feather said, then felt a hollowness at the pit of the stomach as he thought of Lorinda. If Silas Konrad had found the cave, he had also found his Red Blossom! He placed his finger on the trigger of his rifle, hate raging inside him.

"If it is Silas Konrad, what will we do?" Flying Squirrel whispered, tiptoeing stealthily next to Yellow Feather.

"We . . . shall . . . kill him," Yellow Feather whispered unemotionally.

"But we do not kill. . . ."

"To protect our people and our land that has been kept from the white man just *for* our people? *Ay-uh,* I will kill anyone who is a threat to our people's well-being."

"The white woman. She is a threat," Flying Squirrel grumbled, crouching now, so near to the campfire he could hear the crackling of the flames.

Yellow Feather placed a hand firmly on Flying Squirrel's shoulder and stopped him. He faced him squarely and whispered, "I will forget you said that. Now. You must think only of the moment at hand. We must move softly and see how many white man invade our sacred land."

The neighing of a horse close by drew Yellow Feather quickly around. He slipped through the brush to the horse, stiffening inside. He recognized the horse. He recognized the saddle. He had seen Silas Konrad more times than he had wished on this horse and in this saddle. Flying Squirrel came to Yellow Feather's side. "It is . . ." he said, but was interrupted when Yellow Feather placed a hand over Flying Squirrel's mouth.

"Ay-uh," he whispered. "Silas Konrad. We are in luck. He apparently still travels alone."

He removed his hand from Flying Squirrel's mouth, then crouched lower, positioning his rifle. A strange excitement was coursing through his veins. He had been held back by his father. The thrill of the hunt had only been allowed for animals . . . not for man. But now? Hate caused Yellow Feather's heart to race wildly inside him. He was soon to . . . kill . . .

199

"Should I just go shoot him and get it over with?" Flying Squirrel asked anxiously.

"No. We fight valiantly. We will first face him. We will not sneak and kill him as one who does not have honor."

"I thought . . ."

"*Ay-uh.* We *will* kill him," Yellow Feather said. "He will not cause our people any more problems after tonight. He will not be allowed to return to the white man's village to shout to them of this new virgin land. But first, we must approach him." He couldn't tell Flying Squirrel that he feared for Lorinda's life. He *had* to question Silas Konrad first. He had to see if Silas Konrad had found the cave.

With a nod of the head, Yellow Feather motioned for Flying Squirrel to follow him. When they were only a few feet from the campfire, they crouched together in the brush and slowly pulled the leaves aside to get a better look. Yellow Feather blinked his eyes nervously, seeing only the back of this man who sat close to the fire. The shine from a rifle barrel, upright between the man's legs, twinkled in golds against the flames of the fire, causing Yellow Feather to place his finger on the trigger of his own rifle once again.

"There's something different about that man," Flying Squirred whispered, lifting a brow. "But I cannot tell much. The man's hat hides too much from my eyes."

Yellow Feather looked closer. *"Ay-uh,"* he said. "I don't think it's Silas Konrad after all. Silas Konrad is short and round. This man's clothes show that he must be tall and lean."

"Let's circle around and see his face," Flying Squirrel said, inching his way sideways.

Yellow Feather took short, silent steps, then stopped when he was directly in front of the stranger, peering intently through the cover of tall grass. His heart skipped a beat when the stranger's face lifted and began looking cautiously about. This face was *not* that of a stranger after all. He did not understand how . . . but he knew that he was gazing upon the beautiful face of Lorinda . . . his Red Blossom.

"It is . . ." Flying Squirrel gasped softly.

"Ay-uh," Yellow Feather said, rising. He moved from the brush quickly and soon had Lorinda's gun tossed from her grip. He dropped his own gun to the ground and drew her up before him, knocking the hat from her head. As her hair tumbled into lustrous waves of flame across her shoulders, a stab of desire pierced Yellow Feather's insides. "Red Blossom, I do not understand," he said thickly, holding her at arm's length, studying her attire. He had never seen a woman in man's clothing before. *Never.*

His arrival had happened so quickly Lorinda had been left breathless. She gazed into Yellow Feather's eyes, seeing his dark pools so flat, so emotionless, yet his hands were trembling as he held her. "Yellow Feather," she finally said softly. "My God, Yellow Feather."

Tears splashed from her eyes onto her cheeks, glad that he had managed to find her again. If not for the matches she had found in the borrowed man's jacket, she would have had to spend the night in a frightening black silence. Now she had the fire's glow . . . now she had Yellow Feather. . . .

"Red Blossom, what *are* you doing here?" Yellow Feather asked, stepping back, letting his gaze capture the full length of her. "These clothes. The horse . . . ?" His eyes flew open wide. The horse. It *was* Silas Konrad's! He knew that it was. He had seen it many times!

Lorinda moved to Yellow Feather and fell into his arms, sobbing. She laced her arms about his neck and lay her cheek against his chest where his heart thump-thumped, oh, so wildly. "It's so terrible, Yellow

Feather," she cried. "How can I even tell you what has happened."

Flying Squirrel stepped into view. Lorinda caught sight of him out of the corner of her eye. She stiffened and withdrew from Yellow Feather, cowering a bit. She trusted Yellow Feather, but she didn't know enough of Flying Squirrel to also trust him. He was raking his eyes over her as he had the time when he had seen her nude. Even now, she felt undressed as his eyes seemed to be looking through her.

"It *is* the white woman," Flying Squirrel said, moving around her, then laughed aloud. "And in men's clothing?" he said amusedly. "Now I have seen her in two extremes. Without any clothes and in man's breeches and jacket. White woman, you are funny."

Yellow Feather stepped between Flying Squirrel and Lorinda, crossing his arms angrily. "Flying Squirrel, that is enough of your words," he said. He pointed toward the trail where his people waited. "*Mah-szhon*. Return to our people. Ready them to move once again. I will talk with Red Blossom, then we will also be ready to go."

"You are taking her with us?" Flying Squirrel asked sullenly. "She is white. I tell you, Yellow Feather, she should not be permitted to go with our people to where we are to build a life of prosperity. She will only bring sadness to our people."

"Flying Squirrel, enough. Go. Do as I command," Yellow Feather ordered firmly, pointing again.

Flying Squirrel cast Yellow Feather a look of defiance then stormed away.

Yellow Feather turned to Lorinda and offered his arms to her. "Tell Yellow Feather why you have a white man's horse and have on white man's clothes. Tell me. Where is Silas Konrad? It is his horse. How do you have it?"

Lorinda snuggled into Yellow Feather's arms, pulling

202

strength from him. "He is dead," she said softly. "Yellow Feather, I shot him. Silas Konrad is . . . dead. . . ."

Yellow Feather's insides rippled. He held her away from him, studying her eyes and the hurt she held within them. His heart raced. "He is dead . . . ?" he gasped. "You . . . shot . . . him . . . ?"

Lorinda lowered her eyes and told him how it had happened and why Yellow Feather had found her dressed in such a manner. She then pleaded with her eyes as his held her immobile. "It was such a horrible experience," she murmured. "Oh, Yellow Feather, what am I to do?"

"You will go with me. You are my wife. You will share my new wigwam with me and Happy Flower. . . ."

Lorinda pulled free from his embrace and his gaze of steel. "You say I will . . . what . . . ?" she gasped. "Who . . . is . . . Happy Flower?"

"Happy Flower is my other wife," Yellow Feather said flatly. "To Happy Flower *you* will be my other wife."

Lorinda sighed heavily. Her shoulders hunched and her hands went to her hair. "Yellow Feather, I love you, but I am *not* one of your wives," she said. Jealousy crept into her veins like bubbles bouncing. "And where is the *second* Indian wife? What is *her* name? You said you had two Indian wives."

"She grew angry and left. She is no longer wife. Only you and Happy Flower," he said. He began kicking loose, damp dirt onto the fire, then stamped it completely out. He grabbed Lorinda by the arm and forced her gently onward. "Come," he said. "You will travel with me and my people. You will travel on the right of me while Happy Flower travels on the left. You *are* my wife. My people will be watching you. You must act as a wife acts to their chief or they may not approve of you being a part of your village."

He placed his arms about her waist and lifted her onto the horse then trotted back to where the guns lay by the ugly black smoke from the fire. He went to Lorinda and placed her gun in the leather pouch at the side of her horse then took the horse's reins and guided it to where many eyes tried to see who the intruder in the night was.

The dark of the night gave Lorinda a reprieve for now, all except for Happy Flower, who was close enough to see that this person in man's clothing was not a man, but a beautiful woman who had the most unusual color of hair that hung loosely instead of braided across her shoulder.

Lorinda's lips narrowed and her insides knotted when she saw the beautiful, frail Indian maiden who was now on Yellow Feather's left side. Then her gaze lowered and saw the round swell of her abdomen. This Indian named Happy Flower was big with child . . . Yellow Feather's child.

A choking of sorts swept up inside her throat, as she was not able to keep from envisioning Yellow Feather and this beautiful maiden sharing the most intimate of embraces.

Soon they'll even share a child, she thought sadly to herself. She suddenly felt detached, knowing that she did *not* belong. She would *never* belong. She turned her head and let her gaze search through the darkness. She tensed, seeing so many Indians so close. Fear sprang forth. She looked at Yellow Feather, wondering.

"Come. We will travel until we see the swaying yellow meadow beneath the moon's rays, then we will be there," Yellow Feather said, motioning for everyone to once again follow.

"We will be where?" Lorinda asked softly, snapping the horse's reins, feeling the lift of her hair as the horse moved forward in a quiet trot.

"To the land of my childhood dream," he answered, flashing her a quick glance. "Where the cave awaits . . .

204

where the wild rice sways gently in the breeze . . . where the sturgeon are in abundance in the St. Croix River.''

Lorinda swallowed hard. ''You are taking all these people to . . . that . . . place . . . where I killed a man?'' she gasped.

''The spirits are with us. They are also with you because they guided you to me. Do not fear anything, Red Blossom. I will make you happy. You will love my people. They are special.''

''But the . . . man . . . Silas Konrad?''

''I will take care of that for you.''

Lorinda lowered her eyes and placed a hand to her throat. If not by Yellow Feather's side, she would feel she was in a nightmare. But he had a way of making things right for her. He always had . . . surely he always would.

Glancing back around her, she had to wonder how many babies there were in this particular village of Indians. She reached down inside the saddle's pouch and touched Amanda's folded blanket, then turned to face the direction from which she had just traveled. Chills raced through her, remembering how easy it had been to pull the trigger, to kill a man. Had it been so easy for the Indians who had released the arrows from their bows to kill her parents?

Forcing herself to not wonder or think about what was to be, Lorinda held her head high as she traveled beside Yellow Feather. She would show him that she was just as strong as the Indian maiden who so bravely traveled by pony while heavy with child. Did this Indian maiden hate her? Did the Indian maiden even understand who she was? Lorinda had felt watchful eyes on her and knew that they had been Yellow Feather's wife's, but now she felt only the need for sleep lying heavy on her eyelids and wished the journey would be quickly over.

Feeling a sudden jerk of her head, she realized that she

had momentarily dropped off to sleep. She glanced at Yellow Feather, seeing his chin held high and his shoulders squared. She glanced at Happy Flower and saw how she leaned more heavily over her stomach with a hand resting on it as it jiggled clumsily from side to side. Then Lorinda's heart jumped when Yellow Feather moved quickly on ahead of her and shouted something in Indian. She was relieved when he reverted to English and told her they had arrived, as he came racing back to his people. She then ceased to understand him as he spoke to his people in their language.

"We have arrived," he shouted. "My people, see the land that is now yours. It is where our children's children will romp and play. It is where the seasons will come and go with rejoicing with many feasts. Come. We will now move to the meadow where each of you can choose a site to prepare for your wigwams."

He raised his right arm and pointed to the forest from which they had just emerged. "The forest is to our north and will shield us from the north winds,"he shouted further. "The river is to the south of us where we will receive cool, wet breezes in summer. When morning comes, I will show you the wild rice that is waiting to be harvested. But for now, prepare your wigwams. Sleep will come later."

Yellow Feather then lifted his face to the sky. "Thank you, mighty guardian spirit, giant owl of the forest," he whispered. "Thank you for guiding me and my people. I will always be grateful."

Lorinda moved her horse next to Yellow Feather's, watching how the Indians were now swarming around, preparing a large firespace on which to build a bonfire to work by. She then glanced toward the cave, shivering. "Yellow Feather, maybe one day I will understand your ways," she said.

"*Ay-uh*, you will, Red Blossom. You will," he said

dismounting. He reached for Lorinda and helped her from her horse, then Happy Flower from her pony. He brought the two women together, eyeing each one cautiously. "My two wives, we will work together, to prepare our wigwam," he said.

Lorinda's eyes widened. She crossed her arms defiantly as she stared at Happy Flower, then softened a bit when she saw the look in Happy Flower's eyes. Happy Flower was just now understanding why this white woman had traveled at Yellow Feather's right side. She had just now understood that Yellow Feather had already replaced the one wife that had left with another. But this didn't concern Lorinda. She had her own welfare to worry about. "I refuse to share a wigwam with anyone," she hissed. "I shall *not*."

Yellow Feather gazed from one wife to the other. "You *will*," he said firmly. "And you will also help to erect the wigwam, Red Blossom. I now have decided that the burden of the duty should be taken from Happy Flower. The journey has been hard on her. I fear for our child."

Lorinda's face drained of color. "*Ay-uh, your* child," she hissed, stomping a foot. "When you were making love to me you had a woman heavy with child waiting for your embraces. Oh, Yellow Feather, you *are* a savage, heartless Indian. You are!"

Yellow Feather's features grew even more stern. He jerked Lorinda away from Happy Flower's side. He spoke into her face. "I do not have time or patience to deal with a jealous white woman," he fumed. "I have my duties as chief now, as you have your duties of wife. *Mah-bee-szhon*. We will work together. We will build our wigwam next to the forest's door, where we will be a part of nature when making love."

Lorinda jerked and squirmed. "You will never touch me again, Yellow Feather," she argued. "You have one

207

wife. You can *not* have two."

"I am chief. I can have ten if I want."

"Oh!" Lorinda wailed, stumbling as Yellow Feather threw her into the thick of the forest's edge. She composed herself, then watched the Indians all working so quickly and quietly together, cutting ironwood saplings, stripping them, then placing these in many elliptical patterns, to then bring the saplings together in arches, while the women were busy binding the frameworks with green basswood fibers.

Lorinda grumbled as she began to work alongside Yellow Feather until they were draping bark strips over their own structure, securing this by poles and weighted basswood cords. Yellow Feather went and got his rolled-up bark coverings and soon had them secured across the poles, even with deerhide covering the doorway.

"It is done," he said proudly. "See how simple?"

Lorinda was breathless. What had appeared simple had in truth taken many hours. Dawn was creeping along the horizon in pale oranges revealing an almost magical scene now as Lorinda looked slowly around her. She saw many wigwams, and the Indians standing, also gazing about them at this land their new chief had guided them to.

Something swelled in Lorinda's throat, seeing hope . . . love . . . pride in all their eyes. It was touching, knowing that she had been a part of some great movement of these Indians. Yet, she couldn't help but remember her parents . . . and Amanda. . . .

She swirled around and found Yellow Feather gazing intently at her. She flushed a bit, seeing something deep in his eyes this time . . . more than a forced veil over his feelings. He reached for her hand.

"I am proud, my wife," he said. "You worked by my side so skillfully. You have made Yellow Feather proud. My people also see this. There will be a feast to welcome

208

you as my wife. Soon. It will be a joyous one.''

Lorinda felt the sweet ache inside her as one of his hands reached to touch her face. "Yellow Feather, please don't. . . ." she said softly.

"No more words," he said. "I must see to it that my council house is built. A chief must never be without a council house." He looked toward Happy Flower who was stretched out asleep on a spread bullrush mat. "Please see to Happy Flower, Red Blossom. Direct her into the warmth of our wigwam. The child. . . ."

Lorinda sighed heavily. "All right, I will," she said. "But only for the baby. And, Yellow Feather, I tell you, I will *not* share this wigwam with her. I will not."

"We'll see," he said stiffly.

Lorinda glanced toward the cave's entrance. Her eyes wavered a bit as her heart raced. "Yellow Feather, when are you gong to go inside . . . the . . . cave?" she asked softly. "What are you going to do with Silas Konrad?"

"Will it make you feel better if I do it now?"

"*Ay-uh,*" she whispered.

"I will make it my next duty," he said, walking away.

With weakened knees, Lorinda went to Happy Flower and leaned over her. She touched her gently on the cheek. "Happy Flower, come with me to the warmth of the wigwam," she said. "I will even start a fire in the firespace for you."

Happy Flower leaned up on an elbow, frowning. "Me take care of Happy Flower," she said sourly in broken English. "White woman leave Happy Flower alone. Me no like you. Me no like the way Yellow Feather looks at you. Me no like you be Yellow Feather's wife."

Lorinda straightened her back and clamped her lips together tightly. She stood with hands on hips as Happy Flower waddled away with her chin held haughtily in the air. "I don't like the way life has turned out any better than you do," she whispered. She turned quickly to a sound of rushing feet. She took a step forward as Yellow Feather stood before her, breathless.

"What is it, Yellow Feather?" she asked, feeling fear rippling along her spine. She had never seen Yellow Feather in such an anxious state. He was usually so composed, even painfully so.

"You said you left Silas Konrad in the cave?" he asked, grasping her shoulders roughly.

She flinched, then replied, "Yes, I did. Why . . . ?"

"He is not there," Yellow Feather said, panting hard. "There is no trace. . . ."

Lorinda's eyes grew wild. "He has to be," she said. "He *has* to be. I left him lying there."

"No. He is gone. . . ."

Lorinda saw fear etched onto Yellow Feather's face and felt panic rising inside herself. Had someone found Silas Konrad's body and taken it away as proof of her crime. . . ?

"He must not have been dead, Red Blossom," Yellow Feather said thickly. "He has left, now to tell the white man about this sacred place of my childhood dream. . . ."

"No, I'm sure . . ." Lorinda said, but as Yellow Feather released his hold on her and stared across the rippling waters of the St. Croix River, she suddenly realized his fears. . . .

Thirteen

After a hard day's labor in the lumber camp, Lamont Quinby welcomed the isolation of his tiny log cabin that he had built on a hill that overlooked Duluth and the wide expanse of Lake Superior. With land being offered at $2.50 an acre, many settlers were arriving every day, clearly indicating that Duluth had a future as a prosperous city. With lumber and iron ore in abundance, Lamont even looked to this city on the great lake as becoming a busy seaport.

"Damn lucky for me that there's more than one hundred miles that stretches between here and St. Paul," Lamont grumbled as he leaned an arm against his fireplace mantel, staring into the fire on the hearth. He knew that Rettie Odell would see that he hung for sure if he ever set foot in that town of St. Paul again. The miles between the two cities had given him a bit of cover. As far as he knew, so far no one had come looking for him.

"It's best I've kept my true name hid to the men I work with in case that ol' woman does set the law out after me," he grumbled further.

Lamont pulled a cigar from his front shirt pocket and placed it between his lips. He leaned the cigar into the flames of the fire and puffed on it until it was filling the small space around him with the heavy aroma of cigar smoke. He then began pacing the floor, talking in low mumbles to himself. With the forest at his front door and the large body of water at his back, loneliness for a woman had become the biggest problem. He was forever haunted by how it could have been if not for the Indian with the yellow feather.

"I would've won her over. I would've," he said. "If'n that Indian would've minded his own business, Lorinda would be here right now, readying the bed for us to share."

His fingers reached and worked nervously through his wild, sandy-colored hair, then twisted his thick, blond mustache. In his gray eyes lay a torture only evident in a man who has been without a woman for way too long. His loins ached as he continued fantasizing about Lorinda . . . seeing the red of her hair as it would settle like a crown of roses across the bed as he would lower himself over her and possess her first with his eyes. . . .

A scraping noise of sorts at Lamont's cabin door pulled him from his thoughts. He yanked his cigar from his mouth and leaned his ear in the door's direction, listening intensely. When he heard the scraping noise again, he placed his cigar in an ashtray and inched his way toward where he had left his rifle leaning against the wall. Slowly lifting it, he crept to the door and listened again. With his forefinger on the trigger of his gun, he yanked the door open and took a step backwards, shocked.

His gaze quickly raked over the Indian woman, seeing a small bundle in the crook of her left arm and how her clothes were tattered and torn. His eyes then met hers. She was looking upward at him with the darkest of eyes that were visibly full of fear.

"What the hell?" Lamont said quietly, once again taking in the full width and height of her. Her copper-skinned face was quite round and she was a bit on the fleshy side, yet she was beautiful, causing a hunger to gnaw at Lamont's groin. He had just been having the strong need of a woman . . . and one had arrived at his door! Then his eyes narrowed, not ever having had any love for the Indians. Could a squaw be so different from a murdering savage Indian warrior?

Placing his gun on a table, Lamont stepped out onto the ground and began circling the Indian and spat into the wind as he wondered what he should do with her. His eyes suddenly lit up, as he thought that there was only one thing to do with a woman . . . be she Indian . . . or white. A female was a female.

Glancing into the forest, Lamont tensed a bit. Was this a trap? Were there many Indians watching from the cover of the thicket? He grabbed the Indian by the arm and spoke harshly to her. "Are you alone, squaw?" he said. "Is there more of your kind out there waitin' to jump and scalp me?"

Hearing the venom in his voice as he spoke of her Indian people, Foolish Heart felt courage returning to her though she was weary and hungry from the many days of travel. She glared at him with anger flashing in her eyes. She understood English and could speak it, though brokenly.

"Me alone," she stated flatly. "Me travel alone. My people far away. You don't have to worry about being scalped by any of my people. You only have Foolish Heart to worry about, and Foolish Heart only ask for food."

"Well, I'll be damn," Lamont laughed hoarsely. "She talks white man talk." He lifted one of her pitch-black braids, then let it flop back to her shoulder. "Now ain't this interestin'? A squaw all alone with Lamont Quinby. Ain't that somethin'?"

"All Foolish Heart wants is food. Then she will go," Foolish Heart said, taking a step backwards when she noticed the evil glint in the man's eyes. She knew that she had chosen the wrong house. But she had feared the many houses that sat so close together next to the large body of water. She had thought to be safer with one house . . . one family. She hadn't thought to find one man . . .

213

alone. She knew what a man had most on his mind. Hadn't Yellow Feather only used his squaws for the pleasure he drew from them?

Her blood boiled, thinking of how Happy Flower had managed to get Yellow Feather into her bed of blankets more often than Foolish Heart, resulting in her being the first to have become heavy with child. I'm glad I left, she thought angrily to herself. Now Yellow Feather had only one wife, and when Happy Flower had the child, she wouldn't want to accept Yellow Feather into her bed as often. She would only think of the child. How funny it would be to see Yellow Feather all alone on his bed of blankets.

"So's all you want is somethin' to fill your stomach with, eh?" Lamont mocked. "I've got somethin' for you all right. Just step into my house."

Foolish Heart felt the weakness in her knees and the emptiness at the pit of her stomach, yet she began to move steadily backwards, then turned and began to run. She had understood his meaning too well and feared a white man's way of taking a woman.

She panted hard, finding it harder and harder to lift one foot after the other. Her chest was heaving with the exertion and her side ached. Suddenly she couldn't go any farther. She gave in to her weakness and let herself begin falling, only to be grabbed by large, coarse hands around her wrists. With a renewed energy she kicked and scratched but soon became immobile when Lamont pushed her body to the ground and fell across her, leering.

Holding her wrists, he laughed into her face. "Thought you could get away, huh?" he said thickly. "Don't know Lamont Quinby very well, you beautiful Indian squaw." His mouth bore down upon hers in wetness and his one hand released her wrist to move desperately over her body. When his tongue sought entrance into her mouth, her teeth clamped down.

Lamont jumped from her, yowling with pain as blood rushed from between his lips. Foolish Heart rose from the ground and once more attempted to run but her exhaustion from hunger became too great for her. She placed a hand to her head when she began seeing the bare limbs of the trees circling above her as she fell in a swoon to the ground.

"Damn women," Lamont grumbled, wiping at his mouth. He was remembering Rettie Odell's attack with the broom and the fingernails of Lorinda. He still had scars from those women's abuses to his face. And now to have an Indian squaw bite his tongue?

His face flamed red from anger as he loomed over the lifeless body. In one swoop he lifted her into his arms and carried her inside his cabin and placed her on his bed.

"She ain't goin' nowheres," he growled, taking ropes and tying her wrists to the bedposts. He left her legs be, having plans for her lower parts.

He stood over her, nervously twisting the ends of his mustache. His heart pounded with hungry need for a woman. His eyes raked over her, seeing that she did appear clean enough with only a few scratches on her face and hands. The rest of her was fully clothed in buckskin edged with brightly colored beads. Her moccasins showed wear and he wondered how far she had traveled and why? He had never heard of an Indian squaw traveling alone. Had she been cast out of her tribe? She did appear to have a spiteful tongue when she spoke.

Settling down on the edge of the bed, Lamont began tracing her features with his fingers. Her skin was smooth and inviting. He had to see what lay beneath the buckskin even if he would be taking unfair advantage of someone who so obviously was in need of nourishment.

"I'll give her my own kind of nourishment," he chuckled, untying the band around her waist. He then strug-

215

gled until he had her dress pulled down and away from her, leaving only her thigh-high leggings and moccasins.

With trembling, anxious fingers, he completed disrobing her then stood and dropped his breeches to the floor. Taking one last fast glance at the female body outspread before him, he moaned throatily and lowered himself over her. He wasted no time before seeking entrance below and began thrusting excitedly in and out of her while his hands explored her breasts, pinching and squeezing them. He buried his face into the hollow of her throat as he felt his passion rising, anxious for the explosion that had been kept from him for way too long now.

He grunted and groaned, feeling perspiration beading his brow. But something compelled him to slow his pace, and when he brought his face from her throat, he found her eyes watching him with an icy dark hate in their depths. Lamont swallowed hard, feeling pinpricks of fear climbing his spine. Would he ever be able to release her wrists? Would she not find a knife and stab it into his flesh for having taken advantage of her?

He chose to try another tactic. He would not continue taking her so roughly. He would be gentle. Maybe she would like for him to be gentle. Maybe she needed a man . . . as he needed a woman.

He laced his fingers along her body, smiling to himself when he saw the rippling of her flesh with each fresh caress. He moved slowly inside her now and he began talking quietly and passionately as his lips rained kisses on her brow and then the nipples of each of her breasts.

"I only want to make you feel good," he said thickly, kissing her briefly on the brow. His fingers went to her braids and removed the strings from them and skillfully unbraided her hair until it lay in black rivulets all around her face. "You are beautiful. Did your Indian warriors ever tell you how beautiful you are? What did you say your name . . . was . . . ?"

216

4 BESTSELLING HISTORICAL ROMANCES BY YOUR FAVORITE AUTHORS CAN BE YOURS, FREE!

Kensington Choice, our newest book club now brings you historical romances by your favorite bestselling authors including Janelle Taylo Shannon Drake, Rosanne Bittner, Jo Beverley, and Georgina Gentry, just to name a few! Each book is filled with passion, adventure and th excitement of bygone times!

To introduce you to this great new club which is part of Zebra Home Subscription Service, we'd like to send you your first 4 bestselling historical romances, absolutely free! And once you get these 4 free books to savor at home, we'll rush you the next 4 brand-new books a the lowest prices available, as soon as they are published.

The way the club works is that after your initial FREE shipment, you will get our 4 newest bestselling historical romances delivered to you doorstep each month at the preferred subscriber's rate of only $4.20 per book, a savings of up to $7.16 pe month (since these titles sell in bookstores for $4.99– $5.99)! All books are sent on a 10-day free examination basis and there is no minimum number of books to buy. (And no charge for shipping.) Plus as a regular subscriber, you'll receive our FREE monthly newsletter, *Zebra/Pinnacle Romance News*, which features author profiles, contests, subscriber benefits, book previews and more!

So start today by returning the FREE BOOK CERTIFICATE provided. We'll send you 4 FREE BOOKS with no further obligation: A FREE gift offering you hours of reading pleasure with no obligation...how can you lose?

We have 4 FREE BOOKS for you as your introduction to KENSINGTON CHOICE!
To get your FREE BOOKS, worth up to $23.96, mail the card below.

FREE BOOK CERTIFICATE

Yes! Please send me 4 Kensington Choice (the best of Zebra and Pinnacle Books) Historical Romances without cost or obligation (worth up to $23.96). As a Kensington Choice subscriber, I will then receive 4 brand-new romances to preview each month for 10 days FREE. I can return any books I decide not to keep and owe nothing. The publisher's prices for Kensington Choice romances range from $4.99-$5.99, but as a preferred subscriber I will get these books for only $4.20 per book or $16.80 for all four titles. There is no minimum number of books to buy and I may cancel my subscription at any time, plus there is no additional charge for postage and handling. No matter what I decide to do, my first 4 books are mine to keep, absolutely FREE!

Name _____

Address _____ Apt._____

City_____ State_____ Zip_____

Telephone (____) _____

Signature_____

(If under 18, parent or guardian must sign)

KF0197

Subscription subject to acceptance. Terms and prices subject to change.

AFFIX
STAMP
HERE

KENSINGTON CHOICE
Zebra Home Subscription Service, Inc.
120 Brighton Road
P.O. Box 5214
Clifton, NJ 07015-5214

Foolish Heart didn't answer. She just continued to stare icily back at him. Even when he began his eager thrusts inside her again she refused to close her eyes to his manipulations of her body. She lay there, nonfeeling, as she had learned to do for all men. But when she felt the familiar shudder that accompanied a man's release inside her body she puckered her lips and spat onto his face. . . .

Lamont withdrew from her, gagging. He wiped at his face, puzzled. Why did she have to go and do something so uncivilized as spit on his face? He covered his manhood with his hands and walked briskly away, soon in his breeches again. He turned to her, glowering, then went and covered her body with a blanket.

"You're a heathen," he hissed. "All Indians are heathens."

Lamont watched her for a moment then went to lean down over her, knowing that he had to keep her alive, no matter if she was a savage without feelings. He did have further plans for her. Her body was his answer to his loneliness!

"Hungry?" he asked. When she didn't respond, he forced her face around so their eyes could meet. "I asked you. Are you hungry? I have some grub I could share with you. I made me some good bean soup. Could stick to your ribs, it could."

Foolish Heart's eyes widened. "Grub? Stick to my ribs?" she whispered. "Food stick to my ribs? What does white man mean with his funny words?"

"So you're decidin' it's best to share conversation, huh?" Lamont laughed hoarsely. "You know you'll starve if'n you ignore me, huh?"

"Foolish Heart very hungry," she said, lowering her eyes, hating the fact that to remain alive she would have to humble herself to this white man. She would have to be less stubborn and proud and accept whatever he offered.

217

She was far away from her people now . . . and all alone.

"Then I'll fetch us some grub and maybe get better acquainted while eatin'," Lamont said, lumbering over to where a black kettle hung over the flames of the fire. He reached for two wooden bowls and filled both with steaming hot bean soup and placed them on a table beside the bed. He eyed Foolish Heart's bound wrists. He didn't know if it was safe to untie her. He didn't wish to have to force her again as he would have to do if she looked the least bit as though she was trying to escape.

Thinking on it further, he walked to his dining table and poured some cheap wine into two tin cups. He carried them to the table to place beside the soup, then got two spoons and stood over her, studying her with a furrowed brow.

He held a spoon in her direction. "If'n I was to untie you, how can I be sure you won't run?" he asked forcefully.

Foolish Heart cast a fast glance toward her discarded clothes. "Foolish Heart will not go flying from your wigwam unclothed," she said softly. "Me get too cold in the forest. Me not run."

He lifted a brow. "You would grab them then run," he said hoarsely.

Foolish Heart shook her head back and forth. "Me too tired. Me not run," she said softly. She eyed the bowls of steaming soup. "Me very hungry."

Lamont chuckled a bit, liking the sound of her voice as it surfaced from between her lips. Slowly she was looking less and less Indian to him. "Well, okay," he said, settling down on the bed beside her. He dropped the spoons to the bed and began untying her wrists one at a time, eyeing her quizzically. "Your name. It was chosen because of your temperament? Huh?" he said with another lifted brow.

"Yellow Feather called me that because I do foolish things sometimes," she answered. "You do not like my name?" She rubbed her tender wrists as the topes were eased from them.

"I guess any Indian name is a bit hard to understand," Lamont said, shrugging. As the blanket fell from her bare breasts, he swallowed hard and had to fight back the renewed rising heat in his loins. He offered her the bowl of soup and then the spoon. He cleared his throat nervously, trying to focus his eyes away from the pleasant swell of her breasts and the tips of brown on each.

"Who is this Yellow Feather you speak of?" he asked, rising to scoot a chair beside the bed. He settled down onto it and began eating the soup, slurping it noisily from the spoon.

Foolish Heart leaned over her bowl and ate from it hungrily, ignoring Lamont's further words. She was welcoming the warmth at the pit of her stomach and the pleasant glow it was creating. She ate until the bowl was empty and handed it back to Lamont. "More," she said, pleading with her eyes. "Me still hungry."

Lamont laughed as he took the bowl from her. He placed it on the table and offered her a tin cup of wine. "First you should get some different sort of nourishment into your system," he said. "Drink this. It will be good for your blood."

"Good for my blood?" Foolish Heart said quizzically. "White man, you do have a funny way of speaking." She accepted the tin cup of wine and took a fast swallow, suddenly coughing and spewing it from between her lips as it burned and ate away at the insides of her throat and stomach.

She dropped the tin cup to the bed and placed her hands desperately to her throat, eyes wild. "It burns. It no water. What do you give me to drink?"

"Haven't you ever had wine before?" he laughed.

Then he grew somber. "I guess you ain't. I guess you Indians ain't never had much firewater as I've heard tell you call it." He poured her another cup full. "Here. Drink it. It can make you feel good inside." His eyes sparkled with mischief, knowing what he was again leading up to.

"Me want soup. Not firewater," she said stubbornly, crossing her arms across her chest.

Lamont's face grew red, hating for any part of her breasts to be taken from his sight. "Oh, all right," he grumbled. "If'n it's soup you want, it's soup you'll get. But first, I'd like for you to answer some questions."

"What questions?" she asked, setting her lips firmly together, glowering toward him. "What questions does Foolish Heart have to answer to get more soup?"

Lamont placed his own bowl of soup on the table and leaned closer to her. "You spoke of a Yellow Feather," he said smoothly. "Who *is* this Yellow Feather? Someone from your tribe of Indians?"

"Ay-uh," she said.

Lamont squirmed impatiently on his chair. "And just what does *ay-uh* mean?" he said sharply.

"It means 'yes.' "

"This Yellow Feather and yourself. What tribe of Indians are you from?" he asked, lifting a brow.

"The Ojibway . . . the Chippewa," she said quietly.

Lamont's heart was beginning to thunder, remembering the Indian who had abducted Lorinda. That Indian had to have been Chippewa or Lamont knew that he would not have been left alive. His beautiful head of hair would have been on display in a Sioux camp if it had not been a Chippewa who had come upon them on the trail that night. He was suddenly remembering the flash of the yellow feather that had hung from a coil of the Indian's hair as the Indian had raised the gun to his head. Had this been . . . the . . . same Indian . . . ?

"Why do you call this Indian Yellow Feather?" he asked cautiously, leaning even closer to her, eye to eye.

"Because of his childhood dream . . . his vision. . . ." she said. "His guardian spirit presented him with a yellow feather at that time. It was then that he accepted the name Yellow Feather. He has never since been without the yellow feather."

Lamont's insides rippled with eagerness. "And does this Yellow Feather wear this one feather of his, alone, hanging from a coil of his hair?" he asked, wishing his heart would quit pounding so wildly. But he was filled with thoughts of Lorinda. If he could find this Indian with the yellow feather, might he not also find Lorinda?

"Ay-uh," Foolish Heart said quietly, seeing so much in this white man's eyes. Why did the name Yellow Feather mean so much to him? Why did he speak as though he had seen Yellow Feather? Could this white man somehow be a threat to Yellow Feather? A new wave of fright splashed suddenly through her.

"And where . . . is . . . this Yellow Feather . . . ?" Lamont asked, rising, pacing the floor, toying with his mustache.

"Many days away from this wigwam," she answered, rising slowly, seeing a possible chance to escape while he was so engrossed in his thoughts. She reached for her clothes and raced for the door but was soon stopped when he yanked her back around to face him. She breathed heavily as he glared down into her eyes.

"You must take me to him, Foolish Heart," he said flatly. "I must be taken to this Indian named Yellow Feather."

Foolish Heart felt terribly afraid for Yellow Feather and the St. Croix band of Indians. Though she had fled, disgraced, she felt a deep loyalty to them all. *"Gah-ween,"* she hissed. *"Neen gha-ween ee-shee-chee-gay-un."*

221

Lamont grabbed her wrists and squeezed angrily. "What the hell does that mumbo jumbo mean? Speak in a civilized tongue, do you hear?" he shouted.

"Me no tell you where Yellow Feather is," she said stubbornly. "This is what Foolish Heart say."

"And why not?"

"Because he is next chief-in-line," she said, chin tilted haughtily. "Me no cause trouble for next chief-in-line. White man causes trouble. Me no lead you to him."

Lamont laughed evilly. "You are no longer with the Indians for whatever damn reason and you stay loyal to their cause?" he said. "Why *are* you here and not there? What *is* this Yellow Feather to you?"

Foolish Heart lowered her eyes. "He is . . . was . . . my husband," she said softly.

"But he no longer is, huh?"

"Gah-ween," she said languidly.

Lamont threw his head back, sighing with disgust. "There you go again. What did you mean? Yes or no?"

"Foolish Heart say no," she said.

"Then this Yellow Feather has done you wrong? Has he not? Or else why would you be alone while other squaws are sharing this Yellow Feather's bed?"

Foolish Heart flinched as though she had been hit. Jealousy tore at her insides, knowing this white man spoke the truth, though she did not know how he could be so smart in the ways of Yellow Feather. "I no want to talk about it," she said sullenly.

Lamont jerked her to him and placed his arms about her. "This Yellow Feather? He now has a white woman sharing his bed with him," he said quietly, studying her eyes when his words registered inside her brain. He smiled to himself. He had chosen the right words. Now if she would just believe him.

"You . . . say . . . what . . . ?" Foolish Heart gasped. "No white woman in St. Croix village."

"Maybe not when you were there," Lamont persisted. "But there is now."

"How do white man know? How do you know so much about the Chippewa? About Yellow Feather?"

"Your Yellow Feather abducted my woman from me one night on the trail," he said. "Your Yellow Feather now shares his bed with her. He loves my woman now. Not you. Doesn't that anger you, Foolish Heart?"

Foolish Heart began to struggle as she let out a loud wail. "Let Foolish Heart go," she cried. "I no believe you. There was no white woman at the St. Croix village when I left. She not there now. You lie. You cannot know this thing you say about Yellow Feather."

"Only one way to find out, Foolish Heart," he said, whispering into her ear.

"How . . . ?" she said, struggling again. She did not wish to fall into any white man's trap. She hated him. She wanted to kill him. He spoke shamefully of her people . . . of her love, Yellow Feather.

"You must lead me to them," he said firmly.

"No. Me not do this thing you ask of me," she moaned. "Leave Foolish Heart alone. Let me go. Let me leave your wigwam."

Lamont lifted her into his arms and kissed her roughly on the lips as a hand traveled over her flesh. "I cannot do that," he said thickly. "I need you for more than one reason. You need me also."

"Foolish Heart need no one," she screamed, struggling with each added flick of his tongue as he now leaned over her breasts. "Foolish Heart want to leave."

Lamont chuckled as he carried her to the bed and placed her on it. "All right. So I let you leave," he said removing his breeches. "Where would you go? Huh? Do you know that this village of Duluth mostly houses men? Do you know they are hungry for women? Do you know that if I let you go, you will be taken by many men at once? The white man is insatiable for a woman's body especially when he's been without one for as long as most of these man have been. Do you still wish to leave me? To have many men abuse your body? Most men do not respect an Indian squaw as I do you."

"I do not believe what you say," Foolish Heart wailed. She stiffened her body as Lamont stretched out atop her and consumed her flesh with his lips. She flung her head back and forth, fitfully moaning. "Leave me alone. I hate you," she further wailed.

Lamont chuckled. "You *will* lead me to the Indian village," he said. "Or I will turn you loose to the white men in the town of Duluth. Do you want them or me? Huh?"

Foolish Heart sobbed as she pushed at his chest. "Me no want you or the other white men," she sobbed.

He lifted his fingers to her hair and brushed it from around her eyes. "But you have no choice," he said. "You are my prisoner and you will do as I tell you. We will leave tomorrow. We will travel by horseback, you and I. You'll lead me to my Lorinda. . . ."

He gazed with lust into Foolish Heart's dark eyes, wondering what her fate would be upon arriving at the Indian village. But he would not think about that now. He would enjoy her. His days of being without a woman were behind him. Soon the woman in this bed would be none other than his Lorinda . . . his beautiful Lorinda.

Fourteen

The sky was black, void of moon and stars, and the wind whispered through the trees in the forest. Many fires glowed orange inside and outside the wigwams throughout Yellow Feather's new village, yet everybody was asleep, tired from their long journey and their laborings since their arrival in this new land of beauty and promise.

One person in the village was not asleep. Lorinda. The fire warmed her face as she sat cross-legged outside the closed entrance flap. She felt a hammering of her heart, envisioning Yellow Feather inside this newly erected wigwam, embracing his pregnant Indian wife.

Flipping the long, red streamers of her hair around her shoulders, she forced herself to not stare toward the wigwam. She had told Yellow Feather that she would *not* share his wigwam with another woman, and she had meant it!

"But I should have known he'd be as stubborn as me," she whispered to the waving flames of the fire. He had stood as she had, with arms crossed over his chest and chin lifted stubbornly into the air when she had told him she would sleep outside in the cold before sleeping with him and Happy Flower. She now waited for him to come outside to her, to tell her he was sorry.

"But his stubborn Indian pride continues to get in his way," Lorinda sighed.

Pushing herself up from the ground, she began pacing. She pulled at the men's clothing, despising the breeches and sloppy shirt. Oh, how she hated the coarseness of them against her flesh!

Spinning around, she gazed toward the cave's entrance. She was remembering the dress she had worn and the lace of the undergarments. She was remembering how Yellow Feather had looked at her and the passion the dark of his eyes had shown.

"I must go to the cave and change from these ugly things," she whispered. But a shudder rippling through her caused her to remember something else. She could remember pulling the trigger; she could remember the sound as the bullet had found its target.

She closed her eyes and placed her hands to her throat. Would she ever be able to put it all from her mind?

Then her eyes flew wide open, remembering even more. "Though I shot him, he is gone," she murmured softly, once more peering through the darkness, seeing how quiet and dark the cave's entrance was. She set her jaw firmly. Fancy clothing suddenly did not mean as much to her as finding out how that man could have disappeared from the cave after having been shot.

Her eyes frantically searched the ground around her. Before nightfall, Yellow Feather had busied himself making a torch out of a piece of tightly twisted birch bark. Pitch gum from an evergreen tree had been used for making the pitch on the end. He had even shown her how to use it, how it would burn low and bright by lowering and shaking the torch a little before holding it erect.

Seeing it now, Lorinda grabbed the torch and touched its tip to a hot coal. Watching the flames slowly take hold, she inched away from the wigwam. She couldn't stop the trembling in her fingers or her knees. Yet the cold splash of the dew-damp air against her face caused her to hurry her pace. When she reached the cave's entrance she stopped abruptly, remembering all that she had experienced inside this cave. There had been much more than the shooting. There had been Yellow Feather's sweet embraces . . . Yellow Feather's . . .

She shook her head angrily, not wanting to think of Yellow Feather. This night he had once again chosen his squaw over her. "I even think I hate him," she fumed.

A strong determination sent Lorinda on inside the foreboding dark spaces of the cave. Again she shuddered, seeing how mysteriously the torch cast shadows all about her. The crunching of the rock beneath her feet echoed hollowly against the cave's damp walls, and the familiar, strong aroma of mildew burned at her nostrils. But she moved onward, clutching so hard to the torch that her fingers ached, sighing with relief when the cold gray ash in the firespace at her feet told her that she had arrived at her destination.

Lowering the torch, she began to search the cave's floor where she had left Silas Konrad lying there in a pool of his own blood. Falling to her hands and knees, she searched even more closely, gasping when she finally spotted the color of crimson on some loose gravel scattered about.

"It is his blood," she whispered, feeling a bit sick inside. "But where is *he?* Where could he have gone . . . ?"

She rose from her knees and backed away from the blood-covered gravel, then fell backwards against something, landing with a thud atop some piled books. The torch lay sputtering at her feet. She reached for it but stopped when she discovered something that her fall had uncovered. The pearl handle of a gun was reflecting white from its grave beneath the scattering of books.

"A . . . pistol . . ." Lorinda whispered. "A pearl-handled pistol . . ."

Clearing the books away, she reached for the gun and once she held it in the palm of her hand, studied it. It was the type carried by women in their purses. It was small enough for Lorinda to even carry inside a pants pocket!

Couldn't it protect her? Did she truly feel so safe, surrounded by so many Indians day and night? Yes, she trusted Yellow Feather, possibly even Happy Flower, but could she trust Flying Squirrel and others like him who had watched her with cool glints in their dark, fathomless eyes?

"Yes, the gun will be my protector," she whispered. "I won't change into a dress after all. A dress has no pockets to hide a pistol in."

She opened the chamber of the gun and smiled almost wickedly when she counted six bullets still in place. Then as she flipped the chamber shut, a faint, familiar aroma rippled upward from the gun's handle. Lorinda sniffed, over and over again, lifting the gun to her nose.

"It smells of my Aunt Rettie," she whispered. "It does! It smells of lily of the valley cologne!"

A sound of crushing rock drew Lorinda quickly to her feet and away from her thoughts of cologne. She glanced quickly toward the cave's entrance, then down at the pistol she still held in her hand. If the person approaching was Yellow Feather in search of her, she couldn't let him see her standing with the gun in her hand. He would most surely take it away from her. With speed, she dropped the gun down inside her right front pants pocket and pulled her shirttail down over it to hide the bulge, though it was small.

With an anxious heartbeat, Lorinda stood watching, wishing now that she had rescued the sputtering torch from the cave's floor. From where it lay, it wasn't giving out enough light. Lorinda tensed inside, knowing that anyone could be approaching her. Yellow Feather wasn't the only Indian . . .

"You . . ." she gasped noisily, placing her hands to her throat. She watched as Flying Squirrel moved stealthily toward her. The copper skin of his bare chest shone like gold in the soft rays of the torch and his eyes bore

228

down upon her like two dark coals. She took a step backward, forgetting the books and once more lost her footing. Feeling foolish, she caught her fall with a hand and pushed herself back up to a standing position to face him squarely and stubbornly. Her right hand slowly crept to the bulge in her pocket. Yes, she liked the feel of the gun there.

"Flying Squirrel, what are you doing here?" she asked hotly. She let her gaze travel over him, seeing that he was no larger than she. He couldn't be a threat! She wouldn't let him be!

"Red Blossom has been sent from Chief Yellow Feather's wigwam?" Flying Squirrel said mockingly, lifting his lips in a crooked smile. "Has my chief become suddenly *nee-bwah-kah* in the ways of women and sees that the red-colored skin is even more beautiful than the white?"

Lorinda was learning more of the Indian's language as each day passed and knew that Flying Squirrel had just used the word "wise," but not in a flattering way when speaking about his chief. It was as though Flying Squirrel mocked his chief. Had Yellow Feather put too much faith in Flying Squirrel as a friend? Lorinda was beginning to believe so. *"Gah-ween,"* she snapped back at him. "I was *not* sent from Yellow Feather's wigwam. I left because *I* desired to leave. I am not ordered around by anyone."

Flying Squirrel's hands doubled into fists at his side. "White woman, I do not like hearing you speak any of our Indian words," he growled. "You are white. You must not play act at being Indian."

"I would never *want* to be Indian," Lorinda fumed. "I am proud of my white heritage."

Flying Squirrel took a step toward her. "Why white woman stay with Indians if so proud of white way of life?" he grumbled. "Why not go back to your people?

229

Flying Squirrel even get horse for you. You go back to your white village."

Lorinda's heart began to pound. Here was her chance! If she asked, surely Flying Squirrel would even guide her back to St. Paul. Surely he knew every tree and flower in the forest. Wouldn't he know as well where the white man's roads now ran like snakes beneath the trees? She eyed him warily. "But, Flying Squirrel, what . . . ?" she began but was stopped when Yellow Feather was suddenly there, glaring suspiciously from Lorinda back to Flying Squirrel.

"What do my best friend and wife do when Yellow Feather's back is turned?" he accused, crossing his arms angrily across his chest.

Lorinda suspected that Flying Squirrel would be sternly dealt with if he were guilty of what Yellow Feather was accusing him. A wife . . . and a best friend? In the American culture, such things were sometimes dealt with with guns. It could be even worse with an Indian's way of punishment, especially if a chief had been wronged. Lorinda couldn't let anything happed to Flying Squirrel. Hadn't he offered to bring her a horse . . . ?

"It's not what it appears," Lorinda said, reaching to smooth a forefinger over the smoothness of Yellow Feather's cheek.

Yellow Feather knocked her hand away. "My eyes tell me one thing," he said. "Your words say another?"

Lorinda tensed inside, remembering his stubbornness. "He only came to see if I was all right," she tried to reassure. When she glanced toward Flying Squirrel she could see the usual cool glint in his eyes and a slight lift to his lips and hated defending him. She had never liked him, and she trusted him even less! She suddenly felt foolish defending someone who was truly an enemy to her! Yellow Feather swung around and glared down at Flying Squirrel. He clutched at his shoulders. "Flying Squirrel, you speak for yourself," he ordered.

Flying Squirrel's eyes wavered. "I saw Red Blossom come into cave," he said thickly. "She no belong in sacred cave. Flying Squirrel came to tell her to leave."

Yellow Feather stepped away from Flying Squirrel, then looked from Flying Squirrel to Lorinda. "I have heard two different stories here," he said flatly. His gaze settled on Flying Squirrel. "As for you, Flying Squirrel, you leave the cave," he added. "I will forget you were here alone with my woman. You are my best friend and I have to believe my trust in you is wise."

Flying Squirrel mumbled something in Indian as he scurried away, leaving Lorinda and Yellow Feather standing staring at one another.

Yellow Feather broke the silence. "Why did you come to the cave in the dark of night?" he asked, glancing down at the torch and its lingering sparks of flame. He grabbed Lorinda's wrists. "Why do you choose this cave over Yellow Feather's wigwam?"

Lorinda squirmed, struggling with her wrists, only causing them to burn and become raw. "You're hurting me," she whispered.

"You ignore my question?" he said angrily.

Lorinda flinched as his grip strengthened. "Yellow Feather . . ." she said, pleading with her eyes.

He released her quickly, then stepped back away from her. He reached and lifted her hair from her shoulders. "No man is allowed to touch you," he said thickly. "You are mine. Nobody else's."

A simmering passion began to rise in Lorinda as Yellow Feather's fingers went to her face and began a slow tracing of her features. "Don't you know I could never let Flying Squirrel or any other man touch me?" she purred. "Yellow Feather, how *could* you think I was in this cave with Flying Squirrel except for innocent reasons?"

231

"Then Flying Squirrel and you . . . ?"

As his hands began to travel over her body, Lorinda tensed. She was remembering the gun in her pocket. What if he felt it?

"There's only you." she whispered, stepping back. She began to unbutton her blouse, knowing that it had to be her, not Yellow Feather, who would take her clothes from her body, for she could not let him find the gun . . . the gun that she now felt was her only real assurances of safety in this faraway place.

Yellow Feather's gaze raked over her nudity as she stepped clear of everything, then he drew her gently into his arms. His lips blended into hers as the silk of her flesh sent flames burning through his heart. It had been easy to leave Happy Flower, to go to his Red Blossom. He had planned to guide Red Blossom to the romantic shore of the St. Croix River, but since he had found her not by his wigwam but instead in his sacred cave, ah, it was even more perfect. As she laced her arms about his neck and fitted her body into his, his worries of Flying Squirrel were now like puffy clouds breaking away in the blue skies of spring.

"The blankets. They are still spread by the firespace," Lorinda whispered as his lips moved to the hollow of her throat. Sweet threads of pleasure wove in and out of her heart as he lifted her into his arms. Suddenly the cave was once more their lovers' hideaway. Once more she was forgetting all else but the man she loved. She could even forget the haunting beauty of Happy Flower . . .

When Yellow Feather stretched Lorinda atop the bed of blankets she welcomed the warm caress from his lips as he began worshipping her flesh as only he knew how. Her heart thundered against her ribs as his tongue flicked over her, leaving no pleasure spot untouched. Then, when he stepped from his leggings and loin cloth and leaned himself down into her, Lorinda closed her eyes and sighed.

She arched her hips and met his every thrust. She welcomed his fingers twining through her hair to guide her face to his, welcoming even more his fiery, passionate kisses that sent her senses to slowly reeling. The sensuousness of the moment caused her pulse to increase and her eyes to close. When his thrusts became more eager and his lips more demanding, Lorinda smiled to herself, now welcoming the beginning of the quiverings of his body against hers.

As she became aware of the splash of different colors inside her brain from her own desire being spent, she felt the sweet seeds of his pleasure being planted inside her. But then it was over much too quickly, and they both were returned to the present, . . . to white woman and red man . . . two separate people . . . not one as they only moments ago had felt themselves to be.

Yellow Feather leaned over her and framed her face between his hands. "Now you will come back to the wigwam with me?" he said softly. "Wasn't this the reason you wouldn't share the wigwam with me and Happy Flower? Because you wouldn't want to make love to me in front of Happy Flower?"

Lorinda closed her eyes. It had been so simple to put Happy Flower from her mind while she was in his arms, but now her reality was there again in his words. *"Gahween,"* she whispered, trying to shake her face free from his hands. "No, Yellow Feather, that isn't the full reason."

"But . . ."

Lorinda opened her eyes in a flash of anger. "Yellow Feather, you just don't understand," she said hotly. "You just *won't try* to understand. I don't . . . I won't . . . share you with another woman. I just won't."

She once more closed her eyes. She bit her lower lip, realizing what she had just said and the stupidity of it. She *was* sharing him with another woman, wasn't she? She now wondered if he had made love with Happy Flower before leaving her alone in the wigwam. The thought of it tore at Lorinda's heart.

Yellow Feather jumped to his feet and began to dress himself. "You are stubborn white woman," he shouted. "I go. You stay. You keep cold in cave. Yellow Feather will *not* argue with you."

Lorinda leaned up on an elbow, watching him with a breaking heart. She was used to his ordering everyone around and now it seemed that he didn't care enough about her to at least *try* to order *her* around. She watched with trembling lips as he moved in quick, proud steps away from her and disappeared from the cave. He had left her lying alone with only the dim flickerings of the torch as her companion.

She moved to her feet, anger now moving in splashes throughout her. "Oh, I'll never understand him," she argued to herself as she quickly dressed. "First he loves me then . . . oh . . . who even knows?".

Once her shirt was buttoned and the rope secure in her breeches around her waist, she checked to see for sure that the gun hadn't dropped from the pocket while she had undressed in such haste.

"It is still there," she murmured to herself. "At least I have that for protection. It seems Yellow Feather could care less about me any longer."

Pouting a bit, she lifted the torch from the floor and began making her way from the cave. The silence that surrounded her was unnerving. Every step on the crunchiness of rock beneath her feet made her breath stop, as she checked to see if there were any added footsteps behind or in front of her. She still didn't think she should trust Flying Squirrel. He was sneaky! She knew that now!

She moved onward and finally reached the cave's entrance, stopping to glance around on all sides of her before stepping out into the open. Once she saw that nothing moved, she inched her way outside and decided to go stand beside the river instead of going to lie beside the wigwam where she could not touch or embrace the man she loved. But she would not change her mind.

The rippling of the water was dull this night, without the pleasant shine from the moon to settle into it. The water was as black as the night and even moreso, it seemed, as Lorinda made her way toward it. Not only was the night black but it was quiet! Had Yellow Feather led his people to a place of silence? Where were the night sounds of the forest? Where was the haunting cry of a loon?

Lorinda crept to the river's edge and sat down next to it, draping a hand into the water. She ran it back and forth, loving the soft satin of it against her flesh, then jumped with a start when Flying Squirrel suddenly crouched down beside her.

She flashed an angry look in his direction, frowning darkly. "You again?" she snapped. "Flying squirrel you do have a way of sneaking up on a body. Now I know why all the night sounds were silent around me. Because you have been hiding in the brush, watching me."

"I've brought you a horse," he said, glancing cautiously about him. "I waited until I knew Yellow Feather was in his wigwam for the last time tonight. I wouldn't want him to know I am doing this thing for you."

Lorinda laughed sarcastically. "For me?" she said. "You do this thing for me? Flying Squirrel, you know who you do this for, and it most certainly isn't for *me*."

Flying Squirrel pushed himself up angrily. "Take. The horse is yours. Go. Why take time to argue with Flying Squirrel?" he said in a low hiss.

"And when I get into the forest? What then?" Lorinda asked quietly, rising, talking into his face. "Will you then come with bow and arrow and slay me? Will you

235

scalp me? I have seen you looking at my hair!''

"I will even guide your way to safety if that is what white woman wishes,'' Flying Squirrel said. "Flying Squirrel is trustworthy. You know I do not take scalps. You only talk in anger because Yellow Feather found us together in the cave. You are afraid he no trust you as much as he did before.''

Lorinda sighed exasperatedly. "Flying Squirrel, will you just go? Leave me alone?'' she said. "I did at first think you could be the one to help me escape when you made the offer in the cave. But now I am thinking better of it. Now I think you are *not* to be trusted. You are too eager to have me leave. Your hate for me is too great to truly help me find my way back to my people.''

She whirled on her heel and faced the river, feeling tears wetting her cheeks. "Please, Flying Squirrel. Just leave me be. I've so much burden on my heart at this moment.''

Flying Squirrel grumbled in his Indian language and walked away from her. Lorinda settled down on the grass once more, trembling when a brush of air stroked her flesh with its icy bristles. Soon the snows would be settling their shrouds of white around them. Soon no one would be able to venture far from their houses . . . or wigwams.

Lorinda's thoughts went to her aunt . . . wondering about her . . . what she might be thinking at this very moment. Was she sad? Was she lonesome?

Something grabbed at Lorinda's heart. She suddenly remembered the small gun . . . and the aroma that it had seemed to be awash with. She pulled it from her pocket and slowly lifted it to her nose, inhaling. She suddenly felt, oh, so homesick when the fragrance of lily of the valley set her senses to remembering the many hugs from her aunt and how this very aroma had clung to her own clothes for so many hours afterwards.

Lorinda then placed the gun before her eyes, wondering who had worn the same fragrance as her aunt. Had she been a tiny person to match the smallness of the gun? The only type of firearm she could remember her aunt's sporting had been the large bulkiness of a shotgun.

Laughing, Lorinda thought the shotgun a good match for her aunt and her gruffness. Though this gun carried the sweet aroma her aunt had always worn, its personality surely was not that of her aunt. No. Her aunt would have never have been the owner of such a dainty pistol as this one Lorinda held in the palm of her hand.

"But dainty or not, this gun can snuff the life from a body," Lorinda said, curling her nose at the thought. She put it quickly from her sight, hoping to never have to use it.

She sniffed her hands, smelling the lingering aroma of cologne. She rose and went to her arranged bed of blankets next to the wigwam where her love slept away from her and fell into a fitful sleep with dreams pulling her first from her aunt's embrace . . . then from Yellow Feather's . . .

Fifteen

The dewy fresh air drifting in from the river and the aroma of wood fires burning and rice drying had given a contented sense of well-being to Yellow Feather's people. Two days had passed since the first day of the wild rice harvest, and two nights had passed as well, but Lorinda had yet to sleep in the wigwam with Yellow Feather and Happy Flower. Instead, she had stubbornly continued to huddle just outside the entrance flap, while Yellow Feather had just as stubbornly let her.

The outdoor fire had warmed her through the nights but her heart now ached as though it had been packed in ice. She felt that she belonged to no way of life . . . white or Indian. She stared into the fire, then all around her at all the other fires outside each wigwam's closed flaps. Against the black of the forest and the night she could see occasional movement and could hear the low, merry chatter of the Indian families as they shared an evening of peace and happiness inside the close confines of their wigwams.

Pulling the collar of her jacket up around her neck, Lorinda sighed discontentedly. She somehow felt detached from this night, as though she was an observer, outside her own self, watching . . . not doing. Tears shimmered on her lashes, now suddenly aware again of where she was, feeling the aloneness as she heard soft murmurings being exchanged inside this wigwam she had chosen not to be a part of. She wiped her eyes, hating it when the sweet voice of Happy Flower replied to something that Yellow Feather said to her. A muffled female's giggle tore Lorinda's heart to shreds. She rose from the ground and moved swiftly away to the riverbank, where she once more shared the night with the moon and its full reflection that rippled and sparkled back at her, as though smiling.

"Oh!" she said aloud, crossing her arms angrily across her chest. "Everyone is laughing except myself. It isn't fair. What have I done to deserve these things that continue to happen to me?"

"What have you done?" Yellow Feather spoke suddenly from behind her. "Do you ask yourself such a foolish question as that, Red Blossom?"

Lorinda swung around, still remembering the giggles of only moments earlier. Hadn't Happy Flower's teasings been enough for Yellow Feather this night? Lorinda's heart raced as she gazed upward into his eyes. Though they remained flat and expressionless she could sense that he looked back at her with the same rapid heartbeat as she had felt so often as her cheek had rested against his chest. There were many feelings between them. She knew this. But another woman . . . an unborn child . . . continued to stand in the way.

"Yellow Feather, I thought you were still with Happy Flower," she snapped, then placed her back to him, to stare once more into the river. Yellow Feather's reflection shone back at her in the moon's glow in the water as he stepped to her side. "I tell you why your life is now unsettled," Yellow Feather said. "It is because you act as a child . . . not as a wife."

Lorinda sighed exasperately. She turned to Yellow Feather with her hands doubled into fists at her side. "I am *not* acting like a child," she stormed. "And I am *not* a wife."

Her hands relaxed and her gaze lowered. "Anyway, why is how I act any concern of yours?" she asked.

"You *do* have a wife. An Indian wife."

Yellow Feather drew Lorinda around and clasped her shoulders, holding her at arm's length. "In my eyes and in all my people's eyes you are also Chief Yellow Feather's wife," he said firmly. "You must act as wife. Chief Yellow Feather demands it."

Lorinda gasped. Now he chose to confront her with his demands where before he had appeared to care less *what* she did! "You demand?" she said softly. Then her voice rose higher. "You demand?" she shrieked. "Just because you now have the title of chief, you demand me to do this or that? *I will not.* But I'll tell you what I *am* going to do. Tomorrow as the early morning sun rises, I am going to mount my aunt's black stallion and find my way back to St. Paul. I think I'd rather take my chances there than here. No one will know that it was I who shot Silas Konrad."

"You will not take the horse and leave." Yellow Feather fumed. "And even if you did, you would find that you have been worrying needlessly about the death of Silas Konrad. I'm sure he lives. I'm sure it will be he who will guide many white people to this sacred place. But I am ready. I will become a warring chief of the St. Croix if the white man comes with the papers from the place called Washington. And, Red Blossom, I will also show you my determination to keep what is mine if you try to leave."

"Yellow Feather, why do you argue now when you stubbornly refused to these past nights I wouldn't share the wigwam with you and Happy Flower?"

"As new chief of the St. Croix, much is always on my mind," he said flatly. "But now, only Red Blossom is heavy on my mind. You are a big part of my life. Must I always be reminding you of this?"

Lorinda squirmed her way free and bit her lower lip nervously. She stooped and plucked a flower, then tossed it into the river to watch it move slowly away, resembling her heart . . . a heart so fatigued from her endless battles of love and desire for this Indian. "I am not truly a part of your life, Yellow Feather," she murmured. "You have your people. I have mine. I could never be a part of your way of life. I see how your people look at me. It's as though I am not even there. They do not like me, Yellow Feather. They do *not* accept me as your wife."

"If they do not show respect for you as you think they should it is only because you have shown dishonor to their chief by refusing to share my wigwam and bed of blankets," he said. "They have accepted you, a white woman, into the village. They trust me, their chief, and anything I choose to do is accepted. Have I not led them to this land of plenty? They look to you as one blessed by the spirits because they believe you are the only white person to have set foot on this new land of ours. They do not know of Silas Konrad, except for his occasional snooping in our other village where my father now peacefully sleeps. They do not know that he is now a threat to this place that my spiritual guardian, the mighty owl of the forest has so graciously led us all to. But it is my duty as a chief to keep this threat from them, as it is your duty to now behave as my wife."

In one quick movement, Yellow Feather swept Lorinda up into his arms. *"Mah-bee-szhon,"* he said thickly. "I will once again not only take from you, but also give. We will share as man and wife as we have done before. You said you loved me. Do you forget? Does Red Blossom forget how to love?"

"No. I do not forget how to love," she said, struggling as his footsteps carried them away from the river, toward the village. "But I told you before. I thought you understood. I can *not* make love to you while Happy Flower lies heavy with child in the same wigwam." She began hitting his chest with doubled fists. "I won't. I won't," she argued. "Put me down. Let me go. You will not force me to go into that wigwam with you. I don't care if you *are* the chief."

"Bee-sahn," he said, lifting a hand over her mouth, holding it there. "Do you want the whole village to hear you? Do you want them to step from their wigwams and see you still dishonoring their chief?"

Lorinda's eyes widened as he kept her lips sealed with his hand, and she felt defeated as his other hand held her wrists together against her chest. The cool night air lifted her hair as Yellow Feather began a slow trot. When he turned from the circle of wigwams in the village to instead move into the forest, Lorinda watched in confusion as he stepped high and low over brush until an isolated wigwam appeared in a small clearing ahead. Its approach was lighted by a torch attached to a pole next to the wigwam's open flap.

Lorinda eyed Yellow Feather quizzically then glanced back toward the wigwam, now able to see a soft orange glow inside where she knew that a fire in the firespace had already been lighted. She exhaled heavily as Yellow Feather removed his hand from her mouth. "I don't understand," she whispered. "Whose . . . ?"

"It is for you, my stubborn child bride," Yellow Feather replied, bending to kiss her tenderly on the lips. "It is only one gift of the many I will give you to make you a happy wife."

Lorinda twined an arm about his neck and snuggled her cheek next to his chest. She signed leisurely. "Oh, Yellow Feather, I should have known," she said. "I knew you wouldn't let me sleep forever by your wigwam door. I knew you couldn't want to make love to me while another watched."

"This makes you happy?"

"Ay-uh," she murmured. "But I still will have to leave you. No matter what gifts you rain upon me, I still

243

must leave you."

"Do not speak of that to me," he grumbled. "You stay." He bent his back and carried Lorinda on inside the wigwam. She looked around in amazement. Though it was such close quarters, this one room, lined with layers of bulrush mats against the round outer wall, was better than what her mother had lived in after having reached the Minnesota territory. Even the lack of furniture didn't matter. This one room only spoke of comfort and convenience, with many deerskins and colorful blankets rolled up neatly at the sides of the wigwam, and a heavy layer of thick bulrush mats covering the cold, packed earth. A hand drum hung on the wall and strips of meat and little bundles of aromatic herbs and roots dangled from a pole over the fire.

"I will bring you some white man's gifts from the cave tomorrow," Yellow Feather said as he eased her to the floor. "This is now our home, Red Blossom, one we will share alone as man and wife."

Lorinda swung around, eyes wide. "Ours?" she murmured. "Alone?"

"*Ay-uh* . . ."

"But what about Happy Flower . . . ?"

"Before long it will be almost time for our child to seek entrance into this world," Yellow Feather said. "A woman must be left alone at this time. She does not need a man to share her bed of blankets now. Only the child is on her mind."

Lorinda circled her fists to her side as jealous anger seethed inside her. "So that is the reason you've chosen to make *me* feel special," she fumed. "Only because Happy Flower has turned you from her bed. And is that the reason for her laughter of only moments ago? Because she knew that you would only give me your fullest attention because she no longer needed it? Was she making fun of me, Yellow Feather? Was she?"

Yellow Feather grabbed Lorinda's wrists and pulled her hands to his chest. *"Gah-ween,"* he said flatly. "She is only happy because the baby kicks and flutters so inside her womb. Red Blossom, I offer you this wigwam alone with me because I want to make you happy. But you can only fill my dwelling with sunshine and sweetness after your jealousies and doubts are pushed from your mind."

Lorinda's heart raced inside her, once again feeling this strange magic that she and Yellow Feather shared when together. She ached to say that she would, *ay-uh,* share his dwelling with him, knowing how much she loved him, that it was, indeed, an honor to have been singled out by him, after having seen the way his people showed such pride and trust in this young chief and his wise ways.

But the evenings alone beside the fire had given Lorinda much time to think, and she knew the proper thing for her to do was to return to St. Paul, to see if anything was being done about her sister's abduction. Lorinda had very cleverly checked the St. Croix Chippewa's households and had found no white baby among them.

She gazed with longing into his eyes. "Yellow Feather, there's something about myself that I've never shared with you," she said softly. "Now is the time. Then you will understand why I must leave you. You won't even be compelled to force me to stay once you hear what I have to say."

His jaw tightened and his eyes seemed to grow darker as he spoke with even more forcefulness. "Nothing you say will cause my heart to turn away from you. *Gah-ween-geh-goo.*"

Lorinda lifted a hand to his cheek and stroked it. "You always speak so lovingly of babies," she said. "This makes me believe that what I have to tell you will cause you to possibly even lead me back to my people, where hopefully news of a baby awaits me."

Yellow Feather's brow furrowed. "News of a *ah-bee-no-gee?* What baby?" he said thickly as his glance moved quickly over her. When it stopped at her abdomen, Lorinda's eyes widened in green sparkles. A slow smile surfaced as she saw the look of confusion etched across his face.

"No. I am not with child," she laughed. "That is not the baby I was speaking of."

Yellow Feather's eyes softened as he knelt down before the fire. He now remembered having been the first with her and felt a bit foolish. "What baby do you speak of, then?" he grumbled. He stirred the orange embers with a stick, causing smoke to rise and flames to rekindle.

Lorinda positioned herself onto a thickly rolled bulrush mat next to Yellow Feather. She trembled a bit, realizing she had not spoken to anyone of Amanda's abduction since that day with Lamont Quinby. It had been easier on her to not speak of it. Now, to do so, would be reliving that tragic day all over again. She had done this many times in her fitful dreams, but speaking it aloud would be as though she was there once more . . . seeing the bodies . . . the empty cradle's ruins . . .

Lorinda pulled her heavy riding boots from her feet and curled her toes next to the fire. She glanced sideways at Yellow Feather and saw the intensity in the way he continued to look at her. It was as always before. It was as though his dark, imploring eyes could reach into her soul and read her every thought and deep desires and needs. Oh, how it did unnerve her!

She turned her eyes from him and cleared her throat nervously. "The baby I speak of is my five-month-old baby sister," she said softly.

"What about your sister . . . ?"

Lorinda's eyelids grew heavy. She turned her eyes

back to Yellow Feather, near to tears. "I told you of my parents' death" she murmured.

"*Ay-uh*"

Lorinda swallowed hard and lowered her lashes. "It was on the same day," she said. "My sister was surely abducted by the same Indians who killed my mother and father . . ."

Yellow Feather felt a thundering of his heart. He knew that the Sioux had done this many times before. Had they done it again? "And why do you think this?" he asked solemnly.

"Because my baby sister's crib was empty and also the blanket my mother always wrapped about her," Lorinda said in a near whisper. "The blanket that I carry with me . . . to have a part of my sister with me, even though . . . she may now . . . be dead . . ."

Yellow Feather remembered the blanket. He had wondered about its value since it was not large enough to give much warmth. But now he knew that it had helped to warm Lorinda's heart, if not her flesh. He understood. *Ay-uh,* he understood. "It is the Nadoeus-Sioux, our snakelike enemy," he said angrily, rising. "It has to be the Sioux."

Lorinda rose and touched him softly on the face. "I at first thought it might be someone of *your* village of Indians who was guilty," she said. "But I have looked. I have let my eyes scan your village and the cradle boards your women carry. I have seen how wrong I was to think such a thing of your people."

Yellow Feather felt anger rise hotly inside him. He knocked Lorinda's hand away, glowering down at her. "You thought my people guilty of kidnapping a baby?" he grumbled.

Lorinda lowered her eyes. "You kidnapped me . . . why not . . . a baby . . . ?" she murmured.

Yellow Feather settled onto his haunches before the

fire again. "I thought I had rescued you from the evil white man," he said thickly.

Lorinda fell to her knees beside him. "Yellow Feather, you forced me to go with you," she said. "That is called . . . kidnapping . . ."

"I didn't harm you . . ."

"No. You did not. Instead you . . ."

Yellow Feather turned to her and placed his hands to her waist. As he rose to his feet, he urged her upward then drew her into his arms. "My Red Blossom," he said hoarsely. "Instead . . . I made gentle love to you . . . you showed me how a woman can love back."

He framed her face with his hands. His eyes lost their stare of stone as he gazed into hers. "My Red Blossom, I love you, oh, how I love you." His lips met hers in a quiet, soft passion as his fingers weaved through her hair.

Lorinda melted into his embrace, consumed with fiery heartbeats. She had seen the veil lift from before his eyes and knew that in a sense she had become victorious. He had never before let emotion show in his eyes. His brown, smoldering eyes no longer remained flat and untouched. His eyes and his touch spoke to her of his deep love for her. And her body responding in such a wild way spoke to her of *her* love for *him* —but she still had to leave him. She only hoped that she hadn't lingered too long with this Indian. She withdrew from him, trembling.

"Red Blossom, why . . . ?" he asked, still reaching for her.

She rubbed her hands together over the fire. "My sister Amanda," she murmured. "I can't wait any longer. I must try and find her."

Yellow Feather placed his hands to her shoulders and swung her quickly around. "Yellow Feather will help you," he said determinedly. "You will not have to do this thing alone."

Lorinda's heart raced and her eyes widened. "But how

can you?'' she whispered.

"If it was the Sioux who took your sister my brave warriors will get her back for you."

"But, Yellow Feather, I do not know for sure if the Sioux took her. She may possibly have already been rescued. She may already be with my aunt."

"If the Sioux took your sister, they still have her," he said. "They are skillful warriors. The white man would not enter a Sioux camp without much bloodshed. Unless the white man *knows* the Sioux are responsible for the baby's abduction, the white man wouldn't risk beginning a war with the Sioux. The Sioux are not like the Chippewa. They wait to fight the white man. They welcome the fight. My father *ran* from the fight. But *only* with the white man. He welcomed the fight with the Sioux . . .*any*time. I also welcome the fight with the Nadoues-Sioux. I will send a scouting party to first see if a white baby is in the neighboring Sioux camp, then we will make our move."

"You will do this for me?" Lorinda whispered, reaching to touch the softness of his lips.

"I do it also for my people. My warriors have had to go without the fight long enough. They thirst for a battle with our enemy the Sioux. Now we may have a reason."

"You . . . want . . . to fight . . . ?" Lorinda gasped. "Just to be fighting . . . ?"

"It is in our blood to hunger for the fight," he said flatly. "As it is in our blood to hunger for our woman." He drew Lorinda quickly into his arms and sought her mouth with a reckless passion. His hands drew her closer, fitting the curve of her body silkily into his.

Forgetting all else, Lorinda laced her arms about his neck, moaning with ecstasy. She was filled with a consuming need for him. She knew that once more she would be surrendering herself to him . . . fully. She trembled disappointedly as he released his hold on her.

249

"The man's clothing," he said. "It is so ugly. Tomorrow we will give you woman's clothes to wear."

"The dresses from the cave?" she asked, visibly shuddering.

"No," he answered. "Not the dresses from the cave."

"Then which dresses?" she murmured.

"You will not wear white woman's clothes while you are the wife of Yellow Feather," he said. "You will wear Indian clothes."

"But, Yellow Feather . . ."

Yellow Feather began unbuttoning Lorinda's shirt. "No more talk," he said. "Tomorrow we will talk. Tonight we make love." His desire for her kindled into a burning passion as his fingers deftly removed her clothes to reveal the silken pink of her flesh to his feasting eyes.

When she finally stood nude before him, showing the growing rapture in the green of her eyes and in the way her breasts rose and fell, he gathered her into his arms and stroked the curve of her back, raining kisses across her face. He lowered his lips to hers, feeling how hot and demanding hers were as she moaned with quiet ecstasy.

"I will love you *ah-pah-nay*," Yellow Feather said as he leaned back away from her a bit. "You will always be *neen-nee-dah-ee-een*."

"What do your Indian words say?"

"Forever mine . . ."

"Oh, Yellow Feather," she sighed as though in a daze as she watched him begin to disrobe. She loved his tallness . . . his leanness. She loved his shining copper skin and the way his muscles rippled on his chest, arms, and thighs. His blue-black hair was smooth from deer tallow and hung neatly braided down his back. She reached and ran her fingers over the fringe of hair that was held in place by a fillet of beads across his forehead, then she touched his yellow feather and watched him further as he removed even this and stood beautifully nude before her.

250

Her face turned crimson when she lowered her gaze and saw his readiness. She sighed languidly as his hands began to explore her body, cupping her breasts, worshipping them with both hands and eyes. She leaned into his caresses and closed her eyes, letting her hands become her eyes as her fingers sought him out.

She laced her fingers across his face, feeling the prominence of his cheekbones, the hard line of his jaw, the bold, beautiful shape of his nose and the thick softness of his lips. With a rapid heartbeat she moved her fingers lower, to touch the hard erectness of his nipples. She pinched and teased him there, then followed a line downward, smiling seductively to herself when she felt the rippling of his skin as his flesh responded to her fiery touches.

Then with a fever in her heart, causing it to become erratic, Lorinda touched his erect hugeness and gently moved her fingers over it. When Yellow Feather let out a soft moan of pleasure, Lorinda opened her eyes and drew her hand away, so consumed with wanton needs that she threw her body next to his and clung to him as he began to move against her in a slow and agonizing motion.

"Yellow Feather, please . . ." Lorinda whispered, sighing shakily. She was floating . . . drifting. She desired to have him inside her, as well as to feel him against her. She felt brazen as she guided him downward onto the bulrush mats. When he lay over her and drove himself inside her, she felt as though they were becoming one. She was now Indian . . . he was now white. They were the same. Their two hearts blended as they beat against each other's chest. He pressed his lips to the hollow of her throat then sought out a breast and flicked his tongue over the nipple until the pain of desire reached from her breasts to her inner thighs with a fierce, burning intensity.

Lorinda laced her arms about Yellow Feather's neck and clung to him, arching her hips upward with his each added thrust inside her. She cried out with joyous release as her climax was reached, and welcomed his own quiverings as he held her even closer while expressing his pleasure with wild abandonment in a torrent of Indian words.

Lorinda tingled from head to toe as Yellow Feather withdrew from her. When he did his usual worshipping of her with his lips and tongue up and down the full length of her body, she soared further above herself, knowing now that she could never return to the white man's world . . . not . . . without Yellow Feather at her side, and she knew the impossibility of that. She was in love with an Indian chief . . . a chief who was fiercely devoted to his people.

She welcomed his lips against her own as his body once again excited her to another plateau of pleasure, knowing now that she would remain with him.

They would work together to find Amanda. She would fight side by side with Yellow Feather if need be to release her sister from the murdering savages . . . the . . . Sioux . . .

Sixteen

A presence at her side drew Lorinda awake with a start. She turned over on her side on the bed of blankets and saw that the dark eyes watching her were not Yellow Feather's but instead . . . Happy Flower's.

"You . . ." Lorinda whispered, pulling a lively-colored blanket up to her chin. "What do . . . you . . . want . . . ?"

She was afraid that Happy Flower had come to make her feel guilty for having shared a bed with the father of her unborn child. But instead Happy Flower sat docile and lean-faced beside her. Her deerskin dress billowed out around her, showing the proud line of her unborn child beneath it. Lorinda's gaze moved upward. Happy Flower had no braids like all the other Indians. She wondered why.

"Chief Yellow Feather sent me to prepare you for our feast to welcome white woman as part of our village of the St. Croix," Happy Flower said softly. "We will share our morning bath in the river then Happy Flower will give you dress to wear."

Lorinda leaned up on an elbow. "Feast? Bath?" she said, glancing around her. The rays from the morning sun were creeping downward from the smoke hole in the ceiling, blending with the wafts of blue-gray, spiraling smoke, looking almost like ghosts, except that it was day.

"*Ay-uh*," Happy Flower said. "Me take Red Blossom to where the river bends lazily. We will bathe together."

"I will bathe alone," Lorinda said stubbornly, rising,

253

keeping the blanket wrapped snugly about her. She flipped her hair, letting it settle in red rivulets down her back.

"Chief Yellow Feather wants me to stay with you," Happy Flower said meekly. "So me stay. He wants Happy Flower to see that you are readied on time. You do as Happy Flower says because it is what our husband *and* our chief says."

Lorinda stood before the freshly built fire in the firespace, wondering if Happy Flower had done even that service for her chief-husband. "This feast," she finally said. "Yellow Feather didn't tell me the feast would be today."

"Me tell you," Happy Flower stated flatly.

"What will happen at this feast? What does it mean? I am not Indian. No feast will make me Indian," Lorinda said, watching Happy Flower as she pushed herself up from the floor. Each step she took toward the fire appeared to be painful.

Happy Flower's hands went to the small of her back. She breathed hard as she straightened her shoulders. "You go to feast. You *see*," she said. "That's all me tell you."

Lorinda's eyes wavered a bit. "Do you hate me very much, Happy Flower?" she asked cautiously.

"Me no hate you," Happy Flower sighed languidly. "You make Chief Yellow Feather happy now. Soon *me* have *baby*. It will be my duty to raise a healthy son to be next chief-in-line. *You* make Chief Yellow Feather happy *one* way. I make him happy another."

For the first time ever, Lorinda was aware of a new sort of jealousy. She eyed the swell of Happy Flower's abdomen and suddenly realized that she was jealous because it was Happy Flower, not herself, giving Yellow Feather his first child. She had never thought about mothering a child before. Not . . . until . . . now. If she ever did

254

give Yellow Feather a child, it wouldn't be as important to him as his firstborn.

"Mah-bee-szhon," Happy Flower said, lifting the entrance flap.

Lorinda had heard this particular Indian phrase enough to know that Happy Flower had just said "come." "But I only have a blanket. . . ." she argued.

"We will be alone," Happy Flower said. She motioned with her head. *"Mah-bee-szhon."*

The crisp air of morning met Lorinda as she stepped out onto the dew-hung grass. Her toes curled with the cold contact beneath her bare feet and she gave off a deep shudder as the breeze moved up inside the blanket. The days of September had blended much too quickly into the days of October. The days were shorter and the nights were longer. Along with these changes had come the changing temperament of the weather, causing one to shiver one day and bask in a hazy warmth of sunshine the next.

This day that Lorinda had stepped into was a day of sunshine, yet the north wind whistling through the stripped branches of the gnarled oaks gave a taste of what would be offered in full, cold harshness in only a matter of weeks . . . possibly days.

"Through the forest, away from the village," Happy Flower said. Though heavy with child she moved swiftly through the brush. When the sparkle of the river met her gaze she rushed on ahead and dropped her dress to the ground and soon was in the water splashing and giggling.

Lorinda stepped to the water's edge, shivering. "Aren't you afraid you will catch cold?" she asked, unable to stop the chattering of her teeth.

Happy Flower ducked her head then lifted it out again, directing her eyes to the sky as the water ran from her face. "Catch . . . cold . . . ?" she giggled. "White woman play a game where she runs to try and catch the

255

cold air?''

Lorinda sighed exasperately then dropped the blanket to the ground and inched herself into the water until only her breasts lay, as though floating, on the water's surface. Shivers encompassed her as she felt the coldness of the water creep slowly upward into her strands of hair. She closed her eyes as she slowly ran her wet hands over her face. ''What do you do for a bath in the winter?'' she asked, wiping excess water droplets from her lashes.

''Now that we have a river we will take baths in river still,'' Happy Flower said amusedly. ''Then when snows come and river becomes hard like a stone, my people use snow for their bath.''

A crackling of twigs in the nearby brush caused Lorinda's heart to leap and her eyes to search frantically about her. She tensed inside when she saw the flash of copper skin. ''Who's there?'' she shouted. She covered her breasts with her hands when she saw the flutter of leaves as whoever had been watching moved quickly away to the protective covering of the dark of the forest.

Happy Flower's eyes grew wild. ''No scream again, Red Blossom,'' she said quickly.

''And why not?'' Lorinda queried, anger still seething inside her.

''Just do not,'' Happy Flower murmured. ''It is not wise.''

''It is not wise?'' Lorinda fumed. ''Happy Flower, what do you mean? Someone was watching us take a bath. That is not wise.''

''All I say is please do not make commotion over it,'' Happy Flower pleaded.

''And who are you protecting?'' Lorinda asked in a lowered tone. ''You must know who it was or you wouldn't be so determined to keep quiet about the fact that someone was sneaking around while we are unclothed and in the river. Who was it, Happy Flower? I'm sure you know.''

"It was Flying Squirrel," Happy Flower said softly. "But you must not tell anyone. It could get Flying Squirrel in much trouble."

"Flying Squirrel?" Lorinda gasped.

"He no have woman," Happy Flower said wistfully.

"Does he do . . . this . . . on a regular basis?"

"Regular . . . basis . . . ?" Happy Flower said, crinkling her nose with confusion.

Lorinda sighed. "Does Flying Squirrel watch women take baths every day?" she asked, remembering her own baths, alone in the river, early, before she had thought anyone else up and about in the Indian village. She also remembered the one time in the cave when he had seen her nude. . . .

"He no hurt white woman," Happy Flower said angrily. "He good man. He make good husband one day."

"Then why doesn't he take a wife?"

Happy Flower's lashes lowered. "Most Indian squaws are taken," she said quietly.

"So he sneaks around and watches those who belong to another man," Lorinda said, shuddering. "Well, I don't like him watching *me*. I'm going to tell Yellow Feather."

Happy Flower splashed over to Lorinda and clutched at her arm. "No tell," she said anxiously. "No tell you saw Flying Squirrel."

Lorinda's eyes widened. "Why not?" she exclaimed. "He should be reprimanded for his evil actions."

"Me tell Flying Squirrel not watch," Happy Flower said, almost desperately. "No tell Chief Yellow Feather. Please?"

"Well . . . all right . . . but if only you will be sure to warn Flying Squirrel that he is treading in deep water when he chooses to watch *me* in the nude," Lorinda said hotly. She then took a step backwards from Happy

257

Flower, seeing something hidden in the dark of her eyes, and wondered if Yellow Feather knew this Indian wife as well as he thought he did. Her wanting to keep Flying Squirrel's voyeurism a secret made Lorinda wonder what other secrets Happy Flower kept from the man she professed to be obedient to.

Shrugging, Lorinda eased on out of the water. She shivered anew from the cold and wrapped the blanket quickly around her. She watched Happy Flower hurriedly dress then followed, wordless, alongside her until they were once again in the wigwam and the coziness of its warmth.

"Do not dress in man's clothing," Happy Flower said, pulling her dress over her head. "I will soon return with dress for you." She positioned her many rows of beads to hang gracefully between her breasts, then left Lorinda standing with the blanket still wrapped about her, wondering what was to happen next.

Lorinda sniffled, doubting that she could ever survive the winter in this most northern part of the state of Minnesota. She couldn't envision herself bathing in snow! Yet she couldn't envision living at all, without Yellow Feather.

"But still there is this beautiful Indian maiden carrying Yellow Feather's child," she murmured. She felt the familiar dull ache around her heart whenever she let herself think about what Happy Flower had to mean to Yellow Feather. . . .

Voices outside the wigwam drew Lorinda's breathing to an almost halt. She tiptoed to the closed entrance flap and placed her ear next to it, suddenly recognizing the sweetness of Happy Flower's low murmurings and the hatefulness of Flying Squirrel's arguings. Lorinda's skin grew clammy as she listened in disbelief to what they were saying. . . .

"Why you be with white woman at the river?" Flying

Squirrel fumed.

"Yellow Feather told me to prepare her for the feast," Happy Flower whispered. "A bath was required."

"You knew I would be there," Flying Squirrel argued. "We had planned to meet by river. Alone. Now white woman will know. . . ."

"She will know if you don't leave *this* place," Happy Flower said. "She will see us. She will hear us. And, Flying Squirrel, me thought you would *not* come to river when you saw me leading white woman there."

"But I had to see you, Happy Flower," Flying Squirrel grumbled. "It is too long between embraces."

"Me know," Happy Flower whispered.

"Our child. Is it well inside your womb?"

"Ay-uh."

"What if . . . ?"

"Quiet, Flying Squirrel," Happy Flower whispered. "Yellow Feather will never know. Then it will be *our* son who is next chief-in-line. Be proud. We will one day be able to watch our son rule our people."

"Ay-uh," Flying Squirrel grumbled. "One day."

"Till then, be more careful, Flying Squirrel," Happy Flower whispered. "Your death would be swift if Yellow Feather knew of our deceptions."

"Ay-uh," Flying Squirrel said. "He must never know we planned for you two to meet . . . that it was my child you were already swelling inside with."

"Have you always hated him so much?"

"He's strong. In his eyes I am weak," Flying Squirrel growled.

"You *do* hate him then?" Happy Flower persisted.

"Gah-ween," Flying Squirrel mumbled. "No. I do not hate him. I love him as my brother. But I grow tired of him having everything *his* way. This one time I can be proud inside that I have something of greater value than him."

259

"Flying Squirrel, you could have had me as wife. . . ."

"Having a son who will be next chief-in-line is more important than bragging about having wife. . . ."

"But you do still love me, Flying Squirrel?"

"Ay-uh. . . ."

Lorinda knew that the sudden silence meant that they were embracing. She swung around, hands to her throat, unable to grasp fully what she had just heard. A coldness rippled through her, so stunned was she at the treachery planned between Yellow Feather's best friend and his Indian wife. It was unbelievable! How could they do this to their leader . . . the man who trusted them both with probably every fiber of his being!

Then Lorinda remembered the night in the cave . . . the doubt in Yellow Feather's voice when he had found Flying Squirrel and herself alone together. Did Yellow Feather possibly even suspect Flying Squirrel to be capable of deceit?

"But never with the sweet, innocent Happy Flower," Lorinda fumed. She circled her hands into fists at her side, hate bubbling into a scalding liquid inside her. Somehow she had to find the courage to tell Yellow Feather! The deceit should be revealed before the baby was born. Yellow Feather must not be allowed to grow fond of a child that was not his.

"Oh, I must find a way to tell him," Lorinda whispered, pacing. "But when?"

Then she began thinking about his promise to help her find her baby sister. If he was told the truth about his own child now, it could possibly cause him to hate all babies . . . to mistrust all women. Perhaps then he would not lead his men to the Sioux camp . . . he would instead be too busy with warring in his own village, ridding it of *its* vermin. . . .

Lorinda swung around as Happy Flower entered the

260

wigwam. Lorinda's heart raced, wanting to lash out at this woman whose face was flushed from having been in a man's arms . . . other than those of her husband. When Happy Flower smiled sweetly toward Lorinda, Lorinda had to turn and place her back to her. Too much showed in Lorinda's eyes. She just had to keep all she knew to herself. Too much depended on her silence. Yellow Feather had to be in the right frame of mind to help her find Amanda.

"Mah-bee-szhon," Happy Flower said softly. "Here is a gift Happy Flower has made for you."

Lorinda turned slowly around, avoiding Happy Flower's eyes. Instead, she forced her focus onto the dress draped over Happy Flower's arms. "You made a dress for me?" she asked in a near whisper.

"Ay-uh. Yellow Feather commanded Happy Flower to make dress for his new wife," Happy Flower murmured. "Me give it to you. You wear."

Lorinda accepted the dress and held it out before her. It was made of smooth buckskin with beads of all colors sewn onto it in patterns of the rainbow. She eyed Happy Flower quickly, hating to think of wearing something she had made. Surely while sewing it, Happy Flower had been thinking of Flying Squirrel. Oh, the deceit! And yet, whenever the time was right to tell Yellow Feather, Lorinda knew that she would finally have him all to herself! She smiled smugly toward Happy Flower.

"Thank you," she said. Her gaze followed Happy Flower's slow movements as Happy Flower bent and pulled a pair of beautifully beaded moccasins from beneath a roll of blankets.

"These also, Red Blossom," Happy Flower said, handing them to Lorinda. "Big Laughing Star made these for you."

"Big Laughing Star . . . ?"

"She Chief Wind Whisper's widow," Happy Flower said, lowering her eyes. "Yellow Feather's step-mother."

Lorinda accepted this second gift, remembering Yellow Feather's mockery of her boots. "I've not yet met Big Laughing Star," she said.

"She in mourning," Happy Flower said, glancing up again. "She stay in wigwam."

"She won't be at the feast?"

"Gah-ween," Happy Flower said. "She no go. But she already give Yellow Feather his gift of chief's clothing."

"What do you mean?"

"Red Blossom will see. Yellow Feather will wear today. Now you must get dressed. Then Happy Flower will braid your hair."

Lorinda's brow furrowed. "I will wear my hair as I always do," she stated flatly.

"You will wear it in braids," Happy Flower argued, though softly. "You will please Chief Yellow Feather by dressing and looking Indian to please his *people*."

"Oh!" Lorinda fumed. She placed her back to Happy Flower as she let the blanket drop from around her. Not liking being on exhibit she quickly pulled the dress over her head and marveled at how well it fit the curves of her body. She tied its belt at her waist and silently admired the show of beads that decorated the front.

She then stepped into the softness of the moccasins, suddenly realizing that she hadn't been given any leggings to wear as all Indian squaws did. She wondered if the display of legs would set her apart even more from all the other Indian maidens who would surely surround her at the feast. She wondered now about the true importance of braided hair! But her thoughts were quickly erased from her mind when Happy Flower reached over and began to weave Lorinda's hair into place until the task was completed.

"Red Blossom's hair is now two gleaming ropes of red hanging down her back," Happy Flower sighed, clasping her hands together before her. "So *mee-kah-wah-diz-ee. Ay-uh,* so beautiful. Chief Yellow Feather will be pleased."

At this moment, it was hard for Lorinda to believe Happy Flower capable of any sort of deception. Her wide, dark eyes showed such a childish innocence. It was no wonder Yellow Feather had been so easily tricked!

"I'm sure he will be," she replied, a bit too snappishly. "Happy Flower is so good to obey all her chief's commands."

Lorinda saw puzzlement etched across Happy Flower's tiny, frail face. . . .

"*Ay-uh.* Me do these things for my husband," Happy Flower said softly. She turned, motioning with a hand. "We must go. *Mah-bee-szhon.*"

Lorinda sighed laboriously. She indeed knew the meaning of *that* Indian word. She was always being told to "come." She took a step forward, then stopped and glanced toward her bed of blankets. Her hand searched her dress for a pocket, finding none. She would be without the protection of her small gun now wherever she traveled. But as long as Yellow Feather presided over everything, surely she would be safe. His love for her was strong . . . his love for her was true. He would be a shield against all further harm!

Flipping her braids around, she followed Happy Flower out into the sunshine. She walked with head held high next to Happy Flower beneath the moss-fringed limbs of the maples and over the soft cushion of damp leaves. The aroma of this crisp morning was fresh and clean and edged with a mixture of sweetness from pine needles and the crystal-clear waters of the St. Croix River.

Lorinda could hear the merry laughter and chatter of

Yellow Feather's people as the cleared land led Lorinda and Happy Flower on into the village of wigwams. Smoke spiraled upward into curls of gray from the smoke holes, but Lorinda's gaze moved onward to where a larger column of smoke circled upward. As she stepped out into another clearing she saw a large open fire over which food was being prepared for the feast.

Letting her gaze move onward, she saw a larger type of Indian house, nothing at all like the wigwams of this St. Croix band of Chippewa. It was a long and narrow structure handsomely fashioned of snow-white birch bark, and it stood at the far edge of the forest on level ground high above the lake. Outside this house, the Indians who were not preparing the food were already settled in a large semicircle.

As Lorinda grew closer to this circle, her breath caught in her throat, seeing Yellow Feather sitting at the head of this semicircle on a raised platform spread with bearskins and strewn balsam boughs.

"Chief Yellow Feather waits for his wives," Happy Flower whispered, leaning closer to Lorinda. "We must hurry."

Lorinda's knees were weak and her heart had become a bit erratic, still studying Yellow Feather and how different he looked in this new attire. This was most surely being worn this day because he was the chief over them all and had to look the part. With his expressionless eyes and arms folded, he sat beneath a typical tribal headdress of many brightly colored feathers stitched onto leather, trimmed with hundreds of beads of every size and description. He looked, oh, so handsome in a shirt of white doeskin, decorated with fringe and wrought with even more embroidered and colorful beads. His deerskin leggings and buckskin moccasins were fringed with hedgehog quills and his hair was shining brightly from oil. His face showed pride as his gaze fell upon Lorinda as she slowly approached him.

He held his right hand out to her and nodded a quiet welcome. As though in a daze, she accepted the cushions on his right, then felt a jealous bitterness break the magical spell she was momentarily in when Yellow Feather motioned for Happy Flower to take the place on the cushions to the left of him. Lorinda leaned a bit forward and saw the sweetness that Happy Flower reflected and still found the conversation she had heard between Happy Flower and Flying Squirrel hard to believe. But the feeling of many eyes focused on her now drew her eyes around. She gulped hard when she looked into the audience of Yellow Feather's Indians staring toward her.

The chatter had ceased with Lorinda's approach. She looked slowly among the people, seeing how they were attired in their richest raiments, beautifully clad with beads and tassels. Blankets of bold colors were wrapped around many whose round, coppery faces were criss-crossed by networks of furrows and wrinkles. Lorinda studied their eyes more closely than their attire, but she couldn't tell if they approved or disapproved of her presence beside their chief. Like Yellow Feather, these followers of his wore no expression in their eyes.

The raising of his right hand seemed to be the signal from Chief Yellow Feather for the feast ritual to begin. Lorinda sat straight-backed as a drum began its boom-booming, with a stronger accent on the first stroke. Most of the men rose from the semicircle and picked up the rhythm of the drum as they began moving their feet with the beat. Their bodies swayed and their arms tossed first right, then left as they shuffled about the ground chanting, *"Hi-ya-ya-ya, Hi-ya-ya-ya."*

The women picked up the beat and clapped their hands in time with it while the men moved round and round, excitement building with each added movement. This continued for a long while until Chief Yellow Feather once again raised a hand, signaling a change in the celebration. Several children began their own dance in time with the resumed drum beatings. First they danced slowly, stooping, pausing, then, as the drum's beat grew faster, the children's feet moved more swiftly, whirling, spinning them round in circles, even leaping, stamping upon the ground, tossing their braids from their shoulders, until, breathless from their show, they returned, proud, to their seats on the ground.

Yellow Feather rose from his seat and stood with arms crossed, facing his people. "My people, the proud St. Croix band of the Chippewa, we are gathered together here today to have a feast to celebrate many things," he began. "We celebrate life, happiness, and hope for our future generation that will be born here in our new land of promise." He turned his gaze to Lorinda and reached a hand to her.

Lorinda's heart beat wildly as she inched her way up next to Yellow Feather. His hand was warm and reassuring, but she couldn't ignore the nervous shiftings of the Indians as Yellow Feather drew her next to him.

"And, my people, you are already aware of my wife I have chosen to sit on my right side," he said. "Your chief now asks for your approval and for her acceptance into our tribe of St. Croix. You must each pledge your everlasting devotion to her by placing your hand on her shoulder."

Yellow Feather grew silent and looked toward Lorinda. Then he spoke, in English this time. "It is Chief Yellow Feather who asks this of his people," he said more quietly. He tilted Lorinda's chin upward with a forefinger. "It is Chief Yellow Feather who asks that you *let* my people accept you, Red Blossom."

Lorinda's face grew hot and tears sparkled in her eyes. She knew that this was an honor being bestowed upon her. But was she ready to truly become an Indian? It

266

hadn't been very long ago that she had thought of all Indians as savage . . . heathens . . . even murderers! But since Yellow Feather . . . so much had changed in her life. Suddenly she *wanted* his people's approval . . . their blessings. Yellow Feather had become more important to her than even her own life, it seemed.

"Will you accept my people as your own?" Yellow Feather asked softly, turning Lorinda's insides to a river of warmth as the dark of his eyes caressed her flesh.

"Yellow Feather, it is a hard . . ."

"Red Blossom, the time is come to accept my people as you have accepted me," Yellow Feather whispered shallowly.

Lorinda blinked her thick lashes upward at him, forever loving him. "*Ay-uh,* Chief Yellow Feather," she murmured. "Whatever you wish, always. . . ."

Yellow Feather leaned and touched his lips first to one cheek and then the other. "You are now more than my wife," he whispered. "You are also Chippewa!"

Lorinda's insides tingled, hearing the words and realizing their meaning. She accepted Yellow Feather's hand as he guided her from the platform where she stood to receive the Chippewas' acceptance into their tribe. She had already won Yellow Feather's approval . . . she had already been named Chippewa . . . but his people's approval would make it final.

One by one the Indians approached her, moving slowly and with great and solemn dignity. Each placed a hand on her shoulder. Some pledged their friendship, some spoke nothing at all. And when all had made the circle and the task was completed, Lorinda gathered together in her mind the words she could remember in Indian to say her heartfelt thanks. "Red Blossom *mee-gway-chee-wahn-dum geen.*"

This declaration in part Indian was met with great applause and chants, followed by the thunderous pulsating

267

of the drum. Lorinda blushed as children thronged around her, pulling her down to their height to kiss her. And when this was over, she welcomed Yellow Feather's hand as he guided her to where many white man's tables were spread with an abundance of food.

"We will now share in a feast of feasts," Yellow Feather laughed, pulling his tribal headdress from his head. He handed it to Happy Flower who stood quietly by his left side. "Take this inside the council house," he said. "My yellow feather pleases me more."

He now proudly displayed the lone band and the yellow feather hanging that had been hidden by the brief showing of the necessary headdress to please his people during the solemnity of council. But now he would eat and play! His Red Blossom was truly his *and* his people's! He was blessed! Oh, so blessed. He silently thanked his spiritual guardian, the great owl of the forest, then laughed merrily as he handed Lorinda a smoothly polished bowl of basswood and a spoon of horn-of-bison.

Lorinda's gaze raked over the choice of food, seeing fish, venison, sugar cakes and wild rice heaped high in bowls. Corn spiraled smoke from its yellow, sweet kernels, and strips of dried pumpkin lay orange and feastful to the eye.

"Take a little bit of each, then let us go off alone and enjoy it," Yellow Feather encouraged, leaning down closer to her.

"Won't your people miss you?"

"They know you are my new bride," he said. "They would even expect me to carry you away into the brush."

Yellow Feather's deep laughter caused Lorinda's face to fill with more color. "Yellow Feather, you act as though this is a feast of marriage," she whispered back.

"To my people, it *is*," he said. "They only now truly look to you as my true wife. Ceremonies are always necessary to the Chippewa."

"As they are to the white man when a wedding is performed," Lorinda said. "In my people's way, you and I are not yet wed."

"Red Blossom, you are not among your people. We will do as *my* customs require."

Lorinda cast him a sorrowful glance then smiled warmly when she saw the love for her in his dark pools of eyes. She knew him well enough now to understand that it was hard for him to let his eyes show emotion. When he did, it was true.

"Chief Yellow Feather." Flying Squirrel spoke suddenly from behind them.

Lorinda turned with a start, eyeing Flying Squirrel angrily. He was deceitful. He was sneaky. He was all things ugly to her.

"What is it, Flying Squirrel?" Yellow Feather said flatly. "I felt your absence at the celebration. Where were you?"

Flying Squirrel pulled something from behind his back and held it toward Yellow Feather. "I was finishing making my gift to you as new chief," he murmured. "I wanted to give it to you in front of our people but I was delayed by circumstances and only now have it ready for you."

Lorinda grew hot with anger. She was quite aware of what had delayed Flying Squirrel, but she wouldn't yet speak of it. As Happy Flower drew into view at the council house door, Lorinda cast her an angry glance.

"It is a thing of beauty, Flying Squirrel," Yellow Feather sighed, accepting his gift. It was a pipe with a red stonepipe head and stem made of a reed with feathers of the scarlet tanager and the burnished green breast of a mallard duck gracing it. "It will be my peace pipe, forever, Flying Squirrel. Thank you."

"I will take it to the council house and leave it for our

next powwow," Flying Squirrel said, accepting it back into his possession.

Lorinda looked quickly back toward the council house, seeing that Happy Flower had once more disappeared inside it. Lorinda now knew that two in love would soon be embracing inside this house that was meant mainly for council, with Yellow Feather as the one presiding over all. But again, she knew to remain silent. The time would arrive for disclosures, but only after Amanda's rescue. Then, Lorinda would tell all. . . .

"You will eat heartily then make love passionately," Yellow Feather laughed, piling Lorinda's plate full of food.

Lorinda felt the weight of the plate and laughed along with him, once more aware of the merriment around her. The children dashed among them talking and eating. Somewhere along the riverbank a happy tune was being played on a flute. The sun was already losing its strength behind the shadows of trees and more bonfires were being lighted as the celebration continued on into the night.

Lorinda was glad to finally be led away from the songs and laughter of the Chippewa, basking in the warm pleasure of Yellow Feather at her side. "Now it is our time to be alone, my Indian maiden," he said, drawing her next to him. They laughed and kissed, walking in unison until their private wigwam was before them. Then in one swoop, Yellow Feather had Lorinda up in his arms and was bending, entering their love nest that was bathed in a soft glow from the fire in the firespace.

Lorinda's glance moved quickly about her. Yellow Feather had promised her gifts from the cave, and, somehow, while the ceremony had taken place, some gifts had been brought to their wigwam and placed leisurely about it.

"Yellow Feather," Lorinda sighed, taking it all in,

item by item. Some gold-banded china, along with some sandwich glass sauceplates, sat neatly on a table on one rounded, far wall; a pewter coffeepot sat on a piling of bulrush mats next to the stone-lined firespace; and a terry clock sat ticking away next to Lorinda's bed of blankets.

"Yellow Feather," Lorinda sighed again. "It is so grand." Her gaze then caught a stack of books on another space of wall, and she felt as though she did have a little bit of home around her, though she had just been ceremonially changed into a Chippewa Indian.

Lorinda hugged Yellow Feather's neck tightly. "Oh, how I do love you, my sweet gentle savage of an Indian," she crooned.

They then smiled unspoken words of love to each other as Yellow Feather gently placed Lorinda on the ground and began to slowly undress her. Once she was shed of her clothes, she in turn slowly undressed him, then welcomed the hard, lean line of his body next to hers when he roughly jerked ner next to him.

Lorinda gasped as his lips met hers in a frenzy. She locked her arms about his neck, almost breathless from his rougher handling of her. But she liked this stronger, unleashed passion he was revealing to her. Her lips were throbbing from the intensity of his kiss. Her body was becoming inflamed by the searching probing of his fingers. He was no longer the gentle Indian, but one who was demanding, even almost brutally, as he released his lips from hers and forced her down on the blankets.

While his hands moved seductively over her his teeth caught the nipple of a breast and teased her to becoming almost mindless. The continued savagery of his mouth and hands made her moan, and when he lowered his hardness inside her and began to work in and out, she laced her arms about his neck and surrendered her all to him.

She was filled with a strange rapture when his mouth

271

came down upon hers in another fiery, lingering kiss. She was led to pull him closer to her as she lifted her hips, welcoming his eager thrusts with even more blind passion and desire. She could feel the intensity of her feelings growing inside her. She was being lifted, carried above the cool, dark recesses of the forest, to where, by day, the sun's rays danced and leapt about in the sky. She was a part of this dance. She was weaving in and out of what was real and what was not. Her mind was lost to her. All she could feel was a steady warmth humming peacefully inside her brain until her body shuddered and she cried out her love to him as she felt the release that he so skillfully had helped her to find.

"My love," she whispered, clinging.

"Forever. . . ." he said thickly, feeling the pressures building to a crescendo inside himself. Her warm breath caressed his cheek . . . her fingers sent tingles of aliveness across the flesh of his back . . . and the silk of her inflamed his senses into a mind-bursting climax, leaving him panting and winded, stretched out beside her.

"That was a celebration of *all* celebrations," Yellow Feather then laughed, eyeing her passionately as she lay there still so seductive . . . even so wanton. He reached a hand to her braids and began releasing them.

"I won't look Indian any longer," Lorinda teased, casting him a shadowed look through the thick veil of her lashes.

Yellow Feather's fingers spread her hair out about her head and worshipped it with his eyes. "No more braids," he said. "They are wrong for you. I was wrong to ask Happy Flower to braid them for you. You don't have to look Indian to *be* Indian. I *make* you Indian. You are my *wife*."

The mere mention of Happy Flower drew Lorinda's smile from her face. It would be so easy to tell him and have him all to herself. But she had to wait. She reached a hand to his cheek. "Yellow Feather, when will we venture to the Sioux camp?" she asked tentatively.

Yellow Feather frowned down at her as he leaned up on an elbow. "You mean when will Yellow Feather and his warriors go to the Sioux camp," he stated flatly. "Red Blossom will not go. Squaws do not go on warhunts with warriors."

Lorinda sprang up from the bed. "I am *not* a squaw no matter if you *do* call me Chippewa," she argued. "And when *you* go in search of my sister, so will *I* go."

"Gah-ween," he said. He rose and clasped her shoulders angrily. "You will *not* go."

"I have to, Yellow Feather," she murmured. "It is *my* sister who is missing. I must go with you. Only I can recognize her!" She pleaded with the green of her eyes. "And you *must* have a woman along to care for the child on the return trip. This woman must be *me,* the child's blood relative. Her sister!"

Yellow Feather walked away from her and crouched naked before the fire. He kneaded his chin, then cast her a troubled look. "It will be dangerous," he said quietly.

"I must be there for my sister," Lorinda said stubbornly.

"Ay-uh," he said quietly. "Red Blossom can go. But my warriors won't like it."

"I can dress as a warrior," she urged breathlessly.

Yellow Feather went to her and gathered her hair in his hand. "Your hair . . . your skin . . ." he murmured.

"I'll do the best I can," Lorinda said softly. "At least my hair can be blackened. I can use ash from the firespace. . . ."

Yellow Feather drew her into his arms. "Red Blossom is like *no* other woman," he laughed.

"When do we go, Yellow Feather?" she said in a silken whisper.

"Tomorrow. . . ." he replied flatly.

273

Lorinda drew back away from him, eyes wide and heart pounding. "Tomorrow . . . ?" she gasped.

His expression became stern. *"Ay-uh,"* he growled. "Tomorrow. . . ."

Seventeen

The forest trail was narrow but Foolish Heart kept her horse moving at a steady pace next to Lamont Quinby's. She held her head high though many mixed emotions battled inside her. The Indian in her was shamed by what she was doing, yet she knew that she had no other choice. She was at the mercy of the white man who called himself Lamont Quinby. She had to keep urging her horse onward, possibly in the end to cause heartache to her own people.

Foolish Heart did not understand this white man's true motives. Was it for the woman with the red hair? He had spoken with venom when he had mentioned her name. Would this white woman's death come at the end of this trail or did Lamont Quinby in truth hunger for her body? Or was he secretly planning to do harm to Yellow Feather?

Just letting Yellow Feather's name splash through her mind caused Foolish Heart further confusion. She loved him . . . yet she hated him. At this moment her hate was stronger and she couldn't help but taste the sweet succulence of revenge rippling across her tongue.

Lamont grabbed Foolish Heart's horse's reins angrily from her hands and yanked at them, causing her horse to whinny loudly and come to a weaving halt. "Damn it, how much farther?" he growled into her face.

"Foolish Heart get you to the village of my people before the sun sets behind the towering Norway pines," she stated flatly. She held her chin up in a dignified manner, feeling superior to this white man now that she was traveling in her own familiar territory. If she wished, surely she could leave him there and he would not find his way back to the dreary city he had called by the name of Duluth. But she couldn't do this. She feared too much for her own life. He had a gun. He might decide to use it on her if she suddenly tried to escape from him.

Lamont looked upward at the way gray clouds hung low and threatening. "Ha!" he spat. "What sun? I think we might even see some snow before the day is over."

Foolish Heart raised her nose to the sky and inhaled deeply. *"Ay-uh,"* she murmured. *"Goon bay-shoo."*

Dropping her reins, Lamont reached for a half-smoked cigar inside his jacket pocket and placed it between his lips. "Enough of your Indian garbage. When you speak to Lamont Quinby, you speak in English. How many times do I have to tell you that?"

Foolish Heart's eyes snapped angrily back at him. "Me say snow near," she hissed.

"Then we'd better get a-movin'," Lamont said, thrusting his knees into the horse's sides.

"Soon there will be many tracks in the snow," Foolish Heart said, urging her own horse onward.

"Eh?" Lamont said, eyeing her with a lifted brow. He lit his cigar and inhaled the apple flavor of it, letting it snake down his throat and up into his nose.

"The fox and coyote will compete in their hunt for the rabbit," she replied. "Winter is a time of determined hunts."

"I have my own hunt to worry about," Lamont said, peering through the dark of the forest that lay before him. "Yeah. And when it's over I'll show that damn Injun with the yellow feather who truly owns Lorinda."

Foolish Heart's eyes grew wide and her breathing became shallow. Lamont Quinby had spoken with such a hatred about Yellow Feather. Though having only moments ago had thoughts of hate for Yellow Feather, her instinct to always defend and respect the St. Croix Indians' name made a slow seething begin inside her. She glanced a bit sideways at Lamont, seeing how smugly he sat in his saddle, so sure of everything. With her eyes, she took in the wild sandy spray of his hair, his thick, blonde mustache and his broad shoulders. It was the empty gray of his eyes that showed that he had no true soul.

Forgetting that he had a gun, she began to think of escaping. The time was upon her to try to flee from him, for she felt that once she succeeded in leading him to her village, she would be the cause of placing Yellow Feather's life in danger, and certainly, then, her own! If she didn't escape now, she never would!

When he turned his eyes away from her to let them follow a covey of partridges scampering into the low brush, Foolish Heart thrust her knees roughly into her horse's ribs, flipped her reins fiercely against its brown mane and soon found herself traveling at a high rate of speed beneath gnarled branches of oak trees and around scratchy needles of pines that seemed to grab out at her.

She hung her head down low, panting, afraid to look back. She could hear the fierce hoofbeats of Lamont's horse behind her and welcomed a straight, flat stretch of land where the meadow would lead her directly to the land of her people. Surely Yellow Feather wouldn't turn her away again if he saw that she was being pursued by an angry white man. Yellow Feather was known to have hate in his heart for the white man and what they had done to his St. Croix band of Indians. Yet, was he softening? Did he truly have a white woman at his side? Or was she his captive?

The wind rushing against her face caused the coldness of the October day to feel even more intense. Her deerskin dress and leggings were letting the air seep through causing her flesh to feel numb. She hungered for the warmth of a bearskin about her. The one striped blanket tied around her shoulders no longer was protection against the icy fingers of winter that were continually grabbing at her.

Though Lamont's horse was gaining on her, Foolish Heart smiled, knowing that around one more bend in the shadow of the trees she was now riding beneath, the wigwams would come quickly into view. Her heart beat wildly inside her, aching to once more be a part of her people. Surely Yellow Feather had forgotten his anger toward her! She had been taught a lesson. Surely he would know this!

The fresh clearing ahead sent Foolish Heart's head into a strange spinning. Where was her village of people? All that was left standing were the poles of sapling that had been used for the wigwams' frameworks. They were now void of their birch-bark coverings and rolls of bullrush mats. They were now like skeletons, as though left to haunt this land that had been deserted by the St. Croix band of the Chippewa Indians.

Feeling numb and disoriented, Foolish Heart moved on into the village of skeletal poles, shuddering when the wind whistled through them, as though spirits, taunting her. Where had her people gone? Why had they gone? They hadn't traveled with the change of seasons since Chief Wind Whisper had placed his signature in blood on the white man's papers.

"Chief Wind Whisper," she gasped aloud. Her gaze went to where his lodge had stood. It too was a skeleton. "But he was so ill," she whispered. "He would not have stood the strain of moving. . . ."

The pit of her stomach rolled in queasy tremorings, now focusing her eyes on the burial ground. Had Chief Wind Whisper . . . ? Seeing the fresh rise of earth representing a grave, and all the offerings to a chief still spread across it, gave her the answer to her question. When

Lamont's horse galloped to her side, she ignored his presence.

"You damn, stupid Injun," he shouted. He grabbed her by the wrist and forced her eyes around to meet his angry gaze. "What you tryin' to pull runnin' away like that?" He glanced quickly around him, absorbing the emptiness. "And where the hell've you brought me? There ain't no village of people here."

Feeling the need to go to her chief's graveside, Foolish Heart jerked her wrist free. She spoke between clenched teeth to Lamont. *"Koo-gah-bo-win,"* she hissed.

"More Indian garbage?" Lamont shouted. He raised a hand to hit her. "I thought I told you . . ."

Foolish Heart jumped from her horse, out of his range. "Lamont Quinby evil—*mah-gay-i-ee,*" she said. "Me no help anymore. Me now go to Chief Wind Whisper's grave."

"What . . . ?" Lamont said, scratching his head. He spat his cigar from between his lips and dismounted, securing his and Foolish Heart's horse to a sapling pole. He then followed along behind her, now also seeing the grave. He glanced quickly about him, slowly realizing what they had ridden into. It was a deserted Indian village and obviously the village of Foolish Heart. Had she known all along that she was leading them to a dead end? But, no, it didn't make sense. She appeared to be in some sort of state of shock, and over more than finding a fresh grave that she spoke of as being her chief's.

Lamont stood back and watched with mouth agape as Foolish Heart knelt on the ground beside the grave and began a slow rocking back and forth. From somewhere deep inside her throat she began a low, mournful wail, talking in quick Indian chatterings. Something compelled Lamont to leave her be, feeling something strangely eerie about the air around him, as though he and Foolish Heart were no longer alone. Were there spirits dancing around him? Was it true that Indians did have spiritual guardians? Did they even after death? What if the dead chief's spirit was . . . ?

He stepped back a bit, swallowing hard, then rushed to his horse and stood next to it, waiting for Foolish Heart to finish with her grieving, hoping it would be soon. He now didn't only dread the threat of snow but many other things. What if the Indians were still near enough to hear Foolish Heart's cries and come to her rescue? Would they think he was being cruel to her?

But, no, he had to believe the Indians were far, far away from this place. Everything had been taken. They had moved on, to make a village somewhere else.

He peered into the distance, seeing nothing but trees, mountains, and meadow. Disappointment caused him to kick at the dirt at his feet. He had thought to have Lorinda with him by nightfall, and now this! He wouldn't have her at all! Unless . . . yes . . . unless . . .

He looked quickly back towards Foolish Heart. Didn't Indians know ways of tracking? Wouldn't she be able to find her people by searching the ground at her feet? Or did she already know where they were?

Impatience sent him back to Foolish Heart's side, no longer fearing anything but the lonely nights that would follow if he didn't find Lorinda and take her away with him. He laughed at himself for worrying about anything, especially spirits. Wouldn't he be laughed out of the lumber camp if men got word of his momentary weakness?

He placed his hands on his hips, glaring down at Foolish Heart, who still rocked and wailed. ''Get up, you damn Injun squaw,'' he ordered firmly. He watched and saw that this didn't stir her. Her eyes were glassy and her face a strange ashen color. He grabbed both her wrists and drew her quickly from the ground.

''When Lamont Quinby tells you to do something, you do it, damn it,'' he growled. He cringed a bit when her dark pools of eyes returned to their normal, quiet blaze of fury and hate.

"This is sacred ground," she hissed. "Me no do anything white man tell me." She spat at his feet. "Me die first."

Lamont raised a hand and hit her across the face, flinching when he saw the jerk of her neck as her head went with the blow. But he had to show her who was boss. "Now, Foolish Heart, you *will* do as I say," he said thickly. He watched as she cowered a bit beneath his steady stare, rubbing the bright red of her cheek.

Foolish Heart's hate for him was growing, but she now truly did fear him. She felt the tears wanting to escape from her eyes but wouldn't allow them to be set free, for to do so would be to show her true weakness to this man who possessed the only gun between the two of them.

"What you want me to do?" she asked quietly. She glanced quickly around her, seeing the spot where she had shared a wigwam with Yellow Feather for too short a time. Now he would be called Chief Yellow Feather. Oh, why hadn't she had more control of her mouth? Why had she spoken so much in anger? Why had she clipped Happy Flower's beautiful braids? If she had not done any of these things, she would now be the wife of an Indian Chief! How grand that would be! Oh, how grand . . . and, now, oh, how sad!

"Injuns are known for their trackin'," Lamont said, walking around, kicking at the dust with the toe of his boot. "Surely you can find the new home of your people." He squinted his eyes at her. "Or do you already know where they've gone to?" he said.

"Gah-ween," she said, shaking her head back and forth.

"Then, damn it, you will find their tracks," he ordered firmly.

"Me no Chippewa warrior," she said stubbornly,

281

crossing her arms across her chest. "Warriors track. Me no track."

Lamont leaned into her face. "Foolish Heart track," he hissed vehemently. He gave her a shove. "Now. You go by foot and I will follow on horseback."

Foolish Heart clamped her lips together angrily, then began looking toward the ground. How many days ago had her people left? Would the winds of winter have swirled the dust around so that she couldn't find any tracks? Even if she did, what should she do? Lamont Quinby shouldn't be led to her people. But if she did find the path they had taken, wouldn't she be leading herself back to where she belonged? She shouldn't have even left. She had been too stubborn! Too foolish! But she was no longer foolish. She would find her people.

"Well? Do you see any fresh tracks that lead away from this damn isolated place?" Lamont fussed, guiding both horses next to where Foolish Heart still stood, studying the ground.

"Ay-uh," she said, seeing the long, narrow marks ground into the dirt that the many travois had made. She turned and faced all four directions, praying to herself, then to the good spirit Wenebojo, that he would be with her. She needed guidance. She now feared for her life if she didn't find her way to her people.

"So . . . ?" Lamont said with a toss of the head. "Which way?"

"Me take. You follow," she said in a near whisper.

Lamont laughed a bit wickedly. "Now that's more like it," he said, mounting his horse. He clung to her horse's reins as he urged his own onward. He watched her move with head bowed and with feet light on the ground, now also seeing the tracks she was following. He snickered a bit to himself and relaxed atop the horse, feeling confident that all was now well with the world. He would soon have Lorinda with him. He would go by night's cover and

282

sneak her away before the damn Injun with the yellow feather would even miss her. He no longer thought it wise to think about killing the Indian. If only a white woman was taken, surely he wouldn't be trailed and killed. No. The Indian's life would be spared. He only truly cared about Lorinda. And wouldn't she even welcome him . . . a white man come to her rescue? He could just see her now . . . her wide green eyes sparkling with happiness for having been rescued . . . the ruby-red lips that would know how to thank him for being her rescuer. . . .

Dripping gray beards of moss trailing down from the trees in the forest met Foolish Heart's approach, causing her to slow a bit. The air was heavy with the fragrance from the pure, sweet smells of the cedar and pinewood, yet there was nothing at all pleasant about the coldness that the dark forest cover emitted.

She began to shiver, feeling the cold dampness seeping in through the soles of her moccasins. She felt a desperation rising inside her. It seemed that the trail had faded away to a nothingness. How had Yellow Feather guided the full village of the St. Croix Chippewa through this forest? All signs had led her in this direction, but there was hardly room for even herself to push her way through the density of the brush. She cringed when she heard the low grumblings and cursings from Lamont Quinby as he trailed on behind her. She knew that he was battling the low limbs and clinging vines as well as she and even moreso, for the horses needed even more space through which to move.

"Where the hell you takin' me now?" Lamont shouted.

Foolish Heart swung around, trembling. "The tracks led me here," she said softly. "Me no take you in wrong direction. Just be patient. Foolish Heart get there. Somehow. Me will find the village of the St. Croix."

"You sure as hell better," Lamont said, flashing her an ugly sneer. He was beginning to doubt her true worth as a tracker. He wasn't dumb. He knew that for a full village of Indians to move, there had to have been room to walk. But he would wait a while longer before telling Foolish Heart to turn back and try again in another direction.

Foolish Heart swung back around, jumping when a deer bounded ahead of her in the thicket. She smiled weakly then moved onward until she saw nothing different ahead of her. The shadows of the forest were all that was there, and in these she heard too many whisperings. She felt that she had led Lamont Quinby to where the spirits were thick and were growing angry for having been intruded upon. What if they punished her?

When a large owl with widespread wings swooped down above her head, studying her with large, round eyes, Foolish Heart began a mournful cry, remembering Yellow Feather's guardian spirit was the giant owl of the forest. Had the owl come to carry her away, to drop her to her death for having begun this treacherous enterprise of leading a white man to her people?

Turning, Foolish Heart began to run and stumble through the brush, stopping only when Lamont jumped from his horse and grabbed her roughly by the wrists.

"You won't find your people by gettin' scared of your own shadow," he laughed darkly.

"Please let me go," Foolish Heart screamed. "Just let me go. Take me back to your city by the big body of water. Me no want to find my Indian village. They no want me there. The great owl of the forest just warned me of this. Let me go."

"An owl did you say?" Lamont chuckled. He drew her roughly to him and spoke into her face. "Now, Foolish Heart, I know we've taken a wrong turn somewhere. We'll just have to start all over again. Do you hear?"

Trembling from fear, cold, and sudden exhaustion, Foolish Heart stumbled her way back to the deserted village and once more studied the tracks. When she thought she had found her way again, she began the slow walk back into the forest . . . this time only to go in circles and end up once more in the village of skeletal remains.

"You're a dumb Injun if I ever did see one," Lamont said, twisting the tip of his mustache in frustration. He glanced toward the sky and saw that night was drawing near. "We'd best make camp for tonight," he added, dismounting from his horse.

Foolish Heart looked anxiously about her. "Not in my deserted village," she said softly. "Me no want to. Foolish Heart feel . . . spirits . . . are angry. . . ."

Lamont began to unload his horse of camping gear. "You just tell your spirits that I'll only be here one night," he said, spitting on the ground at his feet. "You can even tell your damn spirits that we even give up huntin' for the lost Indian village. Tomorrow mornin', we head back to Duluth."

Foolish Heart's shoulders sagged heavily. She was an Indian without a tribe. She felt defeated . . . useless. She tensed when Lamont came to her and drew her roughly into his arms.

"At least we have each other to keep us company for the full night, eh, Foolish Heart?" he said, crushing his mouth against hers. He laughed to himself, feeling her struggles against him. He loved a woman with spirit.

Foolish Heart squirmed and kicked then succeeded at pulling free from him. "Me no let you make love to me while on Indian land," she hissed. "Me too proud to let you, Lamont Quinby."

Lamont grabbed hold of her wrists and wrestled her to the ground. "I'll show you who tells who what can be done around here," he said, sealing her lips with his once again, letting his fingers search up inside her dress until

285

he had found the soft spot between her legs.

Foolish Heart squirmed her mouth free. *"Gah-ween,"* she moaned. *"Gah-ween."*

"Don't say no to me woman," he sneered. "You see? I *do* know one of your Injun words. You've said it to me enough!"

Foolish Heart's eyes widened when she felt the cold wetness of a snowflake settle on her left cheek. Fear weaved its way through her heart. She feared the white snow more than the white *man.* Death! It could mean death! *"Goon,"* she blurted, frantic. *"Goon!* We must go, Lamont Quinby."

"What's that you're so excited about now?" he sighed exasperatedly.

"Snow. Me said snow," she shouted. "We must not stay here. We must find our way back to your city beside the great body of water before the snows become as ghostly shrouds all about us."

Lamont turned his head and peered upward into the sky, tensing when many snowflakes circled around before his eyes. "Well, I'll be damn," he grumbled. He released his hold on Foolish Heart and began gathering his gear back onto the horse, then quickly pulled himself up on the saddle.

Foolish Heart sighed with relief, pushing herself up from the ground. She rubbed the rawness of her wrists and began to mount her horse, feeling as though she had been saved from one demon, but maybe only to be slain by another . . . if she didn't get to safety before the snows thickened on the ground.

"You're not goin' back with me," Lamont shouted, knocking her from her horse. "You've served your purpose. Get. And I'm tired of your Injun mumbo jumbo."

Foolish Heart fell clumsily to the ground, eyeing him wildly. "You cannot leave me here to die," she cried. She watched him lead her horse away from her. Fear struck at her heart, like many arrows piercing it. "At least leave me a horse. . . ."

"To hell with you," Lamont said. "I've changed my mind about takin' you back with me. I may need both horses to get me back if the weather does worsen." He held to both horse's reins and urged the horses onward in a quick speed. He ignored Foolish Heart's desperate wails. He only had one person on his mind . . . the safety of his own self!

"But, no, there is always another on my mind," he said aloud. "Lorinda!"

He would find her another time. It wasn't as though she had dropped from the face of the earth. He would find her one day. He would never give up the hunt. She had found her way into his blood and he would never be fully washed free of her.

Spring. He would find her then. . . .

Eighteen

The entire night had been filled with shrieking warriors dancing themselves into a delirium of valor to the accompaniment of turtle-shell rattles and pounding drums. Then, earlier in the morning, at the sun's rising, the warriors had squatted around the big war drum listening to Yellow Feather's detailed war plans and to his assurances of their safe return home from the Sioux camp.

Lorinda was now busying herself at blackening her face while Happy Flower stood behind her, braiding her already blackened hair.

"This be foolish," Happy Flower said. "No woman goes to Sioux camp with warriors. Indian squaw stay behind singing songs of farewell. We sing songs of victory and prepare for feast and scalp dance on their return."

"Scalp dance?" Lorinda whispered, shuddering. She lifted her chin and rubbed the cooled ash onto her throat. "You seem to always forget that I am *not* an Indian squaw," she sighed. "I am a white woman and not governed by strict rules set down by men. I do as *I* want to do."

"Yellow Feather not want you to go. . . ."

"I know that," Lorinda said stiffly. "But I *am* going. You know this now. Why not just accept it and quit badgering me?"

"Badgering . . . ?" Happy Flower whispered.

"Oh, forget it," Lorinda sighed. She stepped away from Happy Flower, wishing to have the mirror that she had found in the cave. She most surely had to be a sight.

She glanced down at her attire, liking the warm feel of the fringe-trimmed shirt and leggings against her body. But the breechcloth! She would never feel comfortable with *it* on!

But I must look the part of a man, she thought to herself. If need be, I must even fight like a man. I must do all these things . . . for my sister.

Several muskrat skins, tanned, with the hair left on them, had been sewn into a warm jacket for Lorinda to wear on this expedition, and she accepted it as Happy Flower helped her on with it. She had known that the bulkiness of it would be a good cover for her gun. She went to her bed of blankets and reached beneath it and quickly slipped the gun inside a pouch that she had sewn inside her jacket during the night while Yellow Feather had been away from her bed, preparing his men.

A tremor of fear combined with excitement and eagerness coursed through her. Could this truly be happening? Was she in an Indian village, even part Indian herself now? Was she actually ready to set out with the St. Croix warriors, to travel to a Sioux camp with warring on her mind? Where were the gentle days with her parents . . . with her aunt . . . ?

"Are those days gone forever from me?" she whispered. "Am I so truly changed?"

Familiar footsteps stepping into the wigwam and then behind her drew Lorinda around to face Yellow Feather. She eyed him intently, seeing how warriorlike he appeared today. His face had been painted like leaves of autumn, streaked with crimsons and yellows. His features had never been as stern and set, his eyes so dark and fathomless. His own muskrat jacket pulled on over his fringed shirt didn't hide the proud swell of his chest nor the wide expanse of his shoulders as he stood tall and lean over her. Lorinda's insides quivered with added love for him, knowing that what he was doing, he was doing for her.

His eyes studied her back and she saw a sudden, quiet amusement in their depths. She reached a hand to his face of many colors and hard, lean lines. She traced the fullness of his lips, eyeing him almost sheepishly through her thick veil of lashes. "Am I so funny-looking?" she asked softly.

"Your face with the black ash. It isn't the color of an Indian's," he laughed. "You *have* to know that."

She drew her own lips into a pout and dropped her hand to her side. "It is no longer the color of a white woman's either," she said. "That's what's important, isn't it?"

"Day-bway-win," he chuckled. "That is true."

His expression grew solemn, losing its momentary gaiety. "Red Blossom, you must not go," he said. He clasped her shoulders roughly. "You must reconsider. It could be dangerous. It will even be cold. A few snowflakes with their crystal stars have circled from the sky this morning. Surely you must realize all the dangers of traveling with Yellow Feather and his warriors."

Lorinda set her jaws firmly. "You do see my appearance, do you not?" she fumed.

"Ay-uh. . . ."

"Do you think I'd do this to myself and then stand with the Indian squaws only to sing songs of farewell?" she said determinedly.

"You are stubborn, Red Blossom," Yellow Feather argued, releasing his hold on her.

"It is my sister whom I must think of at this time in my life," she said, slipping into her moccasins. "It is *I* who shall point her out to you. I must go."

"Then you are ready to partake in the final feast . . . the Chippewas' final pledge of their readiness to face death?" he asked, once more showing a strange amusement in his dark pools of eyes.

Lorinda straightened her back and lifted her chin

291

haughtily, wondering what could be so darn amusing about partaking in a feast. "Yes," she said flatly. "I am ready."

Yellow Feather lifted the entrance flap and motioned with a hand for Lorinda to leave the wigwam with him. "Then I hope you will enjoy the dog's head that will be served you. . . ." he said, chuckling a bit beneath his breath.

Lorinda's gut twisted. She spun around and faced Yellow Feather with mouth agape. "What did you say?" she gasped.

"Red Blossom heard me well," Yellow Feather said, guiding her by an elbow away from Happy Flower who stood at the wigwam door, watching . . . listening. . . .

Lorinda stumbled a bit, casting him a sideways glance. "Dog's head . . . ?" she murmured. The thought of eating a dog caused a bitterness to rise in her throat. Would she retch before the whole village of Indians . . . ? Could she take even that first bite . . . ?

"Ay-uh," he said nonchalantly. "We slay the most brave of our dogs. Its spirit joins with us on our journey to the Sioux camp. Its fierceness joins in the fight."

"God . . ." Lorinda whispered, teetering a bit.

The constant boom-boom of the drum and loud songs of hopeful victory greeted Lorinda and Yellow Feather around the swelling bonfire in front of the council house. The aroma of meat boiling in water drew Lorinda's attention to the large black kettle hanging over another smaller fire and she knew that what Yellow Feather had just told her was true.

She shut her eyes, trying to not envision the dog's teeth or the dog's eyes. She would never forget the first time she had seen a *hog's* head boiling over the fire in her mother's log cabin. The teeth had shone back at her in ghostly pearls of white causing her to rush to the door and lose from her stomach all that she had eaten for breakfast that morning.

She forced her thoughts elsewhere. She had to prove her bravery in every way. She *had* to be able to stomach such a meal or most surely they would make her stay behind while they laughed and joked about the weak white woman who had so foolishly painted her face black with ash from a firespace.

"You sit beside me on my right, Red Blossom," Yellow Feather said quietly, urging her down on the ground in front of the fire. "Flying Squirrel will sit on my left."

Lorinda remembered leaving Happy Flower at the wigwam. Yellow Feather hadn't even bade her farewell. "And your Indian wife?" she said quietly to him. "Where will *she* sit?"

"All Indian squaws stay inside dwellings during this feast," he said flatly. "And I've commanded Happy Flower to stay in her dwelling even later when the farewell songs are sung. She has a baby to think of. She needs to avoid all excitement. We will see her on our joyous return."

Lorinda leaned a bit around Yellow Feather and studied Flying Squirrel's solemn expression. Surely *he* had bade Happy Flower a sensual goodbye when Yellow Feather had been busy mingling among his other warriors, handing out individual commands. Oh, if Yellow Feather only knew! The baby Happy Flower carried would no longer be of importance to him!

Lorinda placed such thoughts behind her and glanced quickly about her and saw that all the other warriors' faces were painted like Yellow Feather's. She saw even more than that. She saw a fierceness . . . a burning hatred. Yellow Feather's warriors were ambitious and had been held back from the victories of war with the Sioux for way too long now. The taking of a scalp while on the warpath was known to enhance the stature of the Chippewa male in the eyes of the village maidens. Yellow

Feather had explained to Lorinda that the fight with an enemy was even in part a psychological release for the pent-up bitterness and frustrations of the hard life of an Indian. Lorinda was once more reminded that Yellow Feather not only does this thing for her . . . but also for his people!

Lorinda jumped with a start as one of these warriors stepped before her and began smearing colorful liquid streaks across her face. She now had not only a blackened face, but also one of red and yellow! She murmured a low thank you as the Indian rose up away from her.

Ignoring the occasional glances her way, Lorinda straightened her back and crossed her arms, watching the wooden bowl of freshly cooked meat begin its slow journey around the circle of Indians until it was passed on to her by Yellow Feather. With trembling fingers she accepted it, and, feeling all eyes on her, she chose the smallest remaining piece of meat and hurriedly thrust it inside her mouth.

Staring straight ahead, she tried to not think about the glistening white teeth . . . the snout . . . the ears . . . and swallowed the meat whole. Choking a bit, she emitted a few strained coughs, then sighed with relief that the ordeal was over and passed the dish on to the next person. It hadn't really been all that bad. It hadn't tasted much different than boiled chicken. But she did hope never to have to participate in such a feast again!

Out of the corner of her eyes, she now saw Yellow Feather's large, colorfully decorated pipe being passed from Indian to Indian. The aroma, similar to burned grass, circled around the bonfire and weaved its way up Lorinda's nose. Another bridge to cross before being accepted into the war party! She had watched and wondered about the pipes her father had smoked but she had never dared to try smoking one herself! Would she gag and choke on this also? Why were the Indians' customs so darn strange and undesirable?

She sighed resolutely when the pipe was suddenly fit into her hand with its beautiful, different colors of feathers dangling from the one end. The reed stem was warm to the touch as she placed it to her mouth. She drew from it until she felt she had done her part and exhaled the smoke as swiftly as she pulled the stem from her mouth.

The sage taste and smell of it clung to her lips as she passed it on to Yellow Feather. She was proud. She had not shown any signs of having failed *this* test, though she was beginning to feel quite a giddiness in her head and a queasiness in her stomach. She placed a hand to her temple and watched as Yellow Feather rose to tower over her and all who sat waiting for his final commands of the morning.

"My warriors," he began in his booming voice of authority. "The scouting party has successfully returned and has found the Sioux camp where the white infant is being held captive. . . ."

Lorinda's fingers went to her throat as a low gasp surfaced from between her lips. Tears swam in her eyes, feeling so grateful toward Yellow Feather at this time. He had stood behind his word to find Amanda for her. Lorinda's heart swelled with love and joy. Her sister was alive! But . . . was . . . she well? She swallowed back that fear and listened further to Yellow Feather.

"Though you don't all approve, Red Blossom will go with us to the village of the Sioux. It is only right. It is her sister we will be killing for. Red Blossom must be there to attend to the infant on the journey's return. My warriors, she has shared willingly in our morning feast. She has shared our pipe of loyalty to one another. She has accepted us and our customs as you must also accept her presence at our side while going into battle."

Busy nods and grunts of approval went from man to man all the way around the circle to where Lorinda sat,

295

all warm in heart. She had been coached by Yellow Feather on how to properly say another thank you in Chippewa, since she had known that many thank yous would be in order once she had safely returned with Amanda. She rose to Chief Yellow Feather's side and stood tall and proud next to him. She said in a firm voice, "*Nin-mamoi-awl, nind-awema!*" which, when translated meant, "I thank you, my fellow tribesmen!"

This was met with chants and applause and a sudden pulsating from the war drum. Yellow Feather drew Lorinda next to him, proud.

"You spoke the words well, my Red Blossom," he said, smiling. He turned his gaze back to his people and raised a hand to encourage silence once more to spread among them.

"My warriors, we will move quietly and swiftly once we've arrived at the Sioux village. Since we have my woman and her sister to worry about our war will not be as fierce. We will seek a modest victory this time. We want little loss of lives. Our main concern is to return safely with Red Blossom and her baby sister,"

Low grumblings showed disapproval of this but Yellow Feather ignored them and raised his face to the shallow, blue skies of early morning. "Great owl of the forest, my guardian spirit, hear my prayers. Give my warriors courage and strength to lead them into a victorious battle. I pray that you will be kind enough to help me guide my people, to show them that I am a wise chief and a good leader. Please be kind enough to lead us home again to join together in the celebration with the scalp dance we've been without for too long a time."

Yellow Feather's arm strengthened around Lorinda's waist. "And, great owl of the forest, bless my Red Blossom that she will also have courage and strength to fight right alongside me and my warriors," he added, almost beneath his breath.

All the Indians seemed to rise at once from around the fire. Lorinda observed them closely. They were all buckskin clad and many sported several eagle feathers in the bands at their heads. The ones who weren't armed with rifles had bows and arrows positioned over their shoulders. They were a colorful lot with their painted faces and now they were suddenly embracing their women who had drifted from their wigwams to say their subdued farewells.

Lorinda turned to embrace Yellow Feather but was stopped by a firm, solid hand being laid on her shoulder from behind her. She turned quickly and looked down onto a face still unfamiliar to her despite all the Indians she had met. This Indian squaw was the shortest and fattest of them all, and when she smiled she showed herself to be quite toothless.

Yellow Feather intervened. "Big Laughing Star, I'm glad you've left your mourning behind you," he said, resting a hand heavily on her shoulder.

"Me brought gift to white wife," Big Laughing Star said solemnly, in English. "Then I return to my wigwam of sadness."

Lorinda now understood who this was. It was Chief Wind Whisper's widow, Yellow Feather's stepmother. Looking at what lay in Big Laughing Star's arms, a warmth surged through Lorinda. It was a cradleboard being offered her, for the comfort of her baby sister's return. Inside this straight board of basswood, many rabbit skins had been placed to wrap the baby in. Lorinda had worried about the tiny baby blanket that she had asked Yellow Feather to load with their travel gear. She had feared it wouldn't be enough protection against the bitter winds that swirled around from morning till night now that the season for snow was quickly upon them. But now, Amanda would be both comfortable *and* warm!

"*Mee-gway-chee-wahn-dum,*" Lorinda murmured, accepting the gift into her arms. "Oh, thank you so much, Big Laughing Star.''

Big Laughing Star laughed with her eyes then turned and waddled away with her head bowed, once more to mourn for the loss of a husband . . . a chief. . . .

Yellow Feather reached for his rifle and thrust it into the air above his head. *''Gee-mah-gi-ung-ah-shig-wah,''* he shouted. ''Come. We now go to the canoes!''

Loud excited Indian chatterings followed along with Lorinda and Yellow Feather as they headed toward the banks of the St. Croix River. The women of the village walked along behind, singing their short song of farewell, repeating it over and over again.

''Come,
It is time for you to depart,
We are going on a long journey;
Come,
It is time for you to depart,
We are going on a long journey. . . .''

The odors of the forest, the dew and damp meadow, and the curling smoke from the wigwams were left behind as Lorinda was directed toward the canoes that were resting, gently swaying, at the edge of the clear waters of the river. Yellow Feather had explained that this was the quietest way to approach the Sioux village and would cut the miles they would have had to travel by horseback by at least half.

Lorinda was helped into one of these long, birch-bark canoes. Soft furs covered the floor beneath where she sat, and upon these she placed the baby's cradleboard. Her heart raged inside her to think that soon she might see the sky-blue eyes of her sister staring back at her from the Indian's papoose case. Oh, if only she would be found

298

healthy! How much larger had she grown through these many long weeks of separation?

Lorinda held onto the sides of the canoe as the six canoemen required in this larger canoe manned the oars and pulled the low-riding boat away from the shore. With strong strokes, they dipped the oar tips quietly into the water, sending the graceful canoe forth with each stroke, setting out, paddling upriver.

Glancing at Yellow Feather, who sat directly in front of her, Lorinda felt pride that he was her husband. *Ay-uh,* she had accepted him as any white woman accepts her man, except that he was of a different color and words by a minister had not been spoken over them. But that no longer mattered to her. He had in so many ways proven his love for her. So would she also to him. *"Ay-pah-nay,"* she whispered. *"Ay-uh,* forever. . . ."

The anticipation of what lay before her, even possibly by nightfall, caused her pulse to race. As each oar lifted, so did her spirits. The cold splash of the river's spray against her face caused her no discomfort. She had her thoughts to warm her.

No conversation was shared among the St. Croix band of the Chippewa. Their eyes said it all. The thrill of the conquest drawing nearer . . . nearer . . . danced in each.

The canoes rose and sank with the waves and then slipped along smoothly. They swerved gracefully in and out of the swamp inlets with stiff black skeletons of dead trees rising from the mud. And when night brought with it only the faint sparklings from the stars and a tiny silver of the moon, only then did the canoes begin maneuvering closer to the shore and begin to slow down.

Lorinda's eyes widened and she tensed when she saw some orange reflections against the sky high on the tops of the cliffs on one side of her. She hated breaking the silence, but she had to know the meaning of those lights that now proved to be many fires burning.

She reached and tapped Yellow Feather's shoulder. He turned his dark eyes to her. "I see also," he grumbled. "It is the signal fires built by the Sioux. We are almost there. We must now beach the canoes and go by foot."

Lorinda swallowed hard, suddenly afraid. She glanced upwards toward the fires again and saw many figures silhouetted against the sky. "Did they see us, Yellow Feather?" she whispered.

"*Gah-ween,*" he mumbled. "And that is good for more reasons than one."

"Why . . . ?"

"While these Sioux stand so far from their village we will steal silently in and out of their camp without them even knowing it."

"But your guns. They will hear."

"Our knives will do," he said. "Our rifles we will leave in the canoes."

"Is that wise?"

"Is Yellow Feather chief?" Yellow Feather grumbled, glaring toward her.

"*Ay-uh,*" she said with lowered lashes.

"Then Red Blossom must not question *any*thing I do!"

Lorinda tensed even more as the canoes were one by one beached into thick brush at the river's edge. She sat, trembling, as Yellow Feather went among his men, handing out last-minute instructions. The rifles were placed back in the canoes and a dull shine from the knives was soon reflected in each of their hands.

"Come," Yellow Feather said to Lorinda, offering her a hand. "We know which teepee your sister is in. We go right to her."

"How . . . ?" Lorinda whispered.

"My head scout is good . . . a smart scout," Yellow Feather bragged. "Now you just stay beside me. You don't need knife. *I* protect you fully."

Lorinda's hand went to the lump in her jacket, feeling

her gun. Would he understand her need to carry it? She thought not.

The flickering from a campfire showed through the low brush. Lorinda quickly observed that the Sioux dwellings were different from the Chippewa wigwams. Where the Chippewas' lodges had rounded, domed roofs, the Sioux teepees were in the shape of cones, reaching upward to sharp peaks. These had been built with easy access to the river and sat scattered about. Many horses were roughly fenced in at the far end of the village where meadow met forest. It was late, and only a few Sioux strolled leisurely about outside their dwellings and around the campfire.

"Come," Yellow Feather encouraged her, guiding her on through scratchy briars and low-hanging limbs of willows.

Lorinda was barely breathing, now studying the one Sioux who was within viewing range. He was no different from the Chippewa. The clothing was the same, as were his features and the color of his skin.

"We are now close to the teepee where your sister is," Yellow Feather whispered, drawing Lorinda close to his side. He pointed toward a teepee whose entrance flap was shut. Its outside wall showed a glowing from inside, indicating that a fire burned in the center firespace.

Yellow Feather moved stealthily to where the clearing began, raising his hand, stopping his men. Lorinda's gaze moved quickly on about her, stopping suddenly where two tall poles stood straight up from the ground. Her heart began to race, as she saw the color of the hair swaying gently in the breeze at the top of the one pole. The outside campfire flickered in oranges onto it, making the thick crop of rusty hair even redder than it was.

Lorinda swallowed back a burning sensation in her throat as she began to gasp for air, also recognizing the long, gray scalp of her mother that dangled from the next

301

pole. With a dizziness engulfing her, she closed her eyes and felt a scream rising from her inner depths, but she was silenced just in time as Yellow Feather's fingers clasped tightly over her mouth. Then when the urge had left her and his hand had fallen away from her, she leaned heavily into his embrace and wept quietly.

"I saw," Yellow Feather crooned, cradling her head against his chest. "I knew whose they were the minute I saw. You had described their color. I knew."

He paused a bit, then said, "You must place your grief behind you, Lorinda. We must hasten on. We must move swiftly or we will be discovered."

Lorinda drew away from him, sniffling. She wiped her nose with the back of a hand and straightened her back. For a moment, she had let herself show the weak side of her character. She had to be stronger to continue with the task at hand. "I'm sorry, Yellow Feather," she murmured. "I promise not to slow you any longer."

"There will be Sioux scalps taken, Lorinda," he said thickly. "You must be prepared to witness this. I know it is not the way of your white people."

Lorinda swallowed hard. She cleared her throat nervously and shifted her weight from one foot to the other. "I know," she whispered. "I understand it is the way of the Indian."

She let her gaze move slowly over her parents' scalps again, shuddering violently. "Yes, I understand it's the way of *all* Indians."

Then her head jerked quickly around. She eyed Yellow Feather quizzically. He had twice called her Lorinda instead of his appointed name of Red Blossom. Had he done so to give her more comfort in her moments of grief? He had known all along she had preferred her own name.

"Red Blossom, it is now time," he whispered harshly.

Lorinda smiled to herself, thinking now that she would

302

probably never hear him speak her true name again. For a moment, when she had been grieving for her parents, she had become white again in his eyes. But now that she was showing renewed strength and courage she was *Indian*, ready to join in the attack!

"*Ay-uh*," she replied, squaring her shoulders even more.

Yellow Feather lifted a doubled fist into the air and looked around at all his waiting warriors. His blood had warmed and his heart pounded inside him. How long had he waited for such an opportunity as this! He had hated the Sioux with a deep vengeance since those many long years ago when they would almost monthly sneak into his village and scalp some of the men and steal the women. Chief Wind Whisper had at first retaliated but after the white man came and began pushing the Chippewa around, all the fight had been taken out of the reigning chief of the St. Croix band of the Chippewa. In time, the Sioux gave up the plunderings, having only begun them in the first place to torment the Chippewa into battle, for *all* Indians loved a battle!

Yellow Feather dropped his arm quickly to his side, the signal for his men to attack. He stayed behind with Lorinda, waiting for the right moment to enter the one teepee where he would take his own share of scalps . . . !

Lorinda took a step backwards. She covered her mouth with her hands, suddenly ghastly ill, seeing how quickly the Indians had slain the Sioux warriors who had so peacefully been strolling around the campfire. Each now lay dead of knife wounds, blood seeping from them and void . . . of . . . hair! The scalping had been that swift. The shine of the knives could have been streaks of lightning they had moved so quickly in the hands of the Chippewa.

Lorinda watched, shivering, as Yellow Feather's

Chippewa men sneaked in and out of teepees. She wondered how much blood was being left behind inside of each. . . .

"Come," Yellow Feather said suddenly. "It is now time."

Lorinda felt her pulse race and her face become hot with her own kind of excitement. Soon she would have her sister back with her. All she had to do was recall all the grief these Sioux had caused the Odell family to be able to accept that they were being dealt with fairly. Those who now lay dead would never go on a hunt for more white man's scalps. It was right that they were now without their own!

Stealthily, she moved alongside Yellow Feather. She became breathless when Yellow Feather lifted the entrance flap, wanting to rush on past him, to see for herself that Amanda was there. But Yellow Feather blocked her way with his left arm and, with his right, guided his knife downward, plummeting it into the chest of the male occupant of this dwelling, who had met Yellow Feather's entrance, also with raised knife. But Yellow Feather had been the swifter of the two. . . .

As the Sioux crumpled to the floor, Yellow Feather's arm freed Lorinda, to let her move further into the dwelling. But, instead, she stood as though frozen as Yellow Feather knelt over his kill and quickly rid the Sioux of his coal-black braided hair.

Lorinda gulped back a bitterness rising in her throat, recognizing the savage in Yellow Feather as he stood and held the scalp before his eyes, proud. Then Lorinda's gaze followed his and found a beautiful Sioux maiden, huddled, trembling, against the far wall. In her arms she held a baby, and next to her lay another wrapped bundle that was squirming and emitting soft noises of baby play.

"Amanda . . . ?" Lorinda whispered. The campfire's glow showed the baby in the Indian's woman's

304

arms to be Indian. Lorinda bit her lower lip in disappointment. Then her gaze shifted once more to the other wrapped bundle. Her heart pounded against her ribs as she managed to thaw her limbs of their fear and shock from what she had witnessed Yellow Feather do. She started to take a step forward but Yellow Feather was quickly there, in her way, with his knife poised, moving toward the Indian maiden with the wide, dark eyes and narrow, velvet face.

Lorinda's voice caught in her throat, wanting to yell out at Yellow Feather. But no words would surface as she watched him move closer and closer to the woman. With his knife still raised, Lorinda knew what his intentions were. He was ready to take another scalp!

Two quick steps took Lorinda to Yellow Feather's side. She raised a hand to his arm just as he was letting it move downward to slay another Sioux. *"Gah-ween,"* she whispered harshly. "No, Yellow Feather. You can't kill her. She's so innocent and beautiful. And she's a *mother*. Would you also kill her babies?"

"Her babies?" Yellow Feather growled. "Do you so soon forget that one of these babies is not hers? One is your sister."

Lorinda's eyes wavered. Her heart ached to drop to her knees to pull the blankets aside, to see the face of this second baby, but the sparing of a life had become uppermost in her mind. "Please, Yellow Feather?" she pleaded. "Do not do this thing. Enough blood has been spilled tonight. Let this woman . . . live."

Yellow Feather's dark eyes bore down upon Lorinda in anger. He jerked her hand from his arm, then slowly placed his knife inside the sheath at his waist. He still held the one scalp in his other hand and stepped back away from Lorinda as though he was a child that had been scolded.

"Her life is spared," he hissed.

305

Lorinda inched her way in front of the maiden, eyeing her cautiously, then suddenly fell to her knees and threw the blankets aside from around the other baby. Tears splashed from her eyes and a sudden warmth flowed through her. Amanda lay there without clothes, revealing how fat and healthy she was! Amanda smiled toward Lorinda, showing eight teeth shining back at her, and her sky-blue eyes showed a quiet, content peacefulness.

A keen happiness flooded through Lorinda. She swept Amanda up into her arms and hugged her to her bosom. She clung to her, slowly weeping with joy. Then her gaze met that of the Indian woman, and Lorinda knew that she had been right to save this woman's life. It had been this beautiful mother who had most surely shared her milk-filled breasts with Amanda. She had given Amanda love and tender care, for it showed in how healthy and content Amanda was.

"*Neen mee-gway-chee-wahn-dum,* beautiful Sioux mother," she whispered. "But saying thank you doesn't seem enough for seeing to it that my sister is found alive and well."

A quiet fear was in the Indian maiden's eyes. Lorinda watched her eyes move to the body that lay on the other side of the firespace.

"This is how you thank me," the Sioux maiden said suddenly, in very clear English. "You kill my man."

Lorinda cringed inside, then her eyes flashed angrily back at her. "Your man killed my parents," she hissed. "The proof hangs outside your teepee door. My parents' scalps hang on your scalp poles. The death that came to this teepee tonight is my way of thanking you for my weeks of mourning and grief."

The Indian maiden's eyes lowered. She began rocking back and forth, singing a mournful song, now ignoring any other presence in her teepee.

"You are lucky *you* were spared," Lorinda said flatly.

"Your man was not as kind. *He* slayed a mother . . . *my* mother."

Lorinda reached for a blanket and wrapped it snugly around Amanda, then turned on a heel and looked proudly toward Yellow Feather. "I am ready, my chief," she murmured, tears near as she felt the squirmings of her sister in her arms. Oh, how many nights had she dreamed of this moment? How many prayers had she spoken? And it had been so *easy!* Yes, thanks to Yellow Feather, rescuing her sister had been so easy!

When they stepped outside the wigwam, Lorinda took one more last glance at her parents' scalps, then held her head high and followed Yellow Feather and his waiting, triumphant warriors back to the canoes. Yellow Feather helped her inside and once she had Amanda secured safely on the cradleboard, she held her on her lap and gazed lovingly down at the watchful blue of her sister's eyes.

"Amanda . . ." Lorinda whispered. "Amanda . . . Amanda!"

She loved the sound of her sister's name on her lips, for she was really a part of Lorinda's life again. She was alive! She was well!

Lorinda leaned a kiss onto Amanda's cheek, feeling the softness, tasting the sweetness. She then watched the night gather more darkly around her as the canoes slipped smoothly away from the Sioux camp, leaving havoc and bloodshed behind. . . .

Nineteen

"Well, I'll be damn," Silas Konrad said. He leaned a bit forward on his horse and lifted his knitted hat to scratch his head. "What the hell . . . ?"

His dark eyes moved slowly around him and on through the cover of the low-hanging branches of maple trees, seeing that an Indian village had sprung up where only days ago there had only been the cave, forest, and meadow. Narrowing his eyes, he was now recognizing the wigwams and the two Indians standing guard, hovering over the greatness of an outdoor fire that was turning the dark of the sky to shimmering oranges.

"I thought you said we were going to enter a cave, not an Indian village," a man growled beside Silas. "Damn if I want Injuns takin' *my* hair as a prize." He glanced at Silas's shining bald head and laughed throatily. "Course you don't have no worry 'bout *that,* do you Silas?"

Silas pulled his hat back onto his head, frowning. "Cain't figure it out," he said, ignoring the insulting comment. "The Injuns weren't here before. Damn it, I'd know it. I know where all the Indian villages are. I've traded with 'em all. This particular village was a full day's travel from here."

"Well, seems you ain't as smart as you thought you were," Lawrence laughed again.

"Now I don't know what's happened here," Silas continued, looking even more intently into the village. "But, Lawrence, 'pears we're in luck. The village is deserted of mos' of its braves."

"What Injuns are these?" Lawrence asked, picking at his buckteeth with the sharp point of a knife. His eyes were large and wild and his head bare of a hat, leaving his tousled jet-black hair blowing gently in the night breeze.

"The Chippewa . . ." Silas said. "The St. Croix band of the Ojibway."

"Who's the chief?"

"I imagine you'd now find that answer to be Yellow Feather," Silas mumbled. "If Chief Wind Whisper was still alive, the Injuns wouldn't be here. I've a feelin' this move was guided by the new chief who had hidden his treasures away in a cave." He nodded toward the cave entrance. "That very cave. Where I was left for dead."

"A white woman done and shot you, you said, eh?"

"Yeah. White, with the damnest red hair."

"Got to ask, Silas. Did you come back here for the loot . . . or for the woman . . . ?"

Silas laughed greedily. "Both," he said. "Damn it, I owe that red-haired wench somethin' and I intend to find her and take her back to my ranch and show her she shouldn't mess 'roun with the likes of Silas Konrad."

"What you aimin' to do now that there's an Injun village standin' in the way of the cave?"

"What'd *you* like to do, Lawrence?" Silas chuckled.

"I've always wanted an Injun squaw."

"Well, I've always wanted an Indian *scalp*," Silas sneered. "I've been a trader for way too long. Now I aim to *take* what I want."

A third man with shoulder-length brown hair and a thin build guided his horse and covered wagon up next to Silas. "Well? What's the delay?" he asked, looking from Silas to Lawrence.

"Daniel, ain't you got eyes?" Lawrence fumed, pointing his knife toward the fire and the two Indians.

Daniel lifted his rifle from his lap. "Yeah. I see," he said. "I should be able to pick 'em off from here." He

310

aimed, but Silas knocked the barrel down before he had a chance to pull the trigger.

"We ain't sure those are the only red savages," Silas grumbled. "We must move quietly. Attack 'em from the rear, then look around to be sure we don't get it in the back while emptyin' the cave into our wagon."

"Yeah," Daniel growled. "Guess you're right."

Silas dismounted and secured his horse to a low tree limb. "I guess you gents got to know I'm goin' to find that red-haired wench, don't you?" he said, spitting into the wind. "I'm sure she ain't in the cave no longer. She's probably livin' in *his* wigwam now. What a waste. Tsk, tsk. She givin' herself to a red man instead of white."

"That woman will probably be the death of you yet, Silas," Daniel said, climbing from his wagon. He tied his horse's reins next to Silas's. "If I hadn't been near before, you'd have bled to death."

"Yeah. Some guard you turned out to be," Silas spat angrily. "You were supposed to be standin' guard instead of sleepin'. Why, you didn't even stop 'er when she ran from the cave."

"I didn't even see her," Daniel said. "I was down by the river, lettin' my horse get its fill of water. It was the gunshot that grabbed my attention. You're lucky, Silas, that I even was there. You usually travel alone."

"Yeah . . ." Silas grumbled. "Let's quit jawin' and go to it. I had a reason to bring you along again *this* time, you know."

They all scrambled along together, until they crept to the edge of the clearing. Silas pulled his knife from his pocket and flipped the blade open and tiptoed to where the one Indian stood, yawning. While Lawrence thrust his knife into the other Indian's back, Silas did likewise to this Indian. He then stepped back, breathing heavily, as the Indian crumpled to the ground. Feeling a keen sense of revulsion, Silas kicked the Indian over onto his stomach and left him lying there.

With the fire casting his short, round shadow behind him, Silas went to Lawrence and nudged him in the side. "Whatcha' think? Think the coast is clear to go explorin' inside the wigwams?" He wiped the blood from his knife onto his breeches and held it out ready for whoever might jump out at him from the shadows.

"Looks clear enough," Lawrence said. He glanced from one dead Indian to the next. "Thought you were goin' to take a scalp, Silas." he laughed mockingly. "Ain't got the stomach for it? Eh?"

"I've got more important things on my mind," Silas said stiffly.

"Well, I'm keepin' *my* word," Lawrence said, taking long, confident strides away from Silas. "I'm gettin' me a woman. A pretty, dark-skinned woman. Then I'll be ready to do whatever else you have a mind to do."

"You'll need eyes in the back of your head if you go and take advantage of an Injun squaw," Silas said, peering cautiously about him. "Those Injun warriors can move so quiet and swift, you wouldn't know what hit you if they found you in one of their dwellings with one of their women."

"I knows how to take care of myself," Lawrence chuckled.

Silas tensed when he saw Lawrence lift an entrance flap and disappear from view. He took a step forward and listened. He could hear the throaty laugh surfacing from Lawrence and knew that he had found himself a plaything, all right. Silas frowned a bit. He had never thought he would be doing more than trading with Yellow Feather's people. The thought of being discovered by the dark, emotionless-eyed Indian turned his blood cold. But he did have a reason to be here other than his hatred for Yellow Feather. He wanted that woman, *and* what the cave had hidden inside it. Wasn't it his right to take what Yellow

312

Feather had taken from the white people? Even the woman?

Silas turned with a start when Daniel suddenly walked up behind him. "You'd best go on in the cave and start loadin' the wagon, Daniel," he said, spitting on the ground at his feet, hoping the trembling in his voice hadn't been evident. He *was* a bit afraid. He knew these Indians could have quite a unique way of seeking revenge.

Daniel looked around, eyes wide with consuming fear. "Where's Lawrence?" he whispered.

"He's havin' some fun," Silas laughed nervously.

"Is that wise?"

"Just you worry about unloadin' that cave of its goods," Silas said. "We can get a lot of greenbacks for that stuff that Yellow Feather has highjacked from the white man. Just you concentrate on that while I concentrate on my other thing I've come for."

"I don't like this," Daniel said, lifting his rifle to rest into the crook of his left arm. "I didn't mind coming again to the cave, but I wouldn't have come to this village."

"Well, Daniel, how was I to know that the Indian Yellow Feather would move his camp next to where I found that woman?"

"I'd feel better if you'd just let me shoot them all. It'd be much safer for us."

"Sure. You only feel brave when you have a gun pointin' at somethin', eh, Daniel?"

Daniel stormed away from Silas, leaving Silas to peer cautiously from wigwam to wigwam, wondering in which one he would find his red-haired prize. Surely the Indians inside their dwellings knew they were no longer alone. Surely they knew that the braves who had been left to watch over them were now dead.

Silas kneaded his chin. "Where the hell are the rest of

the Injuns?'' he grumbled to himself. "Where's Yellow Feather? Flying Squirrel?'' He shrugged and decided to move from one wigwam to the next until he found the answers he wanted. In the first several he chose, he found squaws huddled, frightened into silence, then he found the one that held Happy Flower.

Silas stood over her with legs widespread. The fire in the firespace glowed in soft, pale oranges onto her face full of fear. Her eyes were wide as she began scooting back away from him. "What you want, Silas Konrad?'' she uttered softly. She glanced toward the closed entrance flap, oh, so hoping for Flying Squirrel's or Yellow Feather's return. She didn't like the glint in this evil man's eyes, and she had seen him slay the one warrior while the other evil man had slain the other.

Yellow Feather had felt too confident of this new land he had directed his people to. He should have never taken most of his warriors with him. But she knew that all had wanted to go. It had been too long since they had had such excitement to stir their blood. She understood. *Ay-uh,* she understood. But she was afraid! She covered the swell of her stomach with her crossed arms, breathing erratically. Oh, how she was afraid for her unborn child. . . !

"Well, ain't this comfy and cozy?'' Silas sneered. "The pretty Injun squaw Happy Flower and Silas Konrad all alone in a wigwam.''

Happy Flower was so afraid, no more words would surface from between her lips. She just continued staring in silence back at him, having always hated his shifty eyes. She had thought that all white people were probably as unpleasant, having only become acquainted with this one, until Red Blossom. Red Blossom was likable, even trustworthy. Her devotion to Yellow Feather had even made Happy Flower feel ashamed for having tricked him. Such deceit! Oh, how ashamed she was! Though it had

314

been Flying Squirrel whom Happy Flower had at first loved . . . Yellow Feather had eventually stolen her heart. Flying Squirrel had lost his way of lifting her lonely shroud from around her, though she pretended quite convincingly when she was with him. . . .

Silas leaned over, taunting her with his knife. He laughed mockingly. "Wha's the matter? Cat got your tongue? You ain't afraid of Yellow Feather's old faithful trader friend, are you?"

Happy Flower regained a bit of her courage. "Silas Konrad no friend to Chief Yellow Feather or his people," she hissed.

Silas's eyebrows tilted. "Chief Yellow Feather, is it?" he said. "So the ol' man finally kicked the bucket, eh?"

Happy Flower's dark eyes became ablaze with anger. She rose to her feet and challenged him with crossed arms. "Silas Konrad, you no welcome in my wigwam. You go," she stated flatly.

"To hell you say," he laughed. Then his face grew somber and threatening as he took a step toward her. "Silas Konrad'll leave when Silas Konrad decides to leave." He spat on the ground at her feet and placed his knife threateningly close to the swell of her abdomen. "Now tell me, pretty thing, where's Yellow Feather?"

"Me no tell," she said with a haughty lift of her chin.

"Maybe you'll tell me where that red-haired wench is that your chief is acquainted with?" he said sourly. "Surely you don't approve of her shackin' up with your man. Eh? Come on. Tell me which wigwam she's in so's I can go fetch her and rid your village of 'er."

Happy Flower's eyes grew wide as her mouth went slack. "You speak of Red Blossom . . . ?" she whispered.

"Red . . . who . . . ?" Silas said.

Happy Flower didn't know how this man could know of Red Blossom but she did know it was best not to tell

315

him anything about her, though jealousy toward Red Blossom *had* caused much pain in her heart.

She began shaking her head back and forth. "Me no tell you anything," she said. She flinched when Silas's knife moved closer. She eyed it warily, then him. Feeling panic rising inside her, Happy Flower tried to move away from him but tripped on one of his feet and while doing so fell suddenly into him . . . and . . . onto his knife. . . . A low gurgling sound came from the depths of her throat as she clawed at his chest, eyeing him still with the dark browns of her eyes. . . .

"Oh, my God," Silas gasped. He pulled his knife free from her stomach and watched her crumple, lifeless, to the thick pads of bulrush mats at his feet. He stood there, numb, having never had any intention of harming Yellow Feather's Indian squaw. He had meant to scare answers out of her. That was all. Now what was he to do? Once she was found dead by Yellow Feather, Silas knew what to expect.

"I've got to get out of here," he blurted. He took a last look at Happy Flower and then downward at her stomach, realizing that his knife hadn't snuffed the life of just one Indian . . . but two. . . .

With fear lacing his heart, he swung around and fled from the wigwam. Once outside, he closed his eyes and wiped the perspiration from his brow, knowing that his days on earth were probably now numbered. Yellow Feather would seek him out. There was no doubt about it.

A low snicker beside him drew Silas's eyes quickly open. He frowned darkly toward Lawrence who stepped before him, tucking his shirt back inside the waist of his breeches.

"That squaw of mine sure didn't cooperate," Lawrence chuckled. "But that didn't keep me from gettin' my enjoys."

"Did you hurt 'er?" Silas grumbled, peering toward

316

the wigwam from which Lawrence had emerged.

"Naw," Lawrence said, shaking his head.

"Well, you'd best get that smug look off your face, Lawrence? Cause I *did* hurt the Injun *I* was talkin' to."

Lawrence's dark eyes glistened. His lips curved upward into a wicked, sly grin. "You did?" he snickered.

"Ain't like what you're thinkin'," Silas snarled. "I did more'n hurt her." He glanced quickly toward the silence of the wigwam behind him. "She's dead, Lawrence. She's damn dead."

Lawrence's face drained of color. "You . . . killed her . . . ?" he gasped, looking down at the knife in Silas's hand and at the blood drying on it.

"It was a damn accident," Silas growled. He held the knife out before him and suddenly dropped it as though it was a hot coal, no longer wanting any part of it. "She fell on it, herself. . . ." he added softly.

"Let's get the hell out of here," Lawrence said, glancing all around him.

Silas began running toward the cave where Daniel was diligently laboring, loading the wagon with the cave's contents. He went to Daniel and knocked a pile of colorful blankets from his arms. "We're a-leavin'," he shouted. "Get a move on."

Daniel flipped his long hair around and faced Silas. "Huh?" he said, eyes wide.

"We've got us a problem," Lawrence said. "Silas here killed himself an Injun squaw."

"Not *a* squaw," Silas said. "Chief Yellow Feather's pregnant squaw. His wife. . . ."

Lawrence gasped noisily. "Silas, you failed to tell me *that*."

"God . . ." Daniel groaned. He climbed aboard the wagon and jerked and snapped the reins against his horse. "I'm a-gettin' for *sure*," he shouted from across his shoulder.

Silas's short legs wouldn't carry him as fast as Lawrence's and when he finally reached his horse, he found that Lawrence was already gone and out of viewing range. He mounted his horse and followed the sound of the wagon wheels rattling through the forest and soon drew himself up next to Daniel.

"Where's Lawrence?" he asked, wheezing.

"Damn if I know," Daniel said, snapping the horse fiercely with the reins.

"He's done and run out on us," Silas snarled.

"Can't say I blame him none," Daniel replied sourly.

"It's best we stick together, Daniel. . . ."

"Afraid I'll get all the money from these guns and blankets?" Daniel laughed sarcastically.

"Afraid if we travel alone, the Injuns will have the advantage. . . ." Silas said, leaning his knees more heavily against the horse.

Daniel cast Silas a troubled glance. . . .

Twenty

The canoes slipped along smoothly and swiftly through the waters of the St. Croix. The only sounds were those of the paddles striking the water in unison. Lorinda sat behind Yellow Feather, wanting to feel victorious, yet not. She did finally have her sister with her, but a part of her had been left behind, where her heart had slivered into a million pieces when she had recognized the hair hanging from the scalp poles. She had thought of rescuing them also, but she had known that the humility of what had been done to her parents no longer had a role in her future. She had her sister. Amanda and Yellow Feather were Lorinda's future! The scalps only reflected the brief moments in her parents' lives that Lorinda knew they wouldn't want her always to be reminded of, which she would have been, had she taken their scalps with her, to be daily reminders of how they had so terribly died.

Pride swept through her as she looked down at the bundle swaddled up on the cradleboard. Her parents would be proud to know that their older daughter had rescued the younger. "I really always doubted that I could ever do it," she whispered. "I doubted that I would even be given the chance!"

She gazed with a keen sense of appreciation toward Yellow Feather, who continued taking strong strokes, dipping his paddle tips quietly into the waters, sending the canoe shooting forth with each stroke. Even though he was heavily attired in his muskrat jacket, Lorinda could still see the corded muscles of his shoulders and arms. She loved the way in which he sat so proud . . . so handsome. Oh, would she always love him as much as she did at this very moment? Could she ever repay him for his devotion to her?

But his devotion to his people is even greater, she thought to herself. She was remembering the intensity in his eyes when he had commanded his warriors into the Sioux village. He had shown such pride in how quickly and silently his men had slain the Sioux. She shuddered, remembering also how unflinchingly he had slain his own Sioux and scalped him. . . .

Lorinda now felt a bit of guilt ripple through her. To save her sister, death had come to others. Should she feel so proud? She straightened her back and tilted her chin. "Yes," she whispered. "I *am* proud that death came to those who took my parents from me and my sister. . . ."

Yellow Feather's heart thundered with a wild pounding. Only one more bend in the river and he and his warriors would be met with many victory songs. The fires would be built to light the skies as brightly as day, and the scalp poles would be readied for the prizes. The scalp dance would last on into the morning, and then the feast would be great! He was returning the victor. He had proven his greatness as chief!

He smiled a bit to himself. Lorinda had been so involved in rescuing her sister, she hadn't seen him cut a strip of flesh from the back of his slain Sioux's leg at the knee. Would his Red Blossom understand this particular custom . . . that bringing this home to his people was a token of his victory? Before the scalp dance would begin the flesh from the Sioux would be cut into small pieces and passed around to all the notable warriors, who would be obliged to eat them. Those who would keep their pieces down would be honored as highly as the man who had killed the enemy. Those who could not would be derided.

Ay-uh, much death had been left behind at the Sioux camp and the victory celebration would be long and sweet. . . .

The bend in the river was reached and passed. Yellow Feather lifted his eyes to the sky, seeing no color, only the black velvet of the sky and its sequin of stars. The moon had slipped away below the tips of the Norway pines and everything was much too quiet. Where was the steady rhythm of the drums that were supposed to be beating out a welcome? Where were the great fires? Where were the maidens who should be paddling out in their smaller canoes to greet them with their beautiful songs?

A fear was causing a slow rippling of cold to wash through him. He now knew there was to be no greeting for him, the chief of the St. Croix Indians, the proud Chippewa, the Ojibway. He could only think of one reason why. Some sort of disaster had struck his village while he had been gone wreaking havoc on another. Only one sort of disaster could cause such a silence. Death.

He began shouting, feeling breathless from the mounting anxieties over what he would find. "My warriors, *wee-wee-bee-tahn!*" he boomed. "Something is *gee-wah-ni-chee-gay* in our village. *Wee-wee-bee-tahn!* Something is wrong!"

The paddles began moving more quickly and soon the canoes were beached and empty.

Lorinda lifted her sister up into her arms, feeling the contagion of fear and confusion around her. She heard the click of the rifles as they were readied and then rushed to Yellow Feather's side and spoke quietly to him. "Yellow Feather, what's the matter?"

"My village is too quiet," he said. "Something has happened." He placed a hand on Lorinda's arm. "You stay behind. Let me and my warriors see what has hap-

321

pened. I fear for my people. I fear also for you. . . ."

Though it was dark, Lorinda could see the dark of his eyes beseeching her and could feel his fear move from him to her. "I'm afraid, Yellow Feather," she whispered. "I don't want to stay here by myself."

"Flying Squirrel will stay with you," he murmured.

Lorinda's insides rippled with mistrust and hate as Flying Squirrel stepped to her side with his hands clasped tightly onto his rifle.

"Flying Squirrel, *ee-shqueen,*" Yellow Feather ordered firmly. "You stay with Red Blossom and let no harm come to her."

Flying Squirrel's gaze was looking further than Lorinda. His eyes showed worry and concern as he studied the stillness of the night. "Yellow Feather, it is *much* too quiet," he worried aloud. He took a step forward. "I want to go into the village with you. I am no watch dog. I want to check to see if . . ."

Yellow Feather stepped in Flying Squirrel's way. "You do as I say," he snapped angrily.

"Ay-uh," Flying Squirrel growled.

Yellow Feather moved stealthily away and raised a doubled fist into the air then dropped it suddenly, a signal for his armed men to follow after him.

Lorinda's breathing was shallow as she watched . . . Flying Squirrel's pulse pounded out his fear for Happy Flower and their child . . . Yellow Feather's fears were confirmed as he stepped into the clearing . . . and . . . immediately saw his two slain warriors lying beside the soft glow of the one remaining fire in the village. His heart became like a drum, pounding, echoing his sadness over what his eyes had revealed to him, wondering, who . . . why . . . ?

He stretched his arms out on both sides of him, stopping his men's approach. What was the forest beyond hiding? How had anyone found this new place he had

322

guided his people to? Wasn't the great owl of the forest watching over him and his people any longer? But he knew that Chief Wind Whisper's guardian spirit hadn't spared him from all griefs and heartaches. The white man had always seemed to know how to trick even the guardian spirits. . . .

"White man . . ." he whispered harshly. His glance moved quickly to the cave. His hatred swelled when he saw the scattered blankets and strewn pots and pans on the ground at the cave's entrance. "Only one white man knew of this place . . . the cave. . . ." he said aloud, placing his finger on the trigger of his rifle. "Silas Konrad. He has returned. Red Blossom did *not* kill him as she thought."

A loud, mournful wail like nothing he had ever heard before grabbed at Yellow Feather's heart. His head jerked around and he began following the sound, moving even more quickly when he realized from which wigwam the sound of grieving was rising. "Happy Flower," he whispered. "It is Happy Flower's wigwam, but it is Big Laughing Star's voice. . . ."

He rushed to the wigwam and raised the entrance flap with one swift jerk. He stopped abruptly when he saw the scene of death before him. He felt a numbness of sorts enter his legs and move swiftly up to circle his heart when he saw the stilled sweetness of Happy Flower's face and then lower to where the blood had run and spread across the swell of her abdomen where the child had been so peacefully growing.

Big Laughing Star was oblivious to his entrance. She still sat, rocking back and forth on her knees at Happy Flower's side, continuing to wail and grieve.

Yellow Feather dropped his rifle to the floor and went to Big Laughing Star and placed a hand heavily on her shoulder. "Big Laughing Star," he said thickly. "I have returned." He was battling the tears that were swelling in his eyes. He was the chief. He had to show his bravery, even through the loss of a wife and an unborn child. He had to be strong for his people. They would be bewildered and needing reassurances from their leader. If a chief's wife could be slain so easily . . . couldn't they all? He knew that would be the question lying heavily on each of their hearts.

His insides twisted. It seemed that not only a wife and child had been taken from him this night by the hands of an evil white man, but also his acknowledgment of victory by his people upon his return from the Sioux camp. Had the respect for him that accompanied such a victory also been lessened? Had he failed his people by leaving them so vulnerable . . . ?

Big Laughing Star turned her gaze upward, now only sniffling. "Yellow Feather, she is dead," she whispered. "Happy Flower . . . is . . . dead. . . ."

Yellow Feather urged her up and looked intently into her dark, bloodshot eyes. "Who did this thing?" he stated flatly. "Who invades my village and does this thing to my people? Was it Silas Konrad? Was he the one?"

Big Laughing Star's eyes lowered. *"Ay-uh,"* she murmured.

A rush of feet into the wigwam drew Yellow Feather around. He was brushed brusquely aside as Flying Squirrel moved on past him and dropped to his knees next to Happy Flower. Yellow Feather watched in silent confusion as Flying Squirrel began to chant as he bent and drew Happy Flower into his arms, cradling her head on his lap.

Yellow Feather began to reach for Flying Squirrel, to order him from the wigwam, but instead took a step backwards when he heard Flying Squirrel's chants change to low murmurings. What was Flying Squirrel saying about his love for Happy Flower . . . ? What was he saying about . . . the . . . child . . . ?

324

Yellow Feather went to Flying Squirrel and placed a hand heavily on his shoulder, feeling the deception that had just been revealed as though he had been bitten by a poisonous snake. His heart felt heavy and worn as the love he had always felt for Flying Squirrel began to change to hate.

"Flying Squirrel . . ." he said thickly.

Flying Squirrel jumped as though shot. He turned his eyes slowly upward, now realizing that in his tormented grief he had revealed too much. He saw the knowing in Yellow Feather's eyes and slowly released his hold on Happy Flower by gently placing her back onto the bullrush mats.

Swallowing hard, Flying Squirrel rose before Yellow Feather. He gazed once more into his chief's accusing eyes, then fled from the wigwam and mounted a horse. Without looking back, he thrust his knees deeply into the horse's sides and left his village behind him. . . .

Securing Amanda in her arms, Lorinda stepped into the clearing and she saw Flying Squirrel thunder away on his horse. She then moved on toward the confusion around Happy Flower's wigwam and slowly lifted the entrance flap and stepped on inside. Her knees grew weak when she saw Happy Flower's lifeless body, then her heart began a slow aching for Yellow Feather when she saw the grief etched across his face.

Big Laughing Star rose to her feet and went to Lorinda. "You found baby sister," she marveled. "Big Laughing Star happy for you." Her eyes veiled with tears. "But me so sad for Happy Flower." She cast a sideways glance toward Yellow Feather then looked back to Amanda. "Me take *gee-shee-may*," she said softly. "Chief Yellow Feather needs you as *gee-wee-oo*. One wife is all he has left now. Go to him."

Lorinda held Amanda away from Big laughing Star with a nervous heart. She had just rescued her sister from one Indian squaw. Could she so quickly hand her over to another? But one look toward Yellow Feather and she knew that she had to do what she could to comfort him. He had won one victory this night . . . but lost much more.

She yielded the cradleboard to Big Laughing Star and watched her waddle from the wigwam, cooing in soft Indian to Amanda. Lorinda's arms felt too suddenly empty, but she swung around and went to Yellow Feather's side. When he looked her way, she saw more than sadness in his eyes. She saw a look of quiet confusion.

"Yellow Feather, I'm sorry." she whispered. She flinched when he stepped back away from her, now seeing a deep hatred enter his dark pools of eyes. Was he blaming her for being the cause of his not having been there for his people when he was needed? Did he now hate her . . . ? She only wished to be brave enough to tell him that he was mourning a wife and child who in truth hadn't been his. Hadn't he seen Flying Squirrel's reaction to the tragedy? Surely Yellow Feather wasn't so blind.

"It was the white man," he finally said, lifting the entrance flap of the wigwam, peering into the dark of the forest. "I must go after him. I will make war with him. Maybe I will make war with *all* white man. They only bring my people heartache."

"Do you also include me when you speak so harshly of the white man?" Lorinda asked, going to him, touching the corded muscles of his shoulders.

Letting the entrance flap ripple shut again, Yellow Feather turned on a heel and drew Lorinda into his arms. He warmed her cheek with his breath as he spoke. *"Gahween,"* he murmured. "You know how I love you, Red Blossom."

His gaze lowered to where Happy Flower lay so quietly. He had never loved her as much, but he had been

326

fair to her. He would never understand how this thing had happened between his best friend and his Indian wife.

He closed his eyes from his sorrow. He could not let his people know of this deceit. It would make him look weak in their eyes. He would act as though he still believed the child would have been his. And his past brotherly love for Flying Squirrel would keep him from following him and killing him. He only hoped Flying Squirrel had enough sense to know never to return. . . .

"My love for you will always be strong, Yellow Feather," Lorinda whispered. "And because I *do* love you, I want to help you in your grief. Please tell me how I can help."

Yellow Feather withdrew from her and once more went to stand over Happy Flower. "She must be prepared for burial," he murmured.

Lorinda shuddered but stepped courageously to his side. "I will do this thing for you," she said softly.

"Big Laughing Star will find someone among our women who can give nourishment to your sister and leave Amanda in her care, then help you," Yellow Feather said solemnly.

Lorinda's eyes widened in shallow greens. "This can be done?" she questioned. But she already knew the answer. This had also been done in the Sioux camp, for wasn't Amanda a picture of health?

"*Ay-uh*. And she will be chosen carefully. Only one who has enough milk to spare after feeding her own child will place Amanda to her breast."

Lorinda's inner grief for her mother was renewed, as she thought of whose breast should be providing nourishment to her sister. But she had to place such thoughts behind her. Amanda was alive and well, and because an Indian's milk had served her so well. Lorinda was glad that it was now a Chippewa's milk that would be offered. She didn't want ever to speak the name Sioux again . . . !

"And you, Yellow Feather?" she said. "You will seek out the ones responsible for this?"

Yellow Feather turned to her and clasped her shoulders with his fingers. "I did not yet speak the name of the white man to you," he said thickly. "Only one white man would know of this place."

"Who . . . ?" Lorinda said in a near whisper. Then her heart fluttered nervously. The only white man *had* to be . . .

"Silas Konrad," Yellow Feather growled.

"Then I did *not* kill him," Lorinda murmured. A part of her wanted to be glad that she hadn't murdered a man, yet a part of her was angry that she hadn't. If her bullet had found its target, grief would not have been brought to this Indian village of the St. Croix. . . .

"*Gah-ween*, you did not," Yellow Feather murmured. "It is now for Chief Yellow Feather to do. I will track him down. I will show him how the Chippewa deals with evil white man." He took a last lingering look at Happy Flower, sad for her and the child, yet bitter for having been deceived, then spun around on a heel and took a step toward the entrace flap.

Lorinda rushed after him and clung to his arm. "Yellow Feather, please be careful," she whispered. "Please come back to me. . . ."

Yellow Feather tilted her chin with a forefinger and let the dark of his smoldering brown eyes speak his love for her. Yellow Feather had always prided himself on ordering his eyes to remain flat and untouched, *never* revealing his emotions to *any*one, but Lorinda had drawn these feelings from inside him. His self-control was as though blown into the wind when he was with her.

"Red Blossom, you need not fear," he said huskily. "I will move swift and silent. Silas Konrad will be no threat to me. I will return to you." A slow smile curved his lips upward. He moved his hand from her chin and instead lifted her dark braids. "I like you better as white woman," he chuckled. "The flame of your hair is missed."

Lorinda sighed and fell into his arms. "I do love you," she whispered. "When you return I will be waiting with my hair unbraided and washed clean for you, my love. . . ."

He removed himself from her arms and lifted the entrance flap and bent his back to look from it, then looked back to Lorinda. "I must go. . . ." he said, then stepped from Lorinda's sight.

Lorinda turned slowly around and trembled as she gazed sadly toward Happy Flower, realizing that, ironically, Yellow Feather now only had one wife, after having had, so short a time ago, three.

"I am the only wife now. . . ." she murmured. She trembled again. "Why am I suddenly so afraid . . . ?"

Twenty-One

The wagon tracks led from the cave and were picked up again across the St. Croix River and on into the thickness of the forest. Yellow Feather sat straight-backed on his horse, still highly painted with war paint from his attack on the Sioux village. No second war council had been held. Time had not allowed it. Yellow Feather wanted to reach Silas Konrad before the trader-turned-murderer had a chance to arrive at the newly carved road that was used by only the white man.

Though hate was heavy on his heart, Yellow Feather would not involve his Indians in an all-out war with the white man. There was too much to be done in his new village. There were the dangers of winter to fight. At times, its evil was even harsher than the white man's.

Lifting his eyes to the sky, Yellow Feather saw the early morning, low-hanging gray clouds that had taken the place of the velvet canvas of night. "Snow," he said to himself. "We've only seen occasional flakes up till now, but today I fear the heavens will open up and cover everything in its devil's white shroud. . . ."

The wind was blowing in ugly gusts, causing the branches above Yellow Feather's head to creak and groan and the flesh of his cheeks to become chafed and raw. But determination led him onward, knowing that his warriors who traveled behind him would also not bend with the wind, but stay tall and unmoved on their horses until revenge was found and savored.

Yellow Feather's gaze moved forward again, so missing Flying Squirrel at his side. As children, Yellow Feather and Flying Squirrel had become blood brothers. They had shared in joy and sorrow. They had spoken with naked hearts together. Never had Yellow Feather guessed that Flying Squirrel was being anything but honest with him, especially about his wife.

"And a child I even thought was next chief-in-line," he thought sorrowfully. "My love for you has changed to hate, Flying Squirrel. You have torn the right hand of my heart away with your deception. . . ."

A scattering of snowflakes drifting peacefully from the sky and on through the naked branches of the trees caused Yellow Feather's jaws to tighten and his shoulders to square. Swearing to himself never to let his mind worry and wonder about Flying Squirrel again, he urged his men quickly onward, even though the peaceful snowflakes had turned suddenly into a snowstorm, whirling, hissing and drifting.

The landscape was becoming a crystal fairyland as the trees, bushes, grass blades and weed stalks along the trail quickly became encrusted with ice and snow. Yet Yellow Feather would not give up the hunt. The drive inside him was even stronger than when he was on the hunt for food. What he had in mind for Silas Konrad would give him a pleasure far beyond that of entering his village with a slain red deer on his shoulder.

Ay-uh, he would have his revenge, and in a most unique way. . . .

Through the snow-encumbered branches of the trees, Yellow Feather got his first glimpse of smoke wreaths climbing toward the sky. Then, peering around some withered oak leaves, he saw the dancing oranges from a fire against the hanging gray gloom of the day.

With a quick jerk he raised his hand to stop his warriors' approach. He dismounted his horse as did his faithful followers. And once their horses were secured and rifles poised, ready, Yellow Feather motioned for his warriors to move along with him until they were crouching behind bushes, studying the defense of the two men hovering over a fire. The aroma of cooked rabbit and coffee filtered upward into Yellow Feather's nostrils, causing a different sort of hunger to gnaw at his insides. But being strong of mind as well as body he once more concentrated on his purpose for being there.

Shaking the snow from his hair, he looked from warrior to warrior, seeing how their painted, crimson-streaked faces gleamed in the firelight and how their dark eyes revealed a stark readiness. He smiled inwardly, yet wanted to wait a while longer to see if another man might join this party of only two. Somewhere along the trail Yellow Feather had counted the prints of three horses. Now he was only seeing two.

"I don't like it," Daniel said, glancing cautiously about him. "Now we don't have only the Indians to worry about but also the chance we might freeze to death. We should keep on moving. We're wrong to stop."

Silas leaned over and poured coffee into his tin cup. "You'd best quit your frettin' out loud and eat your fill before the fire's put out by the snow," he said. "A man can travel just so far then he needs to give his body a rest. We traveled all night. I know I've got to get some shut-eye before goin' on."

Daniel shook his shoulder-length brown hair to rid it of snow, then wiped the wetness from his nose and eye-lashes. "How are we going to find the road now?" he argued. "All's I see is snow. Just blinding, white snow."

"I know this part of the land, now that we're away from that unchartered land by that cave and river," Silas said, warming his hands on the tin cup that now held steaming, hot coffee. "After we get a bit of shut-eye, I'll lead us on toward Duluth."

"Do you think Lawrence made it safe?" Daniel asked,

stomping a foot, to try and get the circulation moving around in his toes that had grown numb from the snow building at his feet. "Sure wish I'd not been slowed by that damn wagon. If I had been on a horse instead of a wagon, I'd be *long* gone by now."

"I wouldn't be cursin' that wagon," Silas said, glancing toward it. "It's not only filled with valuables, but it will also provide cover for us while we're restin' our weary eyes."

"I still wish we'd keep moving," Daniel whined. "I feel like a sittin' duck here just waiting for the slaughter."

Silas brushed some snow from the shining baldness of his head. He squinted his dark, shifty eyes toward Daniel. "Now you wouldn't be thinkin' on makin' a run for it on my horse once I'm asleep would you?" he sneered.

"I should," Daniel growled. "It was *you* who killed that Injun squaw. Not *me*."

"I told you how she died," Silas said, narrowing his eyes even more toward Daniel. "And don't you forget that even though you didn't kill one of Yellow Feather's braves, you're in just as deep as I am. . . ."

A rustling noise from behind him caused Silas to turn with a start. He dropped the tin cup to the ground, spilling coffee in brown streaks at his feet. "Jesus . . ." he uttered harshly. "Yellow Feather . . . I . . ." His words caught in his throat as Yellow Feather raised the butt of his rifle and brought it down in a loud crack against his skull.... .

Daniel took a step backwards, almost gagging from fear. He let out a loud, blood-curdling scream as an Indian grabbed his long mane of hair, thinking to be scalped at any moment. But a soft prayer of thanks escaped from his lips as his hair was only used to half drag him to a tree. He gulped back his mounting fear as the Indian began to disrobe him, beginning at his jacket, then his shoes,

334

while another Indian held his arms behind him.

"What are you doing . . . ?" Daniel cried. The cold, icy fingers of winter were now caressing his bare flesh but not as a lover might do. There was no pleasure. Only pain.

Yellow Feather stepped before Daniel. He poked at Daniel's now exposed male member with the butt of his rifle. "So you are Silas Konrad's *gee-wee-do-kah-wahn-mah-shee-chee-gayd?*" he said unemotionally.

Daniel wrestled against the leather strappings at his wrists and at his ankles. Though he was completely unclothed and freezing, he still had a flush on his cheeks. With his arms stretched high above his head and his legs widely spread, revealing everything of his body to the group of savage onlookers, he couldn't help but feel an almost unbearable humiliation.

"You speak half-savage and half-white," he said, swallowing hard. "I don't understand everything you say."

Yellow Feather handed his rifle to the Indian standing next to him on his right then slowly removed his knife from its protective sheath. "I said you are Silas Konrad's helper in crime," he said flatly. He teased Daniel with the knife, prodding and poking at the flesh of his lower abdomen.

"Before I left my village in search of you I found that not only my woman had been slain but that another woman had been raped," Yellow Feather said further. His eyes became like dark coals. "Which of these evil things in my village are *you* guilty of?" he hissed vehemently. His knife grazed Daniel's flesh, leaving a narrow, bleeding wound on one of his thighs.

Daniel let another loud scream surface from between his lips then he let his body shake with sobs. "I didn't do anything to anyone," he cried. "I only drove the wagon."

335

Yellow Feather placed the knife at Daniel's testicles. "You lie. . . ." he sneered. "You lie. . . ." He raised his knife to Daniel's throat. "You tell Yellow Feather the truth. Now," he shouted.

Daniel stared into Yellow Feather's expressionless eyes, already knowing that Yellow Feather wouldn't spare his life no matter what was said to him. Tears gushed down Daniel's cheeks as he squirmed and twisted against the rough bark of the tree. He was already feeling numb from his exposure to the cold temperatures. Desperation seized him. "Silas," he cried. "He's the one. Now that I've told you, please let me go. You can't leave me like this. I'm going to freeze to death."

Yellow Feather lowered his knife. "That is why you have been placed there," he said. "That is your punishment for having invaded my village, leaving death behind."

"No . . ." Daniel wailed. "You can't do this thing . . . ."

Yellow Feather took a step forward and lifted Daniel's thick mane of hair from his shoulders. "I would take your scalp," he said. "But that shock would mercifully send you into a darkness that I do not wish to happen so quickly for you. I want you awake to die slowly. . . ."

Daniel closed his eyes and hung his head, moaning, while Yellow Feather walked to where Silas had been unclothed and also secured against a tree, still unconscious. Reaching down, Yellow Feather filled his right hand with the iciness of snow then straightened his back and rubbed the snow all over Silas's face. He then took a step backward and watched with an anxious heart as Silas began coughing and blinking his eyes. A low groan accompanied the opening of his eyes.

"You are now at my mercy, Silas Konrad," Yellow Feather hissed. He once more began teasing with his knife, now circling its tip around a dark, pointed nipple that stood out from thick, curly hairs on Silas's chest. "Your cheating days are over. I should have killed you long ago when I came to realize that you were not trading fairly with my father Chief Wind Whisper. But it wasn't my place to act superior to the great chief of the St. Croix band of the Chippewa."

He paused and shaved some hair from Silas's chest with the sharp blade of his knife. "My father is no longer chief," he added solemnly. "Chief Yellow Feather is now in command. Chief Yellow Feather can now do as he should have done all those years ago."

Silas inched his body back against the tree, terrified. He glanced down and took in his nudity, then across at the next tree, seeing blood dripping from a thin-lined wound on Daniel's abdomen and thigh, then back up again, sighing inwardly when he saw Daniel's hair still intact. A sharp pain in his raised right arm caused his attention to return to himself. His eyes followed the pain upward, discovering an open wound, from which dropped a steady stream of blood.

With wild eyes, he turned his head back toward Yellow Feather. "So you're goin' to kill me one knife wound at a time, are you?" he sneered, trying to hold at least an ounce of bravery intact. But he knew his fate. Showing bravery just wouldn't be enough.

Yellow Feather thrust his knife into Silas's other arm, then wiped the knife free of the blood and placed it back inside its sheath. *"Gah-ween,"* he replied sullenly. "Just enough to let you feel added pain while the cold temperatures slowly snuff the life from you."

Silas flinched as each throb of his wounds sent messages to his brain. "Come on, Yellow Feather," he pleaded, no longer caring about bravery. He *had* to try to talk some sense into Yellow Feather. "You know Chief Wind Whisper would never have approved of you doing such a thing as this. He was a peaceful chief. Will you draw your people into a war . . . ?"

"You come to my village . . . you rape my women . . . you take my possessions . . . you murder my wife . . . ." Yellow Feather stormed angrily. "You deserve to die. I do not bring war to my people. *You* did. So *you* pay. I leave you now to the fate of the north wind."

Yellow Feather swung around and began walking away, having done what he had set out to do. Now he had his warriors to think about. He had to lead them safely home so they, too, wouldn't become defenseless against the swirling snow and wind. He accepted his rifle back into his hand and lifted it into the air and yelled loudly to his men. *"Mah-bee-szhon,"* he ordered. *"Gee-mah-gi-ung-ah-shig-wah."*

All obediently obeyed as Yellow Feather knew they would. They all were ready to return to their people, but sad to know that a burial awaited them. It tore at Yellow Feather's heart to be reminded of Happy Flower. It was a double torment for him. Her death *and* her deceit would weigh heavy on his heart for many moons to come.

"Take the horses and the wagon," he shouted, mounting his horse. He looked at the clothes spread across the snow and dismounted again and placed them in the hot coals of the fire. With hands on hips, he watched them ignite, ignoring the continued cries and pleas from the two white men behind him. A ripple of pleasure coursed through his veins, glad that their deaths would be painfully slow. . . .

Twenty-Two

Flying Squirrel held his head down against the force of the wind and snow. He now felt alone and empty. He had left his heart behind, lying lifeless on the bullrush mats. And he hadn't only lost a love so dear to him, but also the possibility of a son, and his very best friend, to whom he had become traitor.

He shivered as the snowstorm whirled, hissed and drifted on all sides of him. He had no place to go. He was no longer able to say that he was of the St. Croix band of the Chippewa . . . the proud, loving Ojibway. He had the same as cast himself from their midst the day he had urged Happy Flower to play this game of the heart with Yellow Feather.

Oh, if only Yellow Feather hadn't fallen for the softness of her eyes . . . the shape of her body. Then it would have been Flying Squirrel who would have eventually married her, and his wild scheme of one day having a son as chief would have gone from his mind. Oh, how foolish he had been to have thought it could work. Why hadn't he accepted his fate of having been born to someone lesser than Chief Wind Whisper? Why had he longed for more? Now he had *nothing!*

Lifting his head to look around him for possible shelter for the upcoming night, Flying Squirrel's gaze settled on a larger drifting of snow at the side of the trail. Then his heart lurched wildly, seeing that it wasn't a snowdrift at all. It was a body with a covering of snow!

Jumping from his horse, Flying Squirrel knelt at the

side of this mound of white and hurriedly brushed the snow aside. He gasped loudly when he turned the face of the victim to his. "Foolish Heart . . ." he said in a near whisper. "It is you, Foolish Heart. How . . . ?"

Seeing the slight purple cast to her face and the frozen ice at her nostrils, Flying Squirrel felt keenly afraid that she might be dead. Rubbing her face briskly with his hands to try to warm her, his eyes watched for signs of life. When he saw none, he leaned down over her and placed a cheek to where her heart was barely pounding. He sighed with relief, feeling reassured, and grabbed her up into his arms and carried her to his horse.

"I must find shelter of some kind," he mumbled. He draped her across the layer of blankets on his horse then pulled himself on up behind her. He held her there as he began to search desperately around him. He knew this land well and had seen smaller caves than the one he and Yellow Feather had kept filled with the white man's possessions. If he could find one . . . even one just large enough to fit his and her body into . . . at least they could warm each other with their bodies until the storm moved on farther south.

He held Foolish Heart with one hand and guided the horse with the other, still seeing only a mural of white on all sides of him. Then his eyes widened, seeing what he had so desperately been seeking. It was the black mouth of a cave's entrance framed in white. In a flash he had Foolish Heart once more in his arms and was kneeling, entering the cave, already feeling the relief of being in out of the cold.

In the darkness, he felt around with his feet until he found solid ground, gravel free. With caution, he placed Foolish Heart on the floor of the cave and hurried to his horse and grabbed his thick layer of blankets. With only her safety in mind now, he rushed back into the cave and saw to it that she was settled comfortably.

He then went on a wild search of the cave until he had his arms filled with fragments of twigs and debris, and he soon had a fire going, casting a soft, warm glow around him and his female companion, who had also once been of the St. Croix band of the Chippewa.

Lifting her head to cradle it on his lap, Flying Squirrel was reminded once more of Happy Flower and how he had only shortly before cradled her lifeless body in his arms. He shook his head quickly, not wanting to remember. . . .

Foolish Heart stirred, moving her head from side to side, moaning a bit. Flying Squirrel leaned over her and began rubbing her face with his hands again.

"Foolish Heart, wake up," he said anxiously. "It's me. Flying Squirrel. Wake up."

His spirits plummeted, seeing that she had once more relapsed into her deep sleep. He placed her back on the blankets and covered her with another, studying her closely, wondering what to do next. Her color had improved but there was still a pallor about her eyes. Then he noticed something else about her! Her face was no longer as round. Her cheeks were even sunk in a bit. Only the lack of food would be the cause of this. Surely she was poorly in appearance because she had not been eating well. In fact, when *had* she last eaten?

He looked from the cave, seeing the silence of the snow, glad the storm had finally passed on. If he could see fresh tracks in the snow, maybe he could find him a rabbit for supper. Not only for Foolish Heart, but also himself. When had *he* last eaten? He closed his eyes and shook his head. He had to place the past behind him. No good would come from dwelling on his misdeeds, which had led only to misfortune.

Rising, he grabbed his rifle and headed out, wishing snowshoes were a part of his attire. But since they were not, he fought the deep snow in moccasined feet until the crisscross tracks of a rabbit led him to where one was sitting, half-frozen, beneath the cover of a snow-shrouded bush. Lifting his rifle, he only had to fire once, then followed his own tracks in the snow back to the cave.

Seeing that Foolish Heart had not stirred, he busied himself at cleaning the rabbit, then soon had it browned tender and ready for eating. With a piece held at Foolish Heart's mouth, he spoke her name again.

"Foolish Heart, you must awaken," he said. "If you don't soon awaken for nourishment, I fear for your life."

He watched a moment longer then his hunger got the best of him and he ate rabbit until his insides were warm and glowing and he felt as though life was maybe not that bad after all. In fact, he even felt he had a reason to live. He was suddenly responsible for a life other than his own.

His gaze raked slowly over Foolish Heart, seeing her truly for the first time. She was lovely in a different way than Happy Flower had been, an earthy loveliness, one that could make a man kill to make her his own. He just couldn't let her die! With Foolish Heart as his companion he wouldn't be alone, completely away from the Indians he loved. She was Chippewa. He was Chippewa. They could possibly make a future together.

But then, there *was* Foolish Heart's personality! She had caused much trouble for Yellow Feather. But hadn't Flying Squirrel? He was no better than Foolish Heart. *Ay-uh,* maybe they could be traveling companions. Maybe they could even ease the pain in each other's heart. The trail was long and cold. They could warm each other's heart . . . as well as their bodies.

Then Flying Squirrel felt guilty for thinking of another with Happy Flower dead for such a short time. "But she would understand," he thought to himself. "She wouldn't want me to travel alone, especially now that I have had to leave my band of Indians behind. . . ."

When Foolish Heart began stirring under his close

342

scrutiny, a quiver in his loins made him realize that this woman *had* to get well. He had a strong need to possess her, no longer feeling guilty for letting such thoughts enter his mind. Survival had been taught him early in life . . . and to survive . . . a woman was needed.

Flying Squirrel flinched a bit when Foolish Heart's lashes began to flutter slowly open. His pulse raced as he saw her glance quickly upward at him then begin to weep softly. She reached her arms upward and embraced Flying Squirrel, hugging him tightly to her. "Flying Squirrel, oh, how glad I am to see you," she said. "How did you find me? Why are you so far from our people? Are you also lost?"

Flying Squirrel's heart warmed to an almost singing. She was almost surely going to be all right. She was aware of everything around her. "What are *you* doing here, Foolish Heart?" he asked. "You left the village several weeks ago. Surely you haven't been wandering aimlessly about all this time."

Foolish Heart tried to ease up to a sitting position but fell back into Flying Squirrel's arms. She reached a hand toward the fire, trembling. "Evil white man," she whispered weakly. "He brought me to this land and left me. He wanted me to die."

Flying Squirrel leaned his hands over the fire next to hers. "What white man?" he asked. "Was it Silas Konrad? He's the only white man I've known to enter these parts."

"No," Foolish Heart hissed vehemently. *"Gah-ween.* It was *not* Silas Konrad. Had it been, he would not have left me to die. He wasn't *that* evil of a man."

Flying Squirrel's face became darkly shadowed. But it wasn't the time to reveal all that he knew of Silas Konrad to Foolish Heart. It would tear at his heart to speak of all that he had left behind. Yet . . . how could he *not* tell her? He had to have an explanation for his traveling

343

alone, without Yellow Feather. They had ridden together since childhood . . . side by side . . . always as brothers. He slouched his shoulders and began the sad tale, until he ended with why he was in this place . . . at this time. . . .

"Happy Flower . . . dead . . . ?" Foolish Heart said in a strained tone of voice. *"Gah-ween . . . !"*

"Ay-uh . . ."

Foolish Heart reached up to touch the braids of her hair, remembering having so foolishly clipped Happy Flower's from her head. Foolish Heart knew that this was why she was traveling alone, away from the St. Croix band of the Chippewa. It was not Lamont Quinby's fault altogether that she was in this desolate land. She had taken that first step when she had teased and tormented Yellow Feather's pregnant wife.

"The child . . ." she gasped, placing her hands to her mouth. "The next chief-in-line . . ."

"Ay-uh . . ." Flying Squirrel said solemnly.

Then Foolish Heart cast Flying Squirrel a furtive glance. "Flying Squirrel," she said cautiously. "Is there such a woman in our village with hair the color of the autumn poppy?"

Flying Squirrel's head turned with a jerk. He eyed her with a furrowed brow. *"Ay-uh.* But how do you know of this?"

"This white man, Lamont Quinby, he was in search of such a woman," she sighed languidly. "He told me that Yellow Feather was supposed to have this red-haired white woman in the village with him. Is this true?"

"Ay-uh, it is true. And she is his wife," Flying Squirrel said, frowning. He couldn't help but think that if the white woman hadn't shown up, none of their tragedies would have struck. She had brought them bad luck. He had warned Yellow Feather of this. But now Chief Yellow Feather's fate was in his own hands. . . .

344

"Flying Squirrel," Foolish Heart murmured. "Our village. It is gone. . . ."

"*Ay-uh,* but I have explained why."

"Yellow Feather is now Chief Yellow Feather," she whispered. "And he has a white wife. It is not right."

"Much in life is not fair. . . ."

"Flying Squirrel, will you also leave me to die in the snow once you have tired of me?"

"Never. . . ." he said, framing her face with his hands. "Destiny has thrown us together. We shall never part." Leaning, he brushed a sweet kiss across her lips. "It is my promise to you, Foolish Heart. . . ."

Tears sparkled in her eyes. "I will be good to you, Flying Squirrel. . . ." she whispered, reaching a hand to his face.

"To be a good wife you must have strength," he said, straightening his back proudly. "Foolish Heart, I have slain a rabbit for you. Now you must eat it."

Foolish Heart eased up on an elbow, light-headed from weakness, yet she managed a smile. "Foolish Heart will do what Flying Squirrel tells her to do."

"Foolish Heart, when your strength is returned and the sun rises brightly over the snow, we will move onward," Flying Squirrel stated flatly. "We will find a new land . . . our *own* land of promise. . . ."

Twenty-Three

Deeply into winter, Lorinda had adjusted quite well to life in a wigwam. During the day, she did as the other Indian woman did, to assure survival for her husband and the sister that she so dearly loved. She had learned how to pound maize and dress a deerskin, how to fashion garments out of hides and skins with wooden awls, thorn or bone needles, and thread made of nettle fiber or moose and deer sinew.

Most evenings, relaxed beside the warmth of the fire, she had learned the skills of weaving, leatherwork and quill work, and also how to engrave attractive silhouette patterns on birchbark, or dishes.

On other evenings there were social gatherings, when the Indians would travel from one another's wigwams, to exchange stories or jokes. There would always be a drum conveniently near the head of the household, to accompany the older women who were experts in the art of storytelling. Some even acted out their stories, running around the fire, acting while they talked.

But most had survival on their minds at all times. When the men weren't hunting in the snow, they were doing woodwork, making and repairing their snowshoes, as well as their traps. When the women weren't preparing food, they were making basswood cord or fishnets.

The wigwam was, surprising to her, warm enough for Lorinda. It had been readied quite well for winter. Around its circular base, it had been completely banked with moss and cornstalks weighted down with large stones. A generous wood supply had been piled high against the great pines outside the entrance flap, and golden corn lay heaped in a sunny spot in front of the wigwam.

At this moment, Lorinda was quite content. She gazed with deep respect and love toward Yellow Feather as he did a rare thing . . . relaxed . . . reclining across the firespace from where she sat sewing rabbit fur into a new pair of moccasins for him.

Then she looked beside her, at Amanda, who lay wrapped in rabbit skin on the thick padding of a bullrush mat. Amanda's blue eyes studied her back and her face showed its pink shine of health. These times with her sister were savored by her, for during most of the day and night Amanda was with the Indian maiden who so willingly gave of her milk, cradling her own Indian child in one arm and the white child in the other.

Feeling the dark of Yellow Feather's eyes upon her, Lorinda cast him a pleasant smile.

"Gee-mee-nwayn-dum?" he asked, also smiling.

Ay-uh, I am happy,'' she replied, laying her sewing aside. She rose to her feet and went to settle down next to him, lifting the soft deerskin of her Indian dress to wrap snugly around her legs. "It seems your whole village is happy, Yellow Feather. The young men of your village were having so much fun this afternoon playing on the ice."

"The St. Croix River, roofed with ice, is a fun playground I missed as a child," he said sullenly.

"Please don't get moody, Yellow Feather," Lorinda sighed. "Let's be happy for *now*. You've done much for your people. They have an abundance of food to last them through the winter and they are warm. You've proven you're a fine leader. No harm will ever come to your people again."

Yellow Feather leaned up, closer to the fire. He placed

348

more pine cones into the flames and watched the fire begin to eat away at them. "Red Blossom, I fear there was another white man with Silas Konrad," he said softly. He dropped another pine cone into the fire. "I saw tracks that counted three horses, not two. I fear for this, Red Blossom."

Lorinda inched over next to him and laced an arm about his waist. "You didn't tell me this earlier," she said.

"I saw no need to burden your heart with such a worry."

"But surely this man would be afraid to return. Especially after raping one of your squaws and killing another," she encouraged. "Surely there is nothing to worry about."

Yellow Feather turned his eyes to her. "This land we are now on is rich with trees, wild rice, and deer," he said thickly. "If this man returns, he will be accompanied by many. This is why I must be alert at all times. When the snow melts into the river we may have many things to fear. It is then that the paths will be cleared for travel."

Lorinda's insides quivered. "Do you also fear the Sioux?" she whispered. She glanced toward Amanda. "Will they attack our village for what you did to their people while rescuing my sister?"

"Gah-ween," he said, shaking his head. "I never fear the Sioux. Our people are braver. Our people are stronger." His gaze also traveled to Amanda. "You will keep your sister here with us to raise as our own?"

Lorinda rose to her feet and went to drop to her knees at Amanda's side. She lifted Amanda into her arms and held the softness of her cheek against her own. "I don't know what to do," she sighed. "My aunt. I'm sure she has given up hope that either of us are alive. But yet, I feel the need to go to her. Show her. Tell her we are all right."

Yellow Feather went to her and clasped a shoulder

349

firmly. "You cannot do this thing," he said flatly. "When you return to my people the white man will surely follow."

Lorinda broke free from him and rose to her feet, pacing, with Amanda still held lovingly in her arms. "Yellow Feather, there's something else," she murmured. "My parents always prided themselves in seeing that I had proper schooling."

She swung around and boldly faced him. "I'm sure they would want the same for Amanda. I could take her home, leave her there, and then return to you. I could do it in a way that no one would follow. You see, Amanda could be raised by my aunt in St. Paul. She could have all the conveniences she could never have here."

"You are cold? You are hungry?" he stormed, crossing his arms angrily across his chest.

"No," she replied. "I am neither."

"Then your sister stays," he said flatly. "I have thought this thing over carefully. I knew you would want this thing for your sister, but I cannot allow it."

Lorinda's blood began a slow boil. Her face became flushed with a sudden anger. "You cannot allow it?" she fumed. "So I am still considered captive? My sister is also such a captive?"

Yellow Feather went to her and touched her cheek lightly with his forefinger. *"Ay-uh,"* he murmured. "Captive of my heart, Red Blossom." He lifted his hands to her hair and rippled his fingers through the long tresses of red. "As in the beginning, the flame of your hair matches that of my heart. I could never live without you."

Lorinda sighed exasperatedly, feeling the turmoil of her feelings battling inside her. When he was near her, talking so seriously of his love for her, her senses would leave her. She just couldn't let him succeed in getting his way again by the trick of his soft, sweet words.

350

She jerked away from him and went to settle back down by the fire. She smoothed a finger across Amanda's face, smiling as Amanda lifted her tiny lips into a grin.

"I will do what I have to do when spring comes," she said stubbornly. "You say I am captive of your heart. Well, Yellow Feather, Amanda isn't, and she is the true issue here."

Yellow Feather crouched down next to Lorinda. "When spring comes, we shall see. . . ." he said flatly.

A cold breeze suddenly whipping into the wigwam caused Lorinda to look toward the entrance flap. When she saw the tall, lithe Indian brave now standing there waiting, with his copper-toned, expression-free face, she knew her time with Amanda had drawn to a close this night. She knew that the Indian maiden waited with milk-filled breasts. Her husband had come to take the white child back with him for the night, to where Amanda would lie side by side with the male Indian infant, each deriving warmth from the other's body throughout the coldest hours of the night.

Always hating to relinquish her sister into an Indian's arms, Lorinda cradled Amanda next to her and kissed her gently on the cheek. "It's best for you, baby sister," she sighed. "One day you will understand."

She wrapped Amanda more snugly in extra rabbit furs. She then went to the Indian and once more gave her up, never forgetting the gruelling weeks without her, not knowing if she was alive or dead. Slowly her heart had mended from the pain of separation. But could she now, in truth, even give Amanda up to her aunt . . . ? Oh, she was so torn!

With the cold still hovering in the wigwam from the entrance flap's second opening, Lorinda shuddered and moved to stand over the fire, staring blankly into it. "My arms are always so empty without her," she murmured.

Yellow Feather went to her and drew her around and

into his arms. "She is only your sister," he said huskily. "What you need is your own child to fill not only your arms but your heart."

"A child . . . ?" she whispered, casting him a look upward beneath the thick veil of her lashes. "You mean to say . . . *our* child . . . ?"

"*Ay-uh.*"

"Yellow Feather, is this what you want?"

"I want many sons," he said, squaring his shoulders proudly. "I want Red Blossom to bear me the next chief-in-line for our St. Croix band of Chippewa."

"*Our* St. Croix band of Chippewa . . . ?" she whispered further.

"*Ay-uh,*" he said flatly. "You are now one of us. You *are* of the St. Croix. You are the chief's wife. My *only* wife."

Lorinda pulled gently away from him and settled down on the bulrush mats next to the fire. A sudden doubt had seized her, causing her to tremble.

Yellow Feather sensed something was wrong. When his gaze caught her trembles, he knelt down beside her and lifted her chin with a forefinger. When their eyes met and held, he said: "*Ah-neen-ay-szhee-way-bee-zee-en?*"

Lorinda tensed a bit, recognizing his way of asking her what was the matter. He was a smart Indian. He could always read her moods. But this time she was almost afraid to voice her doubts to him. She wasn't sure if she could bear to hear his reply!

She smiled a bit awkwardly toward him. "*Nay-mi-no-mun-gi,*" she replied softly.

He framed her face between his hands. "Red Blossom is *not* fine," he said sourly. "There should always be truth between us. You know I ask this of you. It is necessary that husband and wife be loyal in thoughts and deeds. So you must tell me. *Ah-neen-ay-szhee-way-bee-zee-en?*"

352

Remembering the deceit of Happy Flower, Lorinda understood the importance of proving to Yellow Feather that *she* was a loyal wife. He had never confided in her the truth about Happy Flower and Flying Squirrel, but since Yellow Feather had refused to even speak Flying Squirrel's name since his departure, she had to think that Yellow Feather had somehow become aware of the truth. Yes, it was her place to be open to him at all times, about all things. Doubt was like an open wound that would endlessly fester. . . .

"Yellow Feather, you once told me that a chief could have many wives," she said cautiously. "Does this mean that one day, maybe even soon, you will take another wife, maybe even two? You *did* have two wives when you chose to make me your third."

Yellow Feather rose to his feet and began a slow pacing, avoiding the study of her eyes. "Chief Yellow Feather wants many sons," he said. "But one is all that is required." He stopped and accepted her steady gaze. "I *must* have a son to raise by my side as the next chief-in-line," he added.

Lorinda went to him and spoke into his face. "What are you *not* saying?" she asked.

"I want only you as my wife," he said quickly. "But if no son is born from our union, I will have to take a second wife. It is required. I am the chief of the St. Croix band of the Chippewa. I *must* have a son at my side."

Lorinda circled her fists to her side. Her heart was raging inside her as she glared defiantly back at him. "It is a sort of blackmail, is it?" she said in a strain. "How long do I have to bear you this son, Yellow Feather?"

"Red Blossom, I am not anxious to cater to a wife I could not love," he said. "I will be in no hurry to bring another into my wigwam. I only want you. You have to know that."

Lorinda felt the tensions ebb slowly from inside her,

353

knowing that he was being sincere with her. She fell into his arms and placed a cheek on his chest. "Yellow Feather, I love you so," she whispered. "I couldn't bear to share you with another. I just couldn't. The white man only takes one wife at a time. Why do your customs have to be so different?"

"They are, though," Yellow Feather said. "Just as our skin coloring is different. But that doesn't lessen our love for one another, does it?"

"*Gah-ween* . . ." she murmured.

"We will make a baby tonight?" he asked huskily, lacing his fingers through her hair. He drew her mouth to his amidst her whispers of "*ay-uh.*"

She twined her arms about his neck, slowly losing herself in his kiss. He had this magical way about him that could draw all her worries from inside her to be cast quickly into the wind. The flames of desire crept higher, warming her breasts, desiring his fingers there, then his lips. He would suckle where their son would one day place his lips; he would kiss the nipple to a sharp peak of exquisite sensation.

Pulling free from his tender embrace, Lorinda whispered, "Undress me, my love. Take me. *Ay-uh,* make me with child. . . ."

His eyes were dark coals of passion as his fingers worked eagerly over her until she was standing like pale pink satin before him, statuesque, beautifully naked for his feasting eyes.

"And now, your clothes," Lorinda said silkily, already removing his fringed buckskin jacket. When he was also nude, she wantonly fit her body into the form of his, trembling pleasurably when the readiness of his manhood pressed hard against her flesh.

Once more their lips met, but this time in a heated, frenzied passion. Yellow Feather opened her lips with his tongue and probed inside her mouth, causing a rippling of sensuous pleasure to ride up and down her spine. She had been born to be loved by only him. He had been born to be loved by only her.

When his hands began moving over her, caressing the curve of her buttocks and then on around to where a crazy warmth pulsated between her thighs, Lorinda couldn't hold back a sigh of ecstasy, and she gave way to the further explorings of his fingers. As his fingers moved on her, she felt as though she was on a tranquil body of water, floating, mindlessly floating. . . .

"We must go to our bed of blankets," Yellow Feather said softly. "My body cries for release."

He guided her downward and knelt over her with burning eyes. His mouth then met hers in a fiery kiss as his fingers reached around her and lifted her hips to meet his entrance inside her.

Continued waves of sensuous pleasure swept through Lorinda, threatening to drown her. Her skin quivered as his fingers searched and found a breast. She moaned with rapture as he kneaded and fondled until a sweet pain began to rise inside her, lifting her to the plane of desire only Yellow Feather could take her to.

As his lips trailed downward to place a kiss on the hollow of her throat, Lorinda clung to him, meeting his thrusts until the pounding of her heart warned her of the nearness of her spent passion. . . .

Yellow Feather moved himself in her, feeling the slow burning rising in his loins. He could feel the passion mounting, near to exploding, but he held back, waiting for her with a racing heart. Then, when he felt the vibrations of her flesh against his, he increased his movements and groaned as the warmth of his liquid escaped from him into her. As his movements slowed, he nuzzled her neck playfully, then kissed her and once more gathered her into his arms.

"Please hold me, my love," Lorinda whispered.

"Never let me go. I love you so much."

"You argued that I held you captive a while ago."

"There are different ways of being captive. . . ."

"How well I know," he whispered. His fingers once more began exploring her flesh, causing flames to ignite again inside Lorinda.

"Oh, what you do to me . . ." she sighed, trembling with renewed passion. "You keep this up and there will be no doubt in my mind that this night will create our love child between us."

His fingers continued to travel over the silken flesh of her body, while his lips paid homage to first one breast and then the other. Lorinda's eyes closed. She lay in rapturous ecstasy as she submitted fully to him and his desires.

She twined her arms about his neck when he mounted her again, lifting her hips, meeting thrust with thrust. As her head began the lazy reeling, she cried out his name in Indian and shook violently as he once more came deliciously inside her.

Panting, they laughed and rolled away from one another. "What we now need is an invigorating walk," Yellow Feather said, touching her lovingly on a cheek. "Come. Dress. We will go out into the silent beauty of the snow."

"Yellow Feather, it is so cold. . . ."

"Come. . ." he said flatly.

Lorinda dressed, watching his exact movements as he became fully clothed. Once she was wrapped snugly inside a bearskin and had her snowshoes on, they stepped outside together.

Beneath the light of a full moon the pine trees in the distance resembled wigwams with their cloaks of white snow so beautifully draped. A wolf bayed across the river and the faint sound of a flute being played inside a far wigwam cut through the air almost mystically. The outdoor fire cast orange reflections onto the snow and smoke from the smoke holes puffed gray wreaths up into the sky.

Lorinda clung to Yellow Feather's arm, not at all cold as she had expected to be. She had a warm, contented feeling, proud to be a part of these lovely Indians . . . the Chippewa . . . the Ojibway. Her way of life that had been left behind was only a memory. She couldn't envision herself living any other way now.

Yellow Feather broke through their silence. "I wanted you to share this season fully with me, for soon it will be gone," he said. "When you hear a loud crack like thunder, you will know the ice on the St. Croix River has given way to the welcome hands of *See-gwun*. Spring. It brings us the maple sugar harvest, the planting of maize, and the time for our young men who are of age to travel far into the forest to seek their vision, as I myself did so many years ago."

"This vision. Why is it required?" Lorinda whispered, gazing admiringly into the set features of his handsome face.

"When a boy has his vision . . . his spiritual dream . . . he then becomes a man," he said. "This is when I was given my name Yellow Feather."

"What name were you born with?"

"Little Moon."

"What will we call our son . . . ?"

"A name of strength," Yellow Feather said firmly. "It will not be Little Moon or Wind Whisper, as my father and I were called. Our son will be a great leader. He must have a fierce name from his first breath."

The baying of the wolf they had heard earlier seemed closer, indeed louder, as though an omen of the moment. Yellow Feather's eyes followed the enchantment of the cry. "We will call our son Gray Wolf. . . ." he said flatly. *"Ay-uh*. That name is fierce."

357

He raised his eyes to the sky. "Thank you, my guardian spirit, the great owl of the forest. I know now to expect a son in nine months and know to call him the name you have led me to this night. Thank you, great owl, thank you."

Lorinda felt something similar to a cool breath pass across her face. . . .

Twenty-Four

The smoke in the saloon hung as thick as fog and stung Lamont Quinby's eyes, while the alcohol that he was fast consuming cut sharply into his throat. It had been a long, harsh winter and he was celebrating the melting of the snow.

Drawing deeply from his cigar, he glanced sideways at the man who had been sharing this space at the bar for the past few minutes. Lamont hadn't seen him around, but this wasn't unusual. The town of Duluth was beginning to be a hubbub of activity. New faces and old . . . they now got lost in the crowd. And this had given Lamont the cover he needed in case the St. Paul authorities were still searching for him.

His gaze traveled to the mural painting on the wall opposite to where he sat, causing his loins to ache almost unmercifully. He couldn't help but stare at the red, flowing hair, the eyes of green and the swell of the bare breasts on this beautiful woman stretched out seductively nude on what appeared to be a cloth of crimson velvet. If he didn't know better he would have thought Lorinda had posed for that painting. The hair . . . the eyes. . . .

He turned his head quickly away, remembering the fullness of her breasts. He hung his head into his hands, groaning lightly, knowing he had now almost surely lost her forever. For a while there he had thought he would find her again. But Foolish Heart had only led him to the skeletal remains of a village.

His fingers raked through his coarse hair. He regretted

359

having left Foolish Heart behind. She could have at least given him what all men hungered for. . . .

He crushed his cigar out and tipped his glass to his lips. He emptied it of whiskey in one fast gulp, then slammed the glass back down onto the counter. "Fill 'er up again," he shouted above the noise of a piano's tinkling. He watched the bartender eye him with a tilted eyebrow as he took the glass from the counter.

"Don't you think you've had enough?" the bartender growled. "I open my doors for you lumber gents and 'fore the night's out you sometimes damn near tear up my place 'cause you don't know when to quit tippin' a glass to your lips."

Lamont's gray eyes narrowed. He leaned forward, showing the massiveness of his chest to this short man with a thin face and even thinner frame. "Give me another whiskey," he growled. "Or I'll do more'n tear up your place. . . ."

"Yeah. Give the man another drink," the stranger spoke from beside Lamont. "And give me another while you're at it."

Lamont settled back down onto his stool, eyeing the stranger suspiciously. He had learned to not trust anyone, especially since abducting Lorinda. But this gent with the buckteeth, large and dark eyes, and tousled jet-black hair seemed dependable enough. "That's mighty nice of you," he then said, extending a hand. "Stranger in these parts, ain't you?"

"Been here a few months," the stranger said, accepting the hand of friendship. "But been busy on the docks. And you? You're a lumberjack, I reckon. Am I right?"

Lamont took his hand away and grabbed for the freshly filled glass of whiskey. "Yeah. I'm a lumberjack," he said. "And let me tell you, stranger, it's been a hard, long winter. Too much snow in these parts to please

360

me.''

The man laughed amusedly. "Ice has been my problem," he said. "That damn Lake Superior has had a cover of ice more'n not." He took his glass and lifted it to his lips, pausing to say: "And my name's Lawrence. Call me Lawrence."

Lamont tilted a shaggy eyebrow and glanced slowly around him, wondering if it was safe to reveal his true identity. He was damn tired of using another name. Maybe it was time for him to come out of hiding. It *had* been many months now.

"Name's Lamont," he finally said. "Lamont Quinby."

"Where do you make your residence?" Lawrence asked, wiping his lips free of whiskey.

Lamont tensed a bit, eyeing Lawrence again. "Why's that any of your business?" he snapped, not feeling so smug any longer. Had he chosen the wrong gent to reveal his true identity to? Damn!

"No particular reason," Lawrence chuckled. "All's I know is that I'm livin' in a rat-infested dive and would like to find somethin' more enticin'."

Lamont sighed heavily and took another quick drink of his whiskey. He slammed the glass back down on the counter and wiped the wetness from his thick, bushy mustache. "I built me a place overlookin' Lake Superior," he said proudly. "It's clean enough and sure is a peaceful place." He glanced at the mural, feeling something twisting in his gut. "In fact, *too* peaceful, if you know what I mean."

"Missin' woman companionship, eh?"

"Yeah. . . ."

"There's a few in town that don't expect too much pay for an hour's pleasure," Lawrence laughed, slapping Lamont clumsily on the back. "If you know what *I* mean."

361

"That ain't the kind of companionship I hanker for," Lamont grumbled. He nodded toward the mural. "I'd like to have somethin' like that to keep my bed warm," he added. "Look at that red hair. Ain't it the damnest red hair you've ever heard tell of?"

Lawrence studied the mural. "Heard tell of a woman with such red hair," he said nonchalantly, taking another drink of his whiskey.

Lamont's right cheek twitched nervously. He turned his full attention to Lawrence. "What woman you speakin' of?" he asked cautiously.

"I ain't never seen her," Lawrence said, still studying the painting. "But I come pretty close."

"Where did you know of such a woman?" Lamont asked, turning his attention to the mural again. He knew that he was foolish to think that this stranger could be talking about Lorinda. There had to be many red-haired, beautiful women in the world. But surely not two in this same area of the country. What if . . . ?

"I could've gotten scalped," Lawrence said, emptying his glass of whiskey. "Sure could've got scalped. Maybe Silas and Daniel *did*. Ain't heard tell of them since that damn night."

"Did you say . . . scalped . . . ?" Lamont asked quietly. "Why would you have worried about being scalped?" He tensed, waiting, hoping. What if this man *did* know something about Yellow Feather . . . and Lorinda . . . ?

Lawrence's eyes seemed even larger as he glanced toward Lamont. "This friend of mine told me of this Indian village where there was a cave filled with valuables that an Indian had stolen from stagecoaches," he said. "So we decided to go and steal it back from him. Me, Silas and Daniel. So we traveled there with that in mind. But Silas Konrad had more on his mind than the cave."

"And what . . . was that . . . ?" Lamont asked,

breathing hard.

"A woman. . . ."

Lamont's face flushed to crimson. "A woman?" he said in a near whisper. "And what was this woman's name . . . ?"

Lawrence furrowed his brow and began kneading it. "Damned if I can remember. . . ." he said.

Lamont jumped from his stool and grabbed Lawrence by the collar, jerking him to stand before him. "You have to remember," he snarled. "Tell me. What's her name?"

Lawrence knocked Lamont away from him and worked his shirt back into his breeches. "You're crazy," he said. "What'd you do that for?"

Seeing eyes focused on them, Lamont sat back down on his stool and slumped heavily, hiding his face between his shoulders. He hadn't meant to draw attention to himself in such a way. But the thought of Lorinda drove him insane. She had been like a thorn in his side since the very day he had laid eyes on her. The only way to be rid of that thorn was to find her.

Lawrence settled down on the stool next to Lamont. "I say, what'd you do that for?" he asked, motioning for the bartender to give him another filled glass of whiskey.

Once more Lamont felt the need to be more cautious with his words. Maybe this was a trick of some sort to draw a confession from him. He would not speak Lorinda's name. "Sorry about that," he said, accepting the second glass of whiskey that Lawrence had been kind enough to buy for him.

"Only a woman can send a man into such a rage so quickly," Lawrence said. "Why would the mere mention of a red-haired woman cause you to become so anxious?"

Lamont was eager to hear more, yet he was afraid to make any further references to Lorinda. He didn't wish to be left dangling from a tree. Instead he said, "So you say you went to an Indian village, eh?"

"Ain't told no one but you," Lawrence said, looking slyly around him. "You see, I plan to venture back there when the weather clears. The land the Indians are on is valuable. I'm goin' to get me together some men and go and run them Indians off the land and claim it as my own."

"You don't say. . . ." Lamont said. "Think you can get away with it?"

"Ain't no Indian smart enough to keep land like that away from the white man. And it's this white man sittin' right here that aims to get first chance at that land."

"This Indian you keep speakin' of," Lamont said cautiously, lifting an eyebrow. "He got a name?"

"Yellow Feather. . . ."

Lamont's face flamed red. His fingers tightened around the whiskey glass. "Yellow Feather. . . ." he whispered. "When you aim to go to this Yellow Feather's territory?" he quickly asked. "Maybe you've got your first man to tag along."

"You . . . ?" Lawrence asked. "You want to be my right hand man, eh?"

"Yeah. . . ." Lamont said flatly. "Like I said, though, when . . . ?"

"I told you. When the weather clears."

Lamont looked stealthily around him, then back to Lawrence. He leaned his shoulder over to him and spoke softly into his ear. "You say you've told no one but me about this Indian village?"

"The whiskey spoke for me tonight," Lawrence said sharply. "I didn't want the word spread for fear someone would beat me to the draw." His eyebrows forked menacingly. "And if I hear word that you've told, I'll come knifin' for you. Just you remember that. This can't go no further. You'd best understand that."

Lamont played with his mustache, eyeing the mural once again. He could almost smell the sweetness of Lorinda's flesh . . . he could almost feel the softness of her. "Damn right I won't tell," he snarled. "But, Lawrence, you might as well tell me where this land is now, so's I can be thinkin' on it. Eh? How's about it?" His heart thundered against his ribs, already knowing what he had to do. He wouldn't share Lorinda with anyone.

Lawrence laughed boisterously, then leaned into Lamont's face. "Think I'm some kind of fool, do you?" he hissed. "The whiskey ain't taken that much effect on my brain."

"I give my word that I won't tell," Lamont said blandly. He lifted his glass toward Lawrence. "The word of a gentleman, Lawrence. You can damn trust the word of *this* gentleman."

Lawrence emptied his glass of more whiskey, burping noisily. He wiped at his mouth and lifted an eyebrow toward Lamont. "Aw, guess it won't hurt none to go ahead and tell you," he said with slurred speech, showing the added effects of his last glass of whiskey. "Been havin' the need to talk aloud about it, anyways. It's been eatin' at my insides havin' to keep it all to myself."

"Well? Where we goin' to travel to, Lawrence?" Lamont asked, knowing that he would be making this trip alone. Yellow Feather meant Lorinda! He didn't know how he would do away with Lawrence but he had to find a way. He would not share this treasure with any man. He had known this from the first. It had sickened him to think of her sharing embraces with an Indian. It would sicken him to think of her sharing embraces with anyone, except himself.

Lawrence's eyes got a faraway look in them as he began speaking. "I've never seen such a place," he said dreamily. "Before the Indians, the land had never been touched by man. All virgin and beautiful. . . ."

Lamont listened intently, grasping at every word as Lawrence began to describe the route one would have to take to this land where Lawrence said forest met meadow in an almost perfect setting. In two days, maybe three, Lamont knew that he could be there. Maybe sooner. This time he wouldn't have Foolish Heart to slow him down.

"That's it in a nutshell," Lawrence finally drawled, reeling a bit as he rose from the stool. "But mum's the word, do you hear, Lamont?" he added, placing a forefinger to his lips, ssshhing as he looked cautiously on all sides of him. "We've got to keep this a secret. Least ways until we're ready to round us up enough men to scare them Indians off. Do you hear?"

Lamont scooted from his stool and stepped closer to Lawrence. "Yeah, I hear," he said. "And where are you goin' now?"

Wiping at his eyes, Lawrence began to stumble toward the door. "To get some shut-eye," he said lethargically.

Lamont inched his way next to Lawrence and spoke into his face. "You'll be here tomorrow night?" he asked anxiously. "Maybe we can begin makin' plans."

"Yeah. Sounds good," Lawrence said, yawning. "Won't be long and we can put this dreary town of Duluth behind us. We can begin our *own* town up there by the St. Croix River."

"Then I'll be waitin'," Lamont said, stepping aside. "I'll be here tomorrow night, same time."

"Yeah . . ." Lawrence said from across his shoulder, nodding his head in affirmation. "See ya. . . ."

Lamont watched Lawrence leave the saloon, then left behind him. He looked in the direction Lawrence continued to stagger, until he had disappeared into the dark of the night.

Lamont lit a fresh cigar and began his long, steep ascent up the hill that would take him to his log cabin in the woods. Behind him, he could hear the splash splash of the water against the land. Had it ever sounded so lonely? Had he ever felt so isolated? Yet now he had hope. Though in St. Paul the hangman's noose waited . . . in the Indian's village Lorinda waited. . . .

Lamont puffed eagerly on his cigar as he stepped into his cabin. He placed a match to the wick of a kerosene lamp and sent a soft glow of gold all around him. Soon . . . soon . . . he would have her with him again. He would sneak into the Indian village in the middle of the night and he would take her without anyone's even hearing that first noise.

Dropping to his bed, he stretched out on his back, staring at the dancing, reflecting shadows on the ceiling. "How do I get rid of that man Lawrence?" he whispered. He shuddered violently. He had never once thought himself capable of murdering a man. But for Lorinda? He knew he would be capable of doing anything to have her all to himself again. He was possessed by her and her innocent loveliness. He would have her and to hell with Lawrence!

"Tomorrow night," he whispered further. "I'll have to do it tomorrow night. Somehow."

He spent the full night in the accompaniment of fitful dreams then worked the next day with an anxious, nervous heartbeat, having decided just how he would take another man's life. It would look as though someone else had done it. He wouldn't be charged. He would be free to go to her. . . .

Thunder pealed overhead and lightning sent continuous slivers of white downward into Lake Superior. Lamont buttoned the top button of his red plaid flannel shirt more snugly beneath his chin and hurried his pace toward the town. His eyes were focused on the Silverleaf Saloon, wondering if Lawrence had kept his word and would be there waiting. A shudder rumbled through him, as he thought of his plans. He touched the bulge at his waist, beneath his shirt, and flinched a bit, hoping he would be swift enough with the knife. He had to make it look good. He had to be able to walk away from the crowd a free man. . . .

The noise from the saloons on all sides of him as he stepped into the heart of Duluth's main thoroughfare was that of men already having begun their long evening's vigil at the bars. Drinking had become their substitute for women. Lamont smiled wickedly. He knew that if they all knew of Lorinda, there would be a race to the Indian village to see who would claim her first. But she would be his . . . his. . . .

Stepping on into the Silverleaf Saloon, Lamont looked guardedly around him. His heart pounded in unison with the pounding of the piano and his eyes took in all of the men hovering over their drinks at the many tables in the room, some just drinking and some playing poker.

The stench of the alcohol and cigarette smoke clung to Lamont's clothes as he continued to stand there, studying, trying to work it all out in his mind. Where would be the best place to get a confrontation started . . . ? Would he succeed at drawing most of the men into the fight . . . ?

A set of eyes focused on him drew Lamont on to the bar where Lawrence sat waiting for him.

"Some storm brewin' up out there," Lawrence said, toying with his glass of whiskey.

"Just another spring storm," Lamont said idly, settling down on a stool next to Lawrence. Seeing how friendly Lawrence continued to be made Lamont feel apprehensive about his plans. But in this land where one had to look out for one's self, Lamont had to brush all apprehensions aside.

"Won't be long and we can set out," Lawrence said quietly into Lamont's face. "The rivers and springs should be goin' down soon. Then we can go and take what's too good for the Indians.''

"Yeah,'' Lamont said. He ordered a glass of whiskey and swallowed the sharp liquid down in one gulp. He ordered another for Lawrence and another and another until he was quite sure Lawrence was becoming heavily intoxicated. This was a part of the plan. Lawrence wouldn't know what hit him, it would happen so quickly.

Lamont leaned a bit forward, studying the man on the other side of Lawrence. He smiled to himself when he saw a face familiar to him. It was Pedro, the temperamental, husky Mexican of his lumberjack crew. It didn't take much to rile him. Just a bit of whiskey spilled on the sleeve of his fancily embroidered red shirt and the fight would begin. . . .

Reaching a hand to the bulge of his knife at his waist, Lamont eased his shirttail from beneath his breeches, wishing the trembling would stop in his fingers. Nervous perspiration was beading his brow and his armpits were soaked. He even felt a weakness at the pit of his stomach, knowing that he would soon be taking a man's life.

"Have another drink,'' Lawrence said, scooting a filled glass of whiskey toward Lamont. "We may be here all night by the sounds of the rain.''

Lamont had been so lost in thought he had paid no heed to the sound of the fury of the storm. He looked toward the ceiling, hearing hail bouncing onto the roof in loud thuds. The wind sent whistling sounds and rain through cracks in the walls, while the flooring creaked along with another loud rumble of thunder.

Lamont tensed as he glanced all about him. The boisterousness of the night was at its peak. No one would even notice if the wind blew the saloon from its foundation. Lamont knew that this was the time to make his move!

He got lost in nervous heartbeats as he leaned closer to Lawrence, then in one quick movement he had pushed

369

Lawrence from his stool and against Pedro, at the same time managing to see that Lawrence's drink splashed all over Pedro's shirtsleeve.

Many Spanish words escaped angrily from between Pedro's lips as he flew from his stool. He grabbed Lawrence by the throat and spoke even more angrily into his face, then doubled a fist and sent Lawrence sprawling to the floor.

Lamont smiled evilly and scooted from his stool as he watched small scufflings between men begin all around the room, which soon reached utter chaos. He directed his gaze downward as Lawrence once more went tumbling to the floor where tanglings of feet and hands were thicker than some underbrush in the deepest, darkest regions of the forest.

Slowly, yet deliberately, Lamont pulled his knife from its sheath at his waist. Trembling, he cast a fast glance on all sides of him, then fell to his knees and let his knife find its target. He felt a bitterness rise into his throat when he felt the knife make its way into the flesh and heard the death gurgles in Lawrence's throat as he struggled with his last breaths of life.

Lamont trembled inwardly as he pulled the knife free, wiping it clean on Lawrence's pant leg. He couldn't leave the murder weapon behind. He had to get to the bluff behind his house and toss the knife into Lake Superior. Then he would be free to go once more in search of his Lorinda. . . .

While the scuffling and rowdiness continued on all sides of him, Lamont pushed himself up from the floor. With ease, he slipped the knife back into its sheath, replaced his shirttail inside the waist of his breeches, then slowly began to edge his way toward the door.

Once outside, he ducked his head to the wind and rain, shuddering when the cold of it seeped through his clothes and onto his flesh. Without a look backwards where the fighting still persisted and one man lay dead, Lamont fought the pools of mud at his feet and attempted climbing the steep slope of ground that led to his cabin.

Sinking almost to his ankles with each step and now chilled completely to the bone, Lamont finally reached the bluff. He welcomed rock beneath his feet and hurried to stand directly behind his house, looking downward at the angry waves below him.

"No one will ever find the knife," he whispered. "It will surely be washed away from the land."

Hating to touch the murder weapon again, he cringed as he removed it from its sheath. As though it were a hot coal burning his fingers, he quickly tossed it into the air. It was soon lost from sight in the darkness as it tumbled downward and on into the water.

With a loud exhalation of breath, Lamont made a quick turn and headed for his cabin. "I'll leave tomorrow," he said aloud. "To hell with waitin' for the creeks to recede. Now that I know where I can find Lorinda, nothing will stop me."

He stepped on inside his cabin and to his fireplace that still had embers glowing orange on the grate. He leaned his hands over the warmth, smiling. "To hell with virgin land," he snarled. "I'm goin' to find somethin' way more valuable than that."

A frown creased his brow. "Bet *she* ain't virgin no longer," he growled. "Not after bein' with an Injun for so long."

The thought caused a sharp pain to cut through his loins. . . .

Twenty-Five

Lorinda lifted the entrance flap of her wigwam and inhaled the sweet, fresh fragrance of spring, recalling the old Chippewa song that Big Laughing Star had taught her. She began singing it softly to herself, gazing outward at the brilliant sunshine-drenched morning. . . .

"As my eyes
Go searching through the forest,
I seem to see the summer
In the spring.
As my eyes
Go searching through the forest,
I feel the spring,
Anxious for summer."

In the shade and under the damp thickets of young balsams, delicate flowers now marked the season. Lorinda had sniffed them all on her daily walks . . . the arbutus, claytonia, trillium and the bloodroot, and even the partridge vine.

The sun's warmth had set little runnels of melted snow trickling down sides of trails and small avalanches tumbling from the south slopes of the wigwams. Yellow Feather had told Lorinda that even into early summer one could catch the smell of the snow in the air as it would drift out of the deep forest, where it still lay under ledges of rocks, never touched by the sun.

Lorinda smiled to herself, comparing the fresh, green sprouts of spring to the child growing inside her womb. She touched her stomach proudly. The long and cold winter had given her the opportunity to seek the pleasures of the heart more often than not in the warmth of the wigwam. She knew that many babies could be expected to arrive in this village at about the time the wild rice harvest celebration would begin.

A voice spoke suddenly from behind Lorinda. She swung around and smiled sweetly toward Yellow Feather, seeing his face a mask of desire for her. She stood nude, still slender and beautifully curved, though now four months with child.

"Yellow Feather, my love, it's such a delicious day outside," she said, rushing to him, falling to her knees beside him. Her eyes raked over his nudity, oh, so loving the smooth, copper color of his skin. She twined her arms about his neck and kissed him briefly, then settled down next to him on their bed of blankets.

"*Ah-uh*, the sun warms the earth now, but our sugarbush was slowed in growth this spring," he said. He crossed his arms and stared upward at the smoke hole. "But now the sap should soon begin dripping from the tips of the branches. The succession of melting days and freezing nights have begun to quicken the heart of the maples."

"And the maize is planted," Lorinda said, circling a fingertip around the stiff erectness of one of his nipples.

Yellow Feather turned to her and reached a hand to her abdomen. He touched it gently as his eyes studied it. "It was wise to not let you join the women in the fields to plant the maize," he murmured. "Our child seems to be growing much too slowly. Why isn't there more rise to your stomach? Does it mean you are growing a daughter instead of a son?"

Lorinda's heart fluttered, fear gnawing at her insides.

She had to bear him a son. If not, she could expect another wife to be taken by him. The thought of Yellow Feather sharing embraces with another sent pinpricks of pain throughout her.

Forcing a silken laugh, she purposely ignored his question. Instead she leaned her body toward his and tremored with passion at the mere touch of him. "But I did participate in the blessing of the cornfields, my husband," she purred. "I, alone, the chief's wife, did as you asked. Do you now truly believe the cornfields will be more fruitful?"

Yellow Feather removed his fingers from her abdomen and framed her face between his hands. *"Ay-uh,"* he said hoarsely, devouring her with his dark, fathomless eyes. "You have blessed the cornfields. The passing of your footsteps drew a magic circle around the field of freshly planted maize. No insects or worms shall pass over that magic circle."

Lorinda snuggled next to the lean hardness of Yellow Feather's chest, welcoming his arms about her. She smiled contentedly, remembering her initial response of horror to his request on that cool, spring evening. But in the end she had complied, not only wanting to be the best wife, but knowing to do so would make him even a better husband. He always rewarded her in the most sensual of ways. . . .

When night had fallen in their village and all was silent with the spirit of sleep a companion in all the St. Croix' wigwams, Lorinda had crept from her tent, alone. Once outside, beneath the soft reflection of the April moon, she had laid her garments aside, knowing that Yellow Feather had assured her that no eye would see her. He had told her that all his people realized the importance of this ritual and that any interference from any of them could even cause a failure in the autumn's harvest. . . .

Lorinda's insides quivered as Yellow Feather's lips

375

searched her body, in his usual worshipping fashion, yet she was still remembering that night. . . .

Reminding herself of his promise over and over again, Lorinda had moved swiftly through the village with a thundering heart and trembling knees. The cold splash of the dew-laden air against her bare flesh had sent goose pimples rising and her teeth to chattering. She had known her duty as the chief's wife and was going to go through with it, though she had yet to understand the Indian's customs. The white man's ways seemed so simple in comparison. This was cause for her to admire the Indians more and more each day she was a part of them. She loved their culture. She loved them.

Once she had reached the cornfield and had seen the shadows of the rows and rows of furrowed mounds, she had begun her slow circle of the field, around its borders, having suddenly felt strangely free and uninhibited. She had laughed and enjoyed this freedom, oh, so loving her new way of life. . . .

"What are you thinking about?" Yellow Feather asked, breathing warmth onto her cheek as his fingers combed through her long tresses of outspread red hair.

Lorinda sighed. "I'm marveling at how happy and content I truly am," she whispered. "Yellow Feather, you've completely stolen my heart. Please never return it to me. I so love you."

"The sun rises swiftly in the sky these spring mornings, but I still have time to enjoy my wife this morning," Yellow Feather said, now leaning over her. His hands fit around her hips and lifted her body to his lips. With slow flicks of his tongue he nipped at her flesh, causing her to moan.

She reached her fingers to his back and traced the corded tightness of his shoulders, then downward to the slight lift of his buttocks. With a rising fever inside her, Lorinda inched her fingers around to where a dark, wiry mass of curls circled the treasures of his pleasure stem. She dared a touch to his readiness and then circled it with her fingers and brazenly led it to where her legs were now spread, ready.

When he entered her and began his slow, even strokes, she circled her legs about his body and locked her ankles together. She closed her eyes and let her mind absorb the joy of their union. She was now a part of the meadow, the tall grass . . . weaving, bending. Yellow Feather's breath was the warm breeze . . . warming, caressing.

His lips were the butterfly's touch, so fleeting, darting from one breast to the other, then stopping to taste the sweet pollen of her neck. Lorinda sighed languidly as he circled his fingers around a breast and caused it to come alive with warmth as he kneaded and fondled it. She cried out his name in Indian as her passion began to peak to a fiery climax, but then she was silenced as his lips crushed against hers, and she held back the completion of her pleasure to enjoy the raw passion she was finding in his continually ardent kisses.

Lorinda silkily laced her arms about his neck and drew his chest to hers, feeling his thunderous heartbeat against her breasts. She knew that he was as lost in his desire for her, and she closed her eyes to the ecstasy. . . .

Yellow Feather drew her into his arms, consumed by his uncontrollable need of her. Her body was the soft petals of a rose, her lips the nectar. He explored inside her mouth with his tongue, and when hers met and teased his with swift flicks, he felt the heat rise with even greater intensity inside his loins.

He hastened his strokes inside her and locked his fingers through the soft silk of her hair. Stiffening, then trembling, he released his love for her inside her body, uttering low guttural moans of delight as his thrusts became wild and swift. He smiled to himself when he felt her body also tremor and heard her short gasps and whis-

377

perings of pleasure.

Yellow Feather's lips withdrew from hers and his eyes spoke his love as never before. *"Neen mis-kwah-wa-bee-go-neece,"* he murmured, tracing her face with his fingertips.

She leaned her face into his caress. *"Ay-uh,* I am your Red Blossom," she whispered. *"Ah-pah-nay. Ay-uh,* forever."

"I hate to leave you, but my duties await," he said, raining kisses on her face, throat, and breasts.

"I will go with the women to the 'sugarbush' to help collect the sap," she murmured. "But only after I check on Amanda."

Yellow Feather rose to his feet and began to dress as did Lorinda. "Your sister," he said. "She is no longer a baby."

"No," Lorinda laughed. "She is now a toddler. How sweet it is to see her and Little Red Fox run hand in hand after a ball."

"The carved, wooden ball was one among the treasures I found in the cave," Yellow Feather said, lacing his leggings. "Today I plan to find more useful gifts for my people." He squared his shoulders and went to Lorinda. "Maybe I will even find something special for you," he said thickly. "Would you like that?"

"Ay-uh . . . ."

"Then I must go. . . ."

"I know," she whispered, tiptoeing, kissing him gently on the lips. She watched him bend and step from inside the wigwam, then hurriedly finished dressing herself in the buckskin dress with its trimmings of beads at the hem. She touched her abdomen and smiled. Maybe she didn't show her weight gain, but she could feel it in the tightness of her dress.

"It will be a son," she said aloud. "I will think hard on a son. That will make it so!"

Anxious to see Amanda, she slipped hurriedly into her moccasins. She ran her fingers through her hair as she rushed from the wigwam and on past two others until she saw Amanda and Little Red Fox already outside, romping and giggling.

Lorinda slowed her approach and watched her sister, proud, yet worried. Amanda had grown close to Little Red Fox, so close, in fact, that they still shared their bed of blankets. Lorinda understood how this could happen. It was the way of the Chippewa. They knew ways to melt one's heart. Lorinda and Amanda were fortunate to have shared such a bond between themselves and the St. Croix band of the Chippewa.

Lorinda stopped and gazed upon the gold, bouncing curls of her sister, her cheeks pink from excitement; her blue eyes twinkling as little Red Fox offered her a field daisy. Though they were only toddlers, a love rare and true seemed to be blossoming between them. They had shared the same breast for nourishment and seemed eager to share the rest of their lives. But Lorinda was once more beginning to worry about her sister's future.

Her heart ached, thinking about her parents, always feeling the loss more when she was in Amanda's presence. Amanda's age had been her shield, too young to ever realize that she had at one time known another way of life.

"What is the answer?" Lorinda worried to herself. "What is best?"

The answer in her mind seemed always to be the same. She had to think of what her parents would want for their youngest daughter. Lorinda had to be loyal to her parents' wishes, and she knew that if they were alive they would want Amanda raised in the white man's culture and going to school in a white man's school.

"A proper education," she whispered. "How many times did my mother stress the need for a proper educa-

379

tion?''

Guilt sprang forth. Her parents would also still want this for herself. But then she was reminded of a particular "why" for the need for schooling. Her mother had so often said that while attending school in St. Paul Lorinda might meet a "man of means."

"Was that their sole reason for entering me into school?" she wondered.

Her right hand went to her abdomen and a slow smile crinkled her nose. She had found her man, and not while in school. Yellow Feather was a man of the outdoors, but he was also a man of means. He was the chief of the St. Croix, a very proud people, and she was his wife, already carrying his child. . . .

Lorinda's thoughts were interrupted when she saw Amanda and Little Red Fox being guided back into the wigwam by Little Red Fox's mother, Singing Cloud. Lorinda took a step forward and reached out a hand and began to speak of her presence, but then decided it would be best to wait now until evening to play with and love her sister. She did have her labors to perform as a wife, and she knew that most of the women were probably already busy with their birch-bark buckets at the sugar maple grove, ready to collect the sweet sap.

This day was the beginning of the "sugarbush" rite of spring. Because there was no salt, the Indians used maple sugar as both a confection and as a seasoning for fruits, vegetables and fish. It was now the time of awakening to their needs of the stomach. For most, the needs of the flesh would be set aside for at least a little while.

When Lorinda arrived on the scene, the trees had already been tapped and birch-bark buckets were hanging from the wooden spiles that had been set into the tree trunks. She stopped and looked all about her, seeing and hearing much. After the lean winter months, this sugar-making season was pleasurable. Indians of all ages were enjoying the accompanying dances and other leisure activities. Men were playing lacrosse or gambling with bone dice as the women chatted and cheered them on and the children anxiously waited to taste the sweetness from the first bucket lifted from a tree.

But all was not fun and games. Fires were being tended in a long trench where a hundred-gallon moosehide vat waited for the sap to be emptied into it. The aroma of venison and bear steaks broiling on the coals eased upward into Lorinda's nose, causing hunger to gnaw at her insides. But work came first for the women of the St. Croix. Even for the chief's wife. . . .

Lorinda entered the group with a warm welcome and busied herself going from tree to tree, checking the buckets. She turned with a start when loud cheers suddenly rang out from behind her. Then she smiled when she saw that the first sweet liquid was being poured into the vat over the fire.

It was then that most of the men joined in the labors. They hurried from tree to tree, collecting the sap, then quickly replenishing the moosehide vat. As the men poured, the women stirred with paddles, around and around, while the liquid bubbled and boiled until it reached the proper consistency. The workers then transferred this to a trough in a hollowed-out log and worked it again by paddle into granulated sugar, or poured some of this into molds, if hard sugar was desired.

The day was lost in this continuous effort to capture every sweet drop from every maple tree. When the sunset turned the tips of the trees into flame, Lorinda felt that she had worked her limit. Her back ached and her fingers were callused from tending the paddles, and she knew that for the sake of her unborn child she had to leave the night's vigil to someone else.

Leaving the sweet aroma of maple sugar and the merry chatter of the Indians behind her, Lorinda made her way back to the village. When she began moving around the cluster of wigwams, the sky had just lost its blue and the flickerings of fireflies had begun to rise from the dew-damp grass at her feet.

Though she was tired, she stopped at Singing Cloud's wigwam, where Amanda already lay half-asleep, next to Little Red Fox. Smiling a welcome to Singing Cloud, Lorinda fell to her knees at her sister's side and bent a kiss to her cheek. Amanda opened her eyes sleepily and smiled sweetly up at Lorinda, then closed her eyes again, breathing easily with a contented happiness.

Then Lorinda's gaze went to Little Red Fox, seeing his round, copper face and charcoal-black hair framing it. His sculptured Indian features reflected how handsome he would be one day as a man. . . .

"Oh, what shall I do?" Lorinda argued to herself. "I can't wait much longer. Amanda's first words were even in Chippewa. . . ."

Smoothing some golden curls back from Amanda's face, Lorinda began singing an Indian song to her and Little Red Fox that Yellow Feather had sung to Amanda while they had playfully chased fireflies this pleasant, lovely spring. She sang it softly:

"Oh, little fireflies,
The eyes of night,
Send off your light,
So soft of yellow,
So sweet and mellow.
Oh, little fireflies . . .
Light my child's way
Until the light of day."

She repeated the lullaby, over and over again, until the

peaceful spirit of sleep was causing slow, even breaths to escape from between the two children's slightly parted lips.

Lorinda tucked the colorfully striped Indian blanket more snugly beneath their chins, then rose to her feet, still looking at her sister. Her sister's future was in her hands. She *had* to make the right decision.

Turning on her heel, she moved toward the entrance flap. And without a word to Singing Cloud, Lorinda crept from the wigwam and hurried to her own. When she lifted the entrance flap she found Yellow Feather tending the fire in the firespace. As she approached him her eyes settled on some objects on the bulrush mat flooring next to him. She smiled to herself. She stepped up behind him, draping her arms about his neck. "Yellow Feather, you're so sweet," she purred. "You said you would bring me gifts from the cave and you have."

Yellow Feather took her hands in his and guided her down beside him. He studied her intensely. "I was wrong to let you go to the sugarbush," he said. "Weariness speaks from your eyes. The green is flecked with grays. Are you all right, Red Blossom?"

Lorinda sighed heavily and lifted the palm of his left hand to her lips to kiss it softly. Then she held it tightly as she gazed rapturously onto his face. "Do not fret, my love," she said. "I stayed away from the cornfield. I could not from the sugarbush. It's important to me to look strong in your people's eyes. And I knew when to return to our wigwam. You even seemed to have known when I would return. You are here waiting."

"I've come to add wood to the fire and to bring your gifts to place beside our bed. But I have to go to the sugarbush and help those who must stop to rest."

Lorinda felt a sudden surge of guilt thinking of accepting gifts that were at one time possessions of some innocent traveler along the trail. It was hard to imagine Yellow Feather stealing from anyone, yet he had also taken

383

her, had he not?

She plopped down on the bulrush mats and crossed her legs before her. "Well, then, Yellow Feather, let's see what you have," she said, brushing her guilt aside. Since meeting her, he had stopped stealing from the white man. She had seemed to be enough to quell his hungerings for adventure.

She watched as he reached for a beautifully designed blanket. It was the colors of the rainbow, not unlike the ones the Indians already had, but she knew that each blanket added to the household only meant more warmth for the long winter nights.

As the blanket being lifted into his arms revealed the next gift to be presented to her, Lorinda gasped noisily. Her eyes grew wide and her heart pumped frantically, now even smelling the familiar aroma. She ignored Yellow Feather's outstretched arms that held the blanket, but instead rose to her feet and rushed to where she saw a knitted shawl and, next to it, a cameo brooch. The blanket had hidden these from her view earlier but now she could see that what she was reaching for were . . . her . . . aunt's . . . !

"Red Blossom, what is it?" Yellow Feather asked, also rising to his feet. He dropped the blanket to the floor and leaned down over her as she placed the shawl to her nose.

Lorinda inhaled deeply. She smelled the fragrance of Lily of the valley, her aunt's favorite cologne. She held the shawl back away from her and studied the colors, now knowing whether it was her aunt's. Then her fingers began to travel across the cameo brooch, feeling almost numb inside. How? When? Where had her aunt been when these had been stolen from her?

With a racing heart, she turned and faced Yellow Feather angrily. "Yellow Feather, where did you get these?" she asked in a strained voice. She knew that tears

384

were near but had to show her strength to this Indian who she suddenly didn't know at all. Lorinda knew that Yellow Feather would have had to have stolen these after having been with her, for the last time she had seen her aunt, she had had these in her possession.

"When, Yellow Feather? Tell me when!" she stormed.

Yellow Feather's face became a mask of confusion. He looked first into Lorinda's eyes, seeing a strange torment, then down at what she held, and couldn't understand the connection between her sudden outburst and these possessions of the white man. He had given her gifts before. She hadn't reacted in such a way then. He still didn't know how to understand her and her complex personality! Would he ever?

"These are gifts from the cave," he answered, crossing his arms angrily across his chest. "Red Blossom, you knew I was going to give you more gifts from the cave. Why are you angry with me?"

Lorinda's eyes snapped even more angrily back at him. "Yellow Feather," she said from between clenched teeth. "I know you got these from the cave. But where did you get them from before? *When* did you? I thought you had given up the raids on the white man."

Yellow Feather's eyes narrowed. "Red Blossom, you speak too angrily to the chief of the St. Croix," he snarled. "It is disrespectful for a wife of a chief to question anything he does. You forget your anger or I will walk away from you."

Knowing that he would do just that, Lorinda held the shawl and cameo out before her. In a quieter tone, she said, "Yellow Feather, I have reason to be upset. These were my aunt's. Please tell me when you took these. Where? Is my aunt all right?"

Her lips began to tremble, unable to control her tumultuous emotions any longer. At this moment, she was no longer part Indian. She was all white. At this moment, she missed her aunt with a tortured heart.

Yellow Feather took the shawl and cameo and studied them extensively, furrowing his brow. He then glanced back at Lorinda. "These are not familiar to me," he said. "They were hidden at the back of the cave beneath many other things. I only uncovered them today when arranging things to be taken from the cave to our people."

Lorinda's heart skipped a beat. "Are you saying . . . someone else must have stolen these?" she said softly. "Who? When? Or would you even know to remember all that you stole? Do you have such a memory?"

"Ay-uh," Yellow Feather said. He studied the brooch and shawl again. "When I found them in the cave, my first thought was of Flying Squirrel . . . of his one raid without me." He lifted his eyes back to Lorinda's. *"Ay-uh,* Flying Squirrel must have stolen these from the white man. He did go without me that one night."

Lorinda doubled her fists to her side and swung around. She chewed on her lower lip, then turned once more to face Yellow Feather. "Where did Flying Squirrel go that night?" she asked angrily. "Did he tell you?"

"Gah-ween," Yellow Feather said, shaking his head. "He did not."

Lorinda's voice caught in her throat. "He may have even hurt my aunt," she said, swallowing hard. "I knew that he wasn't to be trusted from the very first. God, Yellow Feather, what if he hurt my aunt?"

Yellow Feather placed the brooch and shawl on the floor. He drew Lorinda gently into his arms. "We never hurt the white man we stole from," he said. "We always waited until they were asleep then crept silently into their camp and took what we could without causing noise to awaken them. I'm sure Flying Squirrel would have followed such rules when working alone."

Lorinda placed her cheek against Yellow Feather's

chest and began a low sobbing. "But what if my aunt awakened while Flying Squirrel was robbing from her?" she murmured. "What would Flying Squirrel have done then? Can you assure me that Flying Squirrel would not have harmed her?"

"*Ay-uh,*" he said. "It is the way of the Chippewa. We are nonwarring with your white people. Flying Squirrel would not have harmed anyone to cause problems with the white man. Believe me, Red Blossom. Believe me that what I say is so."

Lorinda clung to him then leaned her head back away from him to look directly into his dark pools of eyes. "But you cannot be truly sure," she murmured. "You know that Flying Squirrel was different from you. He was capable of many devious things."

Yellow Feather's face shadowed. He was remembering that Flying Squirrel had deceived *him* . . . in the worst way. "I only can try to console you, Red Blossom," he said. "We have to believe that Flying Squirrel would have behaved as all Chippewa."

"But I have to see for myself," Lorinda said firmly. She pulled away from him and began pacing. "Yellow Feather, I must return home. . . ."

He stopped her by grabbing onto her shoulders and held her directly before him. "*Gah-ween,*" he said angrily. "You cannot. . . ."

"I will," Lorinda said flatly. "And soon." She paused, eyeing the closed entrance flap. Swallowing hard, she thought of Amanda. Now was the time to reveal what she had to do to Yellow Feather. She truly knew that this was the right decision. What better time than now, when she had to see if her aunt was all right? She could do both things at once . . . then return to Yellow Feather's side.

She eyed him softly. She had for a brief moment thought him capable of being unfaithful to her by attacking her white people again. But she had been wrong. She should have known! He was good. He was proud. He would never lie to her. She knew that now.

"We have talked about this," Yellow Feather said, taking her gently into his arms. "I thought you could place the white man's ways out of your mind. But now because of these things of your aunt's, you are once again reminded of your past. I do not want you to go. You may not return to me . . . to my people."

Lorinda touched a finger to his lips. "Yellow Feather, I could never live without you now that I've found you," she whispered. Then she cast her eyes downward. "Amanda will be the one who will not return to your village by the St. Croix River. Not I."

Lorinda could hear his quick intake of breath, causing her eyes to move upward once more. "It is the only right thing to do," she murmured. "Amanda must be raised in the white man's culture, not the Indian's."

"You're wrong. . . ."

"No. I am not," she argued softly. "It is what my parents would have wished for their baby daughter. They would want her to have a proper education. Yellow Feather, she speaks more Indian than she does English now that she has begun to talk. If she speaks Indian now, what will she do when her full vocabulary is formed? She will never know how to speak as my people. She will even communicate with *me* in Indian."

She stepped back away from him, lowering her eyes to her aunt's things. "But there is only one problem," she said softly. "If my aunt was harmed by Flying Squirrel, then it must be I myself who makes sure Amanda has a home in the white man's world. . . ."

Yellow Feather stepped to her side and swung her around to face him. "You said that you would return to Yellow Feather," he snapped. "Now you speak as though you will not. How is it to be for you, Red Blossom? Tell me.''

"I have to return to you,'' she said, throwing her arms about his neck. Tears wet his buckskin shirt as they flowed freely from her eyes. "My aunt must be all right. She must. I cannot bear to think of being away from you.''

Yellow Feather stroked her lovingly. "You are with child," he said. "You will return with our child. The spirits will be with you. They will guide your way back to me.''

"Then you understand?" she asked, pleading with her eyes as she looked into his.

"I do not want to say that I do," he said. "I do not want you to go. But if you must . . . you must. . . ."

"Will you help me?"

"I would not let anyone else accompany you on such a journey," he said, glancing down at her stomach. "I must see to your safety. I must see to our child's.''

"How can we do this? When . . . ?"

"Soon. I do not wish to wait until you are swollen uncomfortably with child. We will leave soon.''

"How will Amanda and Little Red Fox exist without one another?" Lorinda whispered. "They have grown so close.''

"I feel they will be destined to meet again," Yellow Feather said sternly. "They have been as one . . . as you and I have become. I am sure nothing will keep them apart.''

"You say that as though you completely disapprove of what I do. . . .''

"*Ay-uh,* Yellow Feather thinks you are wrong," he said. "Amanda . . . White Blossom . . . is more Indian now than white. Her Indian name suits her well. Though her skin is white it is her heart that will always say she is Indian.''

He drew her into his arms once more and kissed her

389

gently on the lips, then said, "I have known for some time now that White Blossom's days were numbered here in our village," he said. "You have spoken of it often enough and I have watched your eyes looking at her. I knew that you were becoming more troubled about her future. Please do not be concerned any longer. We will make things right for your sister. The Sioux were wrong to kill her parents. The Chippewa will set the path straight for her."

Lorinda hugged him tightly. "I knew you would do what was best for her," she sighed. "I should have known all along you wouldn't stop my returning to my aunt. I have had the need to see her . . . to let her know that I am all right."

She then stiffened and gazed upward into his eyes, almost fearful. "But, Yellow Feather, if you travel with me to St. Paul, you could be in danger. What if you are seen? What if I am followed? You don't want the white people to know where our village is."

"You must make your aunt promise not to tell anyone," he said. "I will wait in the forest for you. Then you will come alone to me and we will return to our village. If your aunt is anything like you, she can be wholly trusted."

Tears once more filled Lorinda's eyes. "You mean if my aunt is still alive, don't you?" she said. "What if Flying Squirrel . . . ?"

"She is alive. You will see. Soon. You will see. . . ."

"I only hope you are right," Lorinda said, stepping back away from him, wiping her eyes with the back of her hand. She bent and picked up the brooch and shawl and held them to her, eyeing Yellow Feather warmly. "And thank you for bringing these to me," she added. "These mean more to me than anything else you could have offered."

Yellow Feather walked toward the entrance flap and lifted it. "I must return to the sugarbush," he said. "I will return to you soon. Please rest now."

Lorinda marveled at the smile he directed toward her. When they had first become acquainted, rarely had he smiled! Now he seemed to be doing it all the time. "I will be waiting, my beloved," she said, then watched him disappear from view.

Feeling the full day's labor and the recent strain suddenly causing her to be strangely fatigued, she dropped to her bed of blankets and stretched out, still holding her aunt's brooch and shawl. She watched the fire until her eyelids grew heavy and let herself drift off into an almost drugged sleep.

When a movement in the wigwam drew her eyes slowly open a while later, she turned her body to welcome Yellow Feather's arrival into their bed of blankets. Beneath the soft glow of the dying embers in the firespace, Lorinda couldn't see Yellow Feather's face, only his shadow above her as he knelt over her. She tensed, seeing the difference in the shape of the head and hair, and smelling . . .

Her eyes flew wide open and she gasped noisily. Only one man had smelled so vile. She could so well remember the aroma of alcohol and tobacco on his breath when he had tried to rape her. Even now she could hear his deep, nervous breathing of heated desire and knew that it wasn't Yellow Feather who was looming over her, but the devil himself, that animal Lamont Quinby.

Lorinda raised a knee and struck him in the groin. "You," she hissed. "How did you find me? Get out, do you hear? Get out!"

His low groan of pain didn't slow his attack. "Damn you, woman," he snarled, grabbing her wrists as Lorinda pushed and shoved at him. "I've only come to take what's mine. Now you can't say you're not glad, can

391

you?'' His eyes raked over her, seeing her Indian attire. "But maybe I'm wrong. You're dressed as a squaw. Do you act like one too?''

"Yellow Feather will kill you," she said venomously. "Why have you persisted in your pursuit of me?"

Lamont leaned down and brushed her lips with his, ah, tasting the sweetness. His loins ached. He would first have her then take her away. His mind was now too full of her to worry about being the only white man in the Indian village. He was a white man rescuing a white woman from the savage beast that had dealt him the blow to his head on the trail.

"I told you that no other man could have you," Lamont said smugly. "Especially not a savage Indian."

"You are the savage. Not Yellow Feather," Lorinda said, squirming, but no longer able to kick. He had her legs pinned beneath his. "You vile creature. You'll never get out of here alive. Your thick crop of hair will be swaying on a scalp pole at the rise of the morning's sun."

Lamont's hair raised at the nape of his neck. She sounded more Indian than white! But then a slow smile curved his lips upward, causing his mustache to quiver a bit. He had thought her exciting before, but now she was even moreso with her new wild way of talking. And she now surely knew many ways to set a man's insides on fire.

"I killed for you," he said thickly, kissing her wetly on the hollow of her throat. "Do you think I'd go to all the trouble I've gone to, to just let my hair be taken from my head? It's been a long, hard trail for me while searchin' for you. And now that I've finally found you, you're goin' to be my woman, not an Indian's."

Lorinda's pulse raced. "Who did you kill?" she whispered? "What do you mean?"

Lamont laughed throatily. "There was this man in Duluth," he said. "Seems he was a party of three who had come here to this village. But seems they ran into problems and had gone their separate ways. When he made threats of returnin' I did what I had to do to keep him away from you. I killed him. . . ."

"You are sick," Lorinda hissed, squirming anew. "Let me go. . . ."

"I will, but only after I place a gag over your mouth and tie your hands," he snarled. "You're even more spitfire now than before. I can't have you screamin', now can I?"

Lorinda opened her mouth to do just that but her sounds were stifled by the rough onslaught of his lips attacking hers. A sick feeling began to ripple in her stomach and she suddenly feared for her child. She tried to move but was still pinioned by the steel brute force of his body. She cringed when one of his knees worked her dress up above her thighs and forced her legs apart. She could even feel his male hardness through his clothes pressing against her, ready for the attack inside her.

"I've got to have you," he whispered in her ear. "Please don't scream, Lorinda. I must have you now . . . ."

His hands moved quickly over her, reaching down to free her of her underthings. When she heard the buttons unsnapping on his breeches, she knew there was only one thing left to do. No, she wouldn't scream. She didn't have to. She would defend herself and her unborn child. This man would not brutally rape her. She would not allow it. He had been foolish to release her hands. . . .

Slowly reaching beneath her thick bed of blankets, she searched with her fingers until they came in contact with the cold steel of the pistol. With a racing heartbeat, she circled her fingers around the pearl handle, placed one finger on the trigger and began moving it slowly from beneath the blankets.

She could still smell him, she even tasted his spittle on

her lips, and she could hear his anxious breaths as his hands searched and probed in the soft spot between her legs. When he began to lower his swollen stem downward, already grazing her flesh, Lorinda raised the gun . . . pulled the trigger . . . then cringed when she felt him flinch with the impact.

Trembling, she scooted away from him, now hearing only silence, but smelling more than him. The aroma of gunpowder clung to her hair . . . her clothes. . . .

A rush of feet outside the wigwam and loud chatterings from many Indians drew Lorinda slowly to her feet. She began to inch her way to the entrance flap, sobbing, but stopped when Yellow Feather quickly flipped the entrance flap open and stepped on inside with eyes dark and wide. . . .

Twenty-Six

The fresh green of the trees swayed gently in the breeze above Lorinda's head as she traveled by horseback on Yellow Feather's right side. The cotton of her high-necked, long-sleeved dress billowed around her legs and her hair lifted from her shoulders in lustrous waves of flame. She faced proudly south, knowing that she was finally going home, though it was to be for only a brief visit.

She glanced down at tiny, fourteen-month-old Amanda, who sat straight and beautiful in the saddle in front of her. She was also attired in a dress . . . one that Lorinda had fashioned from a larger one she had found in the cave. They did not represent the Indian way of life this day. They had to be sure they looked like any other woman and child who would be traveling the streets of St. Paul. Lorinda had to make sure no suspicions were aroused. She didn't want to be the cause of anyone's wondering about where she had been or who had guided her back to her aunt's house. Yes, she and Amanda had to look as like mother and daughter out for a day of leisure when they entered the city of St. Paul. . . .

Lorinda looked toward Yellow Feather. He still disapproved of what she she had chosen to do. But his love for her had melted his stubbornness and now he sat tall on a beautiful brown mare, while behind him he lead the black stallion that he had stolen from the trail the same night he had abducted Lorinda.

"Won't you miss the horse terribly?" she asked,

breaking the silence between them. "Do you truly want to part with it, Yellow Feather?"

Yellow Feather held his chin high. *"Ay-uh,"* he said flatly. "By giving back the stolen horse I hope it is a way to steal your aunt's heart. She will not try so hard to keep you from returning to me in the forest if my gift is accepted with eagerness."

"But we've already decided that I cannot take the horse on into town with me," Lorinda said. "There would be questions for sure. Everyone knew my aunt's black stallion. If I was seen with it, all eyes would turn my way."

"She will gladly travel into the forest to get it," Yellow Feather said. "You will see. It will be all right."

"I keep praying that my *aunt* is all right. . . ." she murmured. "That she will be able to join in our plans."

She tightened her arm about Amanda's waist, knowing that the spot she had chosen to leave the stallion was one that her Aunt Rettie would have no trouble finding. The land that had been farmed by her father. The stallion would be left standing there with Yellow Feather until Lorinda returned. Hopefully her aunt would shortly follow. Lorinda had secretly planned a way for her aunt and Yellow Feather to meet. Only by doing this could Lorinda convince her aunt that the man she had chosen as her life's mate was a right choice, one that even Derrick Odell would have approved of had he been given the chance to see the good of this man . . . a Chippewa Indian chief.

Also, Lorinda knew that her aunt had to realize the thanks she owed Yellow Feather. Had it not been for him, Lorinda would most surely be with Lamont Quinby, having been forced to become his wife, and Amanda would still be in the Sioux village.

Yes, the Odell family owed many gratitudes to Yellow Feather and his people.

The thought of Lamont Quinby brought bitter memories to Lorinda's mind. A second time in so few months she had drawn a gun against a man and had pulled the trigger. But this second time her bullet had done its duty.

Being Christian, Lorinda felt a deep regret for having killed a man, but she kept telling herself that she had had no choice. He had been an evil man with only evil guiding his actions. Had she not pulled the trigger, he would have raped her, taken her away from Yellow Feather, and possibly have led the white man back to Yellow Feather's village.

Yes. She had done the right thing. His brutal attack could even have robbed her of her child . . . her and Yellow Feather's child of love . . . possibly the St. Croix band of the Chippewa's next chief-in-line!

Lorinda tensed a bit, seeing where the trail had led her. There were many things familiar to her now as the land showed a thinning of trees ahead. It wouldn't be long now and she would once more see the charred remains of her parents' log cabin.

A tortured ache circled her heart. Could she even bear the pain of seeing it all again? The last time she had been on this strip of land she had said such heartbreaking final goodbyes to her parents.

A renewed burning anger toward Lamont Quinby seethed inside her. He hadn't let her take the time to bury her parents. He hadn't let her return to St. Paul to report the massacre to the proper authorities!

"He was a demon," she hissed beneath her breath. "He surely is burning in hell at this very moment."

Yellow Feather pulled his horse closer to her side. "Are you all right, Red Blossom?" he asked, studying her with his dark, fathomless eyes. "You first look so distraught and then so angry. Maybe returning to your people is not so wise."

Lorinda forced a smile. She had to gain more control of

her emotions. She knew that Yellow Feather worried about their child. He had reason to worry about childbearing. Though the Indian women were known to be strong, so many seemed to fall short of the strength required to carry babies to full term. But Lorinda was white and she was determined to show Yellow Feather that nothing would cause her to lose their child.

Something grabbed at Lorinda's heart. She had forgotten about the many miscarriages her mother had suffered, and *she* had been white. Could this weak trait be inherited. . . ?

She cast Yellow Feather a fast glance beneath the thick veil of her lashes, hoping not. So much depended on her having a healthy baby . . . a son. . . .

Lorinda's attention was suddenly averted. She was seeing the cleared land, the fence her father had built to outline this piece of land, and she knew that she was close. Feeling a pounding of her heart, she let her eyes watch for the first signs of rubble. And when she saw it, the ache that she had felt that day so long ago began anew around her heart and in the pit of her stomach. It was just as she had last seen it. It was apparent that no one was ready to try his hand attending this piece of land that had been desecrated by the Sioux. The fear of Indians would probably prevent anyone's ever beginning anew here.

"I fear we are drawing too close to the white man's village," Yellow Feather said, pulling his horse to a halt. "I must stop here. You go ahead. This will be where you will find me waiting." He pointed toward a cluster of trees that stood back away from the trail. "I will be there. Hidden beneath the safe cover of the trees."

Lorinda eyed him sadly. He didn't know. She drew her horse to a halt next to him and reached to touch the bare flesh of his arm. "Yellow Feather, I am now home," she said in a strained whisper.

Yellow Feather's eyes darkened as he looked her way.

"What do you mean . . . home . . . ?" he asked, tilting an eyebrow.

Lorinda's gaze traveled around her, once more taking in the ashes that were no longer black, but gray, some having become part of the earth as they had been spread beneath the heavy coverings of snows and rains.

Hugging Amanda closer to her abdomen, Lorinda nodded toward the remains of her parents' house. "What you see was once my home, filled with much love and happiness," she said, tears near.

Yellow Feather stiffened his back. "You have brought me to your parents' final resting place?" he asked softly. "This is the house you have spoken of so much in your fitful dreams?"

"*Ay-uh,*" she murmured. She glanced down at Amanda, who squirmed to be released. "And also my sister's house. She was only such a tiny thing when she was taken from her crib." Then she remembered his words: "final resting place." She raised her eyes and began searching frantically around her. Where *had* her parents been placed to rest? Had Aunt Rettie seen to their proper burial? She had to know! Now!

"Yellow Feather, will you tend to Amanda for a few minutes?" she asked, eyeing him with a soft pleading.

"You wish to speak with the spirits of your past?" he asked.

Lorinda smiled weakly. "Yes. Something like that," she said. When he held his arms out for Amanda, Lorinda lifted her from the saddle and toward him. When Amanda was safely hugging him around the neck, Lorinda climbed slowly from her horse and began moving toward the charred remains. Like flashes of lightning, it was all coming back to her. She looked toward the spot where her mother had lain, then where her father had been stretched out on his stomach, without his beautiful red crop of hair.

A choking sensation seemed to be rising in her throat

as she walked slowly across the ground that was ripe with field daisies with their bright golden centers. Then Lorinda found what she had been looking for . . . two mounds on the ground with a stone placed at one end of each.

"It's their graves," she whispered. She placed a knuckle between her teeth to clamp down onto as she fell to her knees between the graves. On one crude stone she read her mother's name and on the other her father's. Lorinda was engulfed with a deep sadness, yet she was relieved. Her mother and father had been found and given a decent burial before any more harm could come to their bodies. At least that was something to be grateful for.

Picking a few daisies, Lorinda placed them on each of the graves, then closed her eyes in a short, quiet prayer. Then, when she felt enough time had been spent in silent mourning, she pushed herself up from the ground and turned and walked away, knowing this was a part of her past that she once again had to learn to place behind her. It was all so fresh again in her mind . . . but she had to remember the future . . . the beautiful, sweet future with Yellow Feather and their child. . . .

Going back to her horse, Lorinda reached inside her travel bag and pulled two sunbonnets out. She handed the smaller one to Yellow Feather and watched him place it atop Amanda's golden curls while she fitted her own over her head, tying its bow beneath her chin.

"Does its brim hide enough of my face, Yellow Feather?" she asked, looking toward Amanda, smiling at her sister's sweetness.

"No one will see enough of your face to recognize you before you reach your aunt's house," Yellow Feather said, climbing from his horse with Amanda still in his arms.

"Will it truly work?" Lorinda worried. "I want to go into town and leave again without anyone having cause to follow me. I don't want anyone finding you here. There's still no way to prove it was the Sioux who was responsible for my parents' death, and I'm sure my word wouldn't be enough."

"You will be safe . . . I will be safe. . . ." he said thickly. "Go. Now. Then return soon. I will be waiting."

Lorinda waited until Yellow Feather had Amanda placed on her horse then she laced her arms about his neck. "I won't be long," she purred. "I promise. . . ."

She let his lips smooth away all the grief she had just been filled with and let hope take its place. She clung to him for a moment longer then drew away from him and settled back on the horse and held Amanda closely to her. She smiled a goodbye to Yellow Feather then headed on toward town, now more anxious than sad. She *had* to find her aunt well. She would *not* think that harm had come to her. Surely Flying Squirrel wouldn't have . . . ! From this point on she would only think on the positive side of life.

Ah, it had been so long since she had seen her aunt. What a surprise this would be for her! But it was going to be hard to explain why the visit would be so short for Lorinda. What would her aunt say when it was explained that an Indian awaited her oldest niece's return . . . ?

Then Lorinda glanced down at her sister, remembering her hugs and goodbyes at the Chippewa Indian village. How was Amanda going to take this new way of life? She didn't even remember an aunt. How sad it had been to pull Amanda away from the embrace of Little Red Fox. Had the two children even understood this was to be a final goodbye for them?

Commanding her horse around a bend, Lorinda saw the familiar stubs of trees poking through the ground as far as the eye could see. This had been where her father had labored . . . where he had lived his dream. His death had come too soon . . . too swiftly. . . .

A spring, rippling clear and fresh along the inside of the fence railing at the side of the small, dusty trail, reminded Lorinda of many more things. Of the butter and milk that she had placed there to cool in the water for safekeeping, of the summer afternoons she had played and splashed in the coolness of the water.

Forcing her eyes to move straight ahead, Lorinda nudged a knee into the horse's side, wanting to speed her journey. This part of the country kept bringing too many sad things to her mind. She wanted to be hopeful for the future. She had to be. The man she loved depended on her.

Lorinda clung to Amanda and was relieved when their hour of travel away from Yellow Feather finally brought them to the edge of town. Lorinda tensed and began watching cautiously around her as she guided her horse down one rut-filled dirt street after another. No one seemed to pay any heed to these two females in cotton dresses and sunbonnets. The people were too busy with their own lives, hustling and bustling along on horseback and in fancy black carriages.

Lorinda took in her surroundings. It was all as she remembered. But she felt a bit strange being among houses instead of wigwams. It was at this time that she realized that she had truly become an Indian, had totally accepted their way of life. She smiled. This was good. Her future lay with the Indians. Not with the white people.

Glancing down once again toward Amanda, Lorinda knew that she had been right to bring her sister back to this life. Though Lorinda was content in her newly found happiness with Yellow Feather and his people, she had to believe that Amanda would find her own kind of peace and love. The conditions were better in the white man's village and food was always there for the asking. With the Indian way of life, one never knew from one season to the next, though Yellow Feather wouldn't admit to this. Yes, Amanda would always be warm. She would always have food. And with her Aunt Rettie, she would always have love.

A deep loneliness for her sister was already beginning inside Lorinda, but she knew that she had to brush such feelings aside. She was now guiding her horse up in front of her aunt's house. Soon she would fill her Aunt Rettie's arms and heart with renewed love!

With a flush in her face and an anxious heart pounding inside her, Lorinda drew the horse to a halt, eyeing the two-storied white frame house. She glanced toward the white wicker chairs on the porch and sighed with relief when she found no one there. So far she was in luck. Now to be able to slip into the house without notice. That would be the final challenge. Hopefully Aunt Rettie's boarders wouldn't be in the sitting room. Surely they would still be at their places of business, leaving the privacy of the sitting room to Aunt Rettie and her two nieces.

Dismounting, Lorinda tied her reins to a hitching post, then lifted Amanda down into her arms. She kissed the soft pink of Amanda's cheeks and whispered into her ear. "We're home, honey," she said. "Please accept Aunt Rettie. Sometimes she sounds a bit gruff but her heart is as large as the moon."

Amanda looked up into Lorinda's eyes and spoke some quick Indian chatter back at her. Lorinda's face flushed even more, knowing that this alone could give them away to passersby. She *had* to get Amanda inside the house. Fast! Her strange words could attract attention faster than anything!

Straightening Amanda's bonnet and fluffing the golden curls that came from beneath it, Lorinda set her on the ground and held the tininess of her hand as they made their way up the steep steps of the porch. Barely breathing, Lorinda slipped quickly into the house. She then stopped and looked cautiously about her, seeing no one. She listened intently and heard noises from the direction of the kitchen. It was midafternoon, and Lorinda knew that her aunt's cook already had to be preparing the evening meal. The aroma of bread baking set her stomach to growling, but her instincts led her on into the sitting room, hoping to find her aunt there, reading or possibly knitting.

With Amanda's hand still clasped tightly in hers, Lorinda looked around her at the plushness of the upholstered furnishings and the white crispness of the crisscrossed priscilla curtains at the windows. She had forgotten about the spaciousness of a house, having grown used to the smallness of a wigwam. She suddenly hungered for a house and knew that she would ask Yellow Feather to build one for her. In such a house she could raise *many* healthy children. Yes, this could be a valid argument to use on a man who seemed to place such importance on sons.

Footsteps approaching from behind her drew Lorinda around with a start. She watched the doorway, breathless. When a man with a thick head of gray hair and the bluest of eyes approached her, carrying, more than using, a gold-tipped cane, Lorinda felt the urge to turn and flee. A stranger meant danger. But his warm smile directed toward her caused the need to trust to flutter at her insides.

"What have we here?" Matthew asked, looking from Lorinda to Amanda. "Are you looking to rent a room? Will there be more than you and your daughter?"

Lorinda looked past him then back at him, puzzled. "And who might you be, sir?" she asked, pulling Amanda closer to her. He appeared to be near her Aunt Rettie's age, with distinguished grooves on his face. Was he a boarder, and if so, who was he to question her? It was as though he thought he owned the place!

"Matthew Toliver's the name," the man answered, offering a hand. "And yours?"

Lorinda took a step backwards, paling. She had feared something like this. She suddenly felt cornered. Where was her Aunt Rettie? Then Lorinda's heart sank. Maybe this man *did* own this boardinghouse now! Maybe her aunt wasn't alive! She forced such thoughts from her mind again, determined not to let herself think the worst!

Heavy footsteps on the staircase right outside the sitting room caused Lorinda to grab Amanda's hand. She ran past Matthew and on out into the foyer and almost ran into her Aunt Rettie as her aunt took the last step from the staircase and made a turn toward the sitting room.

"Aunt Rettie . . ." Lorinda said softly, seeing that her aunt *was* all right! In fact, nothing about her had changed. Her wiry mass of gray hair was circled in a tight bun atop her head and her weight hadn't lessened because of grieving for family. The familiar aroma of lily of the valley floated through the air from her aunt and on up into Lorinda's nose, causing Lorinda to remember, oh, so much.

She then became concerned for her aunt when she saw Rettie's face pale as she grabbed for the staircase bannister. "Aunt Rettie . . ." she said, quickly reaching for her aunt's arm to steady her.

Rettie reached a hand to Lorinda's face, as though testing her presence. "Lorinda, precious, it . . . *is* . . . you. . . ." she said in a low murmur. Then she drew Lorinda into her arms and hugged her tightly, softly crying. "My Lord, it is you. I thought Lamont Quinby or the Indians had done away with you as they did your baby sister Amanda."

Lorinda caressed her aunt's back for a moment, then drew away from her. "Aunt Rettie, I've so much to tell you," she said tearfully. "But, first, I've someone to *show* you." She reached around her and took Amanda's hand and pulled her up next to her. She then untied Amanda's bonnet and let her golden locks of hair fully frame the tiny round face that now appeared to be all eyes of blue as she stared calmly back at her aunt.

Rettie took a step forward, slowly seeing the resemblance between Mavis and this child. Her insides rippled strangely when Lorinda spoke the child's name. . . .

"Amanda, this is your Aunt Rettie," Lorinda said, pushing Amanda toward her aunt. She watched the color rise back into her aunt's cheeks and saw renewed rivers of tears splash from her eyes. Trembling from her own deep emotion, Lorinda busied her fingers by removing her own bonnet, placing it and Amanda's on a rosewood table beside her.

"Amanda . . . ?" Rettie said. "Good Lord, Lorinda, this is . . . Amanda . . . ?"

Rettie fell to her knees and drew Amanda quickly into her arms and cried into Amanda's hair. "How, oh, how?" she whispered. "I had given up. I thought I'd never see either of you again."

When Amanda squirmed out of Rettie's arms, jabbering in Chippewa, Rettie rose slowly to her feet, barely breathing. She looked awkwardly from Lorinda to Amanda, then back to Lorinda. "She's been in an Indian camp?" she whispered. "And you, Lorinda . . . ?"

Lorinda went to Rettie and hugged her, then stepped back away from her, still holding her hands. She looked down at her aunt, having almost forgotten how short she was. "I said that I have so much to tell you," she murmured.

Rettie stole a fast glance at Amanda, who was now walking around, inspecting this new type of house. "Amanda. You've brought her home?" she said. Then her gaze moved upward and studied the green of Lorinda's eyes. "And yourself. Lorinda, precious, I've never been so happy than at this moment.''

Lorinda tensed a bit, realizing now that it was going to be hard to tell her aunt that she would be leaving again, even within the hour. Could she take her aunt's happiness away from her again so soon? But her aunt *would* have Amanda. Surely that would be enough.

The man who had introduced himself as Matthew Toliver moved out into the foyer and stepped to Rettie's side. ''Are you all right, Rettie?'' he asked, framing her face between his hands. ''What's going on here? Why have you been crying?''

Rettie took his hands down from her face and held them tightly. She swallowed back more tears then smiled up into his eyes. ''Matthew, darling, I want you to meet two very special people to me,'' she said softly. Her gaze moved back to Lorinda, then Amanda. ''Matthew, this is Amanda and Lorinda. My . . . two . . . nieces. . . .''

Matthew gasped noisily. ''What . . . ? How . . . ?''

Lorinda studied him quizzically. What was this man to her aunt? There seemed to be a deep affection between her aunt and this stranger. Lorinda didn't know whether to be glad or wary. She still felt that only her aunt should know of her presence.

''Lorinda, I want you to meet my new husband,'' Rettie suddenly blurted. ''Your new uncle, Matthew Toliver. We've now been married for several months.''

''Your . . . husband? My . . . uncle . . . ?'' Lorinda said in a whisper.

''We met in a stagecoach on our way to Duluth,'' Rettie said, proudly locking an arm through one of Matthew's.

Lorinda's heart seemed to shimmy. ''Duluth?'' she said. ''Why were you going to Duluth, Aunt Rettie?''

Rettie reached a hand to Lorinda's face. ''In search of you and that . . . that . . . Lamont Quinby,'' she said. ''But an Indian caused the stagecoach to be turned back to

407

St. Paul.''

"An Indian . . . ?" Lorinda asked cautiously.

"Yes," Rettie snapped. "One lousy Indian. And he was not even as large as a fly and managed to get away with tying me to a tree and stealin' my shawl and brooch.''

"Flying Squirrel . . ." Lorinda whispered to herself. Then a slow smile crept onto her face, wondering what her aunt would say when she was given back her prized brooch and shawl. Lorinda had left them in the travel bag on her horse.

"And he even got away with stealin' my pearl-handled pistol from me," Rettie fumed further. "I had planned to find that Lamont Quinby and kill him dead with that gun. I bought the gun purposely to rid the earth of that vermin. But that savage, red-skinned Indian stopped that right quick.''

Lorinda's smile faded quickly away. The gun! The one she had killed Lamont with had been her aunt's! How ironic that her aunt had purposely purchased the gun to shoot Lamont Quinby . . . and in the end . . . that was what it had been used for!

Matthew broke into the conversation. "Lorinda, where have you traveled from?" he asked, tilting a heavy, gray eyebrow.

Lorinda stepped suddenly back away from him, once more untrusting of him, though he was her aunt's husband. "Aunt Rettie, I have so much to say, but I'm not sure if I want to in front of this man," she said quietly.

"Lorinda, this is my husband, your uncle," Rettie said. "Anything you have to say to me has to be shared with him." Her eyes softened. "Precious, you would never find a finer man than my Matthew," she added. "Don't look as though you are in the presence of the devil.''

"Why don't we go into the sitting room and have a cup

of tea and relax?" Matthew encouraged. "Then we can talk about anything you wish, Lorinda. I promise that anything you have to say won't go any farther."

"Matthew here was a newspaperman," Rettie said proudly. "But he's long since retired since our marriage. So you don't have to worry about him tellin' things you don't want anyone hearin'. We mainly talk between ourselves. That's all."

Lorinda and Amanda were gently ushered into the sitting room where they settled down in a soft chair, Amanda snuggling onto Lorinda's lap. Once tea was served and Rettie and Matthew were sitting opposite them, Lorinda began her long tale, from the very beginning, to now . . . revealing that she was pregnant with Yellow Feather's child. . . .

Watching the color draining from her aunt's face, Lorinda placed her hand to her abdomen, knowing the reason why.

"A child? You are carrying . . . a . . . savage Indian's child . . . ?" Rettie said in a strained whisper. "Lorinda, my precious, how did you let this happen?"

"I told you, Aunt Rettie, I love him," Lorinda said proudly. "He is like no other man you have ever met or *will* ever meet." She glanced toward Matthew and knew that her aunt felt the same way about him . . . *her* husband.

"But he's an Indian," Rettie argued. "White women just don't love Indians. Especially not a white, young thing as pretty and gentle as you!"

"He is not savage . . . he is not *just* an Indian," Lorinda argued back. "Like I said. He is a man. A very special man."

"Their culture so differs. . . ."

"Ay-uh . . . " Lorinda said, then drew in her breath when she saw her aunt's eyes widen and the color rise to her cheeks in fiery splashes. Lorinda knew that she

should have been more cautious. It had been shock enough for her aunt to hear Amanda speaking Indian . . . let alone her adult niece, whom she was finding to have changed so much.

"Lorinda . . ." Rettie gasped, leaning forward, tilting the teacup, spilling tea onto her blue velvet dress.

Lorinda scooted Amanda from her lap and went to her aunt and began wiping the tea from her dress with the skirt of her own cotton dress. "Aunt Rettie, please understand," she said, pleading with her eyes, soaking up even more tea. "I carry the child of the chief of the St. Croix band of the Chippewa. I am proud of this. Please be also proud for me."

Rettie turned her eyes away from Lorinda and swallowed hard. "I cannot. . . ." she murmured.

Lorinda lifted her hands to her aunt's face and guided it around so their eyes could meet. "Aunt Rettie, you *must* accept it, because it is so," she said softly. "I will leave again, in only a matter of minutes, to rejoin my man on the trail. I will once again return to the Chippewa village. It is my way of life now. I want no other."

"Lorinda . . . precious . . ." Rettie said, leaning her face into Lorinda's hands. "You didn't even have a proper wedding ceremony. You are not truly legally married."

"I am," Lorinda said stubbornly. "In the way of the Chippewa tradition, I am. And that is all that matters. You see, I am now of the Chippewa. Their culture is now *my* culture. In their eyes, as in my own, I am married to Chief Yellow Feather."

Rettie shook her face free of Lorinda's hands and closed her eyes tightly. "Do not speak his name to me," she said. "I cannot accept this. I cannot. What would your mother and father say? They were slaughtered by the hands of Indians."

Lorinda forcefully took her aunt's hands in hers. She

squeezed them tightly, causing her aunt's eyes to open again. "They were killed by the Sioux," she said flatly. "I am of the Chippewa. Listen to me! The Chippewa! They are peaceful with the white man. You know that. They are good Indians. Aunt Rettie, won't you please open your heart to what I am saying?"

Rettie's eyes snapped back at Lorinda. "They stole from me . . . they stole from many," she fumed. "And even yourself. Look at what they . . ."

Lorinda interrupted her aunt. 'Yes, they have stolen, but have they done harm to anyone? Have they killed? Have they maimed? I was not harmed by them. You know you weren't harmed by them. You must place your prejudice behind you, Aunt Rettie. You must accept what I am now a part of."

Rettie cast a fast glance toward Matthew and saw his nod of approval, then felt a sinking in her heart. If Matthew understood the pleadings of this niece, surely she also had to try to understand. She didn't want to risk losing Lorinda all over again. To reject her now could mean to never see her again!

"Lorinda, I want to understand," Rettie finally replied. "Please know that I want only what is best for you."

Lorinda smiled warmly. "Then you will come and meet Yellow Feather," she said. "He has a special gift for you. Please come into the forest and meet my husband . . . my very, very special Indian husband."

Rettie glanced quickly toward Matthew once more, catching another nod in her direction. She then looked down at Lorinda, who still sat at her feet. She squeezed Lorinda's hands back. "All right," she surrendered. "If that is what you want."

Lorinda looked warily toward Matthew, still wondering about him, but when she saw even more understanding of her in his eyes than in her aunt's, she felt a sudden liking for this man with the blue eyes and gray hair. She smiled toward him. "And, Matthew, will you please come along also?" she asked.

"You're sure . . . ?" he said, tilting an eyebrow.

"There is only one thing," Lorinda said softly. "We cannot let anyone know where we will be traveling to. Yellow Feather fears for his people. He doesn't want anyone knowing where his new promised land is. So much has been taken away from his people. He must not have that worry again."

"Lorinda, not a word will be spoken," Rettie murmured. "But I will want to ask something of you in return."

Lorinda eyed her cautiously. "And what might that be, Aunt Rettie?" she asked quietly.

"That when it is time for your child to be born, I can be there to assist."

"What . . . ?" Lorinda whispered.

"You must promise to let me travel to your Indian village to assist in the birthing of your child," Rettie said firmly. "It's bad enough that you are going to be living in the wilderness away from civilization. To even think of your bearing a child so far from home makes my insides cringe. You *must* agree to let me come to see you through this thing."

Lorinda rose to her feet. Her hands went to her abdomen. "Aunt Rettie, Yellow Feather wouldn't want this," she said softly. "As I said, he fears for his people. If someone followed you, then all the white men would follow."

"Matthew and I will not tell anyone," Rettie argued, rising, going to Lorinda's side. "Precious, when it nears time for you to have the baby, we will travel with Amanda and spend the time needed with you and see to it that you safely give birth to your child. Then we will return home and leave your Chippewa village in peace. No one will know. You surely will trust your Aunt Rettie."

Lorinda eyed Amanda. It would be nice to see her again. And Amanda would certainly enjoy returning to her village of the Chippewa where she knew that Little Red Fox would always be waiting for her.

"If you are sure. . . ." Lorinda finally replied.

"We won't breathe a word. . . ." Rettie reassured her.

"Yellow Feather will have to approve. . . ."

"He will," Rettie said flatly. "I will convince this Indian that it is the best thing to do. Sons are important to him, are they not?"

"Yes, sometimes even more important than life itself," Lorinda said softly.

"Then take me to him," Rettie said, swooshing the velvet of her skirt around her as she started to rush from the room. "I will leave instructions for the cook to serve my boarders. Then we will go. . . ."

Lorinda's heart pumped wildly, hoping that she had made the right decision. . . .

Lorinda rode on ahead of her aunt's carriage. She had to get to Yellow Feather first and explain. The surprise that she had planned for him might not be welcome after all. Their plans had been to move on north way before her aunt would reach the scene. The black stallion was supposed to be left standing, waiting, alone. But now that her aunt *and* her aunt's husband were going to be there to personally meet Yellow Feather, how would he react?

Her sunbonnet having been tossed aside once St. Paul had been left behind, Lorinda's hair lifted and fell in red splashes against her shoulders as the horse galloped gently along the dirt road. One more bend in this road and Yellow Feather would be waiting. Her heart pounded in unison with the horse's hoofbeats against the ground and then she was there, moving toward the thick cover of maple trees, where Yellow Feather patiently waited. Lorinda glanced quickly around her, wondering about the black stallion. She smiled when she saw it also partially hidden behind a flowering multiflora shrub.

Yellow Feather moved his horse out into the open and went to Lorinda. "It is done?" he asked, touching her cheek. "White Blossom is now safely at your aunt's? And you found that I was right, that Flying Squirrel had not harmed your aunt?"

Lorinda felt color rising in her cheeks. She cast a fast glance over her shoulder, wishing her aunt would hurry. Once Lorinda had explained what was to be, she didn't want Yellow Feather to have time to scold her, or even possibly to ride swiftly away.

She smiled when she heard the creaking of her aunt's carriage wheels and knew that she was close. When she turned to face Yellow Feather her smile quickly faded. He had also heard the sound. It was evident in the dark fear in his eyes and in the way his jaws had set so suddenly hard.

His eyes flashed angrily at her when he spoke. "I thought you said no white man would follow," he said, grabbing her horse's reins from her hands in a quick jerk. "You were only to tell your aunt and she wasn't to follow you. She was to come later. Why weren't you more cautious, Red Blossom?"

"Yellow Feather, it *is* my . . ." she began but was stopped as the carriage came into full view. She watched Yellow Feather's back straighten and his muscles tighten in his shoulders. When he dropped her reins, she rescued them and inched her horse closer to his, to touch his hand reassuringly.

"It is only my aunt, her husband, and Amanda," she said quietly. "It's a surprise, Yellow Feather. I so wanted you to meet my aunt. You see, it is a custom of the white man that once two people are married, the families of the bride and groom should become acquainted. My aunt *is* my family. Yellow Feather, I have accepted your customs, now please bend a little and accept some of mine. It would mean so much to me."

Yellow Feather frowned, then said, "What if they were followed?"

"There would be no reason for my aunt to be followed. Please relax. Our meeting will be short, then I will say my farewell."

"It will be brief?"

"*Ay-uh . . .*"

Yellow Feather's eyes softened. "Red Blossom, I do things for you because my love for you is true," he said. "I will make peace with your aunt only to make you happy."

"And her husband . . . ?"

"You never spoke of a husband before."

"He is a new husband, as I am a new wife."

"Then let's make our peace and go on quickly north. While so far away from my village, my heart is too restless."

"I understand," Lorinda whispered. She leaned a kiss onto Yellow Feather's cheek, then directed her horse toward the carriage to meet her aunt's approach with Yellow Feather at her side. When her aunt's carriage stopped and Lorinda found her husband on display as her aunt studied him with a cautious air, Lorinda interceded and sliced through the silence with her words.

"Aunt Rettie, this is Yellow Feather, my Chippewa husband," she said proudly. Her eyes moved to Amanda who sat next to her aunt, then on to Matthew. It was still hard to accept this new uncle. She had known only one for so many years, and now he was dead. But if this man made her aunt happy, that was what mattered. She nodded toward him and her aunt. "And, Yellow

Feather, this is my Aunt Rettie and Uncle Matthew."
There. She had said it. He was now definitely her uncle.

Yellow Feather had crossed his arms across his chest
and was sitting stiffly in his saddle. His eyes had the same
veil over them as they had had upon Lorinda's first ac-
quaintance with him. He didn't smile, only nodded a
quick, silent hello toward Rettie and Matthew, then
glanced toward Lorinda as though to say that he had done
as she had asked and now he was ready to go.

"So you're Lorinda's Indian husband, eh?" Rettie
asked, leaning forward, studying him even more carefully.

Yellow Feather refused to answer, instead continued
his stubborn pose of silence.

Lorinda inched her way closer to him. "Yellow
Feather, please . . ." she whispered.

"Doesn't he speak English?" Rettie snapped.

Amanda climbed from the carriage and ran to Yellow
Feather, chattering in Indian. She reached her arms up to
him, smiling.

Yellow Feather's wall of stubbornness was quickly
shattered. He reached down and scooped Amanda up into
his arms and held her there while she snuggled next to
him. "I bring White Blossom to you to raise in the white
man's way," he said flatly. "She has become as my own
daughter. You take good care of her."

"My word . . . !" Rettie said with a quick intake of
breath. "He does speak English and he's ordering me
around. And what is it he called Amanda?"

Lorinda laughed a bit nervously. "He only worries
about Amanda's welfare," she said. "And he calls her by
her Indian name as he calls me by my Indian name, Red
Blossom."

Rettie paled. Her fingers went to her throat. "This is
a bit much," she said softly. "Lorinda, I just don't

416

know. . . ."

All grew silent as Yellow Feather turned his horse around and traveled a bit away from them all. Lorinda's heart swelled with pride, seeing where he was headed. When he returned with the black stallion, a low gasp rose from Rettie.

"My horse . . ." she said, rising. She moved from the carriage and went and took the black stallion's reins. "My beautiful horse . . ." she murmured. She stroked its mane, then looked accusingly in Yellow Feather's direction. "You not only stole my niece but my horse as well," she snapped.

"Aunt Rettie . . ." Lorinda said harshly, glancing toward Yellow Feather, waiting for an explosion of Indian words. But he sat, composed, with chin held high, still holding Amanda on the saddle before him.

"Evil white man Lamont Quinby stole this horse and your niece Lorinda," he said flatly. "I bring them both back to you. But you can only keep the horse. Lorinda . . . Red Blossom . . . is now mine. . . ."

"Harumph . . ." Rettie scoffed.

Yellow Feather handed Amanda toward Rettie. "And your other niece," he said. "My Chippewa braves killed for her. . . ."

Rettie accepted Amanda into her arms and hugged her tightly to her bosom. She suddenly felt ashamed. This Indian spoke the truth. He did seem to be as good as Lorinda had said. Maybe it was best to accept him. Her eyes softened. "I'm sorry, Yellow Feather," she murmured. "I do owe you my thanks. You've also returned my youngest niece. I forget too quickly."

Lorinda sighed heavily with relief. She glanced from Yellow Feather to her aunt, seeing a sort of admiration being exchanged between them. The wall of prejudice was gently tumbling down. Her aunt was accepting her Indian husband and Yellow Feather was accepting more *chee-mo-ko-man* as a part of his life.

Lorinda's life was suddenly perfect for the first time in many months. Her hands went to her stomach. Now to . . . only . . . have a son!

Twenty-Seven

It was September, the time of the *Manomin-Gisis,* the wild rice moon. In the shallow inlets of the St. Croix River, the tall, green plants with their heavy tops bending low were swaying to the lapping of the water, filled with grain that somewhat resembled domestic oats. The wild rice, called *manomin,* which, in the Chippewa language, meant ''good berry,'' was now to be the St. Croix band of the Chippewa's staple food.

On the council grounds, the St. Croix were readying themselves for the ancient tribal feast that welcomed the rice into their village. The sun had left velvet streaks of crimson across the horizon, soon to be replaced by a perfectly round autumn moon.

In front of the council house, the grass had been trampled down to form a hard, smooth surface for dancers. The children were already there, chasing each other around and around, screaming and laughing, falling into dance steps their elders would soon be executing.

Fires in long trenches were filled with coals, over which the carcasses of rabbits, squirrel, young bear, and various other animals were roasting, while the women crouched, turning the spits. Village dogs circled about, sniffing, in the way of the tribe as they began assembling, seating themselves on blankets spread before a great pile of wood stacked in a high, teepee-shaped pile.

Lorinda settled down next to Yellow Feather on a deep cushion of skins while her Aunt Rettie and Matthew eased down onto some blankets on the other side of her.

When Amanda rushed to Lorinda, Lorinda urged her to sit on the ground before her, having no room left on her lap because of the large swell of her stomach.

"I'm glad Yellow Feather agreed to let us come," Rettie said softly into Lorinda's ear. She looked down at Lorinda's stomach. "Precious, I just know your baby will be born any time now. You're larger than your mother was before you and Amanda were born, and you're carrying the child much, much higher. Surely it will be a boy."

Lorinda smiled awkwardly. She hadn't told her aunt of the importance of bearing a son. She hadn't wanted her aunt fretting over the fact that Yellow Feather had the right to accept two wives at once. It had been enough that Lorinda had it as a worry day in and day out.

When a tiny, unfamiliar pain shot through her insides, she flinched and grabbed at her stomach.

"Precious, what is it?" Rettie asked, taking one of Lorinda's hands in hers.

Lorinda forced a laugh. "Seems my baby wants to join in the wild rice celebration," she said. "It just gave me quite a hardy kick."

"Are you sure it's nothing else?" Rettie then said, moving her hand to Lorinda's stomach.

Lorinda cast a sideways glance at Yellow Feather, seeing the restful pride in his eyes. This wild rice harvest had been a part of his childhood dream, as she had also been; his people were quite rapidly building a life of prosperity for themselves; and his wife would soon bear him a child. He now appeared at peace with himself. His mighty guardian spirit, the giant owl of the forest, had filled his life with many blessings!

Another pain grabbed at Lorinda's insides, causing beads of perspiration to bead her brow. But she wouldn't admit to this pain. She didn't want to spoil the evening's ritual.

She turned to her aunt and laid a comforting hand on her arm. "Aunt Rettie, just quit fussing over me," she whispered. "I'm all right."

Lorinda watched her aunt tighten the shawl around her shoulders, making sure to not conceal her prized brooch that was pinned to the collar of her high-necked velvet dress.

Lorinda had been proud to surprise her aunt with these things that Flying Squirrel had stolen from her. Even the pearl-handled pistol had been gladly accepted, especially after Lorinda had disclosed to her aunt how it had been used. And, ah, the black stallion. That had been the best gift of all. It had succeeded in joining Aunt Rettie's and Yellow Feather's hearts. . . .

A drum tore Lorinda's thoughts from the past as it began a soft beat, then increased slowly in volume as the moon began to rise, casting pale golden light from the east over the tops of the pines.

Yellow Feather rose suddenly to his feet and stretched his arms above his head to the rising moon and began to chant words that were unintelligible to Lorinda. The drumbeat grew louder. The men of the village then rose to their feet and began their tribal dance, while their shrill voices chanted the strongly accented rhythms of the dance, singing: *"Hi-ya-ya-ya. . . ."*

The cadence of the drum now remained the same, a steady *tum-tum-tum-tum tum-tum-tum-tum*. The aroma of burned grease, baked meat, and parched corn swirled heavily in the air. Then, when the moon finally showed its full face, the drumming and chanting stopped.

Yellow Feather was handed a lighted torch, which he solemnly leaned into the pile of dry wood in the circle of the Indians. All was quiet and everyone looked skyward, and once the sky was lighted orange from the fire, another unintelligible chant rose from between Yellow Feather's lips and the feast was ready to truly begin.

421

Bowls heaped with meat, corn, and crunched maple sugar were passed around. Yellow Feather settled down next to Lorinda, beaming. . . .

"Tomorrow ricing begins," he said proudly. "Today I guided my canoe into the shallows until I was lost in a jungle of rice that towered over my head. When I stripped a husk open it looked like a thin bead, greenish in color, from which protruded a sharp, hairlike tail. *Ay-uh*. It is ready for harvesting."

"I'm happy for you, Yellow Feather," Lorinda said softly. She eyed her bowl of food but suddenly felt nauseated by its strong, overpowering aroma. Again she was racked with pain and this time even felt a strange pressure between her thighs. She couldn't help but give in to this sensation and began bearing down, closing her eyes and gritting her teeth to the intense pain.

Then, once the pain lifted, she breathed easier, glad to see that Yellow Feather had been too absorbed in his pleasure of this proud moment with his people to have even noticed her discomfort. She glanced a bit sideways, glad to see Amanda on her Aunt Rettie's lap, sharing a bowl of sugar crunchies.

Then the pain was there again! And so soon! Lorinda puffed and stretched a leg straight out before her. The bearing down was worse! She didn't think she could stand it much longer. She reached a hand to Yellow Feather's arm and touched him softly. "Yellow Feather, I believe it's time for our child to be born," she whispered, eyeing him warmly.

Yellow Feather dropped his bowl of food to the ground and rose quickly to his feet, drawing her slowly up next to him. "Our child . . . ?" he said thickly. "It is time?"

Lorinda laughed silkily. "Yes, I do believe so," she said. "Now I must return to our cabin with Aunt Rettie. Just you stay here and celebrate with your people. I don't want to ruin what you've been waiting for since your childhood dream."

"Red Blossom, how could you even think I could remain here while you are having our child?" he said thickly. "My son. *He* has also been a dream. I must see my son the minute he is brought into this world. I will go with you. I will even labor with you."

Rettie flew to her feet, seeing how Lorinda clutched so desperately at her stomach. "Lorinda, are you all right?" she murmured.

"Aunt Rettie, I believe you'd best go and tell Big Laughing Star and Singing Cloud that we will need much water boiled, for I am about to have my child," Lorinda said, puffing again when another pain began to tighten inside her. She leaned against Yellow Feather as they moved toward the crude cabin he had built for her upon her request. It wasn't anything in comparison to the houses in St. Paul, but it was built just for her, and that meant more than anything else.

"We must hurry, Yellow Feather," Lorinda said, puffing, sweating.

With one fast swoop, he had her in his arms and rushed through the village of wigwams and into the cabin that he had yet to grow used to. He hadn't liked the fireplace at one side instead of in the middle of the house. He hadn't understood the type of fire hole that had been required. But he had made his Red Blossom happy. That was all that had mattered! With her Uncle Matthew's help in building it, she had been given her dream home!

Easing her down on a bed of blankets and soft pelts, Yellow Feather rushed around the room helping Rettie, Big Laughing Star, and Singing Cloud prepare the water and the clean cloths. He knew that most Indian braves didn't participate in the birthing of their children, but this child was different. This child was to be born of a white woman . . . his white woman. And this child would one day lead his people. *Ay-uh,* this child *was* different!

Once Lorinda was stripped of clothing and lay panting, all that was required was to wait for the baby and its decision to move on out into the world. Yellow Feather paced the floor. Rettie swabbed the perspiration from Lorinda's brow. Big Laughing Star knelt beside her, chanting unintelligibly, and Singing Cloud had ushered Amanda from the room to play with Little Red Fox. And Lorinda pushed and grunted all the while, tossing her perspiration-soaked head back and forth. Then suddenly one more unbearable pain and push and the child was there!

Rettie took the child from between Lorinda's outstretched legs and sighed heavily. Yellow Feather began to chant, flailing his arms wildly into the air, all the while Lorinda lay there, wondering what she had given birth to. Had it been a boy . . . or . . . a girl . . . ?

Leaning up on an elbow, she eyed Rettie quizzically. "Aunt Rettie, the suspense. Please tell me. . . ." she said weakly.

Can't you tell by the way Yellow Feather is reacting?" Rettie chuckled throatily. "Don't you see his happiness?"

Lorinda felt tears stinging her eyes. "Then . . . it is . . . a . . . boy . . . ?" she whispered.

"*Ay-uh,* it is a son," Yellow Feather shouted, falling to his knees at Lorinda's bedside. He clasped her hands in his. "My Red Blossom, my wife, you have made me most proud. You have given birth to my first son . . . a son we have already named Gray Wolf. Gray Wolf will be the next chief. Our son will reign over the St. Croix band of the Chippewa." He leaned a kiss to her lips. "You have made me most proud, my wife. . . ."

"Please let me see him," she whispered. "Let me hold our son."

Rettie wrapped Gray Wolf in a blanket that was oh, so familiar to Lorinda, the baby blanket that she had carried with her for so long while in search of Amanda. Then

Rettie lay the child in the crook of Lorinda's left arm.

Barely breathing, Lorinda pulled the corner of the blanket back and smiled peacefully when she saw that this child was a replica of his father, with beautiful copper skin and wide shoulders. But when he opened his eyes, Lorinda saw a little of herself. She saw the green eyes . . . the beautiful green eyes of her son . . . !

Spring flowers in the meadow were as bright as iridescent butterflies, while other wild blossoms sparkled along the shore of the St. Croix River. Lorinda walked leisurely next to Yellow Feather, leaning into his embrace as he circled an arm about her waist.

"Another spring," she sighed. They moved into the outer edges of the forest. "I don't see how this spring could be lovelier than the last, but it is. It's as though there's a magic wand tapping the trees and meadow, commanding everything to flame with color."

"It is truly no different this season," Yellow Feather laughed. "It only appears to be so because you are happy. Happiness can make the ugliest creature on earth look beautiful."

Lorinda lifted her eyes to the forest ceiling, causing her red mane of hair to hang in lustrous, inviting rivulets down her back. She closed her eyes and inhaled leisurely. "Ah, the smell of the forest," she whispered. "It is the scent of arrowroot." She turned and smiled toward Yellow Feather when she felt his fingers lacing through her hair.

"The true flame is not in the forest or meadow," he said huskily. "But in my heart." He lifted her hair gently from her shoulders and placed a kiss on the nape of her neck then drew her around and embraced her fully and pleasured her with a gentle, sweet kiss on her lips. When one of his hands sought out a breast through the buckskin of her dress she gazed passionately into his eyes.

"Big Laughing Star is tending Gray Wolf in her wigwam," she said teasingly. "I can't think of anything I'd rather do than making love to you." She warmed inside when she saw the lustful gleam in his eyes. Never again could he deny talking with his eyes. They always told her so much.

A stirring in the thickets close to them drew both their eyes in that direction. "Probably a deer," Lorinda laughed nervously. She wouldn't say the word "bear," but it was always a worry. In the spring, it seemed everything ventured out, sniffing the newness of life and nature.

Yellow Feather grabbed Lorinda's arm and pushed her backwards. "It is no deer . . ." he whispered. "A deer does not crouch. A deer does not wear a feather in a coil at its head. . . ."

Lorinda's heart began to thump nervously as her eyes searched frantically around her. "Yellow Feather, what are you trying to tell me . . . ?" she whispered back.

"It is the Sioux," he growled. "I can even smell the stench of him. The Sioux is worse than even the lowliest of forest creatures, the skunk."

A fear was creeping across Lorinda's flesh in the form of goose bumps. She clung to Yellow Feather, eyes wide. "How many do you think . . . ?" she whispered shallowly.

"Only one . . ." Yellow Feather replied. "They would only send a scout."

"Why did the Sioux wait this long . . . ?"

"My guardian spirit led them in other directions," he said. "But I guess the great owl of the forest was also distracted by spring and didn't see this Sioux sneaking around."

"What are you going to do, Yellow Feather?"

"We will pretend we do not see him, then we will do a bit of sneaking," he said, urging her onward, toward a clearing ahead.

"How . . . ?"

"You will see. . . ."

Lorinda walked alongside Yellow Feather to the clearing. Then he began to move in a slow circle back into the forest until he had led her around to behind where the Indian still crouched, staring straight ahead, oblivious to their presence.

Yellow Feather urged Lorinda behind the safe cover of a tree while removing his knife from the sheath at his waist. "I will only be a minute," he whispered. "You stay here."

"Are you going to kill him?" Lorinda asked, trembling inside.

"He will wish I had," Yellow Feather snarled. His eyes were narrow dark coals as he crept on away from her.

Lorinda strained her neck, watching, barely breathing. And when she saw Yellow Feather pounce on the Sioux scout, she had to cover her mouth with her hands to stifle a scream. Stepping quickly from behind the tree, she watched as copper flesh wrestled copper flesh until Yellow Feather stood as the victor, smiling, holding two clipped, charcoal-black braids up into the air as his prize.

Lorinda watched further as the Sioux scout rose from the ground and began shrinking away from Yellow Feather, wordless. Lorinda's mouth was agape, seeing how humbly this Indian looked back at Yellow Feather, and how he was cowering, like a scolded puppy, then inching on away from Yellow Feather until he was gone from sight, deep into the forest.

Yellow Feather squared his shoulders, proud, and went back to Lorinda, smiling. He held the braids before him. "He won't be bothering us anymore," he laughed.

"You let him get away. . . ." Lorinda whispered.

"*Ay-uh*, I did. . . ."

427

"But won't he just return to his village and return with more Sioux?"

"*Gah-ween.* He won't," Yellow Feather said flatly.

"How can you be so sure?"

"He would be a coward in the eyes of his people," Yellow Feather said sternly. "I clipped his braids. No Indian warrior lets another warrior do that without proving himself cowardly."

"Then what will he do?" Lorinda asked quietly.

"He will wander aimlessly in the forest or fall on his own knife in shame."

Lorinda cringed. "How horrible. . . ." she gasped.

"Rather it be him than me," Yellow Feather said angrily.

"*Ay-uh . . .*" Lorinda whispered.

Yellow Feather fell to his knees and dug a small pit in the ground then placed the braids into it. "My people will never know of this," he said, covering the braids with the loose dirt. "They do not need to have a worry of the Sioux. One day we may have to make war with them again and maybe even with the white man. But for now my people will bask in the peace and love my sacred place by the St. Croix has given them." He rose to his feet and embraced Lorinda. "Let us return to our camp and celebrate this morning's victory," he teased laughingly.

"You aren't only a wise chief but a wise husband as well," Lorinda purred. She fell into step next to him, welcoming his arm about her waist. And once inside the cabin with both their clothes shed, they stood and silently admired each other's nudity.

"Bearing our son caused no harm to your body," Yellow Feather said huskily, reaching, tracing her sensuous curves and hollows with the palms of both hands.

Lorinda trembled, already filling with a heated desire for him to do more than touch her. She reached a hand to his body and began studying his flesh with her fingers, smiling wickedly when she felt his tremblings with each added stroke.

"Becoming a father has made *you* change," she whispered. "You are even more handsome in your pride."

Without further hesitation, Yellow Feather drew her quickly into his arms and crushed her lips with his while a hand found a breast and began kneading and fondling it until the nipple rose to a sharp peak and ached for want of his lips. When he lowered his mouth over it, sucking, licking, Lorinda moaned and leaned her head back, consumed with fiery splashes of warmth coursing through her. She was glad to move with him as he lowered her onto the bed. Her knees had become too weak with desire even to hold her up, it seemed.

As his lips then began to lower over the voluptuous curves of her body, letting his kisses fall like soft rain, Lorinda drifted into a tranquil, euphoric state and accepted his gentle, probing tongue moving to all the different pleasure points along her body.

Then the flames inside her began to grow, leaving the euphoric state behind. She lifted her arms to Yellow Feather and drew his mouth to hers as he entered her from below and filled her with his love stem. As he worked with her body they began sharing the exquisite sensations of sensual pleasure until their passion exploded so hard, in unison, that it left them both breathless, lying next to one another. . . .

Yellow Feather's eyes were filled with love for her as she turned to face him. "Yellow Feather, my lovable, Indian husband, please never love another," she whispered.

"One wife is all I desire," he said huskily, kissing her gently in the hollow of the throat.

"One wife can bear many sons," she purred. "Is that what would make you truly happy?"

"Ay-uh."

"Well, my love, I have news for you," she giggled, eyeing him coyly, proud that she never showed with child early in her pregnancies.

He raised himself to gaze with wonderment down at her. "Red Blossom, are you saying . . . ?"

"Ay-uh," she murmured. "I might disturb your next wild rice festival in the same way I interrupted your last. . . ."

Yellow Feather drew her quickly into his arms and began thanking her by making renewed love to her. She was once more a prisoner of his passion, surrendering her all to him. . . .

They were obsessed by their never-ending love for one another. It was . . . a . . . sensuous, savage obsession. . . .

ROMANCE FROM FERN MICHAELS

DEAR EMILY   (0-8217-4952-8, $5.99)

WISH LIST   (0-8217-5228-6, $6.99)

AND IN HARDCOVER:

VEGAS RICH   (1-57566-057-1, $25.00)